To Kyle.

For your continued support, love and many re-reads.

Chapter One

London England - February 16th 1839

"Did you hear that?" A shudder went through Sophia Cole's spine when she stopped in her tracks and looked over her shoulder, only to find an empty path. There was nothing there. Nothing out of the ordinary at least. There were couples walking out from the theatre that herself and her dear friend Jack Green came from, but nothing that would cause her to be suddenly on edge.

"No," Jack didn't even hesitate with his answer. He started tugging on her arm to have her continue their walk back to their home.

Sophia looked over at him, a thin eyebrow raised. "Are you not going to ask *what* I heard?"

A smile emerged on Jack's full lips. Jack was overwhelmingly attractive, something that didn't go unnoticed by Sophia. It was a little bit intense how much of him radiated perfection, from his illuminating blonde hair that didn't have a single strand out of place, and a perfectly chiselled jaw that could cut through glass.

Although the night sky was clear now, it had clearly rained a storm whilst Sophia and Jack were in the theatre. Rivers of puddles were prominent along the cobbled path, and Sophia was extra cautious with her steps. Of course, no matter how careful she thought she was, taking her gaze away from the ground for a single second caused her foot to drop ankle deep into a puddle. The second her ankle made contact with the ice water, Sophia flailed back and released her grip from around Jack's elbow. She picked up the end of her dress and stretched out her foot to reveal her soaking boot, now glossing in the moonlight. Sophia examined the damage and released a deep sigh, "Oh dear."

Jack stopped beside her and dipped his knees to examine the damage caused, leaning most of his weight on his trusty black cane that Sophia had never seen him without. His grin from earlier returned and he was smiling as his bright crystal blue eyes scanned up her dress, "You have made a mess of your dress."

Jack straightened up, raising his cane from the ground and using it to point to the large faded brown stain splattered on the skirt of Sophia's cream and grey pinstripe dress.

A bubble of laughter emerged up Jack's throat and he made no effort to swallow it down. "No need to fret," he dropped his cane back onto the ground. "I am sure Stella can work her magic as soon as we get home."

Sophia's brain still struggled to see the correlation between the word 'home' and the orphanage in which they resided for their entire lives.

Jack was considered by most members as the lucky one, for he is the only person to not only have one parent but two. His mother and father, Cassandra and Albert Green, ran the orphanage. Jack helped too with occasional tasks that his mother insisted wasn't necessary but he always managed to get his own way. It's no surprise that every woman swoons over Jack, all he has to do is enter a room and even ladies of the upper class would have their tongues fall in their soup.

Of course, Sophia wasn't blind, Jack was attractive but it was nothing more than a pleasing sight to her. She often wondered if that's why they became such close friends, because she wasn't pining after him and there was no hidden agenda to their meetings.

All of this talk of stains on her dress didn't distract Sophia from her earlier question that Jack so rudely ignored. "Are you honestly telling me you didn't hear anything?"

Sophia couldn't let this go, it was a simple sound, a long note of someone humming and it lasted for a split second. She may have been willing to walk away from it if a sudden chill hadn't accompanied it.

She looked up at Jack, it was hard to be discreet about trying to catch his expression when her hat acted as an umbrella above her head. What she did manage to see oddly upset her. His brow furrowed like he had just been insulted, his charming smile was a flat line and his nostrils flared slightly.

It was then she noticed the faint limp he walked with, that was so faint on most days Sophia often forgot he had one, had started to become deeper and more weight was being put down onto his left leg.

Jack had made his feelings very clear about not wanting any questions from Sophia about how he obtained the limp, resulting in him requiring a cane even for small trips.

Her boot squelched with every step and her toes were beginning to feel like a prune. She hurried in her pace as she looked up to the dark cloud rolling in, masking the twinkling stars. "I suppose it is rather late," she said, not sure if today had turned into tomorrow. "We should hurry back before your mother worries."

"My mother would worry even if I stood in front of her," Jack tried to joke but his voice was strained, like he was struggling to catch his breath.

Sophia turned to her friend and looped her arm through his. She knew he would refuse her help because he was too proud but Sophia grew concerned for his health. Beads of sweat were starting to drip down his forehead.

Jack lifted his gloved hand, the silver ball atop his cane pressed into his palm. "I'm fine, Sophia."

"Your actions would suggest the opposite," Sophia muttered. She was concentrating on getting Jack back to the orphanage, they weren't too far now. All she had to do was focus on one step at a time, assuring that Jack was doing the same.

Anyone who was not a member of the orphanage would not know that the building in which everyone resides even exists. It is far enough away from the town for it not to be too much of a strain to walk, but not too close for members of the general public to stumble across. It was certainly odd, and something Sophia would question to herself whenever they were walking back from the town.

It's like the orphanage was purposely hidden away, that anyone who didn't live there wasn't even permitted to know the location. It was hidden deep within a plethora of trees that only when you got passed a dozen tall birch trees did the regular dirt path reveal itself.

Walking up the road, and seeing the all too familiar tall black gates that surrounded the church-like building, it filled Sophia with a common sense of dread. A feeling she was all too familiar with when returning from her trips to the town.

Even if it was midday and the sun was as bright as it could ever be, the grey stone walls radiated a gloomy and depressing wave. It was taller than it was wide, with many windows close together, Sophia could see her bedroom window from the gate. The third window on the fourth floor. Oh, how she dreamed of the day she would never have to step through those doors. She had no plan at the moment but she knew one day she could be free from this place.

There was an unspoken rule that whoever resides inside is not permitted to leave. There are orphans that are in their late twenties and are still treated as though they are children. Cassandra pushes no one to seek employment or to seek a partner. If anything, she discourages relationships between each other and certainly no one is allowed inside unless invited by Cassandra.

Sophia was thankful that the end was in sight. As she pushed open the gate, Jack abruptly stopped and leaned his entire weight into the bars, the back of his head leaning against the cold rusting bars. His eyes were pinched shut, causing the corners to crease, and his breathing became heavier than Sophia ever thought to be normal. Jack would occasionally grunt through gritted teeth. To calm himself, he pinched the bridge of his nose and dipped his head.

Sophia didn't know what to do, she had never seen Jack in such a state before. He seemed to be in an unbearable agony. "Jack, what is it?"

Minutes ticked by that felt like a lifetime. Jack pinched his nose harder and it oddly seemed to be working, his shoulders were slowing along with his rapid breaths and he let out one final long breath before lifting himself from the bars, as though nothing had happened.

"Nothing to worry about," he said as he pulled at the collar of his buttoned up shirt. It must have felt restrictive, sitting over his Adam's apple as he struggled to get in the air.

"Jack..." did he think Sophia was stupid? How could he say that was *nothing?*

"It was just...just a terrible pain in my back. I must have sat in an odd position at the theatre."

He stepped in front of Sophia, his sparkling eyes finding hers in the darkness. Jack beamed a toothy grin which made Sophia feel taken aback.

A sudden dull pain emerged under her breastbone. It wasn't physical but it still hurt all the same. Her best friend was lying to her, and so blatantly too. Did he not trust her? She trusted him with all of her troubles and secrets but it's clear he didn't feel the same. In the back of her mind she always knew this, as much as

Jack would deny it, Sophia knew that he was hiding something from her. She didn't know what but she was certain.

"What happened to that beautiful smile?" His free gloved hand hooked under her chin and pulled her to look up at him.

How could he expect her to smile? Act as though her closest friend wasn't in some form of pain?

Sophia couldn't even fake a smile for him, instead she pushed open the gates and they walked up the winding road leading to the front doors. "I wish you would tell me what happened there."

"I did tell you," Jack replied. "I told you it is nothing for you to worry about."

He was using his charming voice, and it certainly wasn't working...not that it ever did. Jack was a glass that Sophia could see right through, but recently that glass has started to fog.

They walked the remainder in silence. The tension could part the thick London fog like the Red Sea.

Every time Sophia walked up the cold grey steps she was reminded of her first day at the orphanage. She was only five years old and anything before that day was a blank space in her memory. It's not that she didn't want to remember a time before the orphanage, if anything she craved to know there was more to

10

her life than this place, but she couldn't. It's like there was a wall built in her mind, a wall not built by herself. She couldn't explain a lot of things, she realised a lot of things in her life didn't make sense and she didn't know where to start to make it make sense.

Sophia always felt as though her life wasn't truly hers, like she was kept a prisoner in the orphanage and the world was simply waiting for her to die so it could move on. She realised how morbid her way of thinking was but it's the only way she could explain the reasoning for the tight rope wrapped around her heart, and every day it was being pulled tighter and tighter until she might burst.

Jack pushed open the doors and before they could close the door behind them Cassandra Green appeared at the bottom of the stairs. Her golden hair that shone brighter than the sun was pulled back into a loose bun, her angelic blue eyes were locked on her son's and didn't even acknowledge that Sophia was with him.

The interior of the orphanage was originally intended to be a cathedral, but there were still remnants of the original design. With golden staircases and marble architecture, and even a handful of religious statues made their way here.

11

No one would believe Cassandra was in her late forties, she could easily pass as someone half her age. There wasn't a single crease on her face, as absurd as it sounded Sophia was certain Cassandra hadn't aged a day since she arrived at the orphanage. There were times where Sophia was certain that Cassandra glowed when she smiled, like she radiated light from her silhouette but Sophia was certain it was just her mind playing tricks on her.

Although Jack inherited most of his handsome features from his father, like his strong jaw and pointed nose, it's clear that his overwhelming beauty came from Cassandra.

Cassandra sprinted to her son, holding up her pale blue gown, and gripped both her hands over his shoulders. She lowered her head, her round eyes were panicked and Sophia didn't see her blink a single time, as though she feared Jack would vanish if she did so.

"What happened?" Cassandra said as more a demand than a question.

"Mother please..." Jack swatted her hands away and opened the gap between them. "I simply require rest, enough with the obsessive pestering."

Cassandra opened her mouth then swiftly shut it, clearly thinking better of arguing in front of Sophia. She dropped her hands down to her sides and looked him up and down, from head to toe, with a single raised eyebrow. Cassandra could be intimidating, Sophia often hid away from her because she could never tell what she was feeling, but not when Jack towered over her.

Suddenly, Cassandra snapped her head to face Sophia, causing her to flinch. An obviously forced smile stretched across her thin lips as she said, "Please go to your room, Sophia. I need to speak to my son...*privately*." She shot her gaze back to Jack, and said the last part as though he knew exactly what she was going to talk with him about.

Sophia didn't want to get in their way, and she certainly didn't want to be on the receiving end of Cassandra's wrath. She bowed her head, not looking up as she scurried to the stairs and headed straight for her room.

An hour had passed since Sophia left Cassandra and Jack to their discussion. She wasn't exactly sure it counted as a discussion when she could hear their booming voices from her room. The front hall was directly below Sophia's room. She was certain she could feel the floorboards vibrating at her feet at some point.

Seated on the edge of her bed, Sophia thought of what she could do to occupy her time before sleeping. She had recently finished her book and forgot to visit the library to pick up a new one.

There was a library within the orphanage, Sophia would often sit alone and lose herself in the work of fiction. It lacked variety though, as there were limitations to what she was permitted to read. An entire section that was completely off limits. She had tried to sneak a peek at what could be so forbidden, but it was as though Cassandra could sense her there. Shortly after, Cassandra barged in and pretended to be interested in the layout of the room. She wasn't subtle about keeping an eye on Sophia, which was unsettling.

It's not like Sophia could read tonight anyway, not with the way her thoughts were occupying her.

Another hour had passed and all Sophia had successfully managed to do was drive herself crazy. At least it was silent now, Jack and Cassandra were done bickering and it was eerily silent. She almost wished they would resume their argument, at least it gave her something to do - trying to hear what they were arguing about.

All Sophia could do was envision the look of excruciating pain on Jack's face.

Had he been injured?

Was he ill?

No, he would have told her. Why would that be such a secret?

She couldn't sit around and wait until morning to see him again. She wouldn't let him sleep away the night. If Sophia left it until morning her dreams would have talked her out of confronting him, which they often did.

It was very late, and Sophia wasn't even sure Jack would still be awake. She couldn't sleep with the weight of what happened tonight on her shoulders, she had to at least try to talk to him.

Pulling out a match from her draw, she lit a thin candle sitting within a silver lamp. When she stepped out into the hall she was cautious with her steps, she was almost certain everyone was asleep. The floorboards were notoriously creaky, so tiptoeing was her best option not to cause a disturbance.

The lamp illuminated the hall, making the doors and paintings seem like they were moving, as if they were alive.

With her bare feet against the cold wooden floors it felt like Sophia was trending on small blocks of ice.

Sophia picked up her pace, only causing a few floorboards to creak. Of course Jack's room was the absolute furthest away from her own, they couldn't be neighbours they had to be divided by a row of empty rooms. Which was another of Sophia's many unanswered questions that plagued her, she was the only member not to have a neighbour. Everyone else had someone directly next to them, the furthest someone had was two doors. But Sophia had to go past seven empty rooms before passing by someone who actually resided inside.

Now standing outside of Jack's door, Sophia just stood there. Her grip was firm around the handle of the lamp, so much so that her hand was starting to hurt.

Her green eyes stared at the golden doorknob, if she desperately wanted to check on Jack's well being all she had to do was turn and push. That was it.

There was something in the back of her mind screaming at her, yelling at her not to open the door. She had no idea why, she had knocked on Jack's door many times before. Something felt wrong about standing out in the hall tonight, perhaps it was because it was so late...or maybe it was something else. Something that has been chewing at her mind for many years...

It was only Jack, a man who she spent almost all of her free time with for the past ten years. Why was she so nervous?

Sophia gathered up whatever courage and strength she found in the darkness and balled her free hand at her side into a fist. She reached up her hand, ready to knock on his door but froze when her eyes caught on the edge of his door...it was open, but only slightly.

It was ajar, if she pushed the door she could peak inside. She really didn't want to wake him, especially after the day she'd had, what harm would it do her to peek inside?

Sophia unwrapped her fist and pressed her palm lightly on the wood of the door. She pushed her hand only lightly, just enough that she could see inside. She could only see through a slit of the open door, she wanted to push more but any further could notify Jack she was there.

Looking inside, her eyes immediately fell to Jack. He was still awake and standing at the end of his bed, his back was to his door.

When her gaze trailed down to the back of his shirt, Sophia had to repress a scream. The back of his once crisp white shirt was stained with a blood red. It certainly wasn't an intentional design of the shirt, it looked wet...like fresh blood.

Everything within Sophia was telling her to shut her eyes, turn around and run.

She couldn't.

Her entire body was frozen, and she couldn't rip her gaze away as Jack started lowering his shirt. It was a slow motion, he hissed out a painful breath as the shirt dropped lower and lower. In one swift motion, the shirt was now crumpled up on the ground, revealing two deep cuts sliced into Jack's back. They were two vertical lines, parallel to one another. Fresh blood was dripping down his lower back and droplets fell to the ground, almost creating a river. The amount of blood falling from his scars made it hard for her to tell where the cuts started and ended.

Sophia had lingered far too long, she was breathing louder with each panicked breath but she still couldn't move. She didn't know what to do. Her heart lurched forward, wanting to console Jack and ask what had caused such violent scars but something in the pit of her stomach was telling her to walk away.

Was it fear?

Sophia's gaze followed Jack as he limped toward his window, pushing them open to let the breeze roll in. He pressed his hands down flat onto the windowsill and dropped his head in between his shoulders, pushing down onto his extended arms. All this did was push the scars further into Sophia's face, they were on full display and she couldn't bring herself to do anything.

Jack began panting heavily, like every breath was a struggle. There was an occasional whimper that escaped as he exhaled.

Should she call for help? It's not like he was being quiet? Surly others could hear his cries. Why had no one come to help him?

Was this why Cassandra was so protective over him?

Did she know this was happening? Why else would she act the way she did? A mother's intuition can be a powerful thing.

Fearfully, Sophia somehow managed to pull her gaze away from Jack. A rush of adrenalin filled her body as she wasted no time in bolting down the hallway, not caring if she woke the entire house, and ran straight to her bedroom.

Once inside, she slammed the door shut and pressed her back against the door, trying to compose herself. Her grip was tight around the lamp and her fast breath was hitting against the flame, causing it to spasm.

Sophia stormed to her bed, dropped the lamp down onto her bedside table and blew out the flame before she escaped under her covers. Pulling up the blanket to cover her mouth she tried to shut out the world, and forget that tonight even happened.

No matter how much she wished for that, it wasn't possible.

Every time she closed her eyes, the horrific cuts in Jack's back flashed directly in her view, like she was standing in front of him.

She tried to conjure what could have possibly caused such a traumatic injury. A whip? A knife? But to be exact lines down his back, almost as if they were placed there on purpose didn't make sense.

None of this made sense.

Sophia was in Jack's company almost every day, and not once had he acted this way. What happened on their way back to the orphanage had never happened before, not in front of Sophia anyway.

Surely an injury that bad would require medical attention, some time in the infirmary?

Was he involved with thugs?

Did he have an unpaid debt?

None of these scenarios fit Jack's character, not the one Sophia thought she knew.

Chapter Two

There is always a door.

In her dreams Sophia is always presented with a large wooden door. It's painted an eggshell white against a grey chevron wall. There are a few chips in the paint, four to be exact.

It's just a regular door, it doesn't do anything in her dreams. It doesn't morph into anything, it's just a door.

It's not a door Sophia has ever come across in her life, it doesn't match anywhere in the orphanage and it doesn't match anywhere she commonly visits.

If it was a one off dream it wouldn't take up too much space in her mind, but was a common occurrence. Each night, the door gets a little bit closer. And each time she prayed she could reach out and open it to find out what was on the other side.

Whenever she thought of what could be on the other side, it sent a dark chill down her spine. She didn't know why, she just felt as though whatever was behind the door wasn't something she wanted to see.

Sophia awoke with a headache, the sun streaming in from her window didn't do much to help.

Pushing herself up and leaning on her elbows, her eyes adjusted to the blurry room. She was all too familiar with this room, she knew it like it was the back of her hand.

Sophia knew there were exactly seven cracks across the ceiling, the striped wallpaper was starting to separate from the wall at each corner and it always had a musky smell that lingered in her nostrils. It smelled like what she imagined the inside of an elderly woman's purse would smell like, which only added to her insecurities. If her room smelled like that it would only mean she too would hold that same musk.

After a few minutes of lying in the same spot, not wanting to get up, she pushed the blankets off from her body and got out of bed.

Sophia sat down at her vanity and looked at her morning appearance, her brunette hair was as wild as a lion's mane and she was not looking forward to taming it. As much as she tried not to look, it was staring her right in the face, the scars that occupied the left side of her face. Two on her cheek that overlapped to look like an X, and three across her chin.

They weren't the only scars she held, she had a couple of sporadic ones on her ribs, torso and inner thigh. All of which were housed on the left side of her body. The scars on her body didn't cause her too much concern, for she could easily cover them up with her clothes but she could do nothing to hide the scars on her face. They were the first thing people would look at when they saw her.

Perhaps what frustrated her most about her scars was that she has no memory of how she acquired them. There is a part of her memory that is wiped from her mind. All she knew was that she had them the day she arrived at the orphanage. She cannot remember a time without them.

Not only did the scars remind her of her deep insecurities, but now she was also reminded of Jack and the gruesome slashes across his back. No matter what excuse she could think of for him, whatever explanation she conjured in her mind, none felt like the correct revelation. The only explanation she could think was reasonable was that he got involved in a fight, or a violent attack.

But Jack was the type of man to walk away from a fight, and not get involved in the first place.

Sophia's head was so full of theories and concern that she was certain her head was going to be anchored down to the flat surface of her vanity table, and not even the strongest men could raise her up.

Thankfully, there was a knocking at her bedroom door. Stella soon entered, her sandy blonde hair was in her usual loose bun, topped with a white cap, and the odd strands dangling over her rosy cheeks.

"Would you like help getting ready today, Miss?" Stella asked, in her usual mouse-like voice.

"Would you be angry if I said yes?" Sophia replied, as she pulled her brunette locks over her shoulder, so her curls tumbled over her chest. "Only so I can steal your time away from others?"

A timid smile grew on Stella's pink lips, she tried to hide it by facing the door to close it but Sophia saw it. Other than Jack, Stella was the only person in this orphanage who spent time with Sophia. She would enjoy their conversations and she wouldn't shy away from her when they would pass each other. Sophia liked to consider her a sister, as she would open up to her about whoas and Stella would listen. Sophia always offered the same to Stella but she politely declined.

She was very much a closed book.

Sophia wasn't sure how much of Stella's kindness was down to her being the maid of the house or because she genuinely enjoyed Sophia's company. She liked to think it was the latter, but considering how everyone else treated her it's hard for her to believe.

"I would actually like help with my hair," Sophia picked up the ends and held it out in front of her face. "I'm not sure what I did in my sleep last night to cause such a mess."

Stella stepped behind her, and Sophia watched her in the mirror as she picked up her brush and got to work in combing out the knots. Stella had a very beautiful face, her lips were full and her eyes were a deep, rich brown. She had the kind of face that was inviting, anyone could sit and talk to her for hours and still find things to admire.

There were a handful of maids who worked at the orphanage, some dealt with cooking, others had allocated rooms to clean and Stella's jobs were to make the beds and assist the household members. Since there were less than a dozen people who lived in the orphanage it wasn't too much of a task to bear.

Stella was the only maid permitted to have her own bedroom, all of the other workers stayed out of everyone's way until it was time to go home. When it came to quitting time they couldn't get out of the doors fast enough, Sophia never bothered to learn any of their names.

Once Stella was finished lacing Sophia's corset, she assisted Sophia in putting on her dress for the day. It had long sleeves which reached to her wrists, made of a soft cotton material that wasn't too heavy to endure. The dress was made for simplicity, a plain lavender colour with a pastel yellow at the chest.

As Stella buttoned up the back of the dress, Sophia's eyes fell onto her jewellery box. She didn't wear jewellery often, only for special occasions like birthday celebrations or trips to the opera. The box was far too big for the small amount of jewellery she owned, with two sets of earrings, three bracelets and a single necklace.

The necklace was the only piece that held any meaning for her, the others she wouldn't even notice if they were stolen.

Sophia opened up the jewellery box, it was slightly stiff as it's been a while since she opened it. Sitting above everything else was the necklace, she pulled it out by the golden chain and held it in front of her face. She forgot how pretty it was.

Sitting on the chain was a simple oval locket. Carved into the back was an inscription of, *always.*

"That's beautiful," Stella said, she was stealing glances in the mirror.

A faint smile danced on Sophia's lips, "It is, isn't it?" She said as more of a statement than a question. "Jack gifted it to me on my fourteenth birthday..." as she spoke those words Sophia realised she hadn't worn it since Jack gifted it to her. There wasn't a valid reason as to why not, it certainly wasn't ugly and it would go with almost every dress in her wardrobe.

"I don't believe I've seen you wear it, Miss."

"I can always change that," Sophia unclasped the chain and wrapped it around her neck. She locked the necklace in place and let the cold locket rest above her cleavage. It was beautiful, but there was something about it that made her feel like she was being weighed down.

An abrupt wave of anxiety washed over her. It didn't take long for her to realise that this stemmed from the knowledge that Jack would see her wear it after four years.

Would he be angry that she hadn't worn it before now?

There was something that made it feel worse if he was happy to see her wearing it.

"It suits you," Stella took a step back and clasped her hands in front of her white apron.

Sophia couldn't bring herself to keep her gaze off of the necklace in the mirror. "Does it?"

It wouldn't take a genius to tell that Sophia wasn't convinced in the slightest.

"Let me fix your hair," Stella said, nervously.

Stella swiftly combed out the knots in her hair, and grabbed two thick locks and pinned them to cross behind her head. She left the rest of her natural curls to tumble down her back.

Stella was happy with her work and lowered her hands back down to her sides, she offered a faint smile to Sophia's reflection but there was something else in her eyes. A sadness that was front and centre, like she wanted to admit something but couldn't. Instead, Stella said, "You look as beautiful as ever, Sophia."

Stella quickly resumed with her chores once she was finished helping Sophia get ready for the day.

Sophia checked her reflection one last time, maybe this time her scars would have magically disappeared. When her gaze fell upon her own face she was severely disappointed to see them still present.

When Sophia stepped out of her room she was ready to make her way downstairs. That was until Robert Shaw caught her eye. He was standing six doors down in front of his sister's bedroom door. His hands were balled into such tight fists that he could squeeze the juice out of an orange. He was pounding on the door, the force in which he was knocking could be enough to send his fist flying through.

Robert's upper lip was curled as he snarled at the door like an impatient dog ready to pounce.

The only way anyone could describe the face he was wearing as pure unfiltered rage.

Sophia looked to the stairs on her left and considered pretending like she hadn't seen Robert, but the look on his face was concerning. He was known for having a short fuse but how could she walk away if anything had happened to his twin sister, Hannah?

As she cautiously approached Robert, Sophia clasped her hands in front of her and squeezed her palms tightly. She couldn't remember the last time Robert and herself had a conversation, she would bet all the money she had saved over the years that there wasn't a single time.

Ensuring to leave a wide gap between them when she came to a halt beside Robert, Sophia asked, "Is everything alright?"

Robert lowered his fist from Hannah's door and brought it up to the bridge of his nose and pinched, tightly. He released a sharp breath, like he found Sophia's presence to be a nuisance. "Hannah won't come out of her room."

Sophia stood awkwardly and just stared at Robert, words were not on her side as she struggled to find anything to say.

Were words of comfort needed? He didn't seem like he wanted them.

Sophia settled on asking, "Is she ill? Does she need a nurse?"

Robert dropped his hand from the bridge of his nose and slapped it against his thigh. He rolled his golden eyes and started shaking his head, like what Sophia had innocently suggested was the worst idea that could ever be conjured by man.

Before Sophia could take another breath, Robert turned to face her and barged past her, his shoulder knocking with hers. If he apologised she couldn't hear it with his grumblings.

Sophia stumbled and was too slow to turn around and yell out the highly inappropriate names she wanted to call him.

Not only had Robert purposely barged past Sophia, Stella had exited one of the rooms at the wrong time. He too pushed past her, causing her to drop the pile of laundry she was holding. It spilled from her hands and gathered around her feet.

Stella let out a defeated sigh as she sank to the floor and began picking it up, she didn't seem shocked by Robert's outburst. It's almost like she would be surprised if he didn't do something like that.

Sophia sank down with Stella and began helping her pick up the multiple pieces of clothing.

"You don't need to help with this, Miss." Stella said, as she picked up her pace.

"It's no trouble," Sophia smiled, sweetly at her. "What kind of friend would I be if I left you like this."

Stella's eyes shot up to Sophia in surprise. When she said nothing in return, a little piece of Sophia's heart chipped away.

She considered Stella a friend but it was the first time she directly referred to herself as one. It was clear from the look on her face that it was a one sided affection.

"Anyway, Robert had no right or reason to barge past you like that." Sophia said, trying to hide the hurt in her voice.

They rose to their feet at the same time and Sophia handed her the clothes. Stella nervously smiled at her, and surprised Sophia by saying, "Mr Shaw doesn't mean it, he's just going through things with Miss Shaw."

How could she possibly know that?

Sophia shot her a quizzical look, as though to ask her that very question.

Stella's cheeks flushed and she dipped her head and excused herself before elaborating further.

There was no point in trying to prod her further, Stella clearly didn't trust her with whatever she was referring to. Instead, she decided to let it go and headed straight for the dining room. She wished she had just gone there in the first place, if she had ignored Robert then she wouldn't be walking through the hall feeling more worthless than she did on most days.

Chapter Three

All of her thoughts vanished when she stepped inside of the dining room and her nostrils were greeted with the smell of toasted buns and the sweet scent of fresh fruit.

The table looked empty today, there were currently only six people present including Sophia. Robert had stormed off to have a tantrum, Hannah locked herself in her room for undisclosed reasons and Sophia hadn't seen Jack all morning. Which she was secretly thankful for. She wasn't sure she was ready to interrogate him in regards to what she had witnessed last night.

Sitting at her usual spot, she could feel the glances from the other members present. Every morning they would do this, like they were waiting for her to have an outburst and Sophia couldn't figure out *why*. She never had a conversation with any of these people, not from lack of trying. And not once had she raised her voice, even at times when she could have.

Scanning her eyes over the long rectangular table, Sophia couldn't help but wonder why there were so many empty seats.

Which brought her to question why so many unfilled rooms that were never occupied.

There were thousands of children and teenagers that were orphans in London alone. Only a dozen orphans claimed shelter here. Many children in the past few years have knocked on the door, pleading for a place to stay but every time they were turned away with no signs of remorse.

Sophia was only certain of this because she had been witness to it.

One night four years ago, a thrashing storm kept her from sleeping so she went downstairs for a glass of water. Before she could even reach the bottom of the stairs, she noticed Cassandra standing at the front door. Her back was straight and shoulders stiff, she stood like that whenever she was lecturing Jack for misbehaving.

Something in Sophia told her to turn around and run back up the stairs but her feet were welded to the floor. She peaked over Cassandra's shoulder and noticed a girl, no older than six years old, standing in the doorway. Her pencil thin fingers laced together, and her scraggly black hair dripping down her face, her eyes were bulging out of her head as she whispered, "Please, Miss, please..." to Cassandra.

Cassandra replied with not a trace of sympathy or emotion in her voice. "There is no room." Followed by her slamming the door in the girls face.

That was the night Sophia saw Cassandra in a completely different light. Before that night she saw her as strict with a big heart and only wanted the best for everyone around her; now that couldn't be further from the truth.

There was always room at the orphanage, there were rooms gathering dust. How could she turn a poor defenceless child into the harsh world, when she herself was a mother?

Sophia thought of that girl every night for a couple of weeks, and prayed to God that she had managed to find a safe place to stay. Deep in the pit of her stomach she knew the harsh realities of what monsters lay deep in London streets and it made her want to throw up. She couldn't look at Cassandra for a while after that night, she had the chance to take in that poor girl and turned her away with no reason.

A jolt flashed through Sophia, shocking her out of her thoughts when Jack abruptly entered the dining room.

He slid into his seat beside Sophia and picked up a roll of bread and immediately began cutting into it.

How could he possibly act so nonchalant, like he didn't have two gruesome cuts deep into his back.

Sophia suddenly didn't know how to act around him, she didn't know how to act in general. She felt like the man sitting next to her, the man she thought she knew for ten years, was a stranger. Anytime she looked at him, or stole a glance she was reminded of last night.

Jack struck up a conversation with Alice Watts, sitting opposite him at the table. She was giggling at almost every word he spoke. She was one of the many girls infatuated with Jack, she would twirl her short red hair around in her fingers in his presence. Whereas she couldn't even greet Sophia with a simple *hello.*

Much like everyone else in the orphanage, Sophia never had the chance to get to know Alice. Not from a lack of trying. Every time she attempted to start a conversation, as if a routine, Alice would drop her gaze, bite her bottom lip then find an excuse to leave or strike a conversation with someone else.

Sophia had no idea what she did to turn everyone at the orphanage against her but she wished someone would tell her so she could at least apologise.

Now she doesn't even bother to say a simple hello, not unless someone else initiates it.

"Sophia?" Jack must have been talking to her but she was too lost in her own thoughts.

She flinched when his hand touched her arm, "Sorry...what did you say?"

Jack noticed her flinch, and there was hurt in his eyes and that sent a spark of anger through her veins. He had no right to feel any sort of hurt toward her, he was the one keeping secrets. Granted he didn't *know* that she knew about his scars, but still.

"I asked if you slept well."

Any other day Sophia would have answered without any scepticism. Now she questioned his intent, was he mocking her?

Did he know that she knew of the scars?

Was he testing her?

"I did, thank you." Sophia answered flatly, and poured herself a glass of orange juice. As she took a sip, as the refreshingly sweet juice trickled down her throat she looked all around the room, completely avoiding meeting Jack's lingering gaze.

More so, Sophia was afraid of what natural expression she would give Jack. She was quite confident that it would consist of a fiery glare with a puzzled brow. Even then he would most likely try and dismiss her in the form of a friendly joke.

She knew she had to bring this up with him, how could she not? It was just about pinpointing when the most appropriate time would be.

Jack didn't take his eyes off her, and Sophia could feel every painstaking glance. His eyes scanned her face for any sign of what was wrong with her.

"Are you alright?" Jack reached out again, placing his delicate hand over her shoulder. She stiffened at his touch.

When she didn't answer right away, Jack retracted his hand and began brushing out imaginary creases in his navy trousers.

Was she being childish? In Jack's eyes he had done nothing wrong. He simply showed up for breakfast like it was any other day. That was the problem. The scars, the intense pain last night...they all seemed to be expected. Jack had no fear in his eyes, like this wasn't something new.

How long had he been enduring this?

How long had he kept this a secret from Sophia?

Why?

"I'm sorry, I...I..." Sophia started but couldn't find the right words. Would it be appropriate to talk about over breakfast buns and orange juice? Was she willing to put him in an uncomfortable situation in front of other household members?

She still loved Jack, she couldn't let her hurt feelings cloud her most important agenda.

Sophia finally turned her head to face him fully, she brought up her shoulder to her chin to shrug. "I simply wanted to check you were alright."

Jack's golden eyebrow shot up, as though he was confused. "If I am alright?"

"Yes," her tone was sharp. Internally pleading with him, she begged he would not make this more painful than it already was. "I heard you fighting with your mother last night, and I was simply-"

Jack waved his hand in front of his face, "My mother and I fight all of the time, I'm almost certain she views it as more of a hobby nowadays."

Sophia forced a smile and laughed along with Jack's joke, although it wouldn't surprise her if that turned out to be the truth.

There was a spark in Jack's eye when he noticed the necklace hanging over Sophia's chest. Of course he recognised the locket immediately, and he certainly didn't hide how happy that made him. "This is the first time I have seen you wear this," Jack pointed to the locket.

Sophia's cheeks blushed as she dropped her head and stared down at her plate, "That is not true," she giggled. "I tried it on when you gave it to me."

Jack nodded, as though he suddenly remembered. "Of course, I suppose all I meant was that it has been a long time since I've seen you wear it. I'd started to worry you had thrown it out."

Sophia snapped her head and looked at him with her mouth wide open, shocked that he would think she would ever throw away something which he had gifted her. "I can assure you that I will never throw this away, it means a lot to me because *you* gifted it to me."

His eyes widened, he wasn't expecting her to say something like that. Even his lips parted slightly as he tried to think of an

41

appropriate response. Suddenly, Jack realised where he was and cleared his throat. "Well, I'm glad," he said, lowering his gaze and resumed buttering his roll. "It looks beautiful on you."

Before Sophia had the chance to protest his compliment, the door leading to Cassandra's office swung open, causing a booming echo across the dining room. Every member had either flinched or dropped whatever they were holding, causing a stir amongst the household.

Cassandra stormed out of her office with a crumpled up letter in her hand. Her hair was twisted up into a bun at the back of her head, and two loose strands outlined the shape of her face.

Her husband, Albert was trailing behind and chirping in his wife's ear. It looked like he was pleading with her to calm down.

It was still surprising that Albert and Cassandra were husband and wife, with her youthful looks she looked like she could be Albert's daughter. He wasn't as blessed with his ageing appearance, his hair was almost a complete shade of white, with only a few strands of brown left.

As Cassandra approached the table Jack began sinking lower into his chair, expecting for his mother's wrath to be aimed at him.

"Sophia," Cassandra announced when she reached the head of the table, her palm clutched tightly around the sheet of paper in her hand.

Everyone turned to look at Cassandra, and a few hushed whispers were hushed between household members.

Sophia tried to remain poised as she waited with an anticipating breath to hear what Cassandra had to say.

"The Council has requested an audience with you," she said through flared nostrils. "We leave immediately."

The Council?

A panic surged deep inside her chest, Sophia was sure she would pass out.

The Council governed the orphanage, they were the ones Cassandra had to deal with on a daily basis. She couldn't make any final decisions on the state of the orphanage, she had to plead her case for any changes that she deemed necessary.

There wasn't much that frightened Cassandra, but it was obvious that The Council was one of those things.

Which of course, didn't fill Sophia with any form of ease. If anything, it poured an extra amount of anxiety into her heart.

Her palms became uncomfortably damp, her heart raced in a panic and she suddenly struggled to breathe in the air around her.

"W-what is the reason?" She did a terrible job in fighting the fear in her voice.

"They only wrote requesting you," Cassandra huffed, and wrapped her hand around Sophia's arm, pulling her up to her feet. Her chair creaked as the legs dragged against the wooden floor, all eyes were on them and Sophia hated that. "We mustn't keep him waiting."

Jack was now out of his chair and smoothing out his shirt. His mother locked a fiery gaze to Jack, a harsh plea for him not to do exactly what she thought he was doing. "Where do you think you are going?"

"I am going to accompany you on this trip." Jack said, smugly.

A choke of baffled laughter raised up Cassandra's throat, her claws still deep into Sophia's arm. "Absolutely not."

When her voice raised past the appropriate level for breakfast she dropped her grip around Sophia's arm. Her crystal eyes scanned the room, only now realising they had an audience, Cassandra snapped her gaze back to her son. She pointed at both

Sophia and Jack and her index and middle finger, and snarled, "You two. Follow me. Now."

Without looking over her shoulder to check that they were following, Cassandra crashed into the door in which she came in from, and slammed it shut as fast as a lightning bolt.

All three of them stood awkwardly and the rest of the room tried to fill the dull silence with idle chatter.

Albert merely shrugged his shoulders, like this was just a regular day, and followed after his wife. Sophia and Jack followed shortly after.

There was only one time that Sophia had ever been called into Cassandra's office, and it was enough to put her off ever stepping foot inside again. She was reprimanded for visiting the town without someone to accompany her. Something that she still considered odd to this day, considering she knew others in the orphanage that had trips alone. They weren't discreet, and Sophia thought it unfair only she was singled out for it.

Her office was very spacious, there was enough room for a floral loveseat and rectangular coffee table in the centre. A mahogany desk took up most of the back wall, with stacks of papers and a quill in ink on display.

The morning sun lit the room with a warming glow, that wouldn't last for too long as soon as the clouds started to roll in.

Cassandra sat at her desk, her arms folded firmly across her chest as her glare focused on her son. Even though she was possibly the most beautiful woman in London, if Cassandra's anger was aimed at you the only option you would have would be to flee the country. Even that wouldn't be enough to escape her.

Albert stood beside her, as always. He was the calmer out of the two, he had a more level head and always did his best to talk his wife down. For Albert was the only person to ever get through to Cassandra, it was clear how much they adored one another.

"The last thing I want is for you to create another scene, Jack." Cassandra finally spoke, her voice laced in warning.

"*Another* scene?" Jack scoffed. "Mother, when have I ever-"

Cassandra raised her hand in the air in one quick motion, "Do not test me. I have enough on my plate with this unexpected call from The Council. "

"Why must Sophia go?"

Sophia felt unsettled by Jack speaking for her, and asking questions on her account. She had not once done this to him, and she couldn't help but feel a little insulted. He felt the need to defend her. Not once did he stop and ask if she *wanted* him here.

She kept her head down, eyeing up the unusual pattern of the carpet. It helped for only a moment to distract from two people talking about her as if she wasn't present. It was what she imagined two parents would do, arguing about what the other believes is best for their child without actually involving the child in the conversation.

"There are two separate issues according to the letter we were sent from Lord Paine," Albert said in a tired breath. When Sophia looked up to Albert as he spoke, she noticed that he had put his hand on the back of Cassandra's chair, he looked to be struggling to hold himself up. It only added to how much older Albert appeared compared to his wife. Where she was blemish and wrinkle free, Albert was an old leather book. With creases at every curve, he looked frail and one slight touch could cause him to crumble.

"Sophia has never visited The Council before," Jack argued. "This might be overwhelming for her. Lord Paine isn't exactly a welcoming and understanding man." He finally acknowledged Sophia's presence by turning to look at her. "Wouldn't you rather me accompany you?"

Why did he have to put her on the spot like this? She met his piercing blue eyes and knew the wave of guilt she would feel if she said no. When she turned back to Cassandra, and the fiery stare in her eyes was enough to make her want to run to her room and lock herself inside for all eternity. Sophia knew that no matter what she chose someone would be angry or disappointed.

And Jack knew her too well. So she looked back to Jack, met his gaze and offered a sweet smile. "I would."

Cassandra released a loud sigh and pushed herself to her feet, the chair almost toppling over from force. She was about to passionately protest, until Albert placed a gentle hand over her shoulder, halting her. "Darling, we will get nowhere with this constant back and forth." He dug his free hand into his coat pocket. "Let's just all go to the town hall and get this out of the way, hmm?"

Pinching the bridge of her nose, Cassandra realised her husband was right - but she certainly wasn't happy about that.

Smacking her hand back down to her thigh she locked eyes with her son again, "Fine. But you are not to request any favours from me, do you understand?"

Cassandra didn't give Jack a chance to agree, before storming out of her office leaving a thunderstorm in her wake.

Albert slowly stepped around to Jack's side and patted him on the back in a sympathetic motion. "You have gotten me into trouble also," he didn't seem too concerned by it though as a ghost of a smile appeared on his lips.

Chapter Four

Inside of the carriage was certainly spacious in appearance, but the thick awkward fog had settled in the empty seats, causing everyone to feel trapped within their own seat.

Sophia sat completely still, keeping her gaze locked out of the window.

No matter how hard she tried not to get carried away with her thoughts, of the worst case scenario as to why she was being summoned to The Council, Sophia couldn't help but fuel the panic already ignited in her blood.

Sophia attempted to gather her thoughts. She never committed a crime or stepped out of line once in her life.

They arrived quicker than she was expecting, The Council was in the centre of London and usually the streets would be bombarded with traffic and drunks passing out in the street, but today was eerily calm. Once she stepped down from the carriage and the cold London air hit her cheeks, Sophia suddenly felt her lungs restricting the amount of air she could intake. A rush of panic filled her chest as she looked up to the marble white building that didn't fit in with the run down houses on the opposite side of the street.

Members of the public were being escorted from the premises whilst shouting and screaming inaudible curses.

Tall white pillars outlined the front doors and statues of angels lined the building, all of which looked down upon those who entered. As if they were casting a harsh judgment of all who dared approach.

Rain trickled down from the clouded skies, soon causing a river in the street.

Jack pulled out his umbrella from the back seat of the carriage and huddled underneath it with Sophia. She was growing increasingly aware of how close he was to her, she could feel his hot breath hitting her face. He met her eyes and offered his arm, "Shall we?"

"I said you could come with us to the town hall," Cassandra stepped in between them, snatching the umbrella from Jack's loose grip, and pushing Sophia into the rain. "I never said you could come inside." Her other hand gripped onto Sophia's arm and pulled her up the steep steps.

Before Jack had the chance to protest they were already inside and slamming the doors to a close.

Sophia's heart was racing in her chest and she felt as though her stomach was in her throat. What she was most afraid of was the unknown. She hoped that she would be seen instantly, that she didn't have to wait around for her fate to be decided for her. A growing need clawed at her throat, to be told what she had done wrong and what her punishment would be. Just to get it out of the way.

Inside was what Sophia would imagine a brothel would look like. People screaming and yelling at members of staff who looked unfazed by the world around them. Sophia found it more disturbing that more than three pools of vomit sat across the floor. Based on the smell she wouldn't be surprised if it were more than a week old.

Outside resembled something as equally regal as Buckingham Palace but inside couldn't be further from that.

The female receptionist was being harassed by two women who - based on their revealing clothing and provocative mannerisms - were prostitutes. One had her arms draped around a security guard's neck and puckering her lips, attempting to kiss him. It would appear that no one was off limits. Whilst the other rested her breasts on the front desk and screamed incoherently at the woman doing her job.

Almost every male that wasn't an employee was drunk and struggling to stand up straight. They were demanding money to feed their alcohol addictions whilst slurring their words.

Sophia felt completely out of place amongst these people. How could The Council be so unorganised? She was on the verge of turning around and locking herself inside of the carriage.

If Jack were permitted inside perhaps she would have felt a bit more at ease. Instead, she had to settle for his mother and father, who weren't exactly in a comforting mood.

They were approached by a gentleman, who looked to be in his early forties. He was dressed in a blue and white tailored suit, with a gold chain hanging from the breast pocket. His hair was thinning and slicked back to hide the bald spot. "Lord Paine requests you in his office." He spoke with a thick northern accent.

Sophia reluctantly followed Cassandra and Albert to Lord Paine's office, they seemed to know the way without the gentleman's assistance.

The office was wide and decorated in shimmering black and gold wallpaper. Lord Paine's desk was cluttered with unorganised paperwork, ornaments gathering layers of dust and an assortment of pens scattered around.

The man, who Sophia presumed was Lord Paine, was sitting at the desk. He held up his head with his fist and watched Sophia enter, wearing a bored expression.

If you exclude the complete mess that this office was, his room screamed wealth, Sophia had no doubt where most of the funding for The Council went to. With the wallpaper alone looking more expensive than the orphanage itself. It's a shame it was wasted on someone with such a disorganised environment.

Sophia seriously doubted there were cleaners working here, or if they did they had a hell of a job to do every day.

The dull silence of the room was quickly filled by an impatient tapping noise, coming from Lord Paine's finger hitting against his oak desk.

Sophia avoided his gaze and took in more of his office. Her eyes trailed along the tall, thin bookcase. She wondered if any of his books could be found in the orphanage's library, and she considered if it would be inappropriate to ask if he had any recommendations.

Eventually she turned her gaze back to Lord Paine and his mouth hooked up to form a half smile. It wasn't a pleasant smile. It was like what you would get from a welcoming grandfather, but something sinister lurking behind it.

Lord Paine's light grey eyes locked on Sophia's as he cracked his slender fingers.

He was dressed more informally that the rest of the room would suggest. He fashioned a simple navy button-up shirt with the first three buttons undone, as if he is already unwinding from a full day at work and it was not even noon. A white overcoat was bound at his waist, certainly not a man of style. His dark red hair was slicked over the left side of his face. "It's a pleasure to meet you, Miss Cole." With such a formality in the way he spoke, it almost tipped Sophia over the edge for the amount of unease she was feeling.

Lord Paine couldn't have been much older than Albert, who was fifty-five years old. Based on looks, Lord Paine was blessed with a minimal amount of wrinkles and not a single strand of grey hair.

Before Sophia could reply, Cassandra cut in. "You have requested Sophia for a purpose. Please could you cut to the chase."

Lord Paine slouched back in his chair and raised one of his thick eyebrows, clearly unimpressed with Cassandra's tone. "Very well," he said in a breath. He opened the draw on the left side of his desk and pulled out a faded beige envelope. Taking his time, he pulled out the letter inside. "Am I correct that you will be turning eighteen within the next few months?

Cassandra was shuffling her feet and let out a sharp and short breath. Everyone could feel Cassandra's frustrations, it was practically in the air they breathed.

"The reason I ask," Lord Paine continued. "Is because five years ago I was given a letter. A...contract or a will. However you would like to say it doesn't really matter."

It was then that Sophia realised her hands were shaking. She clasped her hands behind her back to hide her fear.

"Addressed to you Miss Cole," he looked down his sharp thin nose to the letter and started reading. "I trust my will has made it to the appropriate hands. Once I have passed on, my only request is for my daughter, Miss Sophia Cole, to be married by her eighteenth birthday. If my terms are not met then The Council must refuse shelter and future employment in the United Kingdom and the surrounding areas. This includes any current residency she has. I know my words are harsh and sudden, but I do not want my daughter to be alone in this cruel world. With a husband, she will have someone to guide her. She will take her place in society as a proper lady. Signed by, T.C and endorsed by C.C."

Lord Paine slipped the letter back inside of the envelope and slid out of his chair. With one hand in his pocket, creating a small gap between them where he stood. He handed Sophia the letter and said, "Also known as, Theresa Cole and Christopher Cole." He looked her in the eye, intently. "Your mother and father."

Sophia couldn't catch the gasp before it escaped past her lips. She felt as though a black hole had appeared around her feet, sucking her down to the core of the planet. She was sure she was trembling but she stood motionless, barely breathing. It was the first time in her life she ever truly felt numb.

Marriage. Her mother and father wanted her to marry, within no less than three months. How could she find a husband in three months? She always knew she would marry for love but that seemed to be an out of reach dream, like owning a mansion with horses trotting freely in the garden.

Warm tears outlined her eyes but she forced them back, she refused to show weakness in front of Lord Paine.

"You didn't think to notify her of this sooner?" Albert spoke up, visibly furious at what he had just heard.

Lord Paine pointed at the envelope now in Sophia's tense hands. He tapped his large index finger down five times, almost causing Sophia to drop it, and said, "Do not open until February 17th, 1839." He took a step back and chuckled. "I'm not sure how you run your orphanage but I like to have a level of organisation."

Albert turned his head to signal the chaos in the main hall, and the mess he called a desk. "Clearly."

"In my work." Lord Paine clarified.

Sophia looked up to Cassandra to gain any form of comfort, but her eyes were unwavering from Lord Paine. "What was the reason for my summoning? We've already held our quarterly meeting."

Lord Paine fixed the collar of his shirt and ran a hand through his dark red hair. "There is a...situation that requires your assistance." He flicked his index finger back and forth to signal them to follow him.

They left his office and he led them straight through the vomit soaked main hall. Through one door and down a long corridor. Later they arrived at a dimly lit, bolted metal door. There were three locks securing whatever was being held inside. Whatever was through that door was certainly dangerous enough to warrant all of this protection.

As Lord Paine pulled out a large brass key and released each of the locks, Albert placed a gentle hand on Sophia's shoulders. "It is not wise for you to accompany us."

"Oh it is," Lord Paine chirped. "She will not understand either way, so come along."

Sophia felt insulted by his comment, did he think she was stupid? How could he make such a judgement within minutes of meeting her?

The door shrieked open. Sophia was frightened to be led down into a dark stairwell that this door led to. She wasn't so sure she wanted to be a part of whatever this was.

Albert and Cassandra shared the same troubled look. After a moment of hesitation all three followed him down the dark set of steep cobbled stairs. Without a railing to hold onto Sophia was sure she would tumble down, crashing into everyone in front of her and causing a domino effect.

"Now, I must warn you," Lord Paine's voice echoed. "It's not a pretty sight down here."

Sophia used the condensed walls around her to steady herself down the stairs. She looked to her gloved hands and realised that a black goo had stained the white material.

Candles lit their way down, what felt like, a never ending staircase.

Sophia's foot caught on something, causing her to almost lose her balance. Catching herself on the cold, wet walls she exhaled a shaky breath. She lifted the bottom of her skirt only to find a skull inches away from her foot. One of the eye sockets had collapsed into dust.

Releasing a loud scream and almost falling backwards onto the step, Sophia could not pull her gaze away from the skull. Her body was telling her to run, to flee from this stairwell before they reached the bottom but she froze in place. She prayed it wasn't real and that it was some sick hoax. But no artist alive could sculpt something that realistic.

"Lord Paine, I mean no disrespect but Sophia is not used to this. She should not be here." Albert reached out his hand to Sophia's and held it gently.

And you are used to it? Sophia wanted to say.

"She'll learn soon enough." Lord Paine's voice echoed down the stairwell.

Albert grumbled under his breath.

"Thank you, Albert." Sophia somehow managed to compose herself and let out a weighted breath. "I shall be fine. It was just a shock." As ridiculous as it sounded, finding a skull at her feet was the least of her worries.

His eyes were full of concern. "Are you sure?"

Sophia was anything but sure about these stairs - about her future - but she had to push it aside for now. She just had to walk down these steps, get this over with, and she could return home and bury herself under her covers.

Albert was clearly unsatisfied but they pushed on.

Finally they reached the bottom, Sophia dreaded the thought of walking back up.

Across the large vacant space was a row of cells, each lit with an individual white candle. An eerie silence filled the space, with nothing but the sound of single drops of water hitting a puddle.

The strong scent of manure filled Sophia's nostrils, causing her to instinctively blanket her nose with her hand. When she inhaled through her mouth she could taste the foul stench.

"We have an issue with a recent prisoner," said Lord Paine, leading them to the cell located in the centre of the room. "You see, there has been an increase of murders across London and they are all young prostitutes. They all share a correlation to one another, teeth marks were found in their necks. The most recent murder took place two weeks ago and we found this animal at the scene of the crime. Of course he claims his innocence but due to his..." Lord Paine's eyes locked on Sophia's with a raised eyebrow.

He then shifted his gaze to Cassandra and grinned. "*Background*, I thought you could take him off my hands."

"Forgive me for interrupting," Sophia cut in, timidly from behind. Everyone turned to face her. Cassandra's concerned expression wasn't reassuring. "Are you saying that this man *bit* these women and they died? Also-"

"These questions are not important." Lord Pained waved his hand to signify he was done with her. "All he does is scream, and it is rather disturbing that I can hear him in my office. Considering what type of orphanage you run, I was hoping that you would take him off my hands until we find a way to dispose of him legally."

"What makes you think that I want a screaming murderer anywhere near my orphanage?" Cassandra huffed.

"You care about keeping your orphanage, don't you?"

Albert draped his arm around Cassandra's waist and pulled her close to his hip. "You cannot threaten us."

"I shouldn't have entertained the idea of that orphanage opening its doors in the first place. However, I am a man of business and I would like to offer a deal." Lord Paine turned on the wet cobbled ground and punched his hand into his trouser pockets. His glare focusing on Cassandra's, not hiding that he was clearly trying to intimidate her.

"We have already paid your original debt." Cassandra chimed up, her teeth grinding. She stepped away from Albert's embrace and laced her fingers together at the front of her skirt. "What could you possibly offer us that is equivalent to housing a murderer."

Lord Paine stepped into the light shining from the cracks in the walls. "I am not sure I like this tone you are taking with me," he sounded happy and giddy, which was only the more unsettling. "You seem to forget that I can cancel funding for your orphanage at any time."

Cassandra's jaw locked shut, she hated that Lord Paine was in complete control. She had to bite hard on her lip to prevent from saying anything that could further put her in a tight spot.

"How long would he stay?" Sophia asked, trying to take some of the heat and tension off of Cassandra.

Without taking his gaze from Cassandra, Lord Paine pulled out a set of keys from his pocket. Eventually he had to remove his gaze from Cassandra to hunt for the correct one. When he found it he unlocked the cells and ushered everyone inside.

Sophia was the last to enter, she'd be lying to herself if she said she wasn't terrified for her life.

Inside of the cell was a topless young man hung up in chains against the wall. His wrists were bound in heavy black shackles and pinned on the wall at either side of his head. His skin was covered in dirt and dried blood, with slashes across his torso that ran deeper than the wounds she witnessed on Jack's back.

The prisoner was motionless, Sophia wasn't sure if he was even breathing.

His head hung low between his broad shoulders. His raven black hair was drenched in, what Sophia could only assume was, sweat. Droplets of water fell from the ends of his hair and the tip of his crooked nose.

"Six months should suffice. I can't have him chained up in here for much longer for he will only break out and cause a ruckus." Lord Paine said, running a hand through his hair. "We've managed to sedate him up until now, but we can't keep wasting such valuable doses on him."

"What makes you think he won't escape from my orphanage? It is much less secure than a prison cell." Cassandra said.

Sophia wasn't concentrating on their conversations or arrangement of this prisoner's stay. She found herself blushing when she took in the lines of his torso. Deep and perfectly crafted lines made up his muscled chest.

The prisoner's breathing seemed to intensify as the conversation went on, like the very noise was causing him to become agitated.

Sophia jumped out of her trance when she heard Cassandra shout, her voice echoing across the empty cells. "Are you saying that you are excluding yourself from any responsibility if this prisoner escapes?"

Lord Paine shrugged, "If you don't like it then I will be more than happy to go upstairs and file for funding to stop indefinitely."

The prisoner's chains rattled as his hands formed into tight fists. Suddenly, like he had just been injected with a serum of life, he trashed his pelvis forward and jumped up to his knees. He bared his teeth like a manic dog, hissing with sharp fangs stretching below his bottom lip. A gasp escaped from Sophia when she noticed the prisoner's unnatural stretch of his canines. They looked sharp enough to slice through a plank of wood.

Enough to kill.

The prisoner fought to push himself free from the shackles.

Sophia shrieked and hid behind Albert, as if he would be able to protect her from a raging lunatic.

She couldn't help but look over Albert's shoulder to see what was happening. The prisoner's eyes were a pool of wild black.

The single candle lit his cell, casting a shadow on his face, revealing the deep curves of his cheekbones, and the sharp line of his jaw.

His chains were barely holding him back at the wall. They looked ready to release from their hinges.

Sophia was ready to turn and run the moment his eyes fell on hers. But something about his eyes sent her heart into a pitter patter. She couldn't explain it, but there was a sincerity there. A misunderstanding of sorts.

The prisoner soon slammed back down, resting his head and back against the wall. His once aggressive grunts and hissing were replaced with a deep and husky laughter. Clearly he found this whole situation hilarious, he got a kick out of frightening the people in front of him.

"This is fantastic!" said the prisoner.

Sophia was startled that he spoke in coherent sentences, and he had a formal tone to his voice. It wouldn't be completely unfair that Sophia thought this man was rather attractive, excluding the dirt and blood of course.

"The infamous Cassandra and Albert Green!" The prisoner chimed, as he dipped his head and looked up to Cassandra through his thick eyelashes. A smirk seemed to permanently be painted on his lips as he raised a single bushy eyebrow.

"You will not address us by our given names." Albert snapped.

"Please forgive me," the prisoner chucked. "I am not used to being in the presence of celebrities. We all know how legendary your love story is."

"Enough," Albert warned.

"Do tell," the prisoner continued anyway. "How can you judge my alleged crimes when you yourself have committed the worst crime of all?"

Cassandra and Albert have committed a crime? Sophia thought. She would have dismissed his ramblings but the look on Cassandra and Albert's faces showed a level of shame that Sophia had never seen from them before.

"That is none of your business." Cassandra hissed.

He smiled, as if triumphant.

The prisoner's eyes again locked on Sophia again, and his smirk stretched into a wide grin. "Who is this beauty?" He scanned her up and down from what he could see of her, causing Sophia to blush and suddenly feel naked. "I must say, if you were a prostitute you would be the richest woman in England, for the amount of men that would be begging to bed you."

Her mouth dropped, like she had been slapped in the face with a block of ice. Biting down on her bottom lip, it helped to fight back the words that were far too inappropriate for a young lady to even think.

"Mr Howell," Lord Paine sounded bored as he addressed the prisoner. "You will be staying at the orphanage and you will report to Cassandra every day. If you miss a single appointment you will be put to trial, and trust me when I say that you will not win."

"Why not trial him now?" Albert asked.

"A waste of funds that are required for bigger projects."

"Your back pocket, more like." Albert muttered under his breath.

Lord Paine either didn't hear Albert or pretend like he didn't.

Mr Howell pursed his lips. "No major punishment, I see." He smirked. "So, I will be in a cell at this orphanage? Or thrown into the basement like some disobedient dog."

Cassandra shook her head. "We treat the people who live at the orphanage with respect, regardless of their background. So much as you treat others the same there shouldn't be an issue."

"Will me and this lovely creature be sharing a room?" Mr Howell winked at Sophia.

"Don't be so foul!" Sophia finally spoke up.

Mr Howell only chuckled harder, his shoulders shaking. "Oh, I think I shall be happy at this *orphanage*."

Chapter Five

Sophia was in a complete daze back in the carriage. It was like her whole world had crumbled at her feet and there was no one to grasp onto to help pull her back up to the surface. She had so many questions that haunted her with answers she may never discover.

Finding the words to explain to Jack what had happened wasn't an option at that moment. It didn't help that he bombarded her with questions the minute her foot touched the outside of the town hall. A simple shake of the head was her response as she entered the carriage, using all her might not to cry.

No matter what silver lining she tried to find, her mind always brought her back. She had to find a husband in three months.

It throbbed in her head the idea that she had to be *married* by her eighteenth birthday. This wasn't how she wanted this to happen, forced to give her life away to anyone that would take her. Who would this "husband" be? The more she delved deep into her thoughts of her upcoming reality, the more she didn't want to be there.

Mr Howell traveled to the orphanage in a separate carriage, arranged by Lord Paine. It was a so-called "extra precaution" that he wouldn't escape before he got to the orphanage.

Jack was informed of everything in regards to the plan with the prisoner upon arrival. He instantly demanded that things be changed. He exclaimed that he wasn't comfortable with a murderer living under his roof, especially with a number of vulnerable women present. He proclaimed his disgust with the situation and that his mother should have put up more of a fight with Lord Paine.

"You seem to be under the impression that I want him here," Cassandra stopped in her tracks as they stood in the front hall. Standing directly under the golden chandelier with her eyes glaring through her son. "Just trust The Council and six months will be over before you know it."

"How can I accept that?" Jack scoffed.

Cassandra reached out her fingers and pinched his cheeks, leaving a red mark. It made him look like he was either blushing or flushed. "I honestly do not care if you accept it. You can either get yourself worked up and make yourself ill with fretting, or you can just keep away from this man entirely for the next six months."

Jack let out a harsh breath. "Is there a third option?"

She pulled her hand away from her son's cheeks and clasped them out in front of her. "You can leave if you can't get over your pathetic and childish tantrums." She started to walk away from him, clearly needing time alone to process her situation.

"Mother I-"

"No!" Cassandra abruptly stopped in her tracks, and turned on her heel to once again face Jack. Her eyebrows formed a deep crease in her once smooth forehead, and it was clear she was fighting back from screaming at the top of her lungs. "Go and stay at one of those dusty abandoned houses in the town. It is clear that I am not running a home that meets your standards."

"I did not mean-"

She cut him off with a raise of her hand, silencing him. "No, Jack. I put my heart and soul into running this place. I work every bone in my body to keep it standing whilst having everyone's interests at heart. I *refuse* to let one of your sulking tempers get in the way of my affairs. This is *my* orphanage, and it was *my* decision to go along with Lord Paine and permit Mr Howell to stay here. So, keep your mouth shut."

Sophia didn't dare say that Cassandra didn't have much of a choice to go along with Lord Paine's proposal. Even if she wanted to, she didn't have the energy to meddle in their feud. She had far more important things to worry about.

Without excusing herself, Sophia left the hall and headed straight upstairs to her room. She shut the world out behind her and collapsed onto her bed. She considered falling asleep but that would mean less time to figure out what she was going to do about finding a husband.

She wanted the world to disappear, she wished she could go back to this morning and refuse to visit The Council. Her day would have been normal if she hadn't heard what was written in that letter. How could such a frail sheet of paper hold such significance over the rest of her life.

Why would her mother do this? It seemed so cruel to not only force her daughter to marry but with such a restricted deadline also.

There was a gentle tap on her door, and she swiftly sat up and shuffled to the edge of her bed. There was an attempt to try and compose herself but it was useless.

"Come in."

The hinges creaked as the door opened, she didn't have to look up to know it was Jack. He was the only one - other than Stella - that would visit her.

Jack stopped in front of her.

Sophia's gaze locked on his thick black cane, as she still couldn't bring herself to look at him. She wasn't sure why she felt embarrassed, perhaps it was due to the lack of control she held over her own life.

"Care to accompany me on a stroll?" He said, "I hear that new stalls have opened?"

"Thank you for the offer, Jack." Her tone was as lifeless as the rhythm of her heart beating in her chest. "I really need some time to myself."

Jack let out a sigh and slid down beside Sophia. Her nostrils were treated to his signature smell of fresh pine and soap.

She could feel him watching her with his soft blue eyes. "If you are worried about that prisoner, you have no need to. You could see my disliking to the situation and my mother has assured me that he will be supervised and kept far away from you and-"

"It's not him," she admitted.

The room fell eerily still for a moment.

"Why did The Council request you?" He asked, cutting through their silence.

Sophia chewed her bottom lip, failing to fight the tears that she had been holding back all morning. "A letter was given to them...it was from my mother and father."

Jack's eyes widened with surprise.

"She is requesting that I be married by the time I turn eighteen. If I do not follow her demand then I shall be thrown out to the streets with nothing to my name and no chance of finding work in this country." There was a burning lump that formed in her throat, and each time she swallowed it was like she was igniting a match.

"My mother would never allow that to happen." Jack's tone was low and calm.

"She doesn't have a say. It was signed by my mother *and* father. It is a binding contract for my future." She lightly shook her head, failing to hide her sadness as a single tear trickled down her cheek. "I cannot marry because I am not in love. That *was* the only reason I wished to marry."

Jack was visibly uncomfortable by her statement as he shifted in his seat. His hand gripped tighter around his cane as his eyes lowered to her trembling fingers.

Without another word, Jack got to his feet and left Sophia in solitude.

Jack closed the door behind him. He turned, as if to say something to her closed door, and pressed his forehead against the smooth, hard wood and let out a deep breath.

After a few seconds he pushed himself up and headed down the hallway to his room.

His steps came to a halt when he heard heavy sobs coming from inside of Hannah's room. The realisation dawned on him that he had not seen her all day and that was unusual behaviour for her. She would always wait outside of his door in the morning, and greet him with a bubbly smile. It was as clear as day that she had a romantic affection towards him, one that her brother clearly didn't approve of.

Jack approached her room with caution and knocked on her door. He waited for a response but nothing happened.

Straightening the collar of his shirt, he cleared his throat. "Hannah?" Jack called. "I was just checking that you were alright."

Still no response.

"I haven't seen you today, I am still expecting a smile from you." He said through a tight smile of his own, hoping that would coax her out of her room.

Still nothing.

He pressed his ear against her door, and along with sobbing he could hear furniture crashing, and glass shattering.

"Hannah?"

"I'm fine!" She screamed at the top of her lungs. "Leave me!"

"What are you doing?"

Jack jumped back from the door when Robert approached him, his upper lip curling to a snarl.

Shifting his gaze from Robert and then to Hannah's door, clearly unsure of what to do. "I wanted to check if she was alright, I haven't seen her all day."

"You know that she's not," Robert hissed as he stepped in front of Hannah's door, acting as a form of guard dog.

Jack lowered his head and took a moment to say, "...Is it that bad...today?"

Robert seemed to loosen his tense shoulders. "It's getting worse, it doesn't seem to matter what day it is. I don't know what to do."

"Is there anything I can do?" Jack offered, but he knew the answer already.

Robert shook his head, and turned to face the door. "Just leave her alone, okay? She gets embarrassed when people hear her screaming. Just pretend that you can't hear her."

That was easier said than done but Jack simply nodded and said, "As you wish."

He left Robert soon after with a light pat on the back.

Inside of Jack's room, he lit a match and sparked a flame to light three fat candles on his nightstand.

Pulling off his dark grey coat, he stripped down until he was in nothing but his trousers.

In front of his tall mirror he examined his muscled torso. Clenched fists at his sides, to make his muscles more defined.

Every curve and crease was perfect. He lightly trailed his fingers across his torso, it was like running a feather across a cloud. "I look like a normal person from the front." He muttered to himself.

Pivoting to view his back in the reflection of the mirror, his eyes grazed down one of his deep cuts. "Why must I be...this... *abomination*?" He spat out the last word.

As if on cue, a shooting pain shot up through each of his scars. Like someone had taken a molten sword and dug it deeper into his wounds.

Jack uncontrollably stumbled back, crashing into the desk, the bedpost and finally the wardrobe. Leaving destruction in his path. Frames and vases shattered against the floor, a collection of glass gathered by his feet.

Groaning, he sank to the floor and buried his head in between his knees. It didn't do much to sustain his agony but he found the closer he was to the floor the more comforting it was.

He prayed that soon these attacks would end. They were happening far more frequently as of recent and he had no idea how to make them stop. It wasn't like he could prepare for an attack either, as there was no sign they were coming.

He wondered if his life was worth living if it would be full of agony, but Sophia was the only one keeping his strength up. He lived for her.

Chapter Six

"I am already expecting the answer to be no," Jack said. "But would you please accompany me on a stroll? I can't handle my mother's constant interference."

A walk would help Sophia get her mind off things, such as her impending doom of finding a husband within eight weeks. "I could do with the fresh air," she said.

Raising herself from her seat, she put the book down that she was reading and linked her arm through Jack's. "I could honestly do with a distraction, also."

Jack's smile deepened, revealing his dimples. "We could go to a show? Or treat ourselves at the market stalls?"

Sophia thought for a moment, she hadn't received this week's allowance so she couldn't exactly treat herself to such things. Every week The Council would give an allowance of 5 shillings to each member to purchase new clothes and so on.

"Can we go to the garden and read? Under the tallest willow tree?"

Jack didn't hide his disappointment. "You want to sit in the garden? I was hoping we could be more than two centimetres away from this place."

A giggle arose in her throat, "It will be relaxing," she promised. "We can read together?"

"I can read in my room any time," he huffed.

"You can shop at the market any time too," she looked up at him, batting her eyelashes.

When a faint smile appeared on his lips she knew she had him. "It's going to rain," he said.

The clouds were rolling in but until Sophia saw a single drop fall from the sky she was going outside. "We'll take an umbrella," she offered.

Jack chuckled, "Do you have an answer for everything?"

"Yes."

The second they reached the tallest willow tree, drops of rain fell from the sky and onto the dark green grass. Jack shot her an *Itoldyouso* look as he opened up the large circular umbrella he insisted on bringing, and planted it into the mud.

Sophia knelt down and sat with her legs crossed. It was important she not get the front of her dress wet, as it would certainly make the material almost transparent..

Jack wasn't fast enough to miss a fews drops of rain. His golden hair now glistened with water droplets, and his shoulders were patterned with dark green dots. Luckily the umbrella and some branches of the willow tree managed to block any more damage.

To get comfortable, Jack brushed his shoulders to flick off any droplets of rain and snuggled in until his legs pressed against Sophia's.

The palm of his hand sank into the mud, and as soon as the cold soggy dirt stained his fingers he jolted up. Jack proceeded to rub the palm of his hand against his trouser leg, leaving a brown stain. "You owe me for this."

"Don't be such a prude," she playfully hit the back of her book against his arm. "I am certain when I get up it won't be a flattering sight from the back."

"Ow," he smiled. Taking his book off Sophia, Jack opened up the pages where he last left off.

Jack wasn't as much of a fan of reading, he skimmed a lot of pages and didn't take in most of the words. He just wanted any excuse to be in Sophia's company, as most days he would find her nose deep into a book, completely transported out of this world and into fiction.

There was a question weighing him down that he had to know the answer to. He hated to pull her away from her adventures but he wouldn't settle without asking, "What will you do about the letter? Will you actually look for a husband?"

Sophia didn't lift her gaze from the pages, but she wasn't reading anymore. In a low voice, she said, "I have no choice. I will have nothing if I am thrown onto the streets. I don't know where to start looking for a husband, is there a club or something?"

Jack scoffed in disbelief. Even just that question proved her naivety, how could she make the correct judgment of a man to marry? Not that a man willing to marry in that amount of time would want anything but his own gain.

Even the idea of Sophia in another man's arms made Jack want to punch a hand through a wall.

"What do you want in a husband?"

Slowly closing the pages of her book, she blushed. "Well," straightening her spine and breaking a smile, feeling a child-like glee at the thought. "I imagine him to be kind, thoughtful, caring and charming... I suppose that's what most women want." She shook her head, giggling. "I wouldn't complain if he was handsome too."

Jack mirrored her smile, and decided to be bold and test her reaction. "Not to be too modest, but I would consider myself all of those things."

Sophia shot a wide eyed stare at Jack, whose face was serious. Soon she decided he must have been joking, so she laughed. "That you are." she pulled his hand into her lap. "But what would I do without my dear friend?"

He forced a smile, he expected a reaction like that but he'd be lying if he said it didn't hurt.

They soon went back to the pages of their books and Jack didn't read a single word.

Later that week, when Sophia was trying to sleep there was nothing but the sound of the clock ticking away. Every minute that past felt like seconds, time was truly against her, as her birthday was fast approaching.

It was useless for her to attempt to sleep, her pounding heart was hammering in her ears. The events of the day she met with The Council replayed in her head, and it took a lot of will not to cry. The time restriction was ridiculous, it was like her mother wanted her to fail. What other explanation could there be? Why would she want her daughter to fail, to be homeless, jobless and have nothing to her name?

Suddenly, the sound of her erratic heartbeat was replaced with an enchanting piano playing down the hall.

Sophia raised from her pillow and stared into the darkness of her bedroom. She threw off her blanket and fumbled for a box of matches beside her bed. She struck a match and lit a lantern on her bedside table. The room illuminated from a single flame, a gold and orange flicker brought the items in her room to life. Sophia felt comforted by the light, something about being in darkness unsettled her.

Climbing out of bed she picked up the lantern, using it as a guide to exit her bedroom.

As if the music had put her in some form of trance, she followed the music down the hall. It was like the pied piper was calling out to her.

It led her to a room that had never been occupied for as long as she lived at the orphanage. The room was opposite Jack's, she wondered if the music was keeping him up.

She attempted to knock three times but not once did the music hitch or slow down.

Without thinking, Sophia pushed open the door. Her breath caught in her throat when she found the prisoner gliding his fingers across a black piano, effortlessly. She wasn't sure if she was more surprised by his clean appearance or the fact that one of these rooms contained a black grand piano.

His back was to her as he played, seemingly lost in his work. All she could see was the ends of his black hair that just touched the collar of his crisp white shirt.

"If it isn't the little Gorgon." the prisoner chimed, without taking his gaze from the keys.

"Pardon?" Sophia finally found her voice. With her hand gripped around his doorknob, she was increasingly becoming aware that an accused murderer was permitted to have his door unlocked *and* to be unsupervised.

"Have you not heard of knocking?" She could hear him smiling.

"I-I did knock. Multiple times, actually."

The music came to a halt when he smacked his hands down onto his lap.

An awkward silence filled the air, and with one fist clenched at her side, Sophia blurted, "Why is your door unlocked?"

"Why should it be?" The prisoner turned on the stool he was sitting on, and his deep black eyes immediately locked on Sophia's. He watched her intently with a smile on his razor thin lips.

He was far more handsome than she expected, now that he wasn't dripping with sweat and the filth had been washed away.

Sophia couldn't help but take in his handsome features, his cheekbones curved deep into his face and his jawline was as sharp as a razor blade. Although, he wasn't perfect. His nose was slightly crooked, and she wondered if that was natural or a result of a brawl.

"What is it? You're afraid I'm going to go on a murdering spree?" He mused, pressing his hands into his thighs and leaning the upper half of his body forward.

"Lord Paine said-"

"Do you really believe anything that comes out of Lord Paine's mouth?" The prisoner pushed himself to his feet and slapped his thighs. "You believe I am guilty of murder yet there is no evidence? Oh, how judgemental of you. I feel almost hurt." He placed a hand over his heart, mockingly.

Then he said nothing and just stared at Sophia, his eyes focusing on the scars that occupied her right cheek. He cocked his head to the side. Almost as if he was inspecting them.

Her cheeks burned, "Why must you stare?"

The prisoner raised his index finger and tapped his own cheek, mirroring the position of the scars on Sophia's face. "Any reason for these?"

That was a fatal blow, and certainly not a question she was expecting. She took a step back and covered her scars with the palm of her hand, boiling anger through her blood. "That is none of your business."

With a scoff, and a shake of his head, he said. "Defensive over a question of curiosity?"

The ends of his black hair brushed against his ghostly pale forehead.

"For the insensitivity of your question."

A smile stretched across his face. It must have amused him that he had managed to get under her skin so easily.

"Do not belittle me," she swallowed hard on, what felt like, shards of glass. "I am sure you would share my feelings if I were to come to your home and ask inappropriate questions."

"That is adorable," he raised a thick eyebrow. "You think I have feelings."

"An attitude like that won't get you very far, Mr..." she trailed off, completely drawing a blank on his name. Cassandra had mentioned it earlier but it completely slipped away from her.

"Xavier Howell," he said, still smiling. "Please don't bother with formalities, there is honestly no need for it."

Hearing his name suddenly made her throat tickle, and she couldn't fight the smile that brushed her lips.

"What?" He asked, still with that devilish grin painted on his face.

"I'm sorry," she shook her head at the ground. "It's just an unusual name."

He didn't attempt to hide his smile or even fight it. Running a hand through his thick black hair, he pushed it out of the way of his forehead. Then, he walked around to the side of his bed and sank into his mattress. "Would you mind leaving now?" Tilting his head and flashing a smirk that sent chills down Sophia's spine.

She nodded her head rapidly, so much that she gave herself a headache.

Turning quickly on her heel, Sophia was about to walk away until Xavier's voice called her back. "Oh, and you might want to check on that boy across from me. I heard strange noises coming from his room. Could you tell him if he's going to destroy his belongings could he do so quietly? I had to start playing to drown out the noise."

Jack, a sense of panic filled her body.

Without saying goodbye, she hurried to Jack's room.

Without knocking, she stormed in with her eyes practically bulging from their sockets. She swiftly searched for anything out of the ordinary, expecting him to be found on the floor, cowering in pain.

Quite the opposite.

Jack was sitting on the edge of his bed, his nose deep into a book. His eyes shot up to Sophia, he was visibly startled by her abrupt entrance.

Her lips parted slightly when she realised he was shirtless. She didn't know where her eyes should settle. She couldn't face witnessing his scars again, so she quickly bowed her head and stuttered, "P-please forgive me. I-I did not mean to intrude, I just - I just-"

Jack softly collapsed the pages of his book and got to his feet.

Frozen in place, Sophia kept her eyes locked to the ground. Telling herself to turn around and walk straight back to her room, but she couldn't. It was like her feet were moulded into the floor.

The presence of his eyes all over her face were apparent, and Sophia couldn't fight her flustered face.

"Sophia," Jack's voice was gentle. "You should know that you never need to apologise to me. I was actually hoping to have a moment alone with you anyway."

"Oh?" Still unable to raise her head, her cheeks burned with embarrassment. She didn't want to face what he was about to say.

It was inappropriate for a young lady to be alone with a young single gentleman, especially one that was half naked.

As Jack approached her she felt her heart rate picked up, making it difficult for her to breathe.

He brushed past her to close the door behind her.

Her heart was truly in her throat at this point.

Jack then approached his dresser, pulling out a crisp white shirt and draping it over his shoulders. Once the last button was fastened Sophia felt that she could breathe again.

Shoving his hands into his trouser pockets, he stepped back to face Sophia. His eyes again trailing along her face, drinking in the details.

It alarmed her when he pulled a hand out of his pocket and cupped it around her clear cheek. Making light strokes across her skin, leaving a tingling sensation in its wake.

A gasp escaped from her lips before she could catch it.

His thumb was cold as he grazed it back and forth across her cheek. He shook his head gently, with his eyes still searching her face. "You don't even realise how beautiful you are."

Her eyes shot up to meet him, startled by his words. Not once had he ever spoken to her in such an affectionate way, he was truly acting out of character.

She started shaking her head and ready to pull away, until his other hand cupped her scarred cheek, forcing her to stay.

"Jack," she sighed.

"You know I will do anything to protect you," he began in a hushed tone. "I cannot stop thinking about you being wed to another man, someone who doesn't treat you the way you deserve."

"I have not found a husband yet," her voice was barely above a whisper.

"I am not expressing myself well," he let out a nervous laugh. "What I am trying to say is..." he sucked in a long breath, and as he exhaled he said, "Will you do me the honour of becoming my bride?"

This couldn't be real. He couldn't be serious.

Why did she want to laugh? Maybe to prove that this was some sort of joke. But the look in his eyes she could tell he was deadly serious.

Stepping out of his hands she clasped her hands tightly over her chest to calm her erratic heart. "What are you saying?"

Jack took another step toward Sophia, closing the gap she had created. "I know this is all so sudden and this certainly wasn't how I intended to tell you. Wouldn't you rather marry someone who loves you rather than a stranger?"

Her legs might give in at this point, she could easily collapse on the spot. The blood rushed to her cheeks and her head suddenly felt like a balloon full of nothing but air.

It was all too much. Questions swirled around in her head. Was he telling her he was in love with her? For how long? Was this just a front to protect her?

Her heart was racing and pounding against her ribcage, as if someone had taken a hammer to her chest.

Jack's serious gaze never wavered. "I know this is a shock and it is probably not what you want to hear right now. I...I have been in love with you for many years and as selfish as this will sound..." he trailed off, internally debating whether to finish his sentence. "This could be my only opportunity to have you. I *know* you are not in love with me, but perhaps in time-"

"I will marry you." She couldn't hear any more. Her heart would have crumpled like a biscuit if he said another word.

For her dear friend to pour out his heart, only to not have the feeling reciprocated broke her apart. "I accept your offer of marriage."

Chapter Seven

"Are you quite alright, Miss?" asked Stella, as she pinned up Sophia's curls. "I have noticed you are not quite yourself today."

Sophia stared down at her finger where she envisioned a wedding band would soon reside. The thought made her stomach churn. "Not that there is much point, but may you keep a secret, Stella?"

"Certainly," she said with a hint of scepticism.

"Jack proposed to me." It felt wrong to admit out loud. An engagement should be a happy occasion with the utmost joy pouring out from her. She couldn't be feeling more of a contrast to that. Saying it out loud only made her want to curl up in a ball and do nothing but cry. Admitting it out loud meant it was real, and admitting it to another person was just clarification.

Stella struggled to conjure an appropriate response, Sophia could see her mind working in the reflection of the mirror. "That is...unexpected."

"I know," she breathed. Sophia went on to explain her mother's letter and the reasoning behind Jack's sudden confession of love. "I do not mean to sound ungrateful for his offer of marriage, I will forever be in his debt."

Stella finished styling Sophia's hair and looked at her through the reflection of the mirror.

"Forgive me, if what I say may be inappropriate, Miss. A marriage between two people should not be viewed as a debt. It should be between the happiness of a couple who *want* to spend the rest of their lives together. Based upon what you have told me it is clear that Mr Green wants that with you...are you giving him a sense of false hope?"

False hope.

Stella stepped back, bowing her head. "Pardon me for speaking out, Miss. It was not my place."

"No," Sophia said, quickly. "I appreciate the advice. I think it was something I needed to hear."

Stella left her alone shortly after their conversation.

Sophia pulled a pair of white silk gloves from her dresser and draped them up to her elbows. When she looked down to her gloved hands, she noticed that she was shaking.

"I do say," an annoyingly familiar voice called from her bedroom door.

Sophia turned, surprised to see Xavier leaning his weight against the doorframe. His black eyes comfortably resting on Sophia's. "Have you got any other facial expression than devastation? It does get rather depressing."

She huffed, clasping her hands in front of her casual cotton gown. "You do not have to look at me if I bother you so much."

The corners of his mouth hooked up. "That's not fun. I think you could be rather attractive with a smile."

Grumbling under her breath she stuck up her nose to the ceiling. She stepped in front of him and looked over his shoulder to the empty hallway. "I am going for my breakfast, move."

"There are such words as *excuse me*. No need to be so rude." He was clearly playing a game that she wasn't in any mood to be a part of.

"Please, do not refrain from your opinions of me." She said, sarcastically. "I am highly intrigued to hear how you view yourself."

Xavier pulled his weight from the doorframe and stood with his back held high. He folded his arms over his chest and raised an eyebrow. "Showing interest in me?" He teased. "Well, if you must know, I am eager to get my hands on an alcoholic beverage."

Clearly he wasn't taking anything she was saying seriously, all she wanted was to pass him and eat breakfast. "What a sad life you must lead," she snapped when he still wouldn't budge. "The only thing for you to look forward to is getting intoxicated." She looked deeply into his eyes in an attempt to stare him down, not that it did much, she was a good foot smaller than him.

Sophia considered physically pushing him out of the way, but then she realised how much bigger he was than her. It would be like a single fly trying to push down a house.

Before she could even consider reaching out to him, his hands gripped tightly around her wrists and pushed her back into her room. They came to an abrupt stop before her back would hit the beam of her bedpost.

His breath intertwined with hers and she realised she had never been in this close proximity of someone before.

"Quite a confident way to talk to an accused murderer." A smile curved at his lips as he locked his gaze to hers.

"You cannot hurt me here," Sophia's attempt to exude confidence was tarnished by her shaking voice. "If you were to kill me, everyone would know it was you. You would be taken straight back to that cell and executed right on the spot."

He chuckled, amused by her threat. "You're a sly one. Tell me, where did you learn to run your mouth off to a man?"

She was increasingly growing aware of the limited space between them. "I have spent my life without parents to teach me such things."

Xavier shook his head, the ends of his black hair brushing against his forehead. "Would you say you had a heart of stone?"

"Excuse me?"

Loosening his grip around her wrists, he stepped away from her. Sophia felt like she could take a breath once there was a distance between them.

Xavier bowed and placed a hand over his heart. "Forgive me, it's not my place to get caught up in this pathetic drama."

Everyone wanted to twist Sophia's mind these past few weeks, it was Xavier's turn to leave Sophia in a state of confusion.

What drama?

"Please do not make a show of this," Sophia muttered into Jack's ear.

That night they were joined by Jack's parents in Cassandra's office. Thick white candles filled the room with an orange glow. As if Cassandra didn't already look menacing, the shadows forming around her face made her look like a villain from a children's story book.

Albert was sitting on the windowsill with his arms folded, looking fearful as to why he had been called into an urgent meeting with his son.

"Whatever it is you have to say," Cassandra said. "Please get on with it, I am rather tired."

Jack let out a long breath, he was clearly nervous. "We have some news."

"I gathered that." Cassandra huffed, stretching her arms out across her desk.

Sophia couldn't focus on anything, her eyes were bouncing around the room until she settled on the ground. Her eyes shot up to Jack when he suddenly linked his fingers through hers and clasped his other free hand on top. "We are to be married."

It was like a sharp cold wind was cast over the four of them. The air became uncomfortably thin which was accompanied by a long, horrid silence.

Sophia eventually gathered up the courage to steal a glance at Cassandra, she was surprisingly calm or she was doing a good job at hiding her anger.

Perhaps they knew it was inevitable that Jack would do something like this for Sophia, they must have known he was in love with her. Was it that obvious to everyone but Sophia? Stella only seemed to be surprised by the engagement, and not the fact that Jack had confessed he was in love with her.

Cassandra raised herself up from her chair, the tips of her fingers pressed into her desk. She breathed out through her flared nostrils and said, "I thought I raised an intelligent boy."

"You did." Jack countered.

Cassandra dug her hands deep into her hips. "I didn't think you would be this moronic to propose to a girl who is not suitable for you."

That stung Sophia, like swallowing a bee. Yet again, they were talking about her and insulting her as if she wasn't there. If Sophia had any shred of confidence she would stand up for herself but there was always something inside of her holding her back. Telling her that it was useless to try.

"You may be willing to allow her to live on the streets but I am not." Jack clenched his jaw as his whole body tensed.

It didn't take long for voices to be raised by both parties. Both passionately screaming their points across, neither of them were willing to go down without a fight.

After minutes of listening to the high pitched rants from Cassandra, Sophia couldn't take it anymore. She slipped out of Jack's hands without him noticing and left them to fight. She closed the door behind her and pressed her back against the door. She struggled to hold herself up, she feared her legs would give in from the pressure she was under.

There wasn't enough air, the walls were closing in around her.

She ran up the stairs to the top floor of the orphanage. Bursting through the doors leading to the balcony, she almost tumbled as she stepped through.

Rain hissed down and immediately soaked Sophia like she had just jumped deep into a lake. Drops of water kissed her tear-stained cheeks, as she stopped at the thick black bars that came just above her hips.

The material of her casual gown was cold and sticking to her skin.

Her thoughts were in complete shambles, swirling and wrapping around her brain like an invisible rope. With no way to cut loose or be free from the torment.

The clouds blanketed the city in darkness. There couldn't be a better representation of what Sophia was feeling at this very moment.

She gripped her hands around the black metal railing, and hunched her shoulders in an attempt to catch her breath. The breaths that escaped were fast and sharp, no matter how hard she inhaled she couldn't get enough air. It felt damp in her lungs.

No matter how hard she squeezed her eyes shut she couldn't stop the tears from escaping.

A black fog of loneliness looped around her head like a devil's halo.

Sophia wanted to marry for love. As much as Jack assured her that one day she could learn to love him, she knew in her heart she could never reciprocate his feelings.

She not once imagined that she'd have to spend the rest of her life with Jack in a romantic way. What if he wanted more from her? Like children? She couldn't give that to him, she couldn't *give* herself to him.

What would her life be if it was going to be lived for her?

Suddenly, as if in a trance, Sophia stepped up onto the railing with her heart thudding in her ears.

A small part of her was telling her to consider the possibilities of opportunities in her life, but they were quickly drowned out by the thoughts of not having the life she dreamed of.

Who could she confide in? She felt a level of distrust with Jack, not just for the marriage but the secrets of his scars.

What else was he hiding from her?

Why did everyone around her hate her so much?

She didn't want to see Jack, her lifelong friend, as someone who was taking away her opportunity to love.

It was this moment Sophia realised just how lonely she was. Jack always managed to distract her from her self loathing. Now that a distance had grown in her heart, she realised she didn't really have anyone. Everyone else at the orphanage avoided her at all costs, it seemed to be too much of an effort to greet her. She always ensured she was nothing but polite and respectful to anyone she crossed paths with. What could she have done to make everyone resent her so much?

Why did no one give her a chance?

As these dark thoughts circled her mind she hooked her leg over the railing. Her hands tightly held onto the cold slippery bars. There was nothing blocking her from taking a single step forward and plummeting to her death.

The front garden looked so small from up high.

The more she thought about having an escape from this world of stress and loneliness the more her hands loosened around the bars.

Tears spilled from her eyes and mixed with the drops of rain down her cheeks.

Pinching her eyes shut, she was about to release her grip. When suddenly a cold hand gripped above her elbow, pulling her back.

Startled, Sophia whipped her head around to look over her shoulder. The locks of her wet brunette hair smacking her in the face. She found Xavier holding her back, his clothes were soaked from standing in the pouring rain. His black hair was flat against his forehead and droplets of water fell from his thick eyelashes.

Sophia opened her mouth to speak, to attempt to explain, but the words were trapped in her throat.

Her body was suddenly on fire, what was she doing? She felt a wave of fear and embarrassment as her hands began to tremble.

Xavier slowly guided her to turn around to face him. His grip was firm, afraid of letting go in case she was to fall. An arm slipped around her back and as easily as picking up a feather, Xavier pulled her back over to his side of the railing, the end of her dress catching on the rail and tearing slightly. Sophia was past the point of caring.

Once her foot was back on flat ground Sophia let out a breath and fell into Xavier's chest. She clung to the wet material of his shirt and cried into him. Her shoulders shook in time with the throbbing drums in her head.

Instead of pushing her away and mocking her, like she had come to expect, Xavier wrapped his arms around her and held her tightly against his chest.

She felt comfortable crying into him. She felt safe with his arms cradling her.

The minutes passed and she didn't want this embrace to end.

Soon she realised how inappropriate it was to be held by a man she had only recently met, especially with Sophia's recent engagement.

Her entire body was shaking as she pulled away. As she lifted her head, her eyes scaled up his broad chest, then to his strong square jaw and continued until she met his black eyes. His wet black hair reflected the ray of light shining down from the moon. The ends of his hair were flat against his face, with water trickling down his crooked nose.

His eyebrows knitted together, his mouth a razor thin line. "What the hell were you thinking?"

Sophia sniffled, unable to conjure a response. It was strange to see a softer side to Xavier, it was reassuring that there was more to him than sarcasm and attitude.

The way he spoke to her was laced with concern. Yes, there was a lot of anger in his question, but it was clear that it was born from worry.

Xavier guided her back inside and out of the rain.

Sophia closed her eyes and prayed silently that the world would dissolve at her fingertips or else her embarrassment would consume her.

It was clear that Xavier was furious, but she felt strangely comforted by him being there in a time of desperation.

One thought loomed over her mind as he escorted her down the stairs, leaving puddles behind. Would she have jumped if Xavier hadn't rescued her?

Xavier didn't let Sophia out of his sight as they made their way to her bedroom.

Once arriving at her door, Sophia stared down at the doorknob, she wasn't so sure she was ready to be stuffed away in her compact room, alone with her dark thoughts.

"Thank you for escorting me back," she said to Xavier, sheepishly.

Xavier didn't move as he did a quick glance at her door. "Are you going in?"

She let out an unsteady breath, "I was thinking of stopping by the library before bed," she brought her shoulders up to her ears. "Still feeling slightly overwhelmed."

"I will join you."

Her eyes widened in surprise as she looked up at him.

That irresistible smirk made its appearance as he curved his mouth into a smile. Shaking his head, making the ends of his hair release droplets of rain. "You don't expect me to leave you alone after what just happened, do you?"

What choice did she have? As much as she hated to admit it, he had a point.

Making their way to the library they noticed that Jack and Cassandra had moved their argument to the main hall. Albert must have retired to his chambers, he was never usually involved in their more heated discussions.

Sophia wanted to turn around and run back to her room before anyone noticed; it was too late. Jack's wild eyes jumped to Sophia, taking in her soaking wet appearance and her matching companion. They must have looked like drowned rats.

His glare shifted to Xavier and something inside of Jack snapped. Charging at Xavier, Jack grabbed the collar of his shirt, pushing his back against the wall. His teeth were clenched, resembling a wild animal preparing to sink its teeth into prey.

"And you are..." Xavier drawled, the back of his head pressed against the wall.

"What the hell did you do to her?!" Jack snarled.

Sophia stepped in beside the boys and placed a gentle hand on Jack's tense shoulder. "This is unnecessary, Jack." She said, frantically. "Xav - Mr Howell was simply helping me."

"With what?" His eyes never wavered from Xavier's, who appeared to be bored with this.

Her mind drew a blank. She couldn't tell Jack that she considered throwing herself from the top balcony, he would never forgive her. She couldn't hurt him like that, he would know it was because she didn't want to marry him.

Beads of sweat made a trail down Jack's forehead, Sophia could tell he was resisting the urge to swing for Xavier.

Sophia was surprised when it was Xavier who said, "A large gust of wind took a book she was reading right out of her hand and out onto the top floor balcony. She ran out to retrieve it in the rain, and I simply helped her to her feet after she tripped in doing so. Like any gentleman would do."

Although Xavier's story warranted more questions, and didn't completely make sense, Sophia was impressed with how fast he could come up with a lie.

Xavier just covered for Sophia, but why? It's not like he would care for the consequences of her actions.

"Why would you be on the top floor balcony?"

Jack knew he was lying but before he could query it further, Cassandra said. "Son, you are overreacting. Let him go."

Cassandra didn't seem too fazed by what was going on, it seemed to be an inconvenience to her more than anything.

At first Jack was reluctant to loosen his grip. After a beat, he shook Xavier and released him.

Jack stormed to Sophia's side and draped a possessive arm around her shoulders. He pulled her close to his chest, like he was claiming her as a reward. His grip was firm as his fingers pressed into her arm.

"You will not come near my fiancé again," Jack warned Xavier. Dragging out the word 'fiancé' like he was ensuring Xavier wouldn't misunderstand him. "Do I make myself clear?"

Sophia let out a breath, she felt strangely disappointed. Deep down she didn't want Xavier to know she was engaged, she felt embarrassed by her *fiancé's* behaviour.

Xavier straightened up his now scruffy collar and he appeared to be amused by Jack's threat. "You might want to keep a close eye on your *fiancé.*" Xavier dragged out the word just as much, clearly to mock Jack. "I think that congratulations are in order," stretching out his hand he offered a shake. "Although, by your outburst I'm so sure if it is deserved."

Jack turned his nose up at Xavier's hand. "I will not accept your congratulations." Jack's chest was heaving up and down. Sophia could hear his heart raging through his shirt.

Xavier scoffed, as he dropped his hand down to his side. "How insecure are you? Jealous of a man who has known your *fiancé* for all of five minutes. Are you the jealous type?" He mused. "You must not be a very good lover if you are intimidated by new men."

"Why would I be jealous of a murderer?"

Xavier rolled his eyes and crossed his arms over his soaking shirt. Sophia blushed when she realised she could see the lines of his muscled torso.

"If I truly am a murderer then why am I alive? They would have had me killed by now if they were certain I am guilty."

Jack grumbled under his breath, something about not dignifying him with an answer. With his arm still draped around Sophia he led her to the stairs. Jack abruptly stopped when Xavier called out, "If you are wondering the real reason why I am soaking wet, along with Miss Cole..." Jack froze, his fingers gripping tighter onto Sophia's arm. "Perhaps she shouldn't be so feisty. I am a man after all, and needs must be satisfied."

Like a flash, Jack ripped away from Sophia, causing her to stumble back against the railing.

She called for Jack to calm down as it was clearly a tasteless joke. Xavier was clearly trying to get a rise from Jack and it was working.

But his sights were already locked on Xavier's jaw. His hand clamped tightly into a fist and as soon as he was within reach, punched him across the face.

Xavier didn't put up any sort of fight, he stumbled back and brushed the edge of his hand against his injured jaw. Instead of cowering in pain, he chuckled. "You're attempting to strike a prisoner accused of murder? That was nothing more than a girlish tap."

Sophia had never seen this side of Jack before. She thought she knew him inside and out. Not once had she seen him result to violence. And she has certainly not seen him this angry before.

The breath caught in her throat as her own hands balled into fists.

It baffled Sophia that Cassandra wasn't putting any effort into stopping her son's erratic behaviour. What if someone were to stumble upon this violent confrontation? Surely the other members wouldn't want to be living in fear in their own home.

It was Sophia who broke up the fight. Storming down the stairs, she stepped in front of Jack and locked eyes with him. "That is enough."

Jack's scrunched up face softened. After a small sigh, he turned on his heel and made his way up the stairs.

Xavier's scoff echoed across the hall. "So, that is the man you're going to be spending the rest of your life with?"

Rage boiled in Sophia's blood after that comment. How could he not take a situation like this seriously? Afterall, his cocky words resulted in a punch to the face.

Aside from Xavier's arrogance, something else was eating away at Jack, and Sophia had to know what it was.

Sophia turned to Cassandra, her eyes stinging from the desperate need to cry. "I will see Jack," she wanted to kick herself because she couldn't stop her bottom lip from quivering.

"No," Cassandra barked. "*I* will see him."

Now you decide to step in, Sophia dared not say.

117

Cassandra left Sophia and Xavier standing in puddles of water.

"Still care to accompany me to the library?" Xavier chimed, as if nothing out of the ordinary happened.

"You are unbelievable." She breathed out.

"I save your life and this is how you repay me?" He stepped towards her, his shoes squelching with each step. Where he stood there was a respectable gap between them. Water dripped onto the floor from the tips of his black hair.

On the outside Sophia looked as solid as a rock but on the inside she was ready to break. "You could always make me another one of your victims."

Xavier chuckled, visibly startled by her words. She couldn't tell if her words hurt him. "If I am a cold blooded murder, like you all seem to *think* I am, then why would I have saved you? I would have let you fall and enjoyed your corpse."

"What do you mean by that?"

Xavier was now clearly frustrated. "Whatever you want it to mean, Sophia. Clearly you believe anything that anyone tells you. God forbid, this place has done it to you your entire life."

"What do you mean by that?" She repeated.

His smile returned, only it wasn't out of joy or amusement. "Forget it, I didn't say anything."

Sophia opened her mouth to say something, but the words would not form. She didn't have an answer.

Xavier left Sophia alone.

Shortly after, Cassandra returned with a towel. She handed it to Sophia and she smiled a thank you. The tension could be cut with a knife. Her eyes were glaring through Sophia, she was breathing heavily out of her flared nostrils. Resembling a bull getting ready to charge.

"Cassandra I-"

"You will not marry my son!" she cut Sophia off before she could finish. Her whole body was still, her lips were the only things that moved. It was more of a command than a request.

Sophia's shoulders dropped. "Jack is in love with me, and he has made up his mind that he wants me as his bride. I'm hoping, in time, I can one day fall in love with him too."

Cassandra shook her head, her eyebrows were drawn together and formed a crease in her flawless forehead. "I couldn't care less if my son married a woman who did not love him. I do not want my son marrying *you*."

119

Sophia felt wounded by her words. "I do not understand."

"Of course you don't," Cassandra snarled. "I do not want you falling in love with my son, if that were to happen..." she cut off mid-sentence and her eyes seemed to drift into her own thoughts. Her face looked pained for a long amount of time.

Quickly she shook the thought off and resumed her glare to Sophia. "Long story short, Jack is already getting punished for something I did in the past. I do not want him carrying anyone else's burdens."

"What punishment?"

Cassandra's eyes fluttered closed. "Just...do not marry my son."

If Sophia wasn't confused before, this conversation did nothing to help. Cassandra walked away leaving Sophia quite baffled.

She needed to marry Jack, otherwise she would be out on the streets with no food and no money to her name. She would surely die within a number of weeks. Not to mention the dangers which lurked around every corner, women never felt safe walking alone.

If Jack had such a problem surely he wouldn't have offered her marriage.

Also, what punishment was Jack living through? Was it the scars on his back? But what had Cassandra done in order to have her son punished so brutally?

Sophia knew it wasn't wise to question Jack tonight. She didn't want to put him under any more pressure.

She walked up the stairwell and found Stella waiting in her bedroom. There was little she could do to hide her startled look due to Sophia's appearance.

"I do not require your assistance tonight, Stella." Sophia mumbled. "I wish to be alone."

Stella simply curtsied without question. Sophia assumed she heard all of the commotion that just took place.

"Please remember if you ever need to confide in someone," she said before closing the door behind her. "Don't be afraid to ask me, Miss." she glided out of the room and left Sophia with her own jumbled thoughts.

Pressing her head against the smooth wooden bar of her bed frame, she made a pointless attempt to steady her heart rate.

A whirlpool had formed out of the confusion plaguing her mind. It felt as if her whole world had crumbled the second she stepped foot into Lord Paine's office. Her only holding branch was Jack, and that had now snapped.

Wanting so desperately to cry, she restrained herself. It wasn't enough to let out what she was feeling.

She couldn't believe she attempted something so foolish tonight. The embarrassment to be caught in her actions made her want to dive under the covers and never see the light of day. Of course she'd never have actually *jumped.* But the thrill of being in control was something she desired more of, yet she knew she lacked anything of the sort.

Undressed, and out of her wet clothes she left them in the hall for Stella to collect. She quickly changed into her nightgown and climbed into bed. Her eyes were fixed onto the ceiling as she tried to piece together her thoughts.

If she tried to explain her actions tonight she wasn't so sure anyone would understand. At the time she felt so trapped, so lost that it was the only option for her.

Tossing and turning she cursed herself. Why did it have to be *him* who saved her life? What was he doing out of his room in the first place? Near the top balcony, of all places.

All of the thoughts were hurting her brain.

She couldn't even switch off her confusing thoughts in her dreams. It was like this feeling of pain and confusion was going to follow her for the rest of her life.

Then she thought of Xavier, and his irritating smirk sending her heart into a flutter.

Sophia tossed and turned in an attempt to shake off her persistent thoughts of him. His smile was the main thing on her mind, how could a simple expression make her feel so angry, but fuel such a desire to look at nothing else.

That night, when she managed to fall asleep she dreamed of the door. The same unfamiliar door, only this time it was different. When Sophia's dream-self looked down to her hand she saw a key. She held it in her grasp but wouldn't move any further to unlock the door.

Perhaps soon she would find out what was behind the door.

Chapter Eight

The next day, Jack traveled to the local cathedral alone. He didn't ask Sophia to join him, he knew that she wasn't completely on board with the idea of marrying him. Plus, he was still sceptical as to what happened between her and Xavier in the rain.

It was like iron bars encased his heart, his love for Sophia was trapped within himself. Not a minute past where he didn't have Sophia in his mind. Her timid smiles always made his heart race; her delightful laughter never failed to brighten the darkest of days. There wasn't a moment that went by where he didn't want to hold her beauty filled face and plant kisses in every available spot. He wanted to brush his lips across her scars to show her that she didn't need the insecurities she held onto so tightly.

Jack wasn't a fool, he knew that this whole situation was killing her on the inside. For him to have her as his wife, even if she didn't have much of a choice, was good enough for him. He wanted to prove that he could be everything she ever needed and more, and maybe one day she would love him for it...no matter how dangerous that may be.

When he arrived at the Cathedral he removed his silk gloves and top hat.

The building was extravagant, although in comparison to the orphanage it looked more like a school building. The upper half of the stone walls were outlined with a variety of saints, each holding a book or a staff.

Inside, even the slightest draw of breath would cause a loud echo down the aisles.

Jack proceeded to dip the tips of his fingers into the holy water and made a slow sign of the cross.

There were only a handful of people kneeling at the benches, praying silently for forgiveness, guidance or gratefulness.

Each step Jack took echoed around the cathedral. His eyes trailed across the stained glass windows in admiration, each window telling a story from the Bible. From the birth and death of Jesus.

The man he was here to see, Father Doyle, hobbled down the aisle to meet Jack halfway. He greeted him with a bright toothless smile, and placed his wrinkled hands on his upper arm. "Mr

Green, it's been a while since you have visited. To what do I owe this pleasure?" Father Doyle's snow white hair fell to his shoulders and his wrinkles were reminiscent of broken leather, all of which stretched across his face.

Jack brought his voice down to a whisper, hoping not to disturb those who prayed. "I bring good news, I am to be married."

"Marvellous!" Father Doyle boomed. "You wish to have the ceremony here, I presume. I married your mother and father, you know?"

Jack nodded, unable to contain his smile. It was the vision of Sophia in a luxurious gown, standing in front of him at this very altar, promising her heart and life to him that made his smile grow.

"Who is the lucky lady?" Father Doyle interrupted Jack's vision.

"Sophia Cole..." he suddenly turned sheepish. "...from the orphanage."

Father Doyle's smokey blue eyes changed from excitement to rage in a flash. His bushy white eyebrows furrowed together. "No, I cannot give my blessing to that...that...*thing!*" He turned his back on Jack and began storming away with a hunched over back.

Swinging the door leading to his quarters open, he hurried inside. Just as Father Doyle was about to slam the door shut, Jack stopped him by wedging his black cane in between the door and its frame.

"Father, please," Jack begged. "I know it is against your beliefs but I *truly* love this woman and I want to make her my own. For what I am, surely that should make up for what she is."

Father Doyle's fierce facial expressions were cold and unmoving. "You are a part of Heaven, you will always be welcome in my church but *she...*"

"When she marries me," Jack begged. "She will become a woman of God. She knows nothing about the world around her, she is innocent of whatever opinions you hold over her."

Father Doyle's face slowly fell.

Jack continued, "Please, Father. You have known me since the day I was born. Grant me this favour and I will forever be in your debt." His bright blue eyes were clearly desperate.

There was a long, lingering silence hanging above them.

"You say Miss Cole doesn't know what she is?"

Jack gave a slow nod.

It took another few minutes of silence until Father Doyle said, "I will marry you under one condition."

"Anything!" Jack couldn't restrain his smile.

"You tell her what she is before you are wed." Father Doyle pointed at him with his long scrawny finger.

That smile soon fell from Jack's lips. He couldn't process his words and the world suddenly turned dark. A sickness arose in his stomach, it was like an anchor had been dropped in his gut.

Then he thought of his mother's years of keeping the secret locked away. Working hard everyday to keep everyone in check, for Sophia's sake. Could he discard his mother's work? Making it all for nothing?

He didn't have a choice.

Jack pressed his hand into Father Doyle's door, not to push it open but to hold himself up, he was certain his legs wouldn't be able to hold him up for much longer.

Once he pulled himself together, Jack straightened his posture and pulled out his cane from the door.

How could he tell Sophia? She would never believe him, she would think it was an unusual joke. He could picture it now, that beautiful laugh ringing in his ears.

There was no other choice, he *had* to tell her. All he wanted was to marry her, Jack couldn't have her living on the streets, or worse, married to another man.

"There is nothing else I can do?" Jack said.

Father Doyle's answer was short and to the point. "No." After a beat, he said in a sigh, "She must be willing to denounce the evil within her soul before she can step foot in my church."

Jack's grip tightened around his cane. He tried not to let Father's Doyle's words enrage him so much, he couldn't help but express his frustrations with a tight jaw. "Hold on, Father. Not once have you met Sophia. You know her from rumours and whispers spread by Lord Paine. I can assure you, she is gentle, kind and the most remarkable woman I have ever met."

"Of course you are going to say that," Father Doyle opened the door slightly and stepped into Jack's space. "You will say these things and *believe* these things because you are in love with her. You are blinded by love."

Jack aggressively shook his head. "No, I would see her that way even if I wasn't in love with her, because that is who she is."

Suddenly, Jack felt a shooting pain stab through his heart, the pain he was all too familiar with.

The intensity caused him to take a few steps back and hold a tight grip onto the breast of his shirt. It was like he was trying to reach into his chest, clutch his hand around his heart, and squeeze out the pain.

Not now, he thought. In a failed attempt to steady his breathing, Jack stumbled back. It was a tired effort to calm down the pain. Now spreading faster than ever. His scars throbbed as he hunched over.

Father Doyle's face softened. He placed a comforting hand on Jack's shoulder.

Jack pulled back and quickly straightened up his posture as soon as he felt the slightest touch from him. It was agonising for him to stand straight, enough to cause his left eye to twitch. "Sophia and I shall be married within the week, I expect you to do the ceremony, Father." Jack curled his upper lip. "I will consider your terms."

There it was again. That beautiful, hypnotising music playing from Xavier's room. It was like listening to an angel's lullaby.

Sophia sat at her desk with her eyes closed, listening to the piece. It was unfortunate that the walls muffled the sound, but even with that, the gentle strokes of the keys soothed her.

As much as she loved hearing Xavier play it didn't take long for a wave of guilt to be thrust upon her. This man saved her life when she was being nothing more than reckless.

What would Jack's reaction have been if she told him that she almost took her own life? He would blame himself, that she was certain of.

Sophia was soon pulled out of her thoughts when the music intensified.

She shot open her eyes and stared at her door, internally debating if she should visit Xavier. For nothing more than to hear his song without the many walls and doors in the way, of course.

It didn't take much convincing for her to visit Xavier's room.

Down the hall, her eyes fell on Hannah's bedroom door. She realised it had been days since she left her room, it was an unhealthy amount of time to lock herself away.

Sophia considered knocking on her door, checking to see if she was alright, but then she remembered Robert's snarling face from merely asking about her wellbeing.

She decided against knocking on Hannah's door. What kind of support could she offer that her own brother couldn't provide? Sophia had only spoken to Hannah on a handful of occasions, and striking up a conversation seemed impossible.

Instead Sophia continued to her desired destination, Xavier's room.

The minute she stopped outside of his door the music came to a sudden stop. As if the magic spell of the music broke, she too halted before going any further.

Now in the silence Sophia thought to herself, *What am I doing? This isn't appropriate.*

As she took a step back to turn around and return to her room, Xavier's door flew open. Like a deer caught in the site of a carriage, she looked up with startled eyes.

Xavier stood in the doorway, one hand on the doorknob and the other gripped around the frame of the door. He was looking down at her with a single raised eyebrow. There was always a look of amusement on his face, like everything was funny to him. "Can I help you?" he mused.

What excuse could she come up with? There was nothing past his door that she could claim she was walking to. She could say she wanted to visit Jack and was at the wrong door, but how believable was that?

Opting for the truth, she said. "I heard you playing again and...I...wanted to hear you."

"Oh." Surprise ignited his dark eyes. His face softened as he extended his door and invited her inside.

Sophia stepped in, hugging her arms over her cream nightgown.

It dawned on her once Xavier shut the door behind him that she was alone in a man's bedroom in nothing but her loose nightgown.

She awkwardly looked around his room, it was the same square size as her own, only with much grander furniture. That's not even including the grand piano. "This room is like a palace compared to my own."

"Cassandra mentioned that this was more of a storage room," he said. "Not that I am complaining, if this is considered storage furniture I would *love* to see what her room is like."

Sophia smiled, she had never been inside of Cassandra's bedroom. It's not something she ever wanted to see. That was the only place she and Albert could have any privacy. Cassandra was also very good at keeping her affairs private, not that Sophia was too interested in finding out more about her.

She purposely avoided looking at his double bed, the mere thought caused her to blush an illuminating red.

Xavier brushed past her to the piano, as he sat down on the stool made a loud creaking sound. He shuffled to the edge so his left leg was sticking out to the side. Nodding his head, Xavier signalling for Sophia to sit beside him.

She lowered herself down onto the stool and her knee brushed against Xavier's. It sent a sudden jolt through her entire body. Sophia tried to sit as far away from him as possible, but if she moved another inch away she would fall to the floor. The last thing she needed was another excuse for Xavier to tease her.

Xavier laid his slender fingers down onto the white piano keys, "What would you like to hear?"

Bringing her shoulder up to her ear and dropping it back down dramatically, she muttered "Anything."

"Do you have a favourite song?"

She shook her head, "Not really."

Exhaling a laugh through his nose, a smile crept up on his lips. "You are not very easy to please."

A smile formed on her lips. She lowered her head and looked down at the piano keys. It was looking at these keys that she realised she didn't have any musical talent, or any talent really.

"I'm not so good with remembering the names of songs."

"*Amazing Grace?*" Xavier suggested. "Everyone knows that."

A smile stretched across her lips as she nodded. It would be nice to hear him play something so gentle.

"I'll play it if you sing."

Her head sprang up to meet his eyes. She immediately burst out laughing and said, "No."

"Can you sing?" he pushed.

She shook her head, "No."

His smile deepened, revealing his dimples that she never noticed he had before. "I am sure I have heard worse, sing to me."

Soon after, Xavier began playing the tune to *Amazing Grace*. He never completed the song, he would replay the first part on a repetitive beat. It was clear he wouldn't continue any further until Sophia sang along.

Finally caving in on the fourth replay, she closed her eyes and sang. As time went on and she settled into the song, she felt her hands tense around the material of her nightgown. She grabbed fistfuls of the cotton and tried to block out her own voice with thoughts that brought her joy. Like reading a new book, her trips to the theatre with Jack and...

Sophia was interrupted by a hissing sound coming from Xavier, and she soon realised that he was laughing at her.

Blood rushed to her cheeks and she immediately stopped singing. "I told you I couldn't sing!" she defensively protested.

Xavier removed his hands from the keys and brought his hands up to his face. Laughing hysterically, like he had just heard the funniest joke ever conjured by man. He dragged his thumb under his eyes, in a failed attempt to catch the tears welling up in his eyes. "I thought you were being modest when you said you couldn't sing." He said through his laughter. "It was like hearing a child sing."

Sophia couldn't handle being made fun of. She pushed herself up to her feet and was ready to storm out, only stopped by Xavier's hand lightly wrapping around her wrist.

She looked down at him, with tears stinging her eyes. Why was he so insensitive? Better yet, why was *she* so sensitive? She wished she had more restraint when wanting to cry.

"I'm sorry," he said, still smiling. Bubbles of giggles clearly being swallowed down. "Please sit back down. I promise I won't make you sing anymore."

There was hesitation for a moment, as she watched his face, full of amusement.

Then that all melted away, her embarrassment, his amusement when his thumb began tracing small circles across her wrist.

Swallowing whatever feeling his touch was giving her, with a deep sigh she lowered herself back down onto the stool and gathered her hair around her left shoulder. "You don't sound very apologetic." She avoided his gaze.

"I am, but you have to admit, it was rather funny."

Playfully, Sophia swatted his arm, and pursed her lips to avoid a smile.

Xavier soon grazed his hands across the keys effortlessly. Playing a song Sophia was not familiar with. It was a slow, beautiful melody that Sophia could close her eyes and drift off to. She sat in silence and felt all her worries melt away with each note.

Every few seconds she would steal glances at Xavier. His face was tentative, almost as if he was making up the tune as he went along. With his head hung low the tips of his black hair veiled his face. Dropping a shadow over his strong features.

Sophia never realised how much she loved to look at him, he was ridiculously handsome. A sudden urge arose in her, to reach out her hand and trace the line of his high cheekbone.

With each passing moment she found herself itching closer to him, lowering her gaze to his long slender fingers. She wondered how they would feel against her skin. His hands were much larger than her own. They would surely swallow hers whole if they held hands.

She snapped out of her trance when Xavier stopped playing.

"That was beautiful," muttered Sophia. "Where did you learn to play like that?"

Xavier shifted in his seat, pressing his hand against his flat torso. He cleared his throat and said, whilst not taking his eyes off the black and white keys, "My mother taught me when I was younger. She was quite talented."

A smile stretched across Sophia's lips, imagining Xavier as a child. Even though they were only recently acquainted, she can picture him as a rambunctious child. The idea of him sitting down and learning such a beautiful skill filled her chest with warmth. "It would be wonderful to watch you play together."

Xavier quickly raised and lowered his eyebrows. "It would be." He turned his head to look at her, a sad expression that Sophia wasn't expecting.

Then it hit her.

Out of instinct, she reached over and placed her tiny hand over Xavier's - that was still resting on the piano. Squeezing his hand, it felt warm to the touch.

Xavier's eyes never wavered from hers as she said, "I'm so sorry."

His facial features softened, and his lips parted like he wanted to say something but he forgot how to speak.

"I am sure it is difficult to lose a parent," she continued. "Well, I too have lost parents, but I am sure losing ones you actually *remember* is far more difficult so-"

"Sophia," he cut her off, mid-rambling. The way he said her name sent a shiver down her spine. "You don't have to - it's fine."

Sophia slid her hand back down into her lap, and the warmth from his touch still lingered, like she dipped her hand into a bucket ignited with fire.

"I do so wish I put time into learning something," she tried to change the subject, and forced cheer into her tone. "I'm afraid I have no talent whatsoever."

Xavier cracked a sweet smile, "What do you do for fun then?"

"I love to read, mostly."

"I'd consider that a talent," Xavier said, his black eyes scanning her face. "Most people I've met wouldn't even know what a book is."

They shared a laugh. Not at the expense of the other, but a genuine laugh.

Why was her heart hammering against her chest? It was uncomfortable but not something she wanted to stop. There was also a mixture of glee circling her heart, like she had to repress herself from squealing.

Awkwardly got to her feet, which didn't do anything to make the feeling go away.

"I should really go."

Now her heart was doing cartwheels in her chest, causing her to sound breathless. "I didn't realise how late it was," that was a lie. She realised how late it was before visiting Xavier's room.

Hurrying to exit, when she opened his door to leave his voice halted her.

"Thank you," Xavier said.

Sophia turned back to face him and she was greeted by, not a smirk or a cheeky grin, but a genuine smile.

A rope had wrapped itself around her heart. The longer she stared the tighter that rope was being pulled. Her hand tightly gripped around the doorknob, it was the only thing helping her keep her balance.

The blood rushed to her ears.

Soon she found herself and mirrored his smile. "Thank you for sharing your music with me. You should charge people for that privilege."

"I'll hold you to that," he said as she shut the door behind her.

She laughed and pressed her back into his door, struggling to keep her balance after a wave of emotions flooded her heart.

Sophia placed her hand over her heart, in an attempt to slow down the rapid rate of it's beat, with no avail.

Chapter Nine

The following day, Sophia made a trip to the library located in the east of the orphanage. It was a wide room with a cascade of books outlining every wall.

It was empty today, just like every other day. It was rare that anyone would come to the library, almost everyone found reading boring, but not Sophia. She could spend an eternity diving into different worlds and hearing fictional character's stories she wished were real.

The sound of her heels filled the room with a clapping echo.

She felt at peace when she was surrounded by books, containing the author's vivid imaginations. Sometimes she would wish she could enter a book and live there forever, beneath the soft pages and enter a new realm. That way she would not have to deal with her harsh reality.

For almost two hours she sat in the furthest corner of the library and read silently.

She couldn't stop relaying the encounter with Xavier from last night in her head. How his touch sent a spark through her body that she desperately wanted to experience over and over again.

Frustrated, her book wasn't distracting her from her own thoughts, she slammed the book shut, pressing the pages firmly together. She got to her feet and pulled over the ladder that was resting against the bookshelf.

Often finding that the best books were the hardest to reach.

Climbing up the ladder to the highest shelf, her eyes scanned the spines of the books. Nothing was really capturing her attention.

Just as she was about to give up and climb down, a book out of her reach caught her eye. The spine looked ready to crumble, as if it was handled too aggressively. A lot of people must have read that book, so Sophia assumed it must be a good one.

Sophia saw no harm in reaching for it at the spot she was in. It seemed like a waste of time to climb down from the ladder, move it an inch and then climb back up. So, she clung to the ladder and stretched out her right arm, keeping her left hand tightly wrapped around the wooden ladder. Her fingers brushed the spine but she couldn't quite reach.

When she finally got her hands on it she realised it was wedged between two other books and she had no choice but to yank it out.

With a firm grip on the spine, and all her might, she pulled it out. Overestimating how hard she had to pull.

Although she freed the book, it caused her to lose her footing and fly from the ladder. Her left hand must have not held on tight enough, as she flew freely like a leaf in the autumn breeze.

She was falling from a great height, she knew she would end up with bruises once she hit the floor.

Moments later, she was suddenly cushioned by someone's broad arms holding her up. Her legs dangled over his arms, and a firm hand pressed into her back, keeping her upright.

Sophia found herself being cradled like a child in the arms of a muscled young man. Slowly, she fluttered open her eyes and found Xavier looking down on her. His black eyes were locked on Sophia's, and his razor thin lips hooked up in a relieved smile.

"Looks like you have a habit of getting yourself into awkward predicaments," he teased.

"Looks like you have a habit of saving me." She replied. "May you put me down?"

Without a word he placed her feet on the ground, and she quickly straightened out her posture. "Thank you," she muttered.

"It also seems that you have got yourself into a habit of requiring me to save your life...is all of this to simply grab my attention? Sophia, if you have a crush on me all you have to do is tell me, rather than attempting to throw yourself off the top of a ladder. I must say, I do feel slightly flattered."

"Wha-" she couldn't believe that he was this vain. Also, she couldn't believe the contrast from his gentle behaviour last night.

Was everything to him one big joke?

She wasn't so childish to risk her life just to get a *stranger's* attention.

Why did his words get to her so easily? He loves teasing, especially her.

"Please do not think too highly of yourself. You certainly are too modest, Mr Howell."

"Are you here alone?" Why did her heart flutter at the thought of them being alone?

"I slit the throats of everyone in my way just so I could get my hands on a really good book." His face was like stone.

Sophia dropped her mouth like an anchor. She was sure he was joking but there was a hint of seriousness in his eyes.

Xavier scoffed with a grin. "Clearly you're not used to my humour."

"Clearly." Sophia said, almost to herself.

"Have I ruined your solitude?" Xavier asked, looking around the vacant room.

"No!" she retracted back as she replied far too passionately. "If it wasn't for you being here...who knows what would have happened to me." Her cheeks flushed red.

He merely shrugged his shoulders.

"I have been meaning to thank you for... that night...on the balcony." She smiled, awkwardly. Dropping her head to the floor, she felt a wave of embarrassment. "I suppose I owe you *another* thank you for just now. So...thank you."

Xavier's eyebrows quickly raised, soon chuckling to himself.

Before Sophia could realise what had happened, Xavier's hands were sliding around her waist. He pushed her up against one of the bookshelves. Positioning both of his elbows at either side of her head. His firm body was crushing hers, and his head was tipped low enough that their lips were so close to one another. If she moved even an inch they would be kissing.

Sophia looked up at him with wide eyes, unsure of what this was or what to do.

Once she realised her lips were slightly parted, she clamped them shut. Those sparks she felt from last night were back in full force. Her hands were balled into fists at her sides as she tried to repress them but it was no use.

Trapped beneath him, all she could do was stand there.

"I may consider accepting your gratitude," he muttered. "But...you may have to show me how thankful you are."

Sophia managed to reach up her palm and slapped him across the face.

Xavier didn't move, it only amused him. "What a feisty gorgon."

"That word," she breathed. "You've called me that before. What does it mean?"

He chuckled. His hot breath hit her face. "I must say, Miss Cole. You are very beautiful, it's almost...unnatural."

She opened her mouth to say something, but the words sputtered out. "I-I don't-"

"Understand?" he finished for her with a sinister smile. "You don't understand much, do you?"

Hooking his finger under her chin, forcing her to meet his dark eyes, he said. "You need to look with your eyes at what is really going on around you. Do not just see what people tell you to see." he moved his hand from her chin and cupped her scarred cheek. Gently, he grazed his thumb over the raised texture on her skin. It was so delicate that Sophia felt lost in his touch, every stroke she wanted to close the already small distance between them. Her legs were shaking as her body craved to be tangled up with him.

"How did you get these?"

Realising how this could look to anyone walking in, if Jack walked in, she shook her head. Trying her best to shake off all of the confusing feelings that were in her chest.

"Let go of me."

"Are you sure you want that?" he said.

Without a moment of hesitation, she punched him in the gut, winding him.

Immediately he retreated back, holding his stomach. "Wow, any harder and that would have actually hurt." Xavier said in a strained breath.

"I will not be mocked for showing my gratitude. Now that I have done that there is no need for us to communicate again."

"Why? Are you scared of being alone in a room with a person under suspicion of murdering young women?"

She dropped her head to the ground and sank her teeth into her bottom lip. It completely faded from her mind that *that* was the reason he was here. Sophia knew Xavier was forthcoming with what he wanted, and he was a tease but she couldn't imagine him ever hurting anyone.

Xavier scoffed, taking her silence in the complete wrong way. "Just like everyone else, you're judging me before you have any facts." He scanned the shelves and stormed over to the forbidden section. It was blocked off by a rope, like at the theatre for VIPs.

Sophia stopped in front of the rope and watched as Xavier continued to scan the shelves.

"Xavier, you can't read those books. If Cassandra knew-"

"If Cassandra didn't want anyone in this section so badly, she would do more than put up a stupid piece of rope." When he returned to her he had a book in his hand. Waving it in front of Sophia's face he shoved it into her hands.

The book had a blue and gold spine, it was brand new. That was only made evident by the amount of dust blanketing the top.

Why have all of these books if no one is going to read them?

The book Xavier picked out was titled *Greek Mythology: A Creatures Index.*

"You have reading to do, yes?" Xavier said, running a hand through his long, thick black hair.

She nodded and clutched the book close to her chest. "Excuse me."

Pain.

Day after day after day.

It was becoming far more frequent in the past few weeks. Jack was unsure how much more he could take. He noticed that he had become quick tempered, which was very unlike him. At the smallest of things too. Jack hadn't been attending dinner for the past few days, fearing that he would convulse at the table. Instead he had Stella bring his meals to his room. Last night, she simply asked about his well being, and that resulted in a vase being thrown across the room. Shattering near her feet, and a look of terror washed over Stella's face.

It would surely haunt him.

What was he becoming? A man he despised.

Powering through the agony in his chest and back wasn't doing much. His chest grew tighter as he struggled to take a full breath. Convincing himself that he was going to suffocate unless he made it to his room, Jack tried to quicken his pace to his room.

Beads of sweat dripped down his forehead, as his vision blurred.

Dragging himself up the stairs, desperate to not run into anyone. He'd already lost his strength, he couldn't handle losing his pride.

Just by luck, Stella was walking down the same staircase. The second she noticed him she ran to his side.

Even after last night, she was still caring for him. Jack didn't deserve her kindness, but Stella still placed a delicate hand over his shoulder and attempted to help him regain his balance. "Master Green, I shall call for your mother."

Just as she was about to run back up the stairs, he stopped her by gripping onto the end of her stained apron.

"That won't be necessary," he said, letting out a long breath. Forcing himself to straighten his back, causing sharp pains to snake up his spine. "See? I am quite alright." He said, sounding as if he had a bad case of indigestion.

She wasn't convinced. "Are you sure? Sir, you really do not look well."

He nodded quickly, dropping his hand on her shoulder. "Just some rest. That is all I require." It was tiresome using the same excuse over and over again, not that it mattered. Everyone knew what was wrong with him. Everyone apart from Sophia.

At times like this, he just had to remind himself of the brightness in his life. Most days he could get so clouded by the pain and the darkness swirling around his life. When he thought of Sophia, his main source of light, the world suddenly seemed less dark. Although she didn't realise it, she helped him through the pain, more so now that she was to be his wife.

Sophia.

Perhaps her smile would be the thing to cure the pain in his chest.

Excusing himself from Stella on the stairs, Jack climbed up and made his way to Sophia's bedroom door. Just when he was about to knock his eyes trailed down the hall to where that...*animal* resides.

Suddenly, his bright thoughts were starting to fade when the image of Sophia and *him* together, drenched from the rain. As they wandered into the hall together, so close that their arms almost brushed together.

Gripping his hand over his heart, he walked in stride to Xavier's door.

Without knocking, Jack thrust open the door, almost sending it flying off its hinges.

Xavier didn't as much as flinch when he looked at Jack, now standing in his doorway.

Jack tried not to show he was in any sort of pain which certainly didn't help his situation. As of recently he's tried not to rely so much on his cane, of course he brought it with him everywhere he went but right now all he wanted to do was throw it through Xavier's skull.

"I think I had more privacy in my prison cell," Xavier crossed his arms as he walked to his window, lifting it up and causing a harsh cold breeze to roll in. "I could have been changing for all you know. Is that secretly what you wanted to see?"

Jack marched forward and dug his hand into Xavier's shoulder, spinning him around to face him. "You will look at me when you speak to me," Jack snarled his upper lip. "What happened with Miss Cole? In the rain?"

Xavier was expressionless. "Why don't you ask your *fiancé?*" He couldn't seem to say that word without it being accompanied by a mocking tone.

"I am asking you."

Xavier craned his neck. "You don't have much faith in her, do you?" He laughed under his breath, which only seemed to aggravate Jack more. "Not a good start to a marriage, wouldn't you say?"

Jack stretched out his arm and swung for Xavier's cheek. Before he made contact Xavier cupped his hand around his fist and pushed him back, like he was nothing more than an insect.

"I let you have that punch downstairs," Xavier snarled. "Don't get greedy."

"There are other girls here that you can waste your time with. Leave Sophia alone." Jack spat, he was now hunched over. The pain was now spreading to his legs as they trembled.

Xavier poured himself a drink of whisky from his nightstand. "There is something I have been wondering," he took a sip from his glass. "It is abundantly clear that Miss Cole knows nothing of the world she is a part of, and she knows not of what she is." He swirled his drink around and took another sip. "Of course your mother gave me a lovely lesson in not telling Sophia anything about her life. Why is that?"

"It is in her best interest that she doesn't know." Jack managed to slowly pull himself together.

"Possessive *and* a liar. Isn't she so lucky to be marrying you." There wasn't a word in that sentence that wasn't coated in sarcasm.

Xavier slammed his empty glass down onto his nightstand. "Now that you're done with your outburst, could you be a dear and leave?"

"Don't even think of telling her anything." Jack snapped. "The truth will come out in due course, and I don't want a...a...*blood sucker* like you running things."

Xavier curved his lips and chuckled. "Blood sucker?" He repeated. "Believe me, it is not me ruining whatever balance was originally established here."

Sophia returned to her room, with the book that Xavier picked out for her clutched to her chest.

It had started to frustrate her that her heart would ache at just the thought of Xavier. She didn't understand how he could be so gentle and caring towards her and completely flip after only a day. He was like a playing card, one side was full of intricate details, where it would take a long time to take in each line - each pattern. But when you flip the card over it turns out to be a joker.

Sophia let out a growl and dropped the book onto her mattress. Slumping down onto the bed, she pulled the book onto her lap, taking in the gold foil details across the cover.

Carefully peeling open the first page, she skimmed the introduction and scanned through the contents page. One word caught her eye.

Gorgon.

Xavier's nickname for her.

A frantic desire came over her, as she flicked to page two hundred and seven, and was greeted by a portrait of Medusa's head. Venomous Snakes slithered in her hair, her skin was filled with spots of black. She had frightening, whited out eyes that made Sophia want to shut the book and hide it in her drawer.

It took her a while to look away from the picture, like her whited out eyes were hypnotising her. Eventually, Sophia began reading the text that accompanied the picture:

Medusa is a demon. She is a vicious and dangerous creature known as a gorgon. The well known fact of gorgons is that if anyone, no matter human or otherwise, gazes directly into her eyes then they will immediately turn to stone.

Legends say that Medusa is more than a myth. That there are still descendants of her to this very day, although none can be confirmed. Throughout time, pure gorgon's have become rare amongst us humans. All should beware, as gorgons can disguise themselves as beautiful temptresses. They can breed like anyone else, many have produced demonic offspring with gullible humans.

If anyone within this lifetime was to hold the blood of a Gorgon, something powerful can trigger them in order to turn victims to stone. Based on research, it is believed that any crossbred children don't immediately have their powers activated. It takes something strong to ignite it. What that is, we are unsure. All we do know is that, once the power is triggered, it can never be shut off.

This is due to the Gorgon blood no longer being -

Sophia slammed the book shut, she couldn't read anymore. Suddenly she felt like she wanted to throw up. It was too much for her brain to handle.

The air in the room was suddenly damp, and an odd sense of fear swelled in her veins.

Why would Xavier nickname her after something so hideous?

Why did she care so much about what he thought?

When looking down at her hands she realised she was shaking. This was just a stupid book, possibly another way for him to tease her.

Well, it worked. Her shaking hands are proof of that.

Mythical creatures didn't exist, hence it was made up with the word *myth.*

Sophia snapped out of her thoughts when there was a gentle tapping at her door.

Not wanting anyone to know that this book was from the forbidden section in their library, she hid the book under her pillow.

In a fleeting attempt to compose herself, Sophia looked at her own reflection. With her bright green eyes wide and her brunette curls falling from her bun. She attempted to fix herself but as the seconds pressed on she realised there wasn't much she could do.

Running to the door, Sophia swung it open.

Jack was standing in front of her with a bright smile painted on his lips. There was something off about him that she couldn't quite put her finger on.

That smile soon faded when he saw how shaken up his fiancé appeared to be. Inviting himself inside of her room, he closed the door behind them.

Jack startled her by sliding a hand around her waist, as though they were a real couple.

Sophia wasn't comfortable with this sudden affection from Jack. She still struggled to wrap her head around the fact that they were engaged. Tensing at his touch, she locked her gaze to the top button of his shirt, just below his Adam's apple.

"What's the matter?"

Sophia forced a smile. "Nothing," she lied. "I'm just a bit tired."

Jack closed the gap between them, scanning her face with his familiar blue eyes. "I have some news for you. I spoke to Father Doyle yesterday, and we shall be wed within the week."

Excitement beamed from him out of every corner. She desperately wished she could share in his feelings but she felt numb.

Sophia nodded slowly, as if she was agreeing to a formal wager as opposed to hearing of the place she would be married. It didn't help that the longer he was holding her, the more uneasy she felt. It should be natural for her future husband to hold her and worship her.

It felt wrong, she wanted to push him away and slam the door in his face.

When she finally met his eyes he attempted to read her face. Sophia wasn't good at hiding exactly what she was feeling, and the disappointment that washed over Jack's face was evident of that.

He pressed his forehead against hers and let out a sigh. "You used to be honest with me. Is all of that changing because you are going to be my wife?"

"No," the lie tasted like rotten poison. "I am grateful for what you are doing for me, I just…"

How could something that felt so wrong to her, feel so right for Jack?

No matter what she did, she couldn't shake the feeling that it was like a brother was holding her. That wasn't something a bride should feel toward her future husband.

A sharp bile started to burn in her throat as she pushed herself out of Jack's embrace. "Enough," she cried. "Do not hold me like we are happy and in love." She locked her glare at him.

"I am simply expressing how I feel. For I am happy and in love." He placed a hand over his heart and bowed to her. "I am sorry, I cannot seem to control myself. I have wanted to hold you for so long."

How could she hear such things? It was breaking her heart.

She barged past him, knocking his shoulder as she ran out of her bedroom.

In an attempt to hold in her tears she covered her mouth with her palm. It was a useless attempt as the tears acted on their own accord.

Running down the stairs, through the hall and out of the backdoor, she was greeted by a cold breeze. Running deep into the garden and to the willow tree that they read under. The last time she and Jack were here everything was normal between them. They were friends that enjoyed one another's company.

Now, whenever Jack was in her presence she felt an overwhelming sense of guilt and sadness.

Sophia wanted to escape, she couldn't cope knowing she was hurting her dear friend. They were drifting apart within such a short amount of time, did this mean their friendship wasn't as strong as she once thought?

The bark of the tree was sharp and rough as she ran her hand down the length of it.

Crunching footsteps approached her. She looked over her shoulder and saw Jack running to her without his cane.

"Jack, what if you fall?" She picked up her skirt, and hurried toward him.

"It would be worth it." Jack stepped in her view, taking her hand in his. "Why did you run off?"

Shaking her head, Sophia chewed on her bottom lip. "I cannot stand seeing how much I am hurting you. Giving you false hope after everything you are sacrificing for me."

"Sacrificing?" He scoffed. "Sophia, you are everything I have ever wanted. Even having you like this makes me feel complete."

"In time that will not be enough. It's selfish of me to marry you."

Jack lowered his head, frowning. "I was hoping you would learn to love me...in time."

Tears naturally fell from the corners of her eyes. She shook her head again. "Love should be natural, not something that is learned." Chewing on her bottom lip, she continued. "I feel like I won't give you what you deserve."

"You are the only person I want...how is that not what I deserve?"

His hand was suddenly cradling her cheek, his thumb brushed her skin lightly. By the way he was breathing she knew his heart was racing. "I have endured being your friend for all of these years." The sparkle in his eye was present as he locked his gaze to hers, not once wavering. "You may consider yourself selfish for going through with this. But I too am selfish, for I want you as my wife."

Looking up at him, taking in the sincere way he looked at her made her heart ache. "I had no idea how much I meant to you. I could never imagine how deep your feelings run."

Jack hooked his lips up to a smile. "How much more are you going to make me endure?"

When he lowered his face to hers, Sophia didn't move an inch. Their lips met, he gently brushed his mouth across hers and he instantly melted into her.

Sophia could feel the years of desire in his touch.

Jack's kiss was desperate. He held her like he was afraid of letting go, as if loosening his grip would cause her to flee.

When he parted her lips with his, Sophia felt numb all over.

One hand held her face as his other circled her waist. It took a moment for Sophia to reciprocate his kiss.

This was the first time she had ever kissed, or been kissed. The last person she expected to share this experience with was her best friend.

In her head over the years, she fantasised a handsome prince sweeping her off her feet and holding her in a sweet embrace, giving her a fairytale of a first kiss. She expected to be happily in love, with a man she wanted to spend the rest of her life with.

That's not what this felt like.

It felt like her opportunity of love was slipping through her fingers, like sand. That her fate had now been sealed with Jack. For how could she hurt him after he so desperately wanted this?

Jack truly loved her, she should have been grateful that a caring man like Jack wanted to have her. She could have been stuck with an abuser, or left on the street to perish.

It was with this kiss that she knew she had to stop taking him for granted, even if her heart rejected him.

She didn't love him. That was also made very clear as they kissed. But she wanted to do whatever she could to make him happy, even if it took the rest of her life.

Pinching her eyes shut and unsure of what to do, Sophia kissed him back in the way she imagined the characters in her romance novels would. Sliding her palm up his chest and feeling the erratic beat of his heart against her hand, she grabbed a fistful of his shirt.

The hand that cradled her face made its way to the back of her head, holding her in place.

The wind rustled the leaves which surrounded them, hissing like the sound of snakes circling their feet.

Jack poured out his heart into the kiss. Yet, no matter how hard she tried, Sophia couldn't do the same.

Chapter Ten

Sophia was swimming after her first kiss. Her lips were swollen like she had just been stung by a bee.

When walking back to the orphanage, Jack attempted many times to link his fingers through hers. Each time Sophia slid her hand away and ensured there was a reasonable gap between them.

Not a second went by that she didn't wish she felt some sort of sensation from their kiss, like she read about in all of her books. Something that would make her body tingle, right down to her toes.

Instead she felt guilt with a heavy heart.

Guilt for wanting something that seemed to be so far out of her reach. There was no sign of a slight race of the heart, only an uncomfortable pounding drumming in her ears.

It was when they stepped inside the orphanage that Sophia noticed Jack was struggling to hold up his body. As though he was carrying a human-sized bag, filled to the brim with bricks.

Once they reached Sophia's door, Jack's eyes were rolling around like marbles. His eyelids were gradually drifting shut. The further they walked the more he began leaning his weight against the wall. If he was attempting to hide his poor ability to even stand straight, he was doing a terrible job.

When Sophia noticed this, she stepped into his view and placed a comforting hand on his shoulder. "What's wrong?"

Suddenly, before she had the chance to react, his whole body was pressed against hers. Jack was so firm against her that she had no room to breath. Her back was flat against her door, and discomfort filled her spine as her doorknob dug into her back.

Jack's breath was hot as it hit her face.

Sophia tried to free herself with no avail. Pushing him off her was useless, he didn't even budge an inch. He was far too strong and so heavy that she remained stuck in her current position.

This wasn't her best friend, the man she grew up with. This was someone else. Not once had he ever filled her with such a fear, such a panic of what he would do next. She trusted him like he was a brother.

Jack's breathing grew heavier, more urgent. His hands formed fists, with the material of her dress in his grasp.

If he wanted to, he could rip her entire dress off with one swoop.

His forehead was now pressed against hers, she felt the stickiness of his sweat sticking onto her face.

"Jack please..." she begged.

His blue eyes, now fogged with an unrecognised stare, shot up and locked to hers the moment she spoke. It was like a daemon had possessed his body, he certainly wasn't acting like the gentleman she once trusted.

The free hand at the wall now gripped around the back of her neck, forcefully pulling her head closer to his.

She fought him with all her might. It was as successful as a lamb breaking free from a hungry lion's teeth.

Jack somehow managed to press more of his body weight into her, and she was sure the doorknob would be indented into her back.

"Jack..." she whimpered, wanting this to end.

"Shh!" He hissed through his gritted teeth.

Then, his mouth forcefully pressed against hers. His lips were moving fast, far more animalistic and hungry than how he was outside.

Sophia struggled to breathe with his mouth firmly against hers and his cheek squishing her nostrils. She tried to move her head out of his grasp but there was no use.

"Kiss me," he said against her mouth, his grip tightening around her neck.

Who was this person? She was sure someone had replaced her friend with a monster. Jack had never done anything of this sort in the past.

Why now?

Managing to rip her lips away, Sophia managed to take a big gulp of breath that she was deprived of for a few seconds. Immediately she began punching his chest and pushing him back by his shoulders.

Jack's lips then trailed across her scars as he pressed harder against her.

Realising the gentle approach was useless, she opted for raising her knee and went for the only place she could reach that she knew would cause him pain.

The second her knee made contact Jack stumbled back but Sophia was still in his grip. When his hands released her in one swoop she lost her footing and fell to the floor. Jack tore the sleeve of her dress from the seams when he attempted to maintain his grasp.

Drops of blood fell beside her. Jack must have sunk his nails into her flesh, but Sophia was so dumbfounded and blinded by panic that she didn't feel it.

When she looked back up, it wasn't her best friend standing over her but some kind of animal. "You will do what a wife is supposed to do for her husband!" he yelled.

She sat motionless as Jack charged for her. Reaching down to drag her back up to her feet, she was unable to react. Frozen on the floor as Jack's manic and wild eyes came for her.

After a beat, there was a sudden flash of black. Jack was thrown back down the hall in such a force that any further and he would have fallen down the stairs.

Xavier stood in front of her, with his back to her and fists clenched at his sides.

Jack jumped to his feet, and the men's eyes never wavered from one another.

"That's not how you treat a lady," Xavier chimed. He wore a faint smile on his lips. "Didn't anyone ever teach you manners? A simple please and thank you would suffice, instead of getting your grubby hands in places she doesn't want them."

"Shut up!" Jack spat. "You are *nothing* but a leach! Your soul is a pitch-black hole of *nothing!*" Jack was almost screaming, a frightening display for Sophia to witness.

"That is really not nice," Xavier placed his free hand over his heart, mockingly. "I like to think yellow is a better representation of my soul."

Sophia knew it was inappropriate for jokes at a time like this but she couldn't hold back the snort which escaped.

"Now, Mr Green I suggest you turn around and walk away until you feel you have calmed down." Xavier showed no sign of backing down.

For a long moment they glared at each other in a thick, uncomfortable silence.

Jack knew he had no fight to give. He straightened his posture and gave a quick glance to Sophia. A rush of remorse coated his features, like the real him had returned to his body and remembered what he had just done. The sudden realisation clearly crashed over him like a wave. That wasn't him, he wanted to plead his case but the fear in Sophia's eyes caused him to back away. She looked like a rabbit standing before a hunter, with his shotgun aimed right at her face.

Jack let out a breath, deep with regret and started to walk away.

Xavier turned to Sophia and offered a hand. "He's more of an animal than I am. And I'm the one accused of being capable of murder?"

Before Sophia could reach up and touch Xavier's hand, Jack returned with a charge, resembling a worked up bull. "You bastard!" he yelled and tackled Xavier from behind, causing him to fall flat on his face.

Jack hooked his legs around Xavier's sides, and gripped onto his black hair and began aggressively pulling at it, like a toddler throwing a tantrum.

Xavier let out a yell and tried to turn but Jack's weight was too much for him to roll over. "Get off!" he struggled to say.

Sophia scrambled to her feet and was motionless for a few seconds. She knew she couldn't pull Jack off, how he behaved towards her she was certain he'd swing for her. A devastating thought that not once crossed her mind before today.

Her legs were now shaking, her knees like jelly.. She looked around for something - anything - that could help the situation. Her eyes soon fell on a blue and white vase housing daffodils. It sat beside Hannah's bedroom door.

Without thinking, Sophia ran over, emptied the daffodils onto the floor, causing a giant puddle beside her shoes.

Sophia didn't have much time to hesitate as she feared how far Jack would take this.

Thrusting the vase into the air, Sophia was ready to drop it down onto Jack's head. That was until Cassandra and Albert appeared at the top of the stairs which caused Sophia to freeze in motion.

"What is going on?" Albert's voice boomed. It was rare Albert would be the authority parent, but the flames burning in his eyes showed just how furious he was.

Albert stormed over to his son, who was still attempting to pull out Xavier's hair, and hooked his arms under Jack's armpits.

With a grunt, Albert pulled Jack away from Xavier.

Jack began kicking out his legs, in an attempt to break free from his father's firm grip.

Xavier began rubbing the back of his head as he jumped back to his feet. "I think he pulled out some of my hair." he said as if *that* was the biggest problem.

Cassandra stood in between Jack and Xavier, sticking out her arms signalling for everything to halt. "Whatever this fighting is about, enough. It is childish and disruptive to the household." Her eyes soon met Sophia's, who was still clutching the vase in her fearful grip.

Cassandra stormed over to her, glancing at the puddle of water and flowers on the floor. She lowered her voice and in a hiss said, "It's a good job you didn't do what it *looks* like you were about to do." Cassandra snatched the vase from her, and her eyes shortly fell on the blood dripping down Sophia's arm.

"Clean up this mess, and you-" Cassandra directed at Xavier. "Call Stella to clean up Sophia's arm."

Cassandra left, carrying the vase down the stairs. Soon followed by Albert dragging his son down with them.

Xavier saluted with two fingers to the stairs. "Yes, Ma'am."

Instead of calling for Stella like he told Cassandra he would, Xavier accompanied Sophia into her room.

175

Sitting on the edge of her bed with her hands in her skirt, Sophia was overwhelmed with the events of the day.

Although there was a throbbing cut in her arm, it was her heart that hurt the most. The thought of Jack's aggressive behaviour made her shudder.

After today, the daunting realisation that if she never saw Jack again there would be a part of her that would be happy.

Yet, she knew she couldn't do that. She loved him and it couldn't be more clear that something was going on. Something that he was hiding from her, and she was certain his scars were a factor.

Xavier knelt down in front of Sophia and pulled off his black blazer, and gently gripped Sophia's arm to examine the cut. "With any luck," he began. "You might have another scar to add to your collection."

Frowning at him, she flared her nostrils.

"I may be able to join your club," he pointed to a small scratch flaking across his chin. The result of Jack using Xaver's face as a broom. "I do hope there isn't a splinter, there is nothing worse."

"Shouldn't you call for Stella?"

There was a razor thin smile on his face. "Now, why would I do that? When I can, once again, take the glory for saving you. What was it? Two, three times in the space of a few days?"

"I do not ask for this," she said, dryly.

"Besides," he ignored her. "I like to think I am quite skilled at cleaning up blood from a woman." he smiled to himself, like it was some private joke only he was in on.

"Like sucking the life out of them." Shrinking back when she realised she said that out loud, her mouth began to sputter. She didn't mean to actually say it, it was only meant to be a snide remark for her own mind.

"I ...I am so sorry...I did not mean...I-"

"Why apologise?" he said in a low tone. Was he actually affected by her words? "Everyone else believes I am guilty. What does one more person matter?" That confirmed he was troubled by her accidental outburst.

This angered Sophia.

"What is this sulking behaviour? After every insult you have given me I quite feel like you deserve it."

Xavier shook his head. "There is a *huge* difference between me insulting you and you insulting me."

"And what is that?"

"It's amusing when I do it." his small cheeky grin returned.

They spent a minute in silence. Sophia spent that time thinking about Jack again. Not once had he been irrationally violent...not in front of Sophia, anyway. She hated how much trust had fallen through her fingers. It was like their trust was a solid rock that suddenly transformed into a cold liquid, drenching her hands with doubt.

She always felt protected by him. Now she wasn't sure if the next time he lost his temper, it would be *her* he'd tackle to the floor. There seemed to be nothing he wouldn't do in the hallway.

"Let me tell you a secret." Xavier interrupted her thoughts as he wiped away dried blood from her arm. She hated to admit that there was a spark that shot through her body at the slightest of touch. The spark would cascade through her fingers and toes. Even something as simple as his breath hit her face, it would send her heart into a flutter.

"I am not going to lie to you. I don't usually care what people think of me. But with you...I feel like I need you to believe me." he admitted, so bluntly. Xavier looked up at her through his thick black eyelashes. Shuffling closer to her, he dropped his hands on her knees. "I did not murder those women." he watched her intently and seriously.

The hands on her knees made her body tremble, through her dress she could feel a match that had been struck against her skin.

Sophia tried to read his face, was he toying with her? She couldn't find any indication that he was lying in his eyes.

How could she go from his word? Didn't all criminals proclaim their innocence?

"Why was their blood staining your face as you cowered over them?"

He was amused by her question. "I know the evidence isn't exactly in my favour, and I have no proof that I am innocent."

"You do not deny that you were seen with their blood on your hands and mouth. What other reason would it be for you to do that?"

Xavier shook his head, dazedly. "You still don't know...do you?"

"Know what?"

"About the real world you are living in."

"Enough with these *annoying* riddles. It is clear that everyone is keeping me in the dark about something. I have no idea what it is but it is unfair to be playing with me like this." She let out a troubled sigh whilst clenching her fists. "I wish I understood why people kept secrets from me, why they avoid me. People here must think I don't see them changing course when seeing me down the hall."

"Why are you marrying Jack?" he abruptly changed the subject. He wasn't using his usual sarcastic tone, he was more concerned than anything.

"It was requested in a letter from my mother that I be married before I turn eighteen."

"What is the point in that?"

"I am still unsure but I can only assume it is so I wouldn't have to venture through life alone, and that she wouldn't have to worry about me finding a husband before I am too old to be wanted."

Xavier frustratingly rolled his eyes and slid his hands away from her knees, she felt the ice return to her body once he moved away. Xavier moved his hands to the silk sheets beside each of her legs. His arms completely tensed. "It is not required for you to have a husband. Life would be rather boring if it was planned ahead. I feel it is more exciting to not know which paths you are going to go down."

Just when she thought he was about to remove his hands from beside her, he placed his large hand over hers. Grazing his thumb gently across the back of her hand.

Cursing at herself for the immediate throbbing desire that flowed in her blood, she released a small gasp from her lips.

"Little Gorgon." He whispered.

"Why have you labeled me with that name?" she asked. "I read the book you gave me. They are well known for their hideous appearance and people cannot look at them for they would turn to stone. Is that how you see me? As some sort of hideous demon?"

Xavier pushed himself to his feet and retracted his hands, clasping them behind his back. "You read far too much into things. You try to create a scenario as opposed to *seeing* something right in front of you." he sighed. "People give others names because that is what best describes them. Words such as *ugly* are given to those who aren't pleasant to look at, hence that is the word given that describes what they are."

Ignoring the flaws in his statement, Sophia cocked her head to the side. "Then why do you call me a Gorgon?" her big eyes looked up at him with wonder and disbelief. Her heart was pounding.

She wanted him to tell her, she wasn't sure *what* she wanted him to tell her but she knew there was *something*.

It was on the tip of his tongue, and she could also see the inner turmoil.

"Think about what I said."

Chapter Eleven

The trip to the orphanage's library had not proven to be successful. Sophia scoured the shelves in hopes to find anything that could tell her about gorgons, but alas nothing. She wasn't sure what she was expecting, to find a row of books dedicated to gorgons and their history?

That word that Xavier nicknamed her was driving her crazy. The book he had provided to her told her everything about gorgons and their accent history, but nothing that would be helpful for herself.

What was her next step? She couldn't just walk away, and be satisfied with the possibility she would never find the answers to Xavier's riddles. In her heart she knew that there was something more behind his words, he wasn't only teasing her.

Sophia decided a trip to the local library was her next option.

At the front door, Sophia draped her navy cloak over her shoulders, and slipped into her boots that were neatly put away on the shoe rack. She should have grabbed her hat from her room but her mind was set on getting to the library before it closed.

"Where are you going?"

Sophia snapped her body to spin and faced Jack standing by the staircase. One hand lightly resting on the banister and his other leaning against his cane. His face wore suspicion, as one golden eyebrow was raised and his bright blue eyes took in her attire.

"Oh, only to the library." Sophia stammered, she wasn't sure why she was nervous. She was telling the truth, but the reasons for her visit tasted like a lie.

"It's rather late?" Jack said as a question, and stepped down to meet her.

"You know me," she flashed a toothy smile. "I cannot sleep without a good book and absolutely nothing in our library speaks to me."

Jack chuckled as he dipped his head and shook it. "I will not argue with the fact that you are very difficult to please."

Sophia pursed her lips to fight a smile, and settled on swatting him on the arm.

"What kind of fiancé would I be if I let you go out alone?" Jack sidestepped to the coat rack and picked out his heavy green coat and pulled it over his arm. "As these are dangerous streets you should have an escort." He fixed the collar of his coat and fiddled with the buttons on his sleeves.

Sophia swallowed, before all of the insanity as of recent she still adored spending time with Jack. But this she needed to do alone. She knew he wouldn't approve of what she was going to research, for she felt he was involved with the secrets of this building. Not once had she questioned his loyalty up until she witnessed the horrific scars lining his back, and after what happened outside of her bedroom she wasn't entirely comfortable in his company.

Jack must have read the uncertainty on her face as he stepped uncomfortably close. "Allow me this peace of mind?"

Sophia couldn't fight the gasp that escaped when Jack took her hand and raised it to mouth, brushing his lips across her knuckles.

Snatching her hand back, she clasped it tightly behind her back. Sophia couldn't bring herself to meet his eyes as her cheeks illuminated. How he slipped into the role of a fiancé so effortlessly made Sophia's stomach churn, simply from guilt.

Jack cleared his throat, "Shall we?"

It wouldn't take a genius to know that her reaction had hurt him.

Sophia had to at least try with Jack, he had saved her from a marriage with a complete stranger. Even if she had to fake her affections, she had to give that to him.

Forcing a smile, she snapped up her head and extended her hand. "Are you going to escort your fiancé and not offer your arm?"

Jack's face seemed to brighten, as if his hurt never even existed. A faint smile soon returned. "My sincerest apologies," he bowed and stuck out his elbow for her to take.

Sophia had only half an hour to browse the entire local library for what she was looking for. *What* she was looking for she was still unsure. She abandoned Jack as soon as they stepped inside and picked up her pace into a brisk walk to the history section.

Where would a book like this be?

Scanning the spines as fast as her eyes could read and again, no luck.

Without wasting any time she hurried across every bookcase, turning her head from left to right and up and down trying to find the word Gorgon written anywhere.

Sophia rounded the corner and slammed into Jack's broad chest, his hands caught her upper arms and halted her. "Why are you so frantic? I've never seen you so eager to find a book before."

Sophia was suddenly disgusted with herself that she felt a need to lie to Jack. There was a time that she had no fear in opening up to him but now...with his hands tightly around her arms, she felt like she was being held by a stranger.

Her green eyes rolled as she attempted to conjure an excuse; he was right. She must have looked like an infant that had been let loose in a park. "You're right," she sighed, feeling defeated. "I'm sorry."

Jack reached up his hand to hold her cheek, he kissed her forehead and stepped back. "The library is closing soon anyway, we should leave."

No, they had only just got here. She couldn't leave after accomplishing nothing. "Can we stay for just five minutes? I promise I won't go on a rampage."

Jack's laugh raised in his throat. "Five minutes," he said, and headed for the exit.

Sophia was still internally going on a rampage looking for that one unknown book, but she had the outward appearance of an elegant young lady.

Her five minutes were almost up, but someone - whether it be fate - must have been on her side at that moment. For her eyes caught on the green spine of a book with golden, reflective lettering. It was practically sparkling and drawing her in, like it was an extravagant piece of jewellery.

She pulled out the book that was wedged between a sea of meaningless other titles, and held it in her hands like it was a delicate piece of valuable art that could break with any sudden movements. On the outside, it looked like every other book with a plain green leather but with an odd snake-like design trailing the corners. But when she opened the first page, she felt as though she might cry.

The Untold History of Gorgons

She found it. Again, *what* she had found, she still wasn't sure. Her eyes scanned across the page and her heart almost fell out of her mouth when she read the author's name.

Written by Christopher Cole

Sophia was certain she had stopped breathing for an unhealthy amount of time.

That name.

The name of her father. She had to get this book for that fact alone.

As much as she desired to take this book, she had to come back without Jack. She didn't want him knowing what she was researching. It would only bring up questions that she didn't have the answers for. But with this book, she was hoping that was going to change.

Ever since their trip to the library Jack has barely given her enough time to be alone, and it didn't look like he was going to lighten up any time soon. He was constantly making arrangements in regards to the wedding, and Sophia could tell he was putting all of his heart into it.

Sophia wouldn't be listening most of the time, she was trying to plot out when she could return to the library and pick up the book.

Each day Jack would occupy her time until it was time for her to go to bed. Jack had insisted that they be married that week, to ensure Sophia's future. But Sophia had requested the wedding be pushed back for at least two more weeks. After this discovery, she couldn't jump into a marriage that might not be deemed necessary when she put the pieces together.

Jack was obviously distraught at the news of their pushback, but he accepted as he knew he could not force Sophia up the aisle. And that was the last thing he wanted to do.

Tonight, Sophia decided on paying Xavier a visit before falling asleep.

She debated for days if this was what she wanted to do. What made her think he would help her in the first place? He didn't owe her anything.

Before she could knock on his door, it swung open and he was standing there, his black hair ruffled in multiple directions and his white shirt hanging over his grey trousers. "You linger for far too long," he said with a coy smile.

Sophia looked over her shoulder to Jack's door, ensuring she hadn't disturbed him. She dropped her voice to a whisper and said, "I must request a favour."

"A favour?" he said, seeming delighted. "And what would that be?" he let go of the door handle and crossed his arms over his chest, leaning his bicep against the doorframe.

"I have found a book-"

"A book?' he interrupted with an amused laugh.

"Yes," Sophia hissed. "I listened to you, I am researching gorgons and I found a book in the local library and this book-" she didn't want to go into it, she felt like she might choke on the tears rising in her throat.

Xavier was visibly taken aback when she looked up to meet his eyes again, with tears outlining her deep green eyes.

"Please," she muttered. "I would get it myself but Jack hasn't given me a chance to *breathe* I-"

"What's the book called?" Xavier said. "And where is the library?"

Sophia felt like she might burst with joy, "It's called *The Untold History of Gorgons,* and the library is but a ten minute walk away from here, next to the bakery."

Xavier thought for a moment, as if he might decline but he finally said. "I'll go tomorrow."

Sophia couldn't help but wait for Xavier to burst through her bedroom door and thrust the book into her hands. Her eyes were glued on her door as she waited for him. Every time a person knocked and stepped through that door, it wasn't him. And every time she was disappointed.

Sophia decided to spend some time with Jack in the drawing room. They were putting together plans for their wedding but once again she was too fixated on Xavier getting that book.

What if he wasn't going to get it at all? And this was another tease to get her hopes up and crash them down for his own amusement?

"What do you think, Sophia?" Jack's voice interrupted her thoughts, and she realised she hadn't been listening to a single word he had said. She didn't even realise he had started talking.

"I'm sorry," she dropped her hands into her lap. "Would you mind repeating that? I'm afraid I was off with the fairies."

Jack's expression didn't change, she knew she was starting to frustrate him that she wasn't taking this as seriously as he was. She knew she should have been, but her mind was elsewhere.

"Sophia," Jack's voice was low, and he reached over to hold her hand. She let him and met his eyes. "I know this isn't an ideal situation for you, marrying me wasn't what you were hoping for, but..." he dropped his head, and it took him a moment to meet her eyes again. "I promise I will take care of you, and I will do everything I can to make you happy."

Although she knew Jack had the best of intentions, she knew what he actually meant by the end of that sentence. *I will do everything I can to make you love me.*

Instead of arguing, she squeezed his hand reassuringly and muttered, "I know."

It was almost midnight and Sophia hadn't seen Xavier that day, she was curled up in bed silently kicking herself for believing that he would do such a thing for her.

Just when she was about to fall into a slumber there was a knock on her door.

Suddenly wide awake, as if she hadn't even felt a hint of tiredness, she kicked her covers to the floor, and scrambled out of bed. Almost tripping up over herself she ran to her bedroom door. She must have looked as frantic as she felt when the door swung open and Xavier was standing with his hands behind his back, wearing an expression that was a mixture of confusion and amusement. "Did I disturb you?" he said.

Sophia tucked a strand of her wild hair behind her ear, in hopes of taming her messy locks.

"May I come in?"

Nerves rushed to her chest, the palms of her hands began to sweat as she stepped aside allowing him to enter her room.

When she shut the door, Xavier was facing her with a proud smile on his lips. "You," he brought both of his hands in front of him, revealing the book she had requested outstretched in front of her. "Owe me a favour."

194

Sophia had to restrain herself from not bouncing on her heel and squealing.

Within seconds from taking the book from Xavier, Sophia practically dived into his chest and wrapped her arms around him, holding on tightly in hopes to mask the tears coming to her eyes. She realised to him this must seem like an overreaction to a simple book, but in her heart it held so much weight. Not only could it provide answers to Xavier's riddles but this could be the work of her father, and it meant more that she could say that he would do something like this for her.

It took Xavier a moment, but she was surprised when his arms encircled her back and he held her just as tightly.

Sophia never expected this to last for so long, she found a deep comfort being in Xavier's arms and she never wanted to let go. When Xavier broke the embrace she'd be lying if she said she didn't feel as if something was missing, like being in his embrace was something that she didn't realise that she had craved.

When trying to meet his eyes, Xavier had his head dipped to the floor. "Well, I hope this gives you some clarity."

He began to walk away and stopped in his tracks when Sophia said, "Thank you."

Without looking over his shoulder to Sophia, Xavier replied. "Don't thank me, remember that you owe me one favour."

A playful smile grew on her lips, and as soon as she was alone Sophia hugged the book to her chest and wrapped her arms around herself. When she closed her eyes she imagined she was back in Xavier's arms.

Sophia was left alone shortly after. Xavier's words were still present in the forefront of her mind. *I hope this gives you clarity.*

She read twenty pages of Christopher's book, and it was more of a work of fiction than fact. It was a disappointing realisation that this didn't uncover secrets she needed to know but Sophia was entranced that this could be the work of her father.

Was Christopher a storyteller? Oh, how Sophia would have loved to hear his stories as a child.

Then it only brought up the question, if he was still alive...why wasn't he with her?

No longer could she sit around and wait for the answers to fall into her lap. The conversation with Xavier only made her question everything that unsettled her about the orphanage she lived in all her life. Everyone avoided her because they feared they would be the one to spill the secret *everyone* tried to hide. That much was clear to her now.

Were the rumours in town true that a dark force encircled the building? Was it witchcraft? Was Sophia part of a cult and not realised?

She waited in her room, for what must have been hours. Pacing in circles so much that she was certain that there was going to be a hole burnt into the floor.

It was a few minutes past midnight, she was sure that everyone was asleep. That was when she decided to take matters into her own hands.

Sneaking out of her room, she headed straight for Jack's room.

So built up on a forced confidence, she wasn't afraid of him hurting her. She was ready for answers and she felt ready to fight back this time.

Perhaps it was only adrenaline but that was what she was running on.

Lightly knocking on his door, she received no reply.

The answers she needed were from Jack, she knew he would be the only one willing to talk with her. She wasn't giving up just because there was no reply.

Sophia cracked open the door and had a peek inside. The sheets hadn't been slept in, or even sat on. His books were tidied away on his small shelf. The room clearly hadn't been used since Stella cleaned up on her afternoon chores.

Her nostrils filled up with the smell of Jack, it was an overwhelming scent of pine.

Letting out a deep sigh, she shut the door. She couldn't go back to her room, she had far too many unanswered questions. Fearing that if she retired for tonight, she would never build this confidence again to seek answers.

With her nightgown dragging against the floor she could do nothing but wander around the orphanage halls. In an attempt to clear her head. She had no set destination but she was hoping to stumble across one as she got there.

She made her way to the library and dropped into her usual chair at the head of the rectangular table. Her head was swirling in confusion and frustration as she couldn't piece together her thoughts.

It was like she was given a select amount of pieces to the puzzle but not enough to complete it.

Burying her face in her hands, her eyelashes brushed against her palms as she blinked.

What was happening to her? Her heart was pounding against her ribcage and she couldn't get Xavier's words out of her head.

You still don't know...do you?

What didn't she know? He mentioned something about the world she was in. Was he just babbling to keep her on her toes and to mess with her mind? Yet, when he looked into her eyes she felt a strange sense of safety.

A feeling of truth.

It wasn't clear the feelings she held for him, but there was something locked away in her heart.

It was frightening.

Sophia wasn't sure that this feeling would go away. Perhaps she was afraid because she didn't *want* the feeling to go away.

Slowly, she lowered her hands and found Stella standing in her direct view. Causing Sophia to jolt out of her skin, accelerating her heart.

If her heart raced any more then she feared she might have a heart attack.

She placed her hand over her chest in an attempt to calm herself. "Stella, my God!"

"My apologies, Miss. You should not be wandering around the orphanage late at night."

Sophia watched her, confused. "And why not?" she said, a bit harsher than she had intended. Retracting herself back, Sophia cleared her throat. "It's not like there is any danger here." There was a sudden distrust for everyone she thought she knew, even those she considered friends.

Stella bit hard into her bottom lip and turned away from Sophia. She held her hands in her lap and bowed her head. Her blonde hair was braided down her left shoulder, and her eyes drifted to a close. "It is a full moon tonight, Miss."

"What has that got to do with anything?" Sophia propped her elbow on the table and looked at the back of Stella's head.

Stella paused for a long moment. "Some residents...don't take kindly to a full moon."

"What are you talking about? There have been many other full moons since I have lived here and not once has anyone-"

"Because we do not allow you to hear, Miss. There are things which you are not meant to know."

Sophia got to her feet. Stella knew something, and she was clearly struggling to hold it in.

This only fuelled the fire of rage already bubbling in Sophia's blood. Even Stella, the woman she confided in every morning had been lying to her. Keeping secrets along with everyone else.

Could this be the start to the answers she was searching for? "Stella, what are you talking about?"

She turned to face Sophia, visibly overwhelmed. Her eyes were bloodshot and fresh warm tears were trickling down her rosy cheeks. "Please know that I do not agree with how the people in this orphanage have treated you. Keeping you in the dark. When I saw Master Green get carried away by his father, I...I couldn't help thinking of you. He was shouting for you, screaming that he wanted to tell you the truth. I felt so sorry for you, Miss. That you do not have any idea of what surrounds you." She was frantic, speaking so fast that Sophia struggled to keep up with her words. Stella's chest was heaving up and down in a weighted breath.

"Stella, I don't-"

"Start to understand, Miss!" she barked, with a flood of tears resembling an infinite waterfall. "I fear for Master Green. There is something seriously wrong with him, and I think it is about time you got answers to your questions."

How did she know I was searching? She thought.

"Where is he?" Sophia spoke barely above a whisper.

Stella walked to the door and picked up a flickering candle seated inside a black lantern. "Follow me, Miss."

She did without any hesitation.

An eagerness, and almost excitement, was rising up Sophia's chest. Up until a few weeks ago she never realised how in the dark she was. Not until Xavier started to shine a light into her eyes.

They walked side by side, although Sophia struggled to keep up with Stella's brisk pace.

Sophia followed Stella until they reached the door of the infirmary. There is something unsettling about this part of the orphanage at night. The corridor was lit only by Stella's single lantern.

There was a chill in the air and Sophia hugged herself, more for comfort than warmth.

A lock and chain sealed the door.

Stella pulled out a key from her apron pocket and unlocked it, swiftly. The sound of the chain dropping to the floor echoed through the hall.

"This may be the last time you see me." Stella said, her voice wobbling from crying. "For I will surely be fired for escorting you here."

"To the infirmary?" Sophia watched Stella's glassy eyes. "Stella, I have been down here numerous times when I was ill, I-"

"Alone, Miss," Stella cried. "You've only been here alone. Not when others have been...*sick*."

Sophia opened her mouth, unsure of what had come over Stella's panicked and erratic behaviour. "I wasn't planning on telling Cassandra or Albert. Hand over the keys, and if they question anything I will say I stole them from your pocket."

"I cannot ask for you-"

"You did not ask, I am telling you that is what is going to happen." she grabbed the keys from Stella and shot her a reassuring smile. This certainly didn't reflect how Sophia *actually* felt.

Stella curtsied in gratitude, then handed her the lantern. "Master Green is in there. I must leave, but do tell me what happens when I see you in the morning."

Stella picked up her skirt and apron, leaving Sophia alone.

Chapter Twelve

Stella felt a wave of guilt for leaving Sophia alone in the infirmary. She could see how broken she was, and she could no longer stand by and watch the torment they were putting her through. What everyone had put her through the second she arrived at the orphanage.

Stella remembered that day. She too was only a child, a few years older than Sophia. Everyone was warned of a new addition arriving at the orphanage, and told of what she was. They were all warned to keep their distance, and they were strictly prohibited from forming any type of relationship with her.

Although Stella was under Cassandra's employment, she spent most of her time taking care of Sophia, even at the age of thirteen. She felt a sense of loyalty to her, like a sister. When Sophia called her a friend a few weeks ago it scared Stella, for they seemed to feel the same for one another.

But nothing happened.

All of the horror stories Cassandra told didn't seem to be true, for they locked eyes and nothing happened. Ever since then, Stella has questioned Cassandra's honesty. Which she never thought she would do considering everything she had done for her.

Stella was about to visit Sophia's room and wait for her return. She couldn't wait until morning to find out if she was all right.

That was until she stumbled across Robert lying on the floor, with his back pressed against his bedroom door. He was battered and bruised, with blood dripping from the scars sliced across his arms and face.

Stella hurried over and knelt down beside him. "Sir, are you all right?"

"Do I look alright?" he glared up at her. One bloody scar was carved deep into his square cheek. His once white shirt was decorated with rips and a torn off sleeve. The tanned lines of his torso were fully on display, even when trying *not* to look Stella still found herself blushing. "What happened?"

"Hannah." it was all he had to say. "I can't live my life without worrying about hers." He gritted his teeth and punched the ground below him.

Stella cautiously placed a comforting hand on his broad shoulder and watched him intently. "Sir, you have been a remarkable brother to your sister. You cannot give up on fighting for her."

"After all we've done, I'm not sure why you speak formally toward me." Robert scoffed.

Why did he insist on bringing her down, when all she wanted was to be kind to him?

Robert had been struggling, and Stella was a lonely woman. They found an understanding with one another, and they would meet up for secret rendezvous. It was clear that all it was to Robert was sex, a way of relieving himself from stress. But in the months that they had been intimate, Stella had foolishly fallen in love with him.

She knew she should stop, for nothing good could come of it. Robert would never love her the way she wanted him to. But she still held onto hope that one day he might, because sometimes when she looks into his golden eyes she can see a change in him. A sort of affection that wasn't there at the start.

"Hannah isn't getting better. She can't control it. The full moon seems to come around more frequently." He laughed to himself. "At least, it feels that way." He shook his head, radiating anger. "When she is in that *state* she doesn't see me as a brother..." he lowered his head as if in shame. "and I cannot see her as my sister."

Stella checked his forehead and felt him burning up. "I shall get you some ice-" just as she was about to get to her feet, Robert gripped his hand around her wrist tightly.

She froze, watching him.

"Just...sit with me for a while."

She complied instantly.

Hunching up her knees, hands tightly wrapped around her legs, Stella sat beside Robert and felt the heat radiating from his body.

For a moment they were silent and staring out at the portraits hanging in front of them.

"What happened to that vase that's usually here?" Robert broke their small silence.

Stella glanced over at the vacant space that once housed the prettiest daffodils. "I am sure it has something to do with that prisoner." She gestured in the direction of Xavier's door and buried her nose into her knees.

They soon returned to silence. His chest was heaving up and down. Shifting in his spot and exhaled a sharp breath, Robert wrapped his arm around his bare torso, like he was trying to hold himself together.

"Are you in pain?" Her eyes lingering on his long eyelashes, shadowing his bright golden eyes. They were the first thing she noticed about him when they met. He was such a snobby child, not that much has changed over the years. Robert always saw himself as more mature than the rest of the orphans for he was the oldest.

Stella often wondered if he would have given her a chance if she wasn't put into the position of a maid.

"Yes."

"I'm sure things will be fine," she tried to be comforting.

Robert tilted his head to look over at her. Their eyes locked and Stella was smiling as she spoke, as a way to give him reassurance. "Your sister is strong...much like her brother."

Robert's eyelids widened after hearing her say that. Without warning, he reached over and cupped his hand around the back of Stella's head.

The only thing she was certain of was that her heart ached from his touch.

Although it pained him, he leaned forward until his lips brushed against hers, urgently. Stella's eyes were wide as she tried to wrap her head around what was happening. She told herself that last time was the *last* time.

Who was she kidding?

Robert was like a drug to her, once she had a simple taste she was hooked for life.

Her core ached for him when he pushed his face into hers, and a breathy moan rose up his throat.

They had done this so many times, but Stella was still cautious as she wrapped her arms around his neck and he leaned his body into her.

Without taking his lips from hers, and not caring if anyone left their room and witnessed what was going on, Robert slid his hands under Stella's thighs and wrapped them around his waist. The skirt of her dress gathered at her hips as she crossed her ankles over one another.

Robert picked her up, effortlessly and walked them into his bedroom. He didn't even have to open his eyes to know the way.

Once inside, Robert shut the door behind them by kicking it.

Laying down with Stella still snaked around his waist, he blanketed her body with his. They kissed and created a cloud of pleasure, only accessible by the two of them.

Stella untangled her ankles and released a moan when Robert trailed his lips down her neck.

When he pressed his body firmly into hers, she could feel his erection pressed against her. His hands couldn't decide where to settle, they moved from her cheeks, to over her swollen breasts and to her waist.

Stella slid her hands into his rich brown hair, and held on as the motion of pleasure travelled through her body and between her legs.

Without wasting any time, Robert ripped off his shirt and undid the buttons holding together Stella's dress. In one swift motion he removed it from her, revealing her full naked body.

Positioning one hand beside her head and propping himself up with the outstretched arm, his other hand held her hip. For a moment Robert stared at her, like he was taking in each detail of her face.

Tonight felt different with Robert. Stella was so used to this just being sex, he would barley kiss her but tonight he was really looking at her. Taking in her naked body, and his golden eyes longingly staring at her face.

Stella looked up at him through her thick eyelashes, her mouth slightly open in anticipation. "Robert..." she whispered.

The look of longing was still in his eyes when he removed his hand from her hip and placed it between her legs. Stella trembled, needing his touch. This was all so new, not once had he cared for her pleasure in these meetings. Not that he had to worry, for she was satisfied every time but tonight he was taking the step to seemingly please her.

Robert then stuck two of his fingers inside of her and made fast circular motions, causing Stella to cry out. He swiftly changed his pattern, only causing her body to ache with needing more of him inside of her.

She bucked her hips in response, and Robert covered his body with hers. Somewhere, between all of this he had managed to remove his trousers, kicking them off to the foot of the bed.

When their skin brushed together, it was like feeling the sun on your bare skin in the summer.

Robert removed his fingers, and sat back on his bed with his legs stretched out in front of him. He lifted Stella up and positioned her to sit on top of him, straddling him with both legs around his waist. Her knees sunk into his mattress, as she lightly cupped the sides of his neck.

This certainly felt like something more to Stella. This wasn't just sex, it felt like making love.

When Robert entered her, it was slow and careful. Unlike every other time, where he would slam into her and fuck her until she was dizzy.

This time, Stella felt in control as she rocked back and forth, Robert's hands splayed out on her back and pressed her breasts against his chest.

They moaned and panted in unison, and as Stella kept her gaze locked to Robert's she realised that she was well and truly in love with him.

Jack was glowing, literally. A white and gold illuminated his sleeping body.

Sophia could do nothing but stare. Any reasoning behind what she was seeing was quickly squandered by logic.

He was glowing so bright that it almost blinded her, like she was looking into the golden gates of heaven.

It felt wrong for her to be here.

Is this why Stella was so anxious about Sophia visiting Jack?

Cautiously, she reached out her hand and began stroking his blonde hair that was drenched in his own sweat.

The glow didn't affect how he felt, his skin was still smooth but he had a slight temperature.

He grumbled as his eyelashes fluttered.

There was a dull layer over his sparkling blue eyes. "Sophia?" His voice was hoarse. When he realised where he was, he hoisted himself up so he was propped up on his elbows.

Sophia reached out her hands and gently laid them flat on his chest. "Lie back down. Don't strain yourself."

Without arguing he did as she instructed. But he kept his tired gaze on Sophia.

"You're glowing." Sophia finally addressed it.

Jack smiled, mistaking it for a compliment.

Reading his misinterpretation, she couldn't think of anything else to do but laugh. "No, you are actually glowing."

Why wasn't she more surprised? Perhaps it was exhaustion from the tiresome events of the last few weeks. So much had happened to her in a short amount of time that she was positive she had been teleported into a fantasy novel.

Panic inflicted his face.

Jack shot up completely this time and the glow quickly faded as if it was never there. He was panting, sweat dripping like wet paint from his forehead.

It was at this moment she realised he was shirtless. His chest rising and falling, the lines of his torso resembled the carvings of a greek god statue found in an art gallery. His usually perfectly combed hair was wild and ragged.

"Tell me what is going on," her eyes fell to the scars sliced on his back. Now, dripping with blood like that night in his room.

Following the trail of blood with her eyes, she found an assortment of white feathers sprinkled across the mattress. "What is happening to you?"

"I can't-"

"Jack!" She yelled, startling him and herself. "Please. Enough of the secrets. Whatever it is, you *need* to tell me." Her eyes ringed red. "If you don't and I find out on my own, I will only resent you for keeping me in the dark for longer than necessary."

A sour expression covered his face, like she had slapped him whilst he was already down. "Resent me more than you already do?"

"How could you say that?" She breathed, moments away from tears.

"How could you?"

Jack pinched the bridge of his nose, and gritted his teeth. An action she had seen Cassandra do many times.

"I was not allowed to tell you anything from the day you got here...None of us were." He punched the mattress beside him and swore under his breath. "This was all because of that prisoner. That filthy, arrogant..." his face scrunched up as he spilled out the worst words he could think of.

"If anything *he* is the only one who has been honest with me," Sophia smirked. "Even if it's in his own strange way."

Jack looked up at her, a single eyebrow raised and a look of disdain. "He doesn't take your feelings into consideration."

"He doesn't have to," she barked back. Was she arguing with Jack over Xavier? Oh, if he were here he would be eating this up. It's almost like she could hear the snide comments now.

"Mr Howell owes me nothing."

If at all, I owe him. She didn't dare open that rabbit hole by saying it out loud.

"What is it everyone has been hiding from me?" She pushed. "What is it *you* have been hiding from me?"

Jack opened up his hands, shrugging his shoulders. "I honestly do not know where to start."

"Anywhere," she was crying now, only silently. "Tell me anything."

The blue of his eyes was drowning in sadness, and waves of remorse were crashing through. "You won't believe me."

Angry and now crying, Sophia couldn't settle on which emotion to allow to take control of her. It was like the two were battling it out inside of her chest without a single chance of any other emotion breaking up the two.

"Every person in this orphanage isn't exactly..." he started shaking his head. Unable to meet her eyes, that was usually as easy as breathing for him. "Well, they're not...*we're* not...human."

217

This should have been a joke; it was anything but.

Why had the sudden urge to run spring into her mind? Like this is something she shouldn't be hearing? Because it wasn't.

Was that why only a limited selection of people were permitted to claim shelter within these walls?

Sophia wanted to run and throw up at the same time, that certainly would not make for a pretty sight for anyone she might run past.

It still didn't make sense. When the truth came out it didn't feel like the final piece of the puzzle had been put into place, like she expected. Instead it was like she had the final piece but someone threw the puzzle on the ground, causing the pieces to get mixed up again. Having to start over from the beginning.

Everyone knew. Why?

Jack took her hand in his, to offer support. "Robert and Hannah are werewolves, Alice is a witch, Stella is -"

"What am I?" She cut him off, feeling numb.

All he did was stare at her. Like he was seriously considering leaving it there, but how could he? There was a look on his face now, a desperation, as though he was silently pleading with her to not make him say it.

"Tell me," she could barely say above a whisper. Squeezing his hand, as if ready to brace for a fall. "Please."

It took a few minutes for him to release a long sigh. "From my understanding you're similar to myself. Not that we are the *same* but we share a common feature, if you will. For you have a mixture of human blood in your veins, just as I do." he hesitated. "But...you are a gorgon."

Her first reaction wasn't to scream, or cry. Just a single word repeated in her mind.

Why?

Why wasn't she upset? Why wasn't she surprised? Why did no one tell her? Why did her best friend lie to her? Why was her feeling of loneliness justified to these people?

Why?

Jack read her face. He tilted his head, face full of regret. "Sophia, I'm so sorry I didn't tell you. I promise you if I could have told you sooner I would have." His words picked up in pace, like he was panicking. "My mother ensured all of us it was for your own benefit..."

"Why?" Gritting her teeth, and finally asking the question out loud. "Why does everyone else deserve to know the truth, about who *they* are and who *I* am, but me?"

Jack squeezed her hand tighter, so much that her fingers pulsed at the tips. "It is not as simple as that. There is no...hidden agenda to keep you in the dark."

Snatching her hands away, the warm embrace quickly turned to coal. "Then what was it? Was it some sort of sick joke? A...a bet for how long you could make me suffer?"

"No!" He barked, now enraged. "There's more to your circumstances than just what you are."

"Please explain," she snapped.

"Sophia," he reached for her trembling hand again. She swiftly took a step back, shaking her head. He then pinched the bridge of his nose again, letting out a breath. "No one can love you the way you love them."

"Excuse me?"

Jack suddenly gritted his teeth, signalling that the intense pain had returned. He then placed one arm behind his back to hold himself up. Immediately his hand was coated in a deep red blood that poured from his scars. He arched his body over, with beads of sweat dripping from his forehead.

She choked out a cry. How could that be true?

Why was this kept from her?

Where was the logic?

She couldn't let go of the anger but for now she had to at least swallow it. It hurt, like swallowing a brick, with it's rough edges scratching her throat.

Sophia slid a hand around his shoulder and held him close. Jack nuzzled his head into her stomach, his free hand reaching up and draping around her torso.

"Are the scars and fits a result of...what you are?" She tried to be subtle but was there a need at this point?

"Yes," he pulled away, with his hand resting over her hip. His thumb lightly brushed against the material of her nightgown. "My mother was a Guardian of God. What most people would call a 'guardian angel' and it was her duty to watch over those who were losing their way. During her time on earth she met my father, who is human, and fell in love with him. Which was obviously strictly prohibited." He was smiling, but he clearly wasn't happy. "She then fell pregnant with me, and as a punishment she was stripped of her title as Guardian and exiled to earth, and if she were to die...she wouldn't go to Heaven." He started shaking his head. "As if that wasn't enough, they put a curse on me before I was born. My wings would grow everyday under my skin until they fully formed, tearing open my skin more and more each day.

"Usually, they would grow in the womb and the child would feel nothing. But for her 'crime' her child's wings would grow overtime and into adulthood. Making it a gruelling, dragged out experience."

Sophia's heart ached for him, and Cassandra. She couldn't begin to imagine what that must do to a mother. To be the cause of such harsh and unbearable pain. That would explain why she was so overprotective.

Jack looked over his shoulder as the pain began to settle. "It won't be long until this pain is over. My wings are already feathering."

Their eyes met, "I never apologised to you for what I did to you outside of your bedroom. It's no excuse, but I genuinely can't control myself when I get into these fits." Jack said, dipping his head. "I'm so sorry Sophia. So very sorry. It's all been very difficult."

"It has," she agreed and pressed her lips against his forehead. "You should rest."

Chapter Thirteen

A gorgon.

Sophia was a gorgon.

That blasted word repeated over and over in her head, and the image of medusa's head flashed in her mind when walking back up the stairs to her room. What was she supposed to do now with this information? She could deny it all she wanted to, break it down to Jack's delusions due to his recent outburst. Yet, she knew he was telling the truth. In an odd, and ridiculous way it all seemed to make sense.

But one thing that Sophia couldn't wrap her head around was something Jack had told her in the infirmary.

"No one can love you the way you love them."

What did he mean by that? What would happen?

Her mind was a whirlpool, full of information that her brain was too tired to process.

A Gorgon.

It still didn't make sense. Many times, Jack had looked into her eyes and nothing happened. He didn't turn into a statue. She also stole glances to Xavier's eyes, so many times she memorised them, and nothing happened.

She wished she stayed to ask more questions, but Jack clearly wasn't fit to be pushed further.

What was she supposed to do now? Sit alone in her room and cry?

Even if she wanted to, her eyes felt dry. Plus, she didn't have the energy to cry, it wasn't worth the headache that would shortly follow.

When she entered her room, Sophia immediately dropped to the floor, her back pressed against the door, and she huddled up her knee. Burying her head into her knees, Sophia just sat and stared at nothing. She was frustrating herself the more she didn't understand what had just happened. She didn't know how to process the news that she wasn't fully human.

That wasn't exactly something that was taught to you as a child.

Although she was given an answer, it didn't answer any of her questions.

"I almost didn't see you there," a deep, charming voice called.

Snapping her head up, her eyes fell on Xavier. He was towering over her with his signature lopsided smile.

"I did not see you," she rubbed under her nose with the edge of her hand. "I'm guessing it is some trait from being a creature?"

"Ah!" He clasped his hands together in enthusiasm. "So, you finally figured out my riddles."

"They weren't exactly hard to figure out, considering you outright told me what I am." Sophia grumbled as she rose to her feet. "Multiple times."

The conversation with Jack reappeared in her head and a wave of sadness overtook her. Something she was getting far too used to.

The vision of her best friend surrounded by his own blood, caused by years of agony and suffering. How had she not noticed his behaviour before? The first sign of trouble she witnessed was on their stroll back from the theatre, and that was only weeks ago. By the sounds of it, Jack had been suffering for years, possibly his whole life.

Only now had she realised all of the times he made excuses to leave the room.

It was to suffer alone.

It made her question whenever he would suddenly say he needed to have a discussion with his father, or bring up running an errand for his mother, was any of that true? Was it just a decoy so he could go off to his room and silently suffer? To endure such hardships in solitude?

Xavier took a step forward and reached out his hand. Just as the tip of his index finger brushed her cheek, Sophia flinched back and felt her pulse quicken in her veins.

"What's got you troubled?" he sounded sincere with his question. "Aside from the obvious."

"My whole life has been a lie." She shook her head and shot her eyes up to the ceiling in an attempt to blink away the tears. "I have been given false hope about living a normal life."

Xavier merely shrugged his shoulders and punched his hands in his trouser pockets. "I would say I am sorry but-"

"I already know," she gritted her teeth, dropping her head to the ground. Sophia furrowed her eyebrows. "I do not deserve it for I have been put through exactly what I am putting Jack through. False hope."

Xavier's face hardened. "Doesn't that make you feel better about marrying him?"

"Excuse me?" Sophia shot up her head and met his dark eyes.

"He's given you a false image of your life up until now," he scoffed. "Now you can repay him by providing the rest of his life false hope."

Taking a step in protest, she exclaimed. "He is my best friend."

"Oh, do excuse me," Xavier bellowed, and dramatically shoved his hands on his hips. "I seem to have forgotten we are six years old. What are your plans for tonight? Sitting in the garden making daisy-chains and playing hopscotch?"

"How can this be real?" She ignored him. "Why did no one tell me?"

Xavier sighed, running a hand through his thick locks. "I don't know these people, but I can only speculate that it was to protect you."

"From what?" She wanted to cry again.

Xavier shifted his weight, suddenly serious. "You shouldn't get worked up so easily. Why not let your hair down and accompany me on a trip to the pub?"

"Aren't you confined here?"

The sudden smirk from him sent a tingle down her spine.

Walking to the window with a confident stride, Xavier unlocked the hatch, springing the windows open. "What they don't know won't hurt them." He folded his arms over his chest. "Besides, it will make a change to have a companion when I drink."

Sophia was hesitant but intrigued by his offer. What if someone came by her room and noticed she wasn't here? Would they think she'd run away?

Then she remembered that not one person was concerned for her these past few years. Everyone lied to her every day.

Even Jack.

"May I come with you?" She barely heard herself, she was surprised Xavier did.

The smirk morphed into a pleased grin.

Xavier didn't waste any time in preparing himself to dive out of the window. He hooked his legs out of her bedroom window and sat on her ledge. Looking over his shoulder with a single eyebrow raised, he tilted his head signalling for Sophia to join him.

Sophia pulled out an old pair of boots from her closet and shoved her feet inside. They were cold at her toes, and it took a moment for her feet to adjust in the boots.

Slowly she walked to him, her eyes now locked to the back of his neck. Never before had she been so entranced by the ends of someone's hair, and how he seemed to perfectly sit at the nape of his neck. She wondered if his hair felt as thick as it looked.

Sophia stopped, his scent of fresh spring rain filled her nose. The closer she got, the more pleased her heart seemed to be, which was a frightening realisation.

"Wrap your arms around my neck," he broke her trance with his silk-like voice. "But do *not* strangle me."

Her cheeks illuminated, wondering if he could feel her radiating.

Slowly, she did as he instructed. Her hands slid over his shoulders and joined her hands below his Adam's apple. The edge of her hand pressed against his firm collar bone. She continued to adjust her hands, cautious not to strangle him. She had to fight her instinct to rest her head on his firm back. It was comfortable to hold him like this - just to touch him in general.

Xavier inhaled and exhaled deeply, she wondered if he felt the same as she did. That being this close was torture.

"I'm going to have to hook my arms under your legs," said Xavier. "Or you can rely on your own strength to hold onto me as we jump?"

Sophia instantly shook her head, "I can barely hold up three books at a time."

He chuckled, a sound which Sophia wished she could hear more.

To not frighten her, he slid his hands around her thighs and guided her to position her legs around his waist, her breasts now squished into his back. She wasn't sure why she was smiling, whether it was from fear or genuine happiness. To mask her giddy smile, in fear he would turn and see, she pressed her face into the back of his neck and her entire body began to light a spark. It was like someone got a million thin needles and started poking her around her chest and thighs, not enough to hurt but enough to make her feel uncomfortable.

The hitch in Xavier's breath when she held on tighter to him didn't go unnoticed.

Before Sophia could even question what that meant, Xavier pushed himself from the ledge. Both dropped down from her window in seconds. Xavier landed perfectly on his feet. Sophia knew that if she attempted something like that she would have, at most, broke her ankles.

When Xavier released her legs, Sophia instantly stepped away self-consciously.

Tucking a strand of hair behind her ear she kept her gaze locked to the tall grass. Then she looked up to her bedroom window. It was so high up, and the distance was something no human could survive. Yet, Xavier didn't even flinch. The only time there was a sign of hesitation was when Sophia huddled close to him, and she was certain that had nothing to do with the drop.

"You didn't scream," Xavier chimed. "I am quite impressed." Bowing, he offered her his elbow to take, whilst looking up at her through his long eyelashes. "Shall we?"

They walked arm in arm to the town. Sophia had never been out this late before, it was almost two o'clock in the morning and this simple act made her feel quite rebellious. Although she was excited, she would be lying to herself if she said she wasn't scared.

Xavier held most of the conversation, talking about his favourite bars and places to eat. He cracked a few jokes to make Sophia feel more relaxed.

Finally, they stopped outside of a small cottage with a plank of wood hanging over the door with "The Raven" carved into it, accompanied by a confident raven taking flight.

Once they stepped inside, Sophia was greeted by the sound of lively drunks and music blasting from a far off band that she couldn't find. They were completely out of tune but it sounded as though they were enjoying themselves.

Sophia's nostrils were presented with the strong stinging sense of smoke and beer.

This wasn't exactly what she imagined to be a night of letting go of her problems.

Xavier dropped his hand over hers, lacing their fingers together. "You have nothing to worry about," he yelled over the noise, as if he could read her thoughts. The heat from his hand told her she could trust him, and he squeezed her hand tightly. "As long as I am here you are safe."

She smiled, "I do hope this is not a prank of yours. Once I turn around to find you're not there and I get mangled by these people."

Xavier only smiled and started pushing through the crowd, Sophia stuck to Xavier like glue. One hand clung to his, and the other clutched onto the sleeve of his thick black coat.

Sophia was bumped into strangers more times than she could count, but almost everyone was smiling and allowing themselves to get lost in the drunken cloud. She wondered what it would be like to have that life, to do as you please whenever you please. Not to have a single care about what you must look like to strangers, and not a concern as to where you will wake up in the morning. Just enjoying the moment.

They reached the front of the bar, Xavier pulled out a stool and bowed to Sophia with a hand over his chest. "M'lady."

Rolling her eyes and releasing her grip from his arm, she settled into the seat. Yet, it took her a few seconds to let go of his hand, it felt wrong when she slipped it away. An ice cold chill covered her hand, like she had dipped her hand into a pile of snow after sitting by the warm glow of a fireplace.

She sat with her back to the drunken crowd. Elegantly clasping her hands over the table, she snatched them back when her wrists made contact with a wet liquid.

Xavier was still standing, his profile scanning behind the bar to find the bartender. It was almost frustrating how handsome he was.

"You're not going to sit?" Sophia yelled.

He shook his head. "You can't exactly sit and relax in an atmosphere like this." When the bartender finally approached, Xavier proceeded to order two whisky's. One straight and one with ice. She was grateful that he somehow knew not to overwhelm her with pure alcohol, at least she could wait for the ice to melt and water it down if it was too much. She'd not so much as held a glass of alcohol in her life, and when the short glass was presented to her she just stared at it.

Xavier snorted a laugh, as he held his glass comfortably between his index finger and thumb. "You're supposed to drink it," he then took a sip.

"I am aware of how drinking works," she huffed and - not so confidently - picked up her glass the same way as Xavier. The strong smell caused her to flinch back and turn up her nose. How could a glass, not even a quarter full, smell so strong.

Xavier drank the whisky like it was pure water.

Not wanting to seem like a child in front of Xavier, she brought the glass to her lips and downed the liquid in one gulp. Immediately she began coughing, and her throat burned with an unpleasant taste in her mouth. Shaking her head to try and calm herself, she pressed her palm against her flustered cheek.

Xavier was smiling and shaking his head as he ordered another drink for them both. "Does that orphanage let you have any fun?"

She was about to brave another gulp from her new glass, until Xavier hooked his finger over the rim of the glass and pulled it down before it could touch her lips. "I'd go slow if I were you. I'm guessing you're not used to drinking."

A rush of confidence filled her blood, did alcohol really have this much of an effect on her? "I thought we were going to have fun tonight?"

But he was right, so she waited a few minutes before taking another drink. This was her first night out with Xavier, she wanted to at least remember it.

No big gulps, just sips. Slowly, she was getting used to the bitter taste with each drink.

"It has always been very strict." Sophia felt sad all of a sudden, like her emotions couldn't settle on what she was feeling. "I never understood why until tonight."

Xavier's face slowly fell and looked straight ahead. When Sophia followed his line of sight she realised it was on a waitress. She was very pretty. Young with long black hair that curled up into a messy bun behind her head.

Why did the sight of her seemingly make him sad? Did he know her?

Sophia was aware that he brought her here to get her mind off the events that took place that night. The last thing she wanted was to bring down his kind gesture. "How can you afford these drinks?"

That smirk soon returned. "I have my bill sent to Lord Paine."

"He lets you?"

His dark eyes met hers, causing her heart to pick up its pace.

"He doesn't *let* me. Everyone knows he is practically an alcoholic, so what's a few more drinks to add to his bills? I haven't got caught yet."

"Yet." She took another sip, trying to mask her smile.

As the night went on, Sophia's head began spinning with each drink. Her speech was slurred and she really had to concentrate on what Xavier was saying. He drank the same amount as her but still seemed perfectly sober.

This was what it was like to have fun. Sophia could let loose and be herself for a change. Although she still hadn't figured out what that was.

The music was still going in an upbeat, and out of tune rhythm. "I want to dance!" Sophia yelled, raising her arms in the air. It caused a lot of locals to turn their heads and look her up and down as though she were insane.

Xavier gently grabbed both of her wrists and pulled her arms back down to her lap. Whilst laughing he said, "Shh, this isn't exactly a place for dancing."

Then the realisation hit for how close his face was to hers, she could kiss him. She wanted to.

Instead she stared at him, drinking in his features. It would always slam into her like a meteor how handsome he was. Even his imperfections, like his crooked nose, made him even more perfect. His strong jawline that housed dark stubble that she hadn't noticed before. Her eyes were led straight to his black eyes, they were so unique with how they seemed to suck her in, wanting to find the light in the dark. His furrowed brow and his cheeky smile that always sent her heart into a flutter, like she had a jar of butterflies in her chest.

"You're very handsome," she said, followed by a giggle.

Visibly surprised by her words, he scoffed a laugh.

Sophia's lips parted when she noticed his cheeks flushed red.

He was blushing.

Xavier Howell was actually blushing.

She wanted him to do it more, she wanted to give him all of the feelings he was giving her.

This was how it should have felt with Jack.

Clearly she was drunk, but she knew that if she was sober she would be thinking about doing the same.

Slowly, Sophia reached out her hand and cupped it over Xavier's strong, sharp jaw.

There was surprise in his eyes but he didn't move.

Then, she grazed her thumb lightly over his razor thin bottom lip. It was soft, like a feather. The rest of the pub melted at her feet, all she could see was Xavier. His gorgeous face that she knew she would never tire of looking at. His lips were so soft against her thumb that she wanted to taste him. Kissing him would feel like floating on a cloud, she was sure of it.

"We should go," his voice barely broke a whisper.

Lowering her hand from his cheek and placing it into her lap, she sank her teeth into her bottom lip, nodding. No amount of alcohol could wash away the feeling of rejection and embarrassment.

Xavier helped her down from the stool, and she immediately tumbled backwards, almost falling into someone, until Xavier snaked his arm around her back and held her up.

They made it through the crowd and into the street with Sophia attached to Xavier's hip.

Once the fresh air hit her face she suddenly felt as if she might throw up. She cradled her sudden thumping head and hunched over. The vomit was rising in her throat but nothing came. It was a terrible feeling of anticipation for it, but still no vomit left her mouth.

Xavier gently rubbed her back, stifling a laugh. "It'll pass." He helped her straighten up and walked her stumbling body down the street.

They weren't too far from the orphanage, and when Sophia realised this she stopped in her tracks. She didn't want this night to be over, she was enjoying not thinking about her engagement, or the fact she was a *mythical* creature, or that her father might still be alive. Casual things.

"May we go to the lake?"

Xavier looked her up and down, concerned. "You look like you need rest."

She smiled, "Since when are you concerned about...well...*anything?*"

He paused, thinking. "Fine, but we won't stay too long, you really aren't looking well." He let out a sigh. "I've never known anyone get this drunk from three drinks."

Playfully swatting his arm, she giggled. "Oh, don't be such a mother hen."

The lake was further then she remembered, she felt as if her feet were going to burst out of her boots.

The walk helped her sober up slightly, her head was still spinning from the alcohol. This was her first experience with drinking, and she was confident to say that she wouldn't be disappointed if this was her last. She didn't like the uncertainty of whether she was feeling like she wanted to jump with joy for hunching over and vomiting.

When they reached the lake the world suddenly fell silent, aside from a few leaves rustling and crickets chirping in the distance.

It must have been raining earlier, as Sophia's boots were sinking into the mud and with each step came a squelching sound.

Sophia felt as though her shoes were weighing her down, like she had strapped two anchors to her feet.

In her still drunken state, she clumsily bent down and began unlacing her boots.

Xavier peered over her to see what she was doing, and when he realised he exhaled a laugh. "Your feet will be filthy if you take those off."

She ignored him and persisted.

When her bare toes touched the cold, slippery floor she let out a squeal. She was hesitant at first to allow her entire foot to sink into the mud but eventually she embraced it. Kicking off her second boot, not caring where it landed, Sophia ran across the muddy grass and stopped at the edge of the lake.

Sophia's toes were already starting to prune, like when she had been in the bath too long.

Picking up the bottom of her dress, revealing her legs to the open water, she curled up her toes and dipped her mud covered foot into the water.

"It is as though you *want* to catch a cold," Xavier said, watching her from a distance with his hands tucked away in his coat pockets.

"Be careful Mr Howell, I might confuse your words for care." Xavier smiled and rolled his eyes at that.

Sophia began to sway from side to side, as if dancing to some silent song. Her smile was as bright as the stars that shone behind the fog.

Thinking back to Xavier's face at the bar, how he seemed like a completely different person. He seemed...joyful. How close she came to kissing him there and then, and although he was but steps away from her, she felt like she missed him. Missed being in such a close proximity that all she could see was him.

Sophia wasn't sure whether she liked that her heart would race at the mere thought of him. How she would have to suppress a laugh at his inappropriate jokes, and how she wondered how his hair would feel in between her fingers.

Sophia shook the thought away, like a dog shaking water off its fur.

Turning on her heel, she spun around to face Xavier, almost losing her balance and falling into the river. She managed to save herself, and she extended her arm and pointed her finger at Xavier, singling him out. "You," she called, her words slurred. "Owe me a dance."

Xavier dipped his head, mostly to veil his smile. He walked across the muddy grass and stopped in front of Sophia, "I don't remember owing you anything," he dropped his head down to meet her eyes, not hiding his sweet smile. "If anything, you owe me for the drinks."

"I will repay you by *not* bringing the bill to Lord Paine's attention," her smile was so wide that her cheeks were hurting. Sophia felt her smile fall when Xavier was just staring at her, not moving with a serious expression on his face, like he had some dreadful news to share.

"What's wrong?" asked Sophia.

Xavier reached out a hand from his trouser pocket and offered it to her, "I can't dance with you if you are ankle deep in the lake."

Sophia looked down at her toes, now engulfed by the low river. She accepted Xavier's hand, and his fingers wrapped around her hand, sending a jolt through her arm, as he helped her back onto the grass.

When she found her footing she was certain her heart dropped. Xavier slid his free hand around her waist and held her hand out evenly with his shoulder. He began swaying her from side to side, and only then did she realise he was trying to dance with her.

Sophia was sure it was because she was drunk, but his swaying made her feel as if she was on a ship sailing through a terrible storm.

How she longed to rest her head on his chest, if only to stop the motion sickness.

"You are a terrible dancer," Xavier said, distracting her from the need to vomit.

Before she could respond, her breath caught in her throat when Xavier bent his knees and clutched his hand around her back. Suddenly, Sophia was being lifted until her feet were no longer on the floor. Xavier showed no sign of strain, like it was as easy as picking up a handful of straw.

When he lowered her down, positioning the balls of her feet to stand on top of his. She suddenly feared that she might be too heavy for him, that she might break the bones in his feet.

"Is this alright?" she couldn't speak louder than a whisper. Perhaps it was because she was uncomfortably close to him, her lips were but inches away from his shirt. It was like one big tease, like he read her mind that she wanted to rest her head. Now, in the position she was in, the only logical thing to do *would be* to rest her head.

They started to sway again, and Sophia stopped arguing with herself and slowly pressed her cheek against the material of his shirt.

It was like his chest was made for her cheek to rest on. She felt soothed by the pounding rhythm of his heart beating against her cheek.

"Your shoes will get wet," Sophia sighed.

A husky chuckle rose up Xavier's throat. "I'll charge you for new ones."

A grin stretched across her mouth.

"You seem to know what you are doing," Sophia muttered, her eyes drifting as they moved. She could easily fall asleep in his arms.

His throat vibrated as he made a questioning noise.

"Who taught you to dance?" she clarified.

There was a long pause, and Sophia feared she had offended him.

Xavier rested his chin on the top of Sophia's head, and his grip tightened around her back. She could feel his fingers tense at her spine, and for a while she was sure he would remain silent. Until he said, "My mother."

The world around them went still as they stopped dancing, but neither one pulled away. They stood together, held in a tight embrace.

The sudden pick up in pace of Xavier's heartbeat didn't go unnoticed by Sophia. Then she remembered his odd behavior towards the young woman at the bar, the sadness in the air was almost identical to what she breathed in now.

Sophia lowered herself down from Xavier's feet but didn't step out of his arms. She looked up at him, taking in his still serious expression.

"She taught you a lot," Sophia's smile widened as she slurred her words. "Is that who that woman at the bar reminded you of?"

Xavier looked confused by her question.

"Of your mother?" she clarified.

The way in which his eyebrows raised, the small parting of his lips were enough to give her her answer.

But Xavier was always full of surprises, as he answered. "No," he looked like he was in pain. Like someone was stabbing a knife into his chest. "She actually reminded me of my sister," Xavier dipped his head slightly. "So much so that I thought it was her."

Sophia almost regretted bringing this up, but there was a part of her that didn't. She felt like she was seeing the real Xavier tonight, that behind the snide comments and cynical jokes he had a heart, a warm and caring heart at that.

Suddenly, when looking into his eyes she could see the loneliness. It was staring back at her, a familiar feeling that she had lived with for all of her life. Has it always been there? In his jives, was his darkness lurking behind it? Has Xavier only now allowed her to see it?

"You're alone," Sophia didn't mean to say exactly what she was thinking, and so abruptly too.

Xavier was clearly surprised by her words.

"I-I'm sorry," Sophia stammered, without taking her eyes off him. She was locked to his eyes, like she couldn't pull away even if she wanted to. "I didn't mean that as an insult, I just-" what was she trying to say? She truly didn't mean it as an insult, she found it oddly comforting because... "I feel it too. It's quite...refreshing to know that someone else feels that way. As though...I'm-"

"Not alone?" he finished for her.

Sophia's cheeks flushed a bright pink, "It doesn't make sense, does it?"

Xavier slid his hand up to her scarred cheek, and lightly brushed his thumb along one of her scars, tracing it slowly.

This gesture, it was like he was telling her that things didn't have to make sense, not with him. Because he understood everything, even before she spoke. He understood her, more so than Jack ever could.

When did his lips get so close to hers? Sophia didn't know, but she wanted them closer. So close that she could brush her own across his. When she was certain he was going to give her what she wanted, he paused.

Sophia didn't know why, it was as though he was giving her a chance to pull away.

But she didn't, and she never would.

She wanted him, she needed him like she needed air in her lungs.

After what felt like an eternity, Xavier kissed her.

His lips were gentle as he caressed her mouth.

Sophia could cry at the joy that filled her heart from his kiss. Was it possible to crave something she never knew she needed? She wanted to embrace every second she spent being admired by Xavier's kiss.

For a while Sophia stood still, still surprised that Xavier was kissing her. But quickly she lost herself in him. Taking a small step forward she slipped her arms around his sides and gripped the material of his coat.

Xavier was so soft, so delicate. But there was an unmistakable desire in his kiss, like he had been wanting this for a long time.

When he pulled away, Sophia felt disappointed. She wanted to do this until her lips would fall off.

Xavier rested his forehead against hers with his eyes closed, taking in the night. His breathing was heavy as he dropped both his hands to her waist.

Sophia slid her hands up his chest and over his heart. It was pounding as hard as her own, and she had no doubt that he felt what she did.

Reaching up on the tips of her toes, Sophia kissed him again, and again, and again.

When they finally broke apart, Xavier met her eyes. "We should go."

Her heart sank like a precious jewel had been dropped into the depths of the sea, never to be retrieved again. When they returned it would mean things would have to go back to normal, to deception and sorrow.

She couldn't run away as she still had an endless amount of unanswered questions.

"We should."

Entering the orphanage the way they left wasn't as easy. As Xavier climbed, Sophia found herself slipping and was sure she would fall. Luckily they made it to her window before that happened.

Xavier crawled inside of her open window and Sophia slid down from his shoulders, ungracefully.

Everything was as she left it, which disheartened her slightly. She had no idea what time it was, but she was sure it was almost sunrise.

"I should get back to my room," he stepped in front of her.

"Of course," she said, clutching the skirt of her dress in her hands. Her feet were soaked, her head was spinning and she felt a sadness that tonight may have been a one off with Xavier. Which she knew should. Being engaged to another man wasn't exactly the best time to be kissing another man. No matter the circumstances.

"Are you alright?" Xavier stepped in front of her. Being this close to him only made her heart hurt. "Alcohol is fun until you have to deal with a hangover."

She didn't even think of that, not that she cared in his moment.

When hooked his finger under her chin, he saw disappointment in her eyes. "What's wrong?"

Did he not feel this same aching pull in his chest? Was it not eating him up inside to not be locked in a tight embrace? Because it was for Sophia.

"I had fun tonight."

"Then why do you look so upset?"

Then a separate realisation dawned on her, "I forgot my shoes."

Xavier chuckled. "Is that all?"

Her bright green eyes scanned his face, she worried he could hear her heart pounding from where he was standing. Sophia lightly shrugged, "I'm mostly sad tonight is over."

Tilting his head, Xavier lowered his lips and kissed her. In an instant all of her sadness melted away. She knew she shouldn't enjoy it as much as she did but she couldn't help herself. Each kiss felt more delightful than the last.

With her fingers trembling, she reached up and grabbed a fist full of his coat and pressed her torso flat against his.

It was wrong and she knew it. She should have pushed him away, instead she held on tighter, drowning herself in his kiss.

Their mouths collided in a sharp embrace, but he held her like she was a delicate rose.

Xavier brought his hand to the back of her head and gripped onto the curls of her hair with urgency. As she, in turn, slid her hands up to his hair and felt the thick, smooth locks in between her fingers. Just how she imagined it to be and more.

Swimming in a pool of lust, like this wasn't reality, Sophia concentrated on each of Xavier's movements.

It was as if she was swirling through a fast dream which wasn't coming to an end any time soon.

Xavier held her the way she always wanted to be held, he kissed her the way she had always wanted to be kissed. This was how she imagined her first kiss, this is how it should have been.

Suddenly, her bedroom door swung open. They didn't pull apart fast enough, as Jack was holding the doorknob in his hand.

The look of betrayal would be permanently burnt into Sophia's memory.

Sophia created a large gap between herself and Xavier, and soon dropped her head to hide her wet, swollen lips.

"Jack, I did not expect you to..."

"Walk in on your little love affair?" he snarled. It didn't take Jack long to notice that Sophia was stumbling and struggling to stand still. "Are you drunk?"

"I-"

He didn't give her a chance to explain as he cut her off, "You are to be my wife and *this* is how you show it? By fooling around with a *criminal.*" There was venom in his words. "I left the infirmity early to come and apologise to you, because I felt terrible leaving you with the new knowledge of what you are. Now I wish I hadn't bothered."

"How kind," started Xavier. "You would have woken her up to apologise. Do you not realise the time."

Sophia snapped her head over her shoulder and shot him a look of warning. "Please."

Xavier merely shrugged his shoulders, as if exhausted. "I'm going to anyway," he dropped a hand onto her shoulder, and just the slightest touch filled her body with a fiery warmth.

It was unfair, to have such intense feelings towards Xavier so suddenly, for her heart to constantly play these cruel tricks on her. She couldn't tell whether his simple gesture was one of support, or to annoy Jack, or to help her drunken balance. It could be a mixture of all three.

"Am I correct in assuming that Miss Cole has already expressed that she is not in love with you?" Xavier asked Jack.

"That is none of your concern."

"Unless you are blind as well as stupid, then I think what you just witnessed is proof that is has become my concern." his hand gripped tighter around shoulder, as if growing defensive.

What did he mean by that? Was Xavier confirming that he too held feelings for Sophia?

Jack's hands balled into fists, she was sure he would break the doorknob. "Miss Cole is my fiancé. She has promised to spend her life with me. It is not your place to get involved."

Miss Cole? Thought, Sophia. *He would never speak so formally towards me. Even when we were unfamiliar he would always address me as Sophia.*

Fear for her friendship now troubled her more than ever before. It was becoming clear that this act may be something he cannot easily forgive her for. Not that she could completely blame him.

"If you wish to continue this inappropriate behaviour with Mr Howell," he directed his words at Sophia with a spite in his words. "Be my guest. Just be a bit more discreet about it and find a better hiding place."

With that, Jack was gone in a flash. Slamming the door behind him, resembling the sound of a thunderstorm.

Sophia stood motionless.

What had she done?

A wash of guilt splashed her face, but then she suddenly felt angry.

Angry that Jack had the nerve to speak to her in such a way, after everything they had been through together.

Xavier's lips trailed up the arch of her neck. "Shall we continue where we left off?" he muttered.

As much as Sophia's body was telling her - screaming at her - to give in. She simply shook her head and stepped away from him. It was a struggle but Sophia knew that if she wanted to scrape together the friendship she had with Jack, she had to let Xavier go.

"I have to go to him," she whispered. "He is my fiancé."

Xavier rolled his eyes. "What's the point in marrying him? You will only hurt him more if you do so. He will have to live with his wife resenting him for not allowing her to fall in love with anyone." Xavier ran his hand over the length of his face. "Is that what you want? A life with a man you don't love?"

The anger was still steaming in her stomach. Of course she wanted love, she wanted it more than anyone knew. But she was soon realising that not everything in life goes as well as it does in dreams.

"He is only trying to protect me." She was sure she would scream but managed to bite it back. "For I am nothing more than a hideous Gorgon."

"You are clearly going to believe what you want to," Xavier brushed past her as he started walking away, until he stopped and looked over his shoulder. "But please know that...you couldn't be further from hideous."

"Jack!"

Twenty minutes had passed since Xavier left her. Sophia truly wanted to give Jack space, but she was too anxious to mend his heart.

When she pounded on his door, she wouldn't stop until he answered.

Jack finally opened the door once he realised she wasn't going to go away.

The face she was met with was not the man she grew up with, one that always lit up whenever she entered a room, it was one of loathing and jealousy. "You're drunk," he hissed. "I do not want to see you."

As he began to shut the door, the rage from earlier finally made its presence known. Sophia pushed the door open wide with her hands, even causing Jack to stumble back. Shock was written all over his face, as he clearly didn't expect Sophia to be so strong. She wasn't so sure she was, it was probably the alcohol.

Sophia invited herself inside of Jack's room, just as he had many times in the past.

"Why?" She barked a laugh. "Do you not wish to see me enjoy myself?"

"Oh, I've seen plenty of *that* tonight."

Her hands balled into fists as she glared at him through lowered lashes. "How dare you?"

"How dare I?" Jack's voice boomed on the word 'I.'

"Yes!" Sophia screamed back. She wasn't afraid of hurting his feelings now. "You have lied to me for ten *years,* Jack! You and everyone else in this God forsaken place."

"We had good reason to!"

"Well, I have yet to hear it!" Sophia stormed to his bed, stomping her soggy feet against his floor. She parked herself on the edge of his bed, hooked one leg over her knee and clasped her hands in front of her. "Let me hear *all* about it. I will be the one to judge if you had a good reason or not."

"Why should I explain anything to you after what you just did? Kissing that prisoner? What were you thinking?"

Sophia shot back up to her feet, almost stumbling back from a rush of blood. "I was living! Yes, I kissed him. I have been pushed into a marriage with you that you knew I never wanted. I told you I was not in love with you-"

"So that means I am to be overjoyed when my fiancé sneaks out at whatever time in the morning and kisses other men?" Jack paced back and forth, running a hand through his disheveled hair. "I must have missed that in the husband's guide book."

"Jack, please stop."

"Stop what?" Jack snarled, stopping and turning to fully face her. "This engagement will continue. I am not going to let you throw away your life on some murderer. Who would probably kill you on your wedding night."

"Like I'm not already throwing my life away?"

Jack's face fell, she could see the hurt which her words had caused. She didn't mean to say them, she was drunk and hurt. But she did mean them.

Was it fair that she felt this angry?

"You are wrong if you think I do not love you, because I do. So much." Sophia's voice shook as she spoke. "I ache inside knowing how much I am hurting you. I shouldn't have kissed another man, you are right. Not when I am engaged. I was just...caught up and stressed and..." the lies were coating her tongue like ash. Sophia wanted to kiss Xavier, even before tonight she wanted to. "My actions were selfish by not taking into consideration your feelings. All I can do is beg for your forgiveness."

The moment of silence felt like years of waiting. She wanted him to embrace her and tell her that everything was okay.

That wouldn't happen.

Sophia feared that she may have completely torn apart almost ten years of friendship in one night.

Jack finally spoke. "Please, leave me alone."

Chapter Fourteen

Walking through the stalls on a cloudy Tuesday afternoon would always make Stella feel anxious. Of all her shopping trips, most of the trouble she encountered was on a Tuesday. There was no explanation, it's just how the world was for her.

Today was different. After the night she shared with Robert... how intimate they were, she couldn't wipe the smile from her face. It was like a daze had overcome her senses, walking past all of the drunken men pouring out of bars at three o'clock in the afternoon.

It had been three days since she last saw Robert, and she could still feel the burning touch. His lips on hers and the soft feeling of his skin brushing against her was something she craved.

With a wicker basket hanging from her elbow, she glided through the market stalls, picking up bits and pieces for the cooks.

Stella soon snapped out of her blissful thoughts when she heard a man grunting loudly in an alleyway followed by a weak whimper. There were all types of strange noises in London alleyways but this time Stella felt drawn to it. She peeked around the corner and witnessed a man beating a small, thin grey mutt.

Stella couldn't just stand there and do nothing.

Stepping forward, and placing her basket down beside the wall, Stella barked. "Stop harming that defenceless creature!"

The large man peered over his shoulder, stopping with his hand midair. His face was full of aggression and the air turned tense as he grumbled. "Little woman trying to tell a man what to do?"

"I could not stand by and watch you harm an innocent animal."

He knocked his head back, sticking out his round gut, and let out a piercing cackle.

"I will not cause any hassle," her voice trembled. "Just leave the dog and it will go no further."

Before she had a chance to react, the man tackled Stella to the ground. He pinned her hands over her head and his round gut prevented her from even breathing. As his round belly flattened her torso, all she could do was kick out her legs, and that proved to be useless. The overwhelming stench of alcohol in his breath caused Stella to turn her nose away, but no matter where she faced the smell would follow.

Stella promised herself she would never let herself lose control. However, if this carried on for much longer she could end up dead in the gutter as a result of some lowlife.

As soon as his hand brushed up her leg she felt her heart pounding in her chest. A burst of energy released from her head and filled her eyes until they turned as white as snow.

Feeling the ground rumble beneath her hands, she was overcome with power. A dark power that she tried desperately to hide away in the pit of her stomach.

The drunk was hypnotised by the nothingness in her eyes. She stared at him, breathing in the air from his lungs and releasing a black fog to fill his stomach. Eventually, the drunken man's eyes rolled in the back of his head and he collapsed on top of Stella.

He was still heavy but his limp body made it easier for her to roll him off her.

When she got to her feet, her legs were shaking. Taking a moment to compose herself and get her power back down, she snuffed out any sign it had ever been there in the first place. Stella pushed two fingers into the drunk's neck and found a faint pulse.

A sigh of relief exhaled from her lungs, and brushed out the dirt from her dress. She glanced over at the dog who was still whimpering and watching her with its big black eyes. It was a malnourished mutt and looked days away from death.

Stella sank her teeth into her lip and considered walking away, but she couldn't abandon him.

She squatted down and patted her knees to call him over.

He was sceptical at first and began cowering in the corner.

Getting back to her feet she turned around and grabbed her wicker basket. Squatting back down she ripped off a crust of bread and offered it to the dog. She reached out her other hand as a gesture that she wasn't going to harm him.

Slowly, he tiptoed forward. He gradually sniffed the bread and then took the entire crust out of her hand. He ate so quickly that he almost choked. Once he was finished eating, the dog nuzzled it's dirty head against her palm.

"I have no idea how I am going to convince Mrs Green to let you stay," she gave him a scratch behind the ears. "But I suppose she doesn't have to know for now."

The dog walked with a limp, which wasn't surprising considering the abuse she just witnessed.

Walking up with orphanage steps the dog obediently followed. Before going inside she patted him on the head to reassure him he was safe. This dog must have held a lot of trust for Stella, to follow her into a scary building. Every so often she would scratch behind his ears and stop to make sure it wasn't too much for his malnourished legs to manage.

She pushed open the doors and the dog was shaking upon entering. Stella was thankful that she didn't run into Cassandra. She still hadn't come up with the perfect excuse as to why she should permit a stray dog to stay.

In the meantime, what anyone didn't know wouldn't hurt them. Unfortunately, that statement isn't always correct.

Quickly escorting the dog through the front hall, and past the library, they made it to her chambers without being spotted.

Once they were both inside she shut the door and locked it tightly, ensuring no one could barge in.

The mutt sniffed around as she set up a bed for him, out of spare blankets and a few pillows. The food in her basket had to go straight to the kitchens, but she broke off another piece of bread and handed it to him. The dog hobbled over and ate it in one from her hand. From his visible bones she could tell it had been a while since he was fed.

"You must need more than that," she softly smiled. "Stay here, I'll get you more food and some water."

Stella didn't feel right leaving him alone, when she was leaving he looked up at her with big sad eyes, as though he was afraid she wasn't coming back.

Fighting her urge to stay and keep him company for hours, she hurried out of her room with her wicker basket and sprinted to the kitchen.

As she rounded the corner to the kitchen, her heart stopped when she saw Robert leaning against the wall. His head was down, and his mouth was a flat line as she approached.

Joy filled her heart to see him, she felt foolish that she couldn't hold back her grin.

The sound of her heels clacking against the floor notified Robert that someone was there. When he lifted his head and saw Stella he pushed himself off the wall. "I was hoping to find you here," he said in a low tone.

"You came looking for me?" she had to restrain herself from the excitement bursting from her. "It does feel wonderful to see you." she blushed.

"I need a word with you," he spoke with a hesitation in his tone. "Could we talk in the kitchen?"

Stella looked to the door and immediately feared the other cooks and maids were there. They were not happy when members of the household would intrude on their working space.

Robert saw the uncertainty wash over her face, "I sent everyone inside away for ten minutes, so we don't have long."

Only ten minutes?

The joy that filled Stella's heart was now overcome with worry. This was the first time they had spoken since their passionate night together, and he only wanted ten minutes with her?

Afraid she might break if she spoke, Stella nodded and opened up the door to the kitchen. Stella was so used to seeing it bustling with life, maids and cooks frantically working. But when it was empty like this it felt so spacious. She never realised how large the square room was.

"It is about the other night." Robert said as he closed the door behind them, shifting his weight.

Stella turned to face him, her palms sweating with anticipation at what he was going to say. Was he going to confess that he was in love with her too?

"That can never happen again."

Five words.

Robert dropped her glass heart and shattered it. Not only did he carelessly drop it but he also stomped out all of the hope it held. Sharp shards of glass were now stabbing her chest from the inside out.

Did she really expect anything good to come from this? A parlour maid in a relationship with one of the residences? She wanted to slap herself for considering it for even a second.

"I know that last night wasn't our first time," his tone was barely above a whisper. "But I think it has gone on for long enough. We can't use one another to relieve our stress."

Was he trying to make her feel more worthless than she already was? "You were at the right place at the right time, I suppose."

After using her power this morning she had to be very careful not to completely lose her temper. "How dare you," she glared up at him through her eyelashes.

"How dare you disrespect me. Claim that you were vulnerable? Have you stopped to consider me and my vulnerability? You put yourself into my heart and made me believe that I meant something for once. I gave myself to you time and time again because I had feelings for you." She spat the words, not caring that he could have her fired if he brought this up with Cassandra. "You may have seen what we were doing as nothing more than 'relieving stress' but to me it was so much more."

Robert was visibly baffled. Not once had Stella spoken up for herself, much less yelled at anybody. But it felt good, it felt freeing to speak her truth even if it didn't outweigh the pain.

"This should not come as a surprise to you," Robert's anger was rising up his neck, the vein on his neck was now bulging. "This is hardly new territory for you."

"What is that supposed to mean?"

"I'm certainly not the first man you have..." Robert stopped himself, his words trailing into a faded nothingness. It was only when he saw the tears outlining Stella's eyes, and the hurt wash over her face did he regret ever opening his mouth.

Stella bit back the tears, shaking her head and clenching her hands into fits. "You are right, Mr Shaw. You were not my first. But you were my first by choice." she turned her back to him, hugging her arms over her chest as she glared at the stove, willing herself not to cry. She would not give him the satisfaction of knowing how deep her feelings ran.

"Excuse me." Was all he said as he left the room, leaving Stella with her heart pounding in her ears.

Shortly after, the maids and cooks returned to their stations as if they had never left in the first place.

Biting her cheek, Stella placed the wicker basket down on the side next to the cook chopping vegetables. Her name was Dot, and she was the head cook who didn't waste any time in getting to work and ordering people around.

When Dot examined the items in the basket she looked up at Stella with a raised eyebrow, and pulled out the loaf of bread. "You have an explanation for this, girl?" She said with a huff in her Welsh accent.

"Do not test me today, Dot."

Dot's face shifted like she had just received an electric shot. "Girly, I will talk to you however I want, when I ask for things from the market I don't expect you to get your grubby hands-"

"Enough!" Stella's hands balled into fists, and as her voice boomed across the kitchen. She lost control of her power. The cupboard doors swung open, with plates flying around the room and crashing against the walls. The maids and cooks screamed and fled the kitchen in unison.

When she was alone she managed to calm herself, but not before sinking to the floor and crying into her hands. Stella cried for a good fifteen minutes before looking up to a mirror that was leaning against one of the kitchen counters.

A sharp gasp arose when she took in the colour of her eyes. They had changed from her usual brown to a deep rich red. Stella pressed her hand to her cheek, and just stared at herself hoping it would go away on its own.

After staring at herself for almost an hour, her eyes hadn't changed.

Stella remembered the mutt hiding away in her room. She scarcely looked around for extra pieces of food she could give him. Filling up the wicker basket with meats and extra loafs of bread, she hooked the basket to loop around her elbow and grabbed a big bucket of water.

She was in such a hurry she didn't care that as she fled to her room, drops of water were splashing over the sides of the bucket, causing a mess in the entrance hall.

When she finally arrived at her bedroom, she dropped the basket onto the floor, along with the bucket.

The dog wagged his tail as he devoured the meat first, and took fast gulps of water.

Stella sat at the edge of her bed with her hands in the lap of her dress. Cassandra would surely fire her after everything she had done. She had shown off a small percentage of her power to humans, and they wouldn't keep their mouths shut.

It was an accident. She was so angry and hurt by Robert that she wasn't thinking clearly.

Stella played with the scruff of her dress and thought of knocking Robert unconscious, she certainly had the adrenalin built up. She told herself never to do that again, to get so angry that she wanted to become violent. She couldn't lose control of her powers again, for it could be a lot worse than a few simple plates being thrown around the room.

After a moment in her dark thoughts a wet nose brushed against her hand. The dog rested his head on her knee and sat in front of her. His thin tail was slightly wagging and she felt as if he was trying to cheer her up. She flashed him a half smile and gave him another scratch behind his floppy ears. "I need to give you a name," she muttered. "How about..." she tilted her head to the side as she thought. "Duncan?"

She flashed a bright smile when he released a weak bark. "My friend, Duncan."

Chapter Fifteen

Knocking on Jack's door had become a sort of sport for Sophia. For the past few days she would knock on his door, either be ignored or Jack would exit his room and brush past her. Some days she would wonder how long she could wait patiently for him. Her current record is half an hour.

No answer.

She knew he was there, she could hear movement.

Instead of walking away today and giving him time to come around, she continuously knocked on his door, like a woodpecker.

After a few minutes, the door swung open and Jack's eyes were balls of fury. "What do you want?" he snapped.

She tried to hide the fact his words stung, like her heart was infested with furious wasps. "I want to talk to you," she said. "You've been hiding from me for far too long."

Jack rolled his eyes, gripping his hand around the door frame. "I don't have anything to say to you," he nodded his head, signalling to Xavier's door. "Why don't you see if *he* is home? I'm sure he would be happy to see you."

"Jack, please." She said in a sigh. "How long are we going to be like this? Are we really going to throw away our years of friendship?"

"It's not me that's throwing it away," his eyes shooting daggers through her.

When he saw the hurt in her eyes he let out a deep breath, mad at himself for so easily giving into her.

Jack stepped aside and gestured with his hand for her to enter.

Without a second of hesitation she accepted his offer.

Closing the door behind them, Jack kept his distance and stared out of his window, like that was the most interesting thing to him right now.

"I don't want to fight," she broke the tense silence.

Jack said nothing. He folded his arms over his shirt, looking to his side. Looking anywhere in his room but where Sophia was standing.

"Jack, you know I am not in love with you," she spoke softly. "It would be delusional if you thought I wanted to marry you. I can't pretend this is what I want, but there's not a day I won't try."

Jack shook his head, the ends of his blonde hair brushing against his forehead.

Sophia continued, "Do you remember when we were children, and Robert pushed me into the mud? And when Alice would laugh at me for my scars? You were there, and stood up for me every time. I know it is selfish, but what would I do without you in my life?"

Jack looked up and met her eyes. "This won't go back to normal, Sophia."

She never knew a single sentence could break her heart in two.

That's when the tears began to form, and the back of her throat started to burn. "Please don't say things like that," she whispered.

"What do you expect?" He wasn't angry, more disheartened. His tone was soft and careful. "You think my heart can just mend itself? You think I can just easily fall out of love with you?"

There was little hope in her heart, she couldn't lose him. Not now, not after everything they have been through.

Jack stepped toward her, sliding a hand around her neck. "I'm weak," he said. "It is I that needs you in my life." He leaned his forehead against hers. "Please forgive my ridiculous request. If you are to be my wife, I need all of you. I can't share you."

What else did she expect? A husband shouldn't have to ask a wife to not sneak off with other men. But she couldn't help the sinking ship her heart had become. "It's not a ridiculous request," she said, her voice low.

Taking both of her hands, Jack brushed his thumb across her knuckles. "Maybe, when we are married we should move away from here. We can focus on each other and build a life together."

Sophia was visibly startled, her eyes widened as she looked up at him. If this was an option a few weeks ago, she would have jumped at the chance, for she knew she had nothing to stay for. But now, something was pulling her back, something in her heart.

The uncertainty was written all over her face, like someone had got a pen and wrote her deepest feelings on her forehead.

"You want to stay? Even after all these years of being tormented?"

She released herself from his hands, "Jack, it's not that simple."

"It could be," his eyes now pleading. "Lord Paine could supply us with a home, it may take some convincing from my mother but-"

"I don't want to owe him anything," anger now boiled in her blood. "Let's not make any irrational decisions."

"Like marrying a woman who isn't in love with me in the slightest?"

Curling her upper lip, she told herself that she would not cry. She would not allow him to get to her like this. "That's not fair," she said as a breath.

"It's not," he replied. "Just like it's not fair that I gave my heart to you, and within days of meeting another man you throw yourself at him."

Barking a laugh, she did not find any of this funny. "If you're trying to hurt me, it's working."

"You're hurting?" He scoffed. "Are you truly that selfish?"

Grumbling under her breath, she barged past him to leave.

He blocked her path with his body, "Sophia," his voice dropped to a delicacy.

"You think you can say such harsh things, and I'll come running into your arms?" Balling her hands into fits, repressing the urge to cry. "You seem to be under the impression I can help what I feel." She charged him, shoving him back.

"Why don't I tell you how to feel?"

Shove.

"Stop being in love with me."

Shove.

"Stop, Jack."

Jack gripped her wrists, but she still flailed her body around to release herself.

Pulling her by her wrists, she fell into his chest and he circled his arms around her. Holding on tightly, he allowed her to weep.

Sophia had arranged a meeting in Cassandra's office for every resident in the orphanage. Luckily, there were less than fifteen people that took up space in Cassandra's office. If this were a regular orphanage she had no doubt this meeting would have to take place outside.

It had crossed her mind to consider searching for answers alone, but she knew that wasn't wise since she wasn't sure where to start looking.

It was the first time in days that Hannah had shown her face and she looked as pale as a ghost. Her once illuminating golden eyes were now a lifeless brown, and her auburn hair was all over the place, resembling a lion's mane.

Robert was at her side as always, posing as a guard dog, prepared to take on anyone who tried to get to his sister.

Beside them was Alice and a few other members that Sophia felt guilty she still hadn't learned their names, even after all these years.

Jack and Xavier were also present, and placed themselves as far away from each other as possible. There was a tension that filled the room that could be sliced with a knife.

Albert was sitting at the desk with his elbows resting on the surface. Cassandra was standing at his side looking as radiant as ever. She didn't have to make any effort towards her appearance and she would still be the most beautiful person in the room. Today Cassandra wore a scarlet silk dress complemented by silver jewellery.

Sophia stood in the centre of the office so all eyes were on her.

It was a small room so it wasn't difficult to gather everyone's attention. "I have called this meeting because...." she began.

Everyone watched her intently, an anxiety filled the room as they clearly wanted to know what she was about to say.

This was new to everyone. Only Cassandra ever called meetings, even then it was only to discuss small changes that rarely had an effect on the residence.

"Because I have discovered the truth about this orphanage...and what I truly am."

Gasps hissed across the room.

Cassandra's eyes averted to the ground and her brow furrowed. There was a mixture of shame and anger painted across her face. Sophia wasn't sure which emotion she was truly feeling.

Cassandra's eyes soon shot up to her son, as if the realisation where she had heard this information came from.

Anger.

The shame soon washed away like water down a drain.

"I know I am a gorgon." Sophia continued. It was a strange sense of relief once she said it out loud in front of the people that kept it a secret from her. Like it somehow gave her a sense of understanding, but it still wasn't enough. She had to hear it from the people around her. Have them explain why she was the only one who didn't know.

"I wish to know why you all kept it a secret from me."

Everyone shifted their gazes and murmurs soon filled the small square room. Everyone wondered which one of them was going to share the story.

All eyes eventually landed on Cassandra.

However, to everyone's surprise it was Albert who spoke. "I am assuming that my son is the one who told you?"

Sophia was in pain, unable to meet Jack's gaze. She nodded, "Yes. But I didn't give him much of a choice. How could you all lie to me?"

Albert rubbed his jaw with his fingers. "It is true that we should have informed you of what you are. It was more for emotional reasons that we did not tell you. But please understand that it was for your best interest."

"I have heard that phrase thrown around a lot recently. Please explain how it is *for my best interest*." She spat the last part of her sentence like it was a venom on her tongue.

Cassandra jumped in. "You cannot love."

Sophia couldn't conjure a response.

"We don't know the...science around it," Cassandra clearly couldn't think of any other way to describe it. "All we know is that if you love someone equally it will trigger your heart to turn people to stone." Her tone fell low. "You will never be able to look at someone without turning them to stone...forever."

It felt as though her heart had sunk to the bottom of the ocean, never able to retrieve it.

"Because you have half human blood," Cassandra continued. "You can't control it when it does trigger. So, one day it will be inevitable that the person you fall in love with turns to stone."

That's why you don't want me to marry Jack, Sophia thought. *You're afraid I'll love him in return and kill him.*

"How could you not tell me?" Sophia barely heard herself whisper.

"How could we tell you that we are not permitted to love you? You would have closed yourself off and not allowed yourself to love anyone. It would have driven you insane." Cassandra was harsh but to the point with her words. "We all have not loved you and forced ourselves not to in any capacity. It is too dangerous. In return we allowed you to love us in order to have something to hope for."

Sophia wasn't sure why she glanced at Xavier then. He was watching her, his black eyes intently staring at her face. With an expression she couldn't read.

Sophia turned her attention back to Cassandra and Albert. "You gave me false hope. I cannot have a loving marriage or ever have true love. If I would have known I would not have gone insane, I would have dealt with it. You have done nothing but crush all of my hopes of living a life of happiness."

"And all of you," she turned around the room and captured glances from each individual member. "You're all some sort of creature?"

"Don't refer to us as though we are dirt on your shoe," it was Robert who spoke up. "For you are a *creature* also."

"What are you and Hannah?" Sophia was told by Jack what they were, but she needed to hear it from each of them.

Hannah huddled closer to her brother, like she was afraid everyone would turn on them.

"We are werewolves," Robert said, simply. "We can shift into a wolf form every full moon. But if we learn to control it, we can decide when we shift."

That wasn't a complete lie for Robert. He could control his wolf form, but as for Hannah...

Sophia didn't say anything. She only nodded and went around the room asking each member to tell her what they are. There were witches, even goblins that used magic to hide in a human form.

Then she stopped in front of Xavier, who kept his head down the entire time.

Sophia could feel Jack shifting on the balls of his feet on the opposite side of the room.

"Xavier?" Her voice was timid.

Xavier let out a sigh, and without warning extended his canines so they reached below his bottom lip. It didn't startle her as much as she expected, for she remembered she had seen them from him before in his cell.

"Vampire." He simply said.

There was a brief silence, when Sophia turned her back on everyone and took her spot in the centre of the room again. The room suddenly felt a lot more intimidating. With creatures that were written for horror stories surrounded her. If they wanted to, they could kill her on the spot.

"Is there anything else you have kept from me?"

Cassandra's eyes told the truth she didn't want to reveal.

There was more.

"What is it?"

Albert ordered everyone else to leave. It took them a few minutes to clear out as they wanted to hear but Albert escorted everyone out.

"Jack," his mother called for him before he left. "We need you here." Jack lingered at the door for a moment. There was a reluctance in his stance. After a few heartbeats he shut the door and leaned back against the corner of the room. He crossed his arms over his chest, keeping his gaze to the floor. Closely resembling a sulking child.

Albert stepped in front of Sophia and offered her a seat on the sofa.

She was stiff as she sank down into the fluffed seats. Albert sat beside her and placed a comforting hand over hers, "We do not want you to think that because we cannot love you that it means that we do not care. It has been hard for all of us, Cassandra and I especially." He began, he spoke like what she imagined it would be like being lectured by a father. "Every child that was brought

287

into this building, we considered ourselves as parental figures. Even to you."

"But there is one thing we have actively lied to you about," Cassandra stepped in, sitting on the coffee table. "You are not an orphan."

Again, Sophia said nothing, unable to find the words. Like the English language fell from her mind and she did not know how to speak.

"Your father is very much alive. We have reason to believe that that note from your mother came from him."

So much life altering information all at once, she wasn't so sure she could handle it.

Cassandra curved her hand under her eyes, wiping away tears. It wasn't right to see someone as strong as Cassandra cry. This must have taken such a toll on her over the years.

"Lord Paine ordered all creatures to be housed here. To keep the streets clear of *things like us.*" She quoted his words in a mocking tone, her voice shaking. "For a long time, creatures were hunted and killed on the spot. That was until I fought to protect us, transforming this building into a sanctuary for creatures. Everyone here is truly an orphan, apart from you and Jack."

"Why isn't my father here?" That word felt wrong to escape her lips. Her father. A man she doesn't remember, a man who she convinced herself didn't exist on this earth.

"He's human."

Now she was angry. "Albert is human, are the rules only twisted to suit your family?"

Albert and Cassandra's facial expressions mirrored. Shocked by her harsh tone, Albert looked at Jack - clearly annoyed. "How much did you tell her?"

His son scoffed, "As much as I could."

As the Green family bickered between themselves, Sophia's palms became clammy. "I wish to see Lord Paine." She fired out. "I need to find my father."

"Absolutely not," Cassandra laughed, not that she found anything about this even slightly amusing. With her her golden hair was twisted at the back of her head, it really showed off her fierce features. "You are lucky to have even discovered what you are. It is far too dangerous."

Sophia pushed herself from her feet, snatching her hand away from Albert's. "It is a bit late to show concern for my wellbeing. You hardly have a better judgement."

Her words stung Cassandra, she was visibly offended. "You have a roof over your head because of what you are, were my services all in vain?"

"No," Sophia said, immediately. "I am grateful for the shelter. I do not want to continue to live within a lie." she felt Jack's eyes on her. She quickly glanced over and held a strong breath.

Cassandra and Sophia locked eyes for a moment. It was clear how serious Sophia was, everyone knew she wanted nothing more than to have a normal life. Even before she found out about what was coursing through her veins.

"Your father knows you are here, Sophia." Albert said with sadness. "He's always known you are here. I promise you, if you seek him out you will only be disappointed."

He knew? And he never tried to come and see me?

"That is my decision to make."

"You're selfish." Jack said to himself, but loud enough for all to hear.

"Jack..." Albert began.

"Don't," he threatened. Jack continued to direct his words at his fiancé. "At least you can live your life without any physical pain. You can still fall in love, it will only come at a cost. Everyone here is struggling with what they are, even knowing all their lives. Don't you dare act as if you have it the worst."

Sophia couldn't believe this was the man who would defend her no matter what. How could he turn hostile against her in such a short amount of time? She wasn't sure how to respond, "I didn't mean to offend you, Jack."

"You do not mean that," he continued to glare. "For you will still go in search of answers that will prove pointless."

Truly, the words were lost on her tongue. She felt saddened that she had managed to offend almost everyone in the orphanage in such a short amount of time.

Albert raised himself up from the sofa. "If you truly desire to seek out your past, you have my blessing-"

"Albert!" Cassandra barked in protest.

He continued anyway, and ignored his wife's clear disapproval. "I will schedule you to meet with Lord Paine tomorrow morning, and wherever they send you I will have Jack escort you."

"What?" Jack snarled.

"Sophia cannot go alone," his gaze locked on his son. "Everyone else has other priorities, plus you are the one that revealed everything to her so this will be a punishment of some sort."

"Father," Jack stepped forward in immediate protest.

Albert erupted and his eyes were piercing through Jack. "I am your father and you do not, and will not question my decision. For once you will do as you are told!"

Cassandra, much like everyone else in the room, was startled by Albert's outburst. He stormed out of the room with his shoulders arched off. Cassandra stared blankly at the door and then followed after him.

Chapter Sixteen

The next day, Sophia fashioned a light pastel blue dress with her brunette curls tucked away under her white oval hat.

Sophia was waiting by the carriage for Jack. He was taking his time in getting ready, more so than usual. With her impatience growing, she began kicking the cobbled ground at her feet, and gripped her hand around the open carriage window.

The driver was growing frustrated, they were scheduled to leave ten minutes ago.

After a number of minutes of waiting, Xavier exited the orphanage and skipped down the steps.

Sophia was surprised and confused to find him here, dressed in his usual black and white attire. One of these days Sophia will convince him to add some colour into his wardrobe.

Jack followed shortly after, and once he noticed Xavier walking to the carriage he and Sophia would be entering, the look of disdain was something no artist could capture.

"Why are *you* here?" Jack snarled.

"I was about to ask the same thing," Sophia raised an eyebrow.

"Were you not informed?" He patted Jack on the back, and swiftly Jack shoved him back by his chest. This only seemed to entertain Xavier, as he chuckled. "Seems like your dearest mother requested I tag along for extra support."

"Most likely because she is afraid you'll try to murder people whilst I'm away."

"Like you could stop me if you were there?"

"Please," Sophia chimed in. "Enough of this. Can we leave now?"

Jack brushed past her, his icy glare sent a chill down her spine. He doesn't seriously think that it was her idea to bring Xavier along?

Jack climbed into the carriage first.

Sophia looked up at Xavier who was still smiling, like this was one big show. "Try to contain yourself. We do not want Mr Green getting jealous." he muttered, and Sophia followed him into the carriage with radiating cheeks.

Jack and Xavier sat opposite one another and exchanged glares. Sophia was torn as to who she should sit next to. Xavier was more welcoming as opposed to Jack whose stare resembled daggers. If she sat beside Xavier it would only anger Jack more. She had no choice but to try and defuse the situation. She settled in beside her fiancé.

Jack crossed his arms over his dark green coat and his eyes focused out of the window. He couldn't make it much clearer that he didn't want to be in the same space Xavier. Sophia wasn't so sure he wanted to be in the same space as her either. As his eyebrows were sewn together, the creases were forming in his forehead.

Xavier was sitting across from them and twiddling his thumbs. The silence of the carriage was soon replaced by a whistle. His eyes were intently focused on Jack's, an obvious attempt to get a reaction from him.

Sophia kept her head down and feared that this carriage ride was going to become violent very quickly. He began patting his knees with the palms of his hands to go along with the rhythm.

"Stop it." Jack was much calmer than Sophia expected.

"I thought I would make the journey go quicker by coming up with my own song. I was hoping you'd become my number one fan."

"I would not become an adoring fan. Even if you made me the richest man to walk this earth, *and* paid me thousands to hear nothing but that God awful tune."

Do not encourage him, Sophia thought.

Xavier crossed his arms over his chest and leaned back, with a raise of a single eyebrow.

This felt like some travel game you would play with children.

"You despise me, don't you?" Xavier said as more of a fact than a question.

Jack looked away in a huff, not wanting to continue this pointless conversation.

Xavier scoffed. "Look at his face, he can't even stand to be in the same room as me."

"Mr. Howell..." Sophia began as a warning.

"How can you despise someone whom you do not know?" he ignored Sophia.

Jack's jaw tensed and his fists clenched around his arms.

Sophia hoped that journey wouldn't last for too much longer, she didn't know how much more of this she could take.

Lord Paine was tapping his index finger against his desk, in rhythm of the ticking clock hanging on the wall. He sat with his back against his chair with his eyes on Sophia. He looked as if he had been disturbed from a long awaited nap. "What do you want?" he drawled.

"The letter," Sophia began, with her shoulders broad and not prepared to let her guard down. "I wish to get in contact with the man who sent it to you."

He rolled his eyes around in his head and pressed his back deeper into the chair. "And the purpose of this is..."

"She has it in her head that this man could have some connection with her mother." Jack spoke, in a formal business matter, with his arms behind his back and a straight spine.

"Some connection?" She scoffed at Jack's insensitive words. "This man is-"

Lord Paine got to his feet with his nostrils flaring. He pulled out a crystal-like glass from the wooden cabinet and poured himself a glass of brandy. "Do you insist on wasting my time?" he scoffed. "What makes you assume I could help you with that?"

"You had an encounter with him-"

"What does that matter?" he cut Sophia off before she could finish. "That was over ten years ago. You expect me to remember every person that waltzes into my office?" he shrugged his shoulders. "Could be dead for all I know.

Sophia refused to accept this, she wasn't prepared to walk away with nothing. She needed to learn about her past and uncover the lost memories blocked in her mind. "This should be a priority, you should keep a record of everyone."

"Do not tell me what should be a priority, little girl." Lord Paine's eyebrows knitted together. "I run this Council and I have far more important matters to attend to than help a stupid girl."

"The council is supposed to help -"

"Miss Cole, if you continue to test my patients then I will see that funding for the orphanage will cease, do you want that on your shoulders?" he said, in a raised voice.

Sophia lowered her head and dropped her shoulders in a sigh.

"You don't remember anything about this gentleman?" Jack was the one to ask.

"What would you plan to do if I gave you the details? Go see him? Then what? Do you even know what you're seeing him for?"

"I need to know who I am, that man must be my father. How else would he have gotten such an important letter from my mother?" Sophia spoke up with no filter. "I am certain he can tell me of my gorgon heritage."

Lord Paine's face hardened. She quickly worried that she opened up too much to Lord Paine. Like that information was something she wasn't supposed to know.

It was like he lost a battle he thought he could win. He opened up the draw from his desk and rummaged through until he pulled out a sheet of crinkled paper. He scribbled something down and shoved it into Sophia's hands. He dropped back into his chair as if defeated. "Now get out."

Xavier bared his fangs. "You could have said that with some manners."

"I can have the guards in here in five seconds." Lord Paine said, flatly.

"I can kill you in three."

Lord Paine rolled his eyes. "You are not helping yourself Mr Howell. Don't make me regret my leniency." He looked back over to Sophia. "Now, I remember encountering this man and he wasn't the most normal of people. I do not care for you creatures in the orphanage but if I must say anything, watch your back if you find him. He has a knack for swindling people."

"Are you going to stop cradling that sheet of paper and read it?" Xavier huffed as he stomped down the town hall steps.

Sophia stopped on the final step and lowered the sheet of paper from her chest with trembling hands. Her eyes were shaking, like she couldn't concentrate. When her eyes finally focused she read the note, and her fingers were now trembling.

"This is his address...Christopher Cole." she looked up to find Jack and Xavier staring at her in awe and mild confusion. "He shares my last name."

"As do most children with their father." Jack's tone was to the point. He shifted his weight and shoved his hands in his coat pocket.

Xavier stormed over and snatched the sheet from her light grip. "Yes, yes that's all well and good but I am more interested in how far we have to travel to meet him." his eyes scanned the page. "I do not know about either of you but I certainly do not want to be sat in a stinking carriage for more than an hour."

Jack snatched the sheet from Xavier. "I thought you would have taken this opportunity, so you can escape."

"If this keeps me away from that dreadful orphanage, I will be happy. Besides," he chirped, looking at Jack. "Why would I want to leave when I can spend more time with *you?*"

Jack read the paper and his face dropped. "It'll take longer than an hour." He said in a low tone. "If you decide to seek him out, it looks like we've got a wonderful trip to Derbyshire ahead of us." He glanced over at Sophia, for only a moment.

"Looks like your wedding may be put on hold," Xavier smirked.

Chapter Seventeen

"Derbyshire?" Xavier sulked with his arm crossed over his chest. "I suppose it could be worse."

They were on their way back to the orphanage, and Sophia couldn't stop re-reading Lord Paine's careless writing of her father's home address. Her father, a man who she presumed was dead all her life, very much alive and living in Derbyshire. She almost wanted to scream with excitement but knew that she shouldn't get too carried away, this could be misinformation for all she knew.

Xavier began hitting the back of his head against the window of the carriage with his eyes firmly shut. "It will be infuriating if this is a hoax from Lord Paine. If we arrive and he is not there."

"It would be rather foolish for me to pack a bag and leave immediately," Sophia said, as a matter of fact. Yes, that's what she wanted to do. But what would her father's reaction be if his daughter arrived at his doorstep with no warning. Desperately wanting to meet him, she had to come up with a plan to at least warn him of her arrival. Then it would give her enough time to prepare for his rejection,

Jack took the note from Sophia's grasp once again and cast his eyes across the wrinkled page. "I agree, plus we cannot trust what Lord Paine says is true," there was a hitch in his voice as he spoke, like a panic that didn't miss Sophia's ears. "This could be a cruel trick."

"What makes you so certain?" Sophia looked up at him with an unbelievable expression. He knew how much she desired to find out about her past, that she craved answers for her lost memories. This could be an opportunity for her to discover everything that she did not know about herself, and Jack seemed bothered by it all, like it was an inconvenience.

Jack didn't respond, instead he put the letter back onto Sophia's lap and locked his glare out of the window, watching as the London streets passed them by.

Sophia excused herself the second she walked through the orphanage doors. She was so eager to be alone in her room that she didn't even hang up her coat.

Unintentionally slamming her door, she fell into her desk and pulled out a fresh sheet of paper. There was so much to say, and yet so little also. She thought she had a clear message for the man believed to be her father, but the minute her quill touched the paper, her mind filled with doubt.

What if this man wasn't her father? What was she basing this belief on? Because Lord Paine had said so, he could say anything he liked, that didn't make it true.

What else did she have other than to believe him? Sit in her room and think about what could have been? Her life was bland and empty, the least she could do was try to uncover her past to make sense of her future.

Sophia spent most of her evening trying to conjure up an appropriate letter to send to Christopher; everything she wrote felt too childish, like she was writing a letter to Father Christmas by telling him everything that she wanted most.

"Sophia?" Jack's voice called from behind her door.

"Yes?" she called back.

Her door creaked open and Jack was soon by her side, looming over her shoulder and taking in the countless balls of screwed up paper scattered around her desk. "You're making a mess," Jack's tone was playful. "Would you like my help?"

"What could I possibly say to him?" Sophia buried her face into her hands, and swiftly snapped her head back so her eyes trailed across the cracked ceiling. "*Dear Mr Cole, I am Sophia Cole. I have reason to believe that I am your daughter, would you be so kind as to invite me to your home?*" Although Sophia tried to sound humorous, it hurt her heart to think of what his response would be to that letter.

Jack dropped his hand onto her shoulder, "Yes, well. Have you considered that he might not want to see you? My mother was telling the truth, he's known where you are all these years."

"I know that," Sophia grumbled.

"You could just request a meeting with him?" Jack suggested. "That you have urgent matters that you wish to discuss."

"That is far too vague."

Jack chuckled and sat down at the edge of her bed, "It doesn't have to be word for word." He let out a sigh as he placed his cane down next to him. "My mother didn't provide me with much information on your father. Apparently he is an inventor of sorts.

Why not pretend like you are interested in the field and wish to learn from him?"

"I know nothing of science," Sophia felt like a deflated balloon. "He would tell instantly."

"Not all inventors talk only in science," a thin smile stretched across his lips. "Believe it or not, they do in fact have regular conversations."

Sophia shot him an evil look, and soon followed it with a laugh. "If you are such an expert why don't you write the letter?"

For whatever reason, when Jack's face fell into a serious expression and he got to his feet, Sophia's heart picked up in pace.

Jack stopped in front of her, and hooked his finger under her chin and raised her head to meet his eyes. A ghost of a smile tickled his lips as his bright blue eyes scanned her face, "You've read plenty of books," his voice barely broke a whisper. "I have faith that you can articulate what you want to say in a letter."

As he lowered himself down, Sophia's eyes widened in a panic. She swiftly swivelled around in her seat and dipped her head, pretending to be interested in her blank sheet of paper. Clearing her throat, she could feel the tension crawling around her neck like a spider. "Thank you, you always offer the best advice."

Although she couldn't see him, she knew Jack was hurt. His tone was formal, like he was about to present a speech, "Be sure to let me know if you get a meeting with him. I would be delighted to meet my future father-in-law."

When Jack left, Sophia cried.

For she couldn't deny one of her many reasons for wanting to find her father, yes she wanted to discover the past but just as desperately, she wanted to find a way to not have to go through with this marriage to Jack.

Dear Mr Cole,

I hope this letter finds you well. Please excuse the abrupt nature of this letter, but I have recently been made aware of your efforts as an inventor and it is something that has recently captivated my interest.

If you are willing, I would be honoured to meet with you and discuss the fascinating inventions that you propose to bring to the market.

Yours Sincerely,

Sophia Cole

It took three days for Sophia to write a satisfactory letter. The countless drafts that she accumulated in her room would be enough to fill pages in a book. Should she sign it with her last name? If he knew he had a daughter would he recognise her? Of course she wanted him to recognise her but she didn't want to scare him away.

Eventually she went with signing her full name, what was the point in dancing around the fact when she would eventually have to tell him anyway.

Sophia had requested Stella send the letter immediately, and now she was in a void waiting for a response. As the days passed by, she was beginning to think that her letter had gone unread, or thrown away without even a glance. *Was* it too bold of her to give away her last name? Would Christopher think it was a hoax?

Sophia was sitting under the shade of the tall willow tree in the garden, with her back pressed against the rough bark. She stared out to the vast green grass that led up a hill that seemed to span as far as the imagination.

Sophia looked up to the clouds rolling in, it was surely going to rain but she didn't want to go inside just yet, only when she felt a drop would she bolt for her solitude.

"This has arrived for you," she didn't notice Xavier standing beside her until he spoke, outstretched in his hand was an envelope.

Her heart practically leaped into her mouth as she reached up to snatch it out of his hand. Sophia fumbled forward, landing on her palm when Xavier raised the envelope in the air, like a teasing brother would to a younger sibling. He had a devilish smirk across his lips as he waved it from side to side, "I require payment first."

"Please, Mr Howell, I *need* to see what is in that letter." she looked up at him, her eyes begging.

"Formalities will get you nowhere Miss Cole," Xavier took a step back and started walking away, practically dangling the envelope in Sophia's face as he held both hands behind his back, and the paper in her direct view.

Sophia grumbled as she scrambled to her feet and followed after him, picking up her thin cream dress to ensure she would not trip. She caught up to him and stopped directly in his path, halting him. Just by the look on his face she could tell he was loving this.

"I'm afraid you are getting far too greedy, Miss Cole." said Xavier. "I played for you free of charge and now you expect my delivery services to go unpaid?"

Sophia only glared at him, as she folded her arms like a pretzel and stuck out her chin.

Xavier let out a playful, exasperated breath, "Oh fine. But one day I will cash in on all of these unpaid debts." he handed Sophia the letter, and she almost tore the paper from snatching it so swiftly. "Manners," Xavier commented, but she ignored him and proceeded to open the envelope.

At first she didn't read or take in a single word out of excitement. It was on her third attempt that it sunk in what the note had said:

Dear Miss Cole,

My deepest thanks for your letter, it is always motivating to receive praise from an up and coming inventor and from a woman, nonetheless.

I believe you could show promise in this field with time, and I would be more than happy to share any advice that may assist you.

As you have my home address I would like to invite you to stay
for a few days. Please visit me at your earliest convenience so we
may discuss your future possibilities.
I only ask that you give me a few days notice for when you arrive
so I can welcome you accordingly.
You must know that I am one who enjoys a good party, so please
bring as many ballgowns and guests as you need.
Yours Faithfully
Christopher Cole
P.S. It is a small world, isn't it?

Sophia choked out a laugh, not because she found any of this amusing but because she was truly shocked. All of these years, all she had to do was simply request the information of her father's whereabouts and he would write back to her.

It wasn't quite what she was expecting. The letter seemed so formal, like it truly was between a scientist and his prodigy. Not a father receiving a letter from his daughter.

And the last part of his letter:

It's a small world, isn't it?

What did he mean by that?

"I must say," Xavier said, breaking her thoughts. "It was bold of you to give him your last name. Do you think he suspects?" he had clearly read the letter over her shoulder without permission.

"I have no idea," her hands were shaking as she clutched the letter. "But did you see? He wants me to visit him? *At my earliest convenience.*" she began bouncing on her heel like a sugar filled toddler. "Well, I must go straight away." She took a few steps forward and quickly retracted as she thought about the situation at hand. "No, it would be rude if I just showed up and he *did* request a letter in advance to my arrival-"

"Sophia," Xavier's curt voice halted her. "Please think about what you are doing. Do not get yourself so excited, just because he may be your father…it doesn't mean he is the nicest of people."

Her mouth opened slightly, surprisingly hurt by his words. "If he truly wanted nothing to do with me he wouldn't have written back. How convenient is it that a girl writes him the exact name and surname of his daughter? And if he knew I was here, my address itself is a huge giveaway."

"Well, he certainly hid it well within his writing." Xavier was visibly agitated. "You must ask yourself the question of *why?* Why now has he only decided to write to you, or have any form of conversation with you?"

Sophia didn't have an answer, for she too had these questions in the back of her mind.

Xavier's face softened, and he dropped a hand onto her shoulder. Even in her most vulnerable state she still felt the sparks ignite from his touch. She wanted to kick herself that she immediately was brought back to their kiss by the lake, and she wondered what he thought of it.

Did it mean as much to him as it did to Sophia?

Without looking at her he said, "I only request that you be careful. Don't rush into anything and get yourself hurt."

This caused a ripple in her heart as she watched him walk away. He must have cared for her; when she thought back to his words, she wondered if he meant rushing into finding out about her father or rushing into her marriage with Jack.

Chapter Eighteen

Xavier rolled his eyes, annoyed by the idea. "I think I would have preferred to reside in a prison cell."

"There is no issue with us turning around and dropping you off." Jack's comment was snide.

The three of them were on their way to Christopher's address. Sophia had taken up her father's offer of visiting his home. She almost showed up without warning, she didn't want to wait for his reply. But the second she received the confirmation by letter, they packed a bag and headed straight for Derbyshire.

They had been on the road for over an hour, and time seemed to slow down. Sophia was ignoring most of the jabs Xavier and Jack would give one another, she was too focused on how she would present herself. How she would introduce herself, she still hadn't decided when to reveal that she was his daughter. Or, would he recognise her as his own?

All of these questions only made her more nervous.

Xavier scoffed.

"I gave the driver Christopher's instructions on the fastest route to the address," Jack said.

Sophia's mouth opened as if ready to say something. Suddenly, the carriage was hit with a mighty force and Xavier, Jack and Sophia found themselves tumbling and rolling inside the carriage. Sophia's head was hit many times against the walls of the carriage and her vision soon clouded.

Finally when the carriage came to a shocking halt there was a high pitched ringing that filled Sophia's ears. She landed flat on her back and her eyes were drifting into unconsciousness.

Fighting to keep her eyes open, she squirmed in an attempt to lift herself. It was like the inside of her body had become stone, and she was too weak to even raise a finger. Soon, she let the darkness consume her. Sophia was sure that she heard Jack's voice, but it was too muffled for her to make out what he was saying, if he was saying anything at all.

Darkness surrounded Sophia on her blank path. The further she walked the more it consumed her. There was nothing beneath her feet and it felt as if she was walking on air. Her brunette hair had

tumbled down her shoulders and her eyes were searching for
anything to look at. She became dazed and confused and found
herself spinning around and around in circles. On her final turn,
the door from her dreams appeared with nothing behind it.

She stepped towards it. This was the first time she had mobility
in her dreams.

Her hand touched the doorknob, it was cold. As though it had
been standing in a snowstorm.

There was a second of hesitation, but for the first time she
managed to open the door. Behind it led a flight of stairs, shortly
followed by a woman's cry echoing from down below.

Sophia shot up from her dream drowning in her own sweat. A sudden rush of fatigue took its claim over Sophia, when she realised she got up too quickly. Bringing her hand to her forehead she flinched at the touch, a small cut sat below her hairline, and her fingers were painted with blood. At this rate, she was certain her entire body would be covered in scars. Her brain throbbed as she pushed herself up to her feet with dirt smeared on her hands and clothes.

Cradling her head with her hands, she attempted to soothe the ache with no avail. It was like someone was smacking the inside of her head with a tree branch.

When her eyes fell upon the carriage, now on it's side, it dawned on her that she must have been flung out of the window.

Forgetting all feelings of pain, she ran to the crash site. Frantically searching for a sign of life, and was distraught when she found nothing. Trying her best to look inside of the carriage, one window against the ground, and the other was facing the sky. Sophia was too short to reach up and climb ontop to check. For all she knew, Xavier and Jack could be so badly injured that they are trapped inside.

"Jack!" she called out.

There was no response.

Scanning the area and over her shoulder she found a familiar black cane stabbed into the bark of a hollow tree. This only caused a rush of panic. Even if Jack was fine, what if he too got flung deep into this forest, and without his cane it would be difficult for him to find his way around.

"I'm fine by the way," an annoyed voice huffed from behind her.

With tears staining her cheeks she saw Xavier emerge from behind one of the trees.

"Quite a journey getting back here." He said as he brushed off the dirt from his shoulders. "I was certain I'd been flung halfway across England."

"Are you hurt?"

He opened his mouth to say something but was cut off by the sound of groaning coming from inside the carriage.

Sophia jumped like a startled cat and followed the sound. Falling to her knees and pressing her ear against the walls she listened for the sound. It came again shortly after, and Sophia began pounding on the walls. "Jack! It's me. We'll get you out, I promise."

Grabbing onto the roof of the carriage to hoist herself up, Xavier's hand gripped onto her waist and dropped her back down to the leaf covered ground, like she was a child misbehaving.

"Don't be stupid," he snapped and pulled her up by the shoulders to look at him. "You think you're strong enough to pull him out of there? Stop being irrational and use your brain." Releasing her, Xavier startled Sophia by leaping up, like a bird taking flight, and landing on top of the carriage. Shrinking down to his knees he looked through the shattered window.

In one effortless swoop, Xavier ripped open the door with a grunt and reached his arms inside. He stretched his arm as far as it could go, almost certain he would pull it out of his socket. Still his fingers couldn't quite reach Jack. He was wedged in the furthest corner away from the door.

Jack would have to meet him halfway if Xavier had any chance of rescuing him.

Xavier rolled his eyes and huffed, "Are you purposely being awkward? Just reach up your arm a little so I can pull you out, stubborn bastard."

Jack let out a pained amused laugh.

Xavier smirked. "You just like to see me suffer. Reach up your hand."

After a beat Jack raised a weak hand, and Xavier only just managed to snatch it into his own. Xavier hooked his fingers around Jack's limp hand and started pulling.

As Xavier pulled up, Jack released a painful groan.

Xavier was lucky not to dislocate any joints in Jack's arm as he hoisted him up and through the carriage window.

When Jack's limp body was on the outside, his legs dangled over the side of the window like a ragdoll. Xavier looped his arm around Jack's stomach, positioning his back flat against Xavier's chest.

Xavier dragged his entire body out of the window and dropped down with him to the ground with a thud.

Sophia hurried to her friend, cupping her hands around his cheeks to examine him for any cuts and scrapes. There seemed to be no major wound or injury as she searched, only a few scratches along his jaw and some torn clothes. But he was severely dazed from a bump on the head.

"Are you all right?" Sophia spoke quickly.

He weakly pushed her hands away. "I am fine, please do not fuss."

Sophia was wounded by his response, which hurt more than the cut along her forehead. Perhaps it was just an impulse, for he would be irritated when Cassandra would coddle him. Jack must have wanted to prove he was strong enough to handle anything on his own.

Xavier tilted his head and examined the sky. "It is getting dark, it's not wise to be in a forest at night. Never know what might be lurking about."

"We also cannot go wandering around either, with no sense of direction or any clue of where we are." said Sophia, feeling defeated.

"What do you suggest we do?" Xavier said in a defeated breath. "With a dead driver and a runaway horse?"

Unfortunately, her mind drew a blank and she knew he was right. They couldn't stay in a forest at night, especially with the state Jack was in. If they were to encounter anything there was no chance for Jack to stand up for himself.

Sophia grabbed one of Jack's arms and draped it over her shoulder. He was heavier than she had expected. It was a struggle for her to straighten her knees, how she was going to walk like this was beyond her.

Suddenly Jack felt lighter and Xavier was at his other side assisting her.

Jack couldn't bring himself to place one foot on the ground so they had to drag him through the forest, ruining his brown leather shoes.

They were practically wandering around hoping they'd find any form of shelter. Nightfall was almost upon them and the sound of owls hooting, echoing around them made it feel like a scene from one of Sophia's horror novels.

"This is all my fault," Sophia said in a low tone.

Xavier looked past Jack's dangling head, with surprise in his eyes.

She stared out at the dirt road in front of her. "If I hadn't been so foolish to try and uncover my past this wouldn't have happened." She shrugged her shoulder that wasn't fully occupied by Jack. "We didn't even get to my father's door, and look at us."

Xavier said nothing. He clearly had something on his mind but thought better of saying anything. Nothing he could say would make this situation better. Jack had fallen unconscious only minutes before, and Sophia didn't have the strength to walk like this for too long, although Xavier seemed to carry the brunt of his weight.

After what felt like hours of walking they finally stumbled across a run down building. Based on appearance, it used to be a hotel. A hotel which seemed to have been hit by a bunch of bandits, with its caved in windows and black soot coating the walls. It had a collapsed stable beside it, where riders could once tie up their horses if on a journey into town.

"There must be a town nearby," Xavier said. "But we can't drag him around looking for it."

Above the front door was a mosaic tile with the pattern of sun shining over a small town.

They dragged Jack up the dirt covered steps and Xavier knocked three times. After a few minutes of silence he pushed open the unlocked door and pigeons swooped down and soared through the rafters.

"Ugly little beasties," Xavier said under his breath.

"We should find him a bed so he can rest," Sophia said dazedly.

"I wouldn't trust those stairs," said Xavier. "They look ready to collapse. As much as I don't like the guy, I don't fancy finding him through rubble."

Dragging Jack's body into the drawing room was like dragging the corpse of a dead man. They dropped him down into a dusty red velvet settee and a cloud of dust filled the room, causing Sophia and Xavier to cough up a storm.

Sophia positioned her friend flat on his back and watched him for a moment as he remained in his blissful sleep. When she was assured he was breathing, with the steady rise and fall of his chest, she brushed her hand over his sweaty forehead and pecked a kiss on his forehead.

Xavier drew the moth-eaten curtains which made the already dark room even darker. Xavier found a candle and some matches and placed it down in the middle of the room. It filled the room with a comfortable golden glow, and provided a small bit of heat for the room that no one had entered in months.

Xavier sprawled out on the floor with his eyes locked to the cracked ceiling.

Sophia sat on the carpeted floor beside Xavier, with her back straight and staring at the candle flickering from the breeze rolling in from the broken windows.

The once floral wallpaper, what still existed of it, was hanging by a thread and it smelt like someone ignited a casm full of cigarettes.

"It wasn't foolish of you to try and find out about your past," Xavier broke the empty silence. "It's brave, if anything. One bump in the road shouldn't stop you," he scoffed. "Is it too soon to say, one crash in the road shouldn't stop you?"

Sophia shook her head with a laugh. She wasn't sure why she thought back to the passionate kiss they shared, it wasn't an appropriate thought but she wanted nothing more than to do it again.

Shuffling closer to him, a light breeze tickled up her dress from the material being ripped in various places.

"Why were you dangling over the balcony that night?" Xavier finally asked.

The question stung her heart as she thought back to that night. It was like she was reliving that moment, her heart felt heavy and she had an overwhelming feeling of confusion filling her thoughts. "I didn't want my life to be lived for me. I'd rather not have one at all."

"You didn't? Does that imply you are happy with what is happening now?"

"Of course not," she said, defensively. "At the moment, I am trying to figure out things in my life. Past and present."

He said nothing, and continued to stare at the blank ceiling.

"Why did you kiss me?"

He said nothing.

"To mock me?"

"Why must you always think I do things to mock you? You are much like Mr Green."

"In what way?"

"You are both much too sensitive."

"I was simply confused as we do not know anything about one another."

"I wouldn't say that," he grinned. "Besides, you don't have to know a lot about a person to want to kiss them. There is no course, although some people could do with one."

Sophia shook her head and watched him with the glow of the candle light flickering across his face. His black eyes were watching her softly, and his lips parted. For a moment she sat and stared back, internally pleading he was going to kiss her.

"You are a dreamer," he said, abruptly. "You want your life to go a certain way but if it comes down to someone telling you what to do, you politely nod your head and go along with it because you don't want to upset another person. You care for others over yourself, you focus on others so you don't have to deal with your own burdens. I also knew that you had the blood of a gorgon in you, I knew what you were before you did. So, I know more about you than you probably realise." Xavier dipped his head and leveled his eyes with Sophia's. There was a shadow under his high cheekbones. "Plus you are very beautiful, that is the main thing you do not know about yourself."

"I cannot be because of-"

"Your scars don't define you." his eyes never wavered. "You'd be beautiful even if a thousand scars coated your face."

A blush ignited her cheeks and she couldn't fight back the smile which grew on her lips. Shaking her head in denial and hiding her face with a veil of her hair.

Xavier let out a small, sincere laugh.

"I wish I could analyse people like you can, for I don't even know how old you are and you have picked me apart as if you have known me since birth."

"I am twenty, if that helps."

They shared a small laugh and as the night passed by they stayed up for hours just talking. Most of the time it wasn't about anything in particular but they would just talk about whatever popped into their minds. They sat next to one another with the wax on the candle slowly burning out. They stared at the flickering flame and watched it dance in front of them.

"I do not want to marry Jack." she looked over her shoulder and watched Jack still in a peaceful slumber. "I love him dearly, I just do not want to marry him."

"Then don't," Xavier said, as if it was that easy.

She looked back to the candle and shook her head. "I have to."

"Surly Cassandra would not throw you out," Xavier seemed disheartened. "All because of an insignificant letter? To me it sounds like some ridiculous excuse just so *he* can have you."

"It will make Jack happy."

"But not you."

Sophia was drawn to look at Xavier's face, the light from the candle was showing off the broad line of his jaw, a shadow darkened under his strong cheekbone, and she could see the flame in his eyes. "Jack is helping me find my past, the least I can do is return the favour in marriage."

Xavier rolled his eyes to the back of his head and punched a hand through his black hair. "Why must you see marriage as some form of bargain? It doesn't work like that."

He didn't give her the chance to respond, as Xavier continued. "Sophia," the way he said her name sent a tingling sensation through her chest. "I kissed you because I wanted to."

328

How was she supposed to respond to that? So, she just said the first thing that came to her mind. "I am very glad that you did."

Sophia was the first to fall asleep, she was curled up in a ball and Xavier was quite happy watching her for a while.

He noticed her shudder from the rolling breeze. Raising to his feet he found a ratty old blanket draped across one of the armchairs. He shook out the years worth of dust until it was clear.

Just as he made his way to Sophia, a firm hand gripped around his wrist. Xavier turned to see Jack glaring up at him with the fire of hell in his eyes.

"Jesus," he exclaimed. "You scared the life out of me."

"Do not think you can worm your way into her heart." Jack snarled.

Xavier hooked up a satisfied smile. "Jealous that she has opened her heart to me within such a small amount of time? Besides, can't two friends share a heart to heart?"

Jack painfully propped himself up on his elbow. "She is more than a friend to you, that much is true."

Xavier tried to pull his hand away but Jack's grip was too firm. "I do not know what you are talking about."

"The kiss was enough evidence."

"Perhaps it is a lesson for you to knock before you enter a room, didn't your mother teach you manners?" Xavier shrugged. "I suppose she didn't see the point, considering she knew one day your wings would kill you."

Jack grabbed him by the scruff of his shirt and pulled him down until their noses were inches apart. "Consider this my final warning," Jack growled. "Sophia is *my* fiancé, she is soon to be *my* wife. If you even breathe in front of her without it being necessary, I will have Lord Paine and his men take you away and rip you limb from limb. Have I made myself clear?"

Xavier paused for a moment, knowing his threat was real. "Crystal."

When Jack was satisfied he released his grip and shoved his hand away.

Xavier turned back to Sophia and rested his eyes on her sleeping figure. He draped the blanket over her shoulders and she eventually stopped shaking. His face hardened as he breathed in how beautiful she looked by simply sleeping.

"We should really check on the carriage," Xavier said without even glancing over his shoulder to look at Jack. "Safe to say it wasn't a swerve in the road which caused the crash."

Jack abruptly froze in place and let out a small grunt. His eyes dragged down until they reached the floor.

"If I didn't know any better," Xavier continued. "It seems that someone was trying to put a stop to Sophia visiting Christopher. Don't you care for her safety that we at least investigate it?"

There was a moment of silence as Jack took his words into consideration. "When the sun rises we'll investigate."

Xavier shot up his eyebrows in surprise. "Need me to hold your hand?"

"I would not give you the satisfaction."

Jack and Xavier visited the crash site as planned, and were both examining the remains.

Xavier squatted down over the toppled carriage and ran his fingers across the puncture. "It would seem a meteor decided to fall and crash into the carriage at the exact moment we were on the road."

Jack rolled his eyes and limped towards his cane stabbed through the tree. With a small amount of force he pulled it out and leaned the majority of his body weight onto it. He hated how relieving it was to not have to rely on his own strength.

"You're more of a moron than I assumed. My apologies for misjudging you."

"You're more possessive than I assumed, it should be you accepting my apology." Xavier bowed his head then examined the corpse of the driver. "Sadly, our poor carriage driver didn't make it. Do you think this is Lord Paine's doing?"

Jack joined Xavier to look down on their carriage driver. His legs and torso were squashed by the carriage and he was drenched in his own blood forming a river either side of him.

"If he truly didn't want Sophia visiting her father he would not have given her the letter," Jack glanced around the site for any more clues. "I'm not so sure this was an attempt to stop her from visiting."

"How so?"

"I'm not sure," Jack said. "But what better way to get Sophia alone than knocking her unconscious."

Xavier wasn't fully following Jack's logic. "You think Christopher had a part in the crash? Why would he encourage Sophia to bring others if he wanted her alone?"

"To make himself seem trusting. For he knew that she wouldn't be alone even without the recommendation."

Xavier eyed Jack for a while, trying to figure out his logic. "You know more about Christopher than you're letting on, don't you?"

Jack didn't respond. Instead he began poking the dead driver with the end of his cane, and his lifeless head tilted so he was not facing them.

"I wonder what happened to the horse?" Xavier looked either side of him, and didn't see a trace of him.

Jack dipped his cane into the pool of blood and raised it so it was level with Xavier's face. He watched Jack with confusion and saw drops of blood falling at his feet.

"Will the smell of this blood tempt you into going back and draining Sophia?" Jack's hatred poured out through his glare. "Do not pretend as though you are worthy of her. The second you can't control your bloodlust you will kill her."

Xavier shifted his weight out of irritation.

"Like the animal you are," Jack pushed. "Can't control the monster that lives within you."

"You truly are an idiot." Xavier spat. "I can see exactly what you're trying to do."

"And what is that?"

"You're willing to put your darling fiancé's life in danger just because your insecurities can't put up with the fact that she is not in love with you, and she never will be. Willing to have a vampire be tempted into sucking her blood just to prove a point." Xavier clenched his fists and his pulse was hammering through his veins. "Do you even love her?"

"Do you?"

The question took Xavier by surprise. Any answer he could conger left his head. He wanted to say *Don't be ridiculous*, but he couldn't bring himself to say it. For some reason, he thought it would be too big of a lie for him to deal with.

"Well, do you?" Jack pushed, as he lowered his cane to the ground.

Xavier rubbed the bridge of his nose with two fingers. "I wouldn't say I am in love with her...but she is the one thing that occupies my mind and I cannot seem to think of anything...other than her."

They were both taken aback by his answer. He was mostly thinking out loud.

Sophia's face appeared in Xavier's mind and he spoke like he was talking to her. He couldn't help the pounding rhythm he felt in his heart whenever he saw her. It was something he had never experienced before. In his past, he had met countless women with varying types of beauty but no one ever lasted longer than a week in his mind. But Sophia was always there, she was the first thing he thought of in the morning and the last at night. There were days he realised he hoped he'd run into her, and his heart would skip whenever he did.

Jack's nose crinkled into an animalistic snarl. Raising his cane again, line a sword, he dug it into Xavier's chest and persisted in pushing him back forcefully.

With the strong pressure against his chest, Xavier lost his footing and fell back into the mud, soaking his clothes. Jack never wavered, he persisted in pushing it into his chest.

"I am so tempted to keep on pushing until it pierces your heart," Jack snarled.

"Do you honestly think I'd let you do that?" Xavier looked amused by his actions. "If you haven't noticed, I am a lot stronger than you. In more ways than physical."

Jack gritted his teeth harder. "What is that supposed to mean?"

"Any feelings I have towards Sophia are controlled, because I am strong enough to control them. Whereas with you, one small sign that someone is getting in the way and you throw the toys out of your pram." he smirked. "It is as clear as day Sophia reciprocates my feelings."

"She must not care for you that much if she is still going to be my bride."

"You seem to forget that she feels as though she *has* to marry you. If it wasn't for that letter do you think she'd even consider having any form of romantic relationship with you?"

Jack pushed the cane harder into his chest. "Shut up!" he yelled.

Xavier grabbed the cane and pushed it off his chest, like it was a measly twig poking him. Snatching the cane out of Jack's firm grip, he threw it with such a foresity that it disappeared behind the trees. "Fetch."

"Do not attempt to intimidate me."

Xavier began quickly patting his knees and watched him with wide and playful eyes. Like he was in fact playing with a dog. "Go on boy, fetch the stick!"

Jack charged at Xavier and grabbed him by the collar of his coat and pushed him up against the side of the carriage. "Don't think because I am a Nephlim it means I won't kill you. I'll be disposing of a demon from this world and I am sure God will be more than understanding."

The corner of Xavier's mouth hooked up. "Don't think you're so special. That's only because your mother is a whore and slept with the first human who made contact with her."

Jack shook Xavier so the back of his head hit hard against the carriage.

"Are you trying to hurt me?" Xavier teased. "Because that was a pathetic attempt."

After a beat Jack released his grip. He turned to the grass and found his cane not too far from where they were standing.

Jack then left Xavier at the site, with nothing but the sound of the gust of wind rustling the leaves.

Sophia awoke with her heart heavy in her chest. Her head was spinning and she couldn't bring her eyes to focus on anything in her view. Xavier's face immediately came to mind, she began picturing what it would be like to be close to him and to be held romantically by him again. Yet, guilt filled her as soon as that thought popped into her mind.

She thought of Jack, how much these thoughts would hurt him if he truly knew how she felt. Every time she tried to force herself to think of Jack and the possibilities with him, her mind jumped straight back to Xavier. Picturing his hands all over her body, him pulling her into a passionate kiss.

"Sophia," Jack's voice echoed through the room. She turned to see him at the doorway with sad eyes resting on her.

"Jack," she breathed. "Are you well enough to stand?"

He joined her on the floor. "I shall be fine," he assured. "I've been through worse pain than this." There was clearly something bothering him, he was frustrated and in an agitated state.

Sophia reached over and placed a gentle hand over his. "What is it?"

"I need to ask you a question."

She nodded with a worried smile.

He gathered her hands in his lap and squeezed like he needed some form of support. "If it wasn't for your mother's letter...would you even consider me as a partner?"

Sophia sat there, gawking at him. Her mouth opened as if to say something but nothing left her mouth. She sank her teeth into her bottom lip and held her ashamed gaze to his. How much more could she hurt him? Hadn't he endured all the hurt any man could take?

"It had not crossed my mind," she admitted. "However, no one knows where our paths lead and maybe at some point in the near future our paths will have crossed. For I love no one more than I love you."

Jack lowered his eyes. He knew that would be her answer, a rejection but an attempt to see a brighter side. Even if it was a lie.

"Just not the same way I love you." he said as a fact, rather than a question.

Her silence gave him the answer he was looking for. When he leaned over and brushed his lips across her forehead, the wound now dried, he breathed in her sweet scent.

"That will have to do," he muttered.

Closing her eyes, feeling another piece of her heart die, she allowed her friend to hold her. The least she could do was give him this moment. She clutched onto his shirt and felt the soft material slide through her fingers. She rested her head in the arch of his neck and closed her eyes within his embrace.

"I wish," he began in a low and husky tone. "I wish you could understand the amount my heart aches for you."

Her eyebrows arched. "It's not that I don't understand, it's that my heart doesn't reciprocate it." she held a breath. "If you cannot marry me because of the ache I give you, I understand. Knowing how much I hurt you is more than my heart can take."

Jack cupped his hand around her cheek and pushed her back so she would look at him. "You deserve no such punishment. I do not wish for your sympathy, I wish for nothing more than your happiness."

"I cannot be happy knowing I have hurt you." her bottom lip trembled.

The spark in his blue eyes returned for a moment, but it wasn't a spark of love, it was of hatred. "What do you feel for *him?*" he asked with poison stinging his lips.

Just the image of Xavier had brought her heart hammering against her ribcage. Like it was captive in a strong prison and it was aching to break free. It was a feeling she couldn't explain because she had never felt this way before. Whenever she tried to see a future with Jack, or even the idea of creating happy memories with him, Xavier always found a way to crawl into her mind. With his dashing lopsided smile and his mysterious dark eyes. He was someone no woman could keep away from, his charm was like a magic spell that had hypnotised her. She was drawn to him like he was forever tempting her in just his presence.

"I do not know."

"Do you love him?"

"No," she was certain of that, but she knew there was something strong there for him. "He just has this...power over me."

"I'm sure he did that to all those women he murdered." he dropped his hand from her cheek.

"But, he didn't murder them. He is innocent."

Jack's face turned sour. "What makes you think that?"

"He told me."

Jack barked out a laugh of disbelief. "Because he told you that means it is true? Well, I am the King of France."

"Jack..." she started.

"No, I have said it so it must be the truth." he pushed himself out of her embrace.

"Why do you despise him so much?" she created more of a gap between them. "He has only been *accused* of murder, there has been no solid proof that he killed them. If he was a murderer he would be in prison right now, or worse...."

"He will slip up and show you what a monster he truly is." Jack pushed himself to his feet. "Do not get too used to his presence. I guarantee he will not be here for long."

She watched him with wide eyes and her mouth slightly gaping. "How can you be so cruel?"

"Anyone who tries to take my fiancé away from me deserves to be thrown into a pit. Which is where he will end up as soon as people realise he is guilty."

Sophia silently prayed that Xavier wouldn't purposely try to push Jack's buttons anymore than he already had, he was on thin ice with his temper these last few weeks.

It was growing more apparent how much of a box Jack was placing Sophia in. His jealousy, and possessiveness felt like a poisonous snake lacing it's way around her heart. Keeping everyone else away, not even the people she wanted there were permitted.

"You cannot control me Jack." Sophia said as she too got to her feet.

"You are my *fiancé!*" He spat the final word out, his face reddening. Sophia had never seen Jack so angry.

These days he was so quick to anger that it was jarring. She never knew when to expect his temper to rise up.

"You are to act as such!"

Sophia scoffed. Her hands balled into tight fists at her sides, her fingernails almost drawing blood. "And how is that Jack? Do enlighten me how one is supposed to act!" She yelled so loud that it made her ears ring.

"With loyalty!"

Sophia just stared at him for a moment. How had they come to this? Screaming in each other's faces, when there was a time that she adored him. Now she couldn't look at him as nothing more than a selfish man taking her future away, and there was little she could do to stop it.

Jack may have been selfish with his intentions, but so was Sophia.

Sophia dropped her voice to a hushed snarl as she took a stride toward him, locking her fiery gaze with his. "You expect me to express loyalty to a man whom I have been engaged to for a matter of weeks? When there was no foundation of a loving relationship to start us off on?"

When Jack dropped his head to hide his face, Sophia made sure to dip her head and force his gaze back to her. She had to make sure he understood her, that there was no doubt with what was between them. "I told you from the very beginning that I hold no romantic feelings for you."

Jack flinched, and it made Sophia second guess her harsh words but she knew she could not lie to him. She could not give him a false hope of a marriage.

"I do love you, Jack." she was softer now, to emphasise that she meant it. "I love you more than anyone in this entire bleak world. But you can't expect me to fall in love with you just because of how you feel." Tears were welling up in her eyes, as the sparkle in his eyes was fading.

Waiting for him to speak was like torture, every minute that passed filled Sophia with a lingering sense of dread.

Jack eventually lifted his head, his shoulders were back and his eyes were fixed ahead of him. He was doing his best to avoid Sophia's gaze as he stared out at nothing in particular. "Don't take me for a fool, Sophia. Don't for one second think that I don't know where this is stemming from."

"What are you-"

"From *him!*" Jack boomed, hurling himself around to fully face Sophia. His face creased with rage, his upper lip snarled and his breath was sharp and fast. Sophia was frightened that he might lash out at something - or her.

"He has nothing to do with this," Sophia didn't dare speak his name out loud, for Jack may actually tear this room to shreds.

Jack barked a laugh but there was no amusement on his face. "Oh, really? I confided in you about my love for you these past ten years. On the very day I proposed to you. You said nothing. You accepted my proposal and I took that as a pretty clear sign that we could have a life together one day. Then *he* shows up and-"

"Our engagement wasn't born out of love. You may have taken this opportunity to quench your ten year thirst of wanting me as your wife but you know damn well that I accepted out of fear!" Sophia didn't wipe away any of the tears that were streaming like a waterfall down her cheeks. "You said so yourself, that you didn't want me in the arms of a stranger who could use me or abuse me. And as for *him* that you so confidently speak of as though he is...he is...some *monster*."

"Which he is," Jack snarled. "He is a demon."

"Jealousy is not flattering."

Jack gawked at her, seething with boiling rage. "You think so little of me that I would be *jealous* of that? Jealous of a creature who can't control his thirst for blood? I am certain you aren't stupid enough to forget *why* he is here in the first place."

"He is innocent of any such crime." She said, flatly.

"Why is that?" Jack bounced on his heel. "Oh yes, that's right because he told you so...how silly of me. Be sure to tell me of how innocent he is when he has his beastly fangs in your neck."

346

Sophia raised·her palm to silence him. "Not everyone is as they appear. Have you forgotten that the entire time I have known you, the past ten years I thought you were the most honest man in my life and you were *lying* to me every single day! You knew of my father, you knew of what I am and you said nothing. You saw the torment which I faced every single day and you stood by and watched, not once trying to relieve me of it. *He* is the only one whom has been truly honest with me, in his own peculiar way. This man that you call a *criminal* and a *demon,* has shown me true honesty in the past few weeks than you have in the past ten years."

"He is a DEMON Sophia!"

"SO AM I!"

This struck Jack like a lightning bolt. The hurt was written all over his face. He didn't even try to defend himself, as one second he was there and the next he was gone. Slamming the door behind him, sending a wave through the house which almost caused it to crumble.

347

Chapter Nineteen

There was something unnerving about being in an abandoned hotel alone. There was an uncomfortable presence filling the air. Contorted shadows formed on the dusty ground from the light streaming through the broken windows.

Pushing cobwebs out of her way, Sophia searched the empty rooms that weren't barricaded by rubble.

Dusting the cobwebs from her hands, she entered what used to be a kitchen. The second she stepped foot inside her nostrils filled with the stench of rotten apples and bananas. It was a cocktail of smells, she was sure she would gag.

It wasn't in her nature to rummage through strangers' cupboards but since this place was clearly abandoned she didn't feel as guilty.

Finding anything which wasn't rotten was her main goal, her stomach growled with impatience and she was losing faith the more empty cupboards she found. Kneeling down to the bottom shelves she wasn't surprised to find nothing, not even a crumb.

"You're wasting your time," Xavier said from the door. When he stepped inside, he too was greeted by the vile stench. Covering his nose with the collar of his jacket, the smell caused him to break out into a coughing fit. "Not that I would trust anything in this kitchen."

Sophia pushed herself to her feet and met Xavier at the door. "I wish we stumbled across a functioning hotel, at least there would be real services."

Xavier scratched the edge of his crooked nose with a wide smile. "The best things in life are free," he dropped his hand. "When you get to my age you will understand."

"Do not try and act as though you are full of wisdom," she said. "You are only two years older than me."

"A lot of experiences can be had within two years," he reached out a hand and pinched her waist, causing her to squeal like a mouse. "I am sure you can manage a few hours without food."

Her eyebrows flicked up. "Are you implying I am fat?"

"No," he chuckled. "I am saying you are not malnourished, there is no fear of you breaking like a twig."

Sophia cocked her head to the side, trying her best to read him. "Why must you settle on such cruel and dark humour?"

"Cruel and dark?" Xavier wondered as he pursed his lips. "I thought my humour was quite uplifting."

Sophia wasn't sure why she smiled at that, "I can assure you it is not."

The conversation was interrupted by a beast growling in Sophia's stomach. She pressed her hand hard against her torso, in a failed attempt to silence the noise. Her cheeks flared as she dropped her head to the dust covered floor. "My apologies."

Xavier only laughed. "I found a town not far from here this morning. Why don't we grab some supplies?"

"How will we get there, we have no carriage?"

Shifting his weight, and trailing his eyes down the front of her skirt, he said. "Is there something wrong with your legs?"

Xavier turned to leave until Sophia's voice called him back. "What about Jack?"

With a sinister smile, Xavier turned his head to look over his shoulder at her. "What about him?"

It was enough to make her heart come to a halt. She ran her tongue across her top row of teeth, feeling guilty for not wanting

Jack to come along with them. In an attempt to comfort herself, she told herself it was because of the tension that would come along with him.

Secretly, she wanted time alone with Xavier.

"Nothing," she settled on saying, and followed Xavier out of the hotel.

The air was surprisingly cool once they reached the miniature town.

Embarrassment flooded Sophia's bones when she noticed people staring at her torn dress. She was thankful people had a reason to stare at her, and not because of where she lived. It was reassuring when she looked up at Xavier as he browsed the buildings, not seeming fazed by the stares in the slightest.

Sophia was carrying a wicker basket that she picked up from the kitchen back at the hotel.

Xavier insisted on buying exactly fifteen succulent red apples. "Why fifteen?" She asked, looking at the fresh fruit. She was surprised the rotten fruit hadn't put her off her appetite.

"I thought I would show you one of my hidden talents."

"Cooking?" She had to hold back a laugh.

Xavier took note of her snickering. "Don't act so surprised. I wouldn't call myself a master chef but I can cook up some delicious apple pies."

"It's a good job you're not modest, Mr Howell."

He smiled.

What do vampires eat? From the stories she was familiar with, Sophia assumed blood was their source of nutrition. Why would he bother learning to cook anything?

"Do you eat the pies you make?"

A puzzled expression masked his face, "What would be the point if I didn't eat them?"

"Well, because you're..." she lowered her voice and wasn't confident in saying what species he was in front of a crowd.

With his signature smirk he said, "Of course I smother my pies in blood, I even inject little drops of blood into the apples for that extra spice."

Sophia abruptly stopped in her tracks, her heart hammering against her ribcage.

When Xavier noticed he was a couple of steps ahead, he stopped and turned to face her. "I'm joking, Sophia." Running a hand through his disheveled black hair, he dipped his head to meet Sophia's eyes. "Just because I am a vampire it doesn't mean I live off blood alone. Blood is more like...my strength. I'll become weak without it, but I don't need it every single day. I can go a solid month without a drop."

Anxiety filled her face as she closed the gap between them. "Keep your voice down."

"They shouldn't be eavesdropping," he said, hooking out his arm as a gesture for her to take it. "I've never been a fan of the orphanage. Hiding creatures away like we don't exist. Funnily enough," he continued, when Sophia looped her hand around his elbow. "My family was offered a place when I was a child. They said no, of course."

The idea that Sophia and Xavier could have met as children filled her mind with wonder. If they had met earlier, would everything be different today? Jack would have no reason to hate him, and perhaps they would have fallen in love over the years as they got to know one another.

They pushed forward through the market stalls and browsed the signs of the shops. Xavier was clearly looking for a place that supplied alcohol.

"Why did they decline?"

He shrugged, "Like I said, they didn't want to be hidden away like they were prisoners. When our family had done nothing wrong..."

There was pain in his voice, and a sprinkle of anger. Clearly, there was more to just his family declining a spot at the orphanage. Xavier couldn't mold the perfect mask to shield his pain, for it was too prominent.

"I suppose you're getting used to feeling that?" That sounded more condescending that she intended. She clutched tighter onto his sleeve to assure him she meant nothing by it.

It was odd to be clutching Xavier and not Jack, in a new town nonetheless. It was like a breath of fresh air, refreshing. To everyone else they appeared to be a regular couple taking a stroll.

After browsing the stalls, and buying the supplies they were about to head back to the hotel.

Xavier abruptly stopped in front of a dress boutique and his face hardened as his eyes locked onto a horse and carriage parked outside of the store. It was certainly a posh carriage, with slick black doors and large golden wheels, and a white horse that seemed more elegant than Sophia.

"Do you see what I see?"

Sophia confirmed his line of sight when she followed it to the horse and carriage. "A horse and carriage that doesn't belong to us."

Xavier pulled Sophia to the front of the horse. He began stroking his hand down his long black and white nose. The horse stomped his hoof several times as he blinked with his long eyelashes.

Sophia couldn't get her eyes off Xavier, he seemed so giddy as he lightly ran his hand up and down the horse's face. "He's the most beautiful horse I have ever seen!"

A giggle arose in Sophia's throat.

In a flash, Xavier swiftly moved away from the horse and climbed up to the driver's seat. His black eyes scanned the area, checking no one was a witness.

"What are you doing?" Sophia hissed. "The driver will see."

"Ah!" He picked up a pair of black gloves and a tall top hat. Putting them on he jumped back down onto the ground. The top hat was far too big for his head, it dipped down below his eyebrows. He had to constantly adjust it so it didn't fall over his eyes.

Striking a pose, Xavier spun around whilst popping the collar of his jacket.

"Xavier!" She was doing a terrible job fighting her amusement. He looked rather ridiculous.

The devilish smirk returned as he took her hand and led her behind the carriage. He opened up the door and pushed her inside, all the while laughing. Before he closed the door she looked at him with an unsure expression.

"It has been a rather depressing couple of days," he said. "What's wrong with *borrowing* an unattended carriage?"

She clearly wasn't convinced. With her conscience screaming at her that this wasn't the right thing, this was stealing.

"Besides, the horse is beautiful and I want to keep him."

A long breath escaped her lips. Still her conscience was crying out, pleading for her to leave the carriage and walk away, but that was overpowered by her desire to run away with Xavier. To be bold and take a chance on a journey and let go.

Taking a seat in the green leather booth, Xavier smiled and slammed the door shut.

It was clear from looking at it that this carriage belonged to a person of wealth. Fresh white roses decorated each corner and not a single trace of dirt could be found. The silk curtains matched the seats.

And here Sophia was, in a torn dress that certainly wasn't worthy of sitting in such luxury.

This carriage was slightly bigger than the one they crashed, she actually had enough room to stretch her legs.

Xavier climbed back up to the driver's seat, without checking who was around he snapped the reins and the horse shot into a fast gallop.

Sophia held the walls to brace for the rocky ride. She assumed Xavier knew how to drive but based on the recklessness she feared she would be in another carriage accident.

They left the town and led the horse past a row of tall trees leading deep into a forest.

Sophia felt an odd thrill from the uncertainty of where they were going.

Xavier drove the carriage to an unknown location, and Sophia was feeling the thrill of it. So much sadness and anxiety had taken control of her life these past few weeks, she was happy to let loose.

When the carriage came to a sudden stop, there was silence. Sophia waited for Xavier to meet her at the door, but he never did. Out of a growing concern, she climbed to the blacked out driver window and pulled it down, only to be greeted by the back of Xavier's head. A giggle arose when she noticed he was still wearing the oversized top hat.

His eyes were transfixed on the lake, mesmerised by the water. It certainly was beautiful, a lot nicer than the one back in London. Sophia wondered if lakes held a special meaning in Xavier's heart, or if he just personally found them pleasing.

Sophia's eyes were unmoving as she watched him. She wondered what he could be thinking.

Was he as nervous as she was? Coming down from her high, she followed Xavier's gaze to the ripples on the lake. Could he be thinking about their kiss too?

Hypnotised by the rising and falling of his shoulders as he breathed, Sophia tapped his shoulder, and Xavier quickly spun in his seat to face her.

"Thinking of swimming?"

Xavier dipped his head, the top hat tipping over his eyes. "Yes, actually."

Suddenly, he dropped the reins and jumped down from the driver's seat. He broke out into a run to the carriage door.

Sophia was bubbling in excitement, and her heart thrashed against her chest when Xavier opened the door, stepped inside and wrapped his hands around her waist. Soon she realised he was hoisting her out of her seat and carrying her out of the carriage.

"And you are coming with me."

Sophia laughed as she kicked her legs, and held onto his tight arms at her stomach. "Xavier, no!"

"You have many unpaid debts," Xavier was smiling as they approached the water. "Now it is finally your time to pay them."

Sophia shrieked, as she fought back to prevent getting dunked into the lake. When she dropped her foot down to the ground, it tangled with Xavier's ankle. She felt his grip losen, but she wasn't fast enough to break free from his grasp as they fell to the ground together.

Xavier landed on his back, making an *oof* sound, and Sophia landed with her back against his chest.

They lay there for a little while, staring up at the white clouds over the blue sky. Being outside of London certainly seemed brighter, even though they had no idea where the crash had landed them.

Sophia rolled over so her stomach was flat against his chest. She looked down at him, her head casting a shadow over his face, and for a while he kept his gaze to the sky. It was obvious he was lost in thought, something that was troubling him, and Sophia wanted to know all of his secrets. But she would never push him.

Sophia's grin widened when she picked up the top hat that had fallen beside Xavier's head. Placing it on top of her own, it sat over her eyes where she could see nothing but darkness. Just the thought of how she must look sent a giggle up her throat.

"I love it when you laugh," he said.

Unfortunately, this hat wasn't big enough to hide her rosy cheeks.

Then, the hat was lifted above her eyes and she was looking directly into Xavier's. Positioning the hat so it rested on the back of Sophia's head, making her entire face visible.

Xavier looked at her longingly, and brought up his hand to her cheek. "I prefer it like this."

She couldn't stop the gasp before it escaped. Her heart was thrumming as she watched him carefully take in every detail of her face. All of her insecurities he seemed to admire, each scar, each blemish he was captivated by.

"I was warned away from you," Xavier's voice was a low rasp. "Mr Green made it very clear that if I am alone with you he will have me sent back to Lord Paine."

This contorted her heart, but then it made her mind wonder. "Why are you risking that now?"

He smiled her favourite smile, bright and tooth-filled. The genuine smile that never failed to make her heart race. "Because I want to."

"Is that all it takes to do something?" It was only then she realised she was inching closer, her hand now gripping the material of his torn jacket. "Simply wanting it? Like kissing me that night?"

Instead of allowing him to answer, she picked up his hand that was flat against the grass and brought his fingers to her lips. She slid the glove from his hand and dropped it to the ground. Slowly, she began trailing kisses along the tips of his fingers and embraced his touch. "I was worried," she said against his skin. "That you hadn't attempted to kiss me again because you thought I was acting out of intoxication."

"It had crossed my mind," he laughed.

She shook her head, looking down at him with her big green eyes. "I may have to add another request onto my pile of debts."

"Oh? And what might that be?"

"Kiss me."

Xavier would have done that without the request. He was so captivated by her that he wanted nothing more than to feel the soft brush of her lips against his own. It was true that he thought of nothing else but her, and their first kiss did nothing to help matters.

Slowly, Xavier pulled her cheek down until their faces were but inches away from one another. Then he kissed her slowly at first, but as swift as the current in a nighttime storm, it intensified.

It was natural how they melted into one another, with Xavier's free hand sliding around her waist, pressing her body firmly against his. Each kiss was something new, a new setting of a celebration. Wild, with fireworks exploding in the distance.

Xavier rolled her onto her back, with his hands still cradling her close to him. Not once did their lips break apart, and in the split seconds that they did for air, they missed the others touch.

This was everything Sophia wanted, she felt like her heart might burst and scatter glitter into her bloodstream.

His skin was smooth against her fingers as she brought her hands around his neck. Searching his mouth with her own unlocked secrets to her heart that she never knew existed.

All the while the back of her head was uncomfortably being propped up by the top hat, she was sure she had crushed it at this point but she didn't care.

When the hand at her waist slid up over her breast, Sophia felt a new pleasure that awoke within her body. It startled her, causing her to pull away.

"I'm sorry," he whispered out of breath, and immediately put his hand back to its original position. "I got carried away-"

"No," she met his eyes, and she smiled. "I-I don't mind. I was just surprised. I've never..."

Xavier dipped his head and kissed the side of her mouth, "I won't do anything you aren't comfortable with."

Something new had awoken in Sophia from that simple touch. A fire that made her crave more, like she wanted their kiss to lead to an unexpected place. She wanted that thrill.

Sophia reached for Xavier's hand, and guided it back over her swollen breast. She kept her gaze on his, enjoying his reaction to touching her intimately. Shortly after, Xavier engulfed her mouth and rocked against her as they kissed.

Xavier groaned against her mouth, and she could feel his hard excitement pressing into her.

He kissed her mouth, her jaw and began trailing hot kisses into the curve of her neck.

Sparks flew in her vision as she embraced his touch. She had to sink her teeth into her bottom lip to prevent crying out in pleasure.

A sudden panic scurried across her heart, only for a brief moment but once she realised it was there she couldn't ignore it. "I don't want to mean nothing to you." she admitted.

When Xavier raised his head, and for a second time removed his palm from her breast, a flash of pain rippled across his face. Taking her hand in his, he placed it over his heart. It was beating just as fast as hers. It was like it was trying to burst out of his shirt.

At that very moment she realised how easily she could fall in love with him. It should have been a thought that brought joy, instead it frightened her. What if he falls in love with her and he looks directly into her eyes? He would turn to stone.

Then guilt mixed into the emotions, was what she was doing with Xavier considered cheating? Was she having an affair? She made it clear to Jack that she was not in love with him, and she thought he understood that she was only marrying him because she had to. They were still engaged, she still agreed to marry him.

Confusion was ingrained into her head. She wanted Xavier so badly, but she needed Jack. "Am I a bad person?"

"No," Xavier didn't take a second to think about it.

Her eyes trailed along his lips and she wanted nothing more than to kiss him over and over again.

"What you said before, about meaning nothing to me? I wouldn't be here with you if I didn't feel something. I wouldn't be open with you, I wouldn't want to get to know you." His black eyes scanned her face as his eyebrows pricked up. "But I do."

He didn't have to say anything else, she believed him. Tilting her chin she found his lips and they resumed to consume one another. Even if this was just another moment that only lasted by the lake, Sophia would cherish it.

They returned the horse and carriage back to the rightful owner. Luckily no one had noticed that it was missing. Well, Xavier and Sophia fled the scene before anyone would catch them. They were in such a rush they left the basket full of apples in the backseat.

Instead of heading straight, Xavier took a turn on a dirt filled road. Sophia stood in the path they originally took and watched him curiously. "The hotel is this way."

"Short cut."

It took a moment for her to consider it, but she followed him anyway. She was worried about what Jack's reaction would be with them being gone for hours, and turning up with swollen lips. With Jack's threat to Xavier in the front of her mind, she knew it wasn't going to be pleasant back in that hotel.

They were walking for a good ten minutes until Xavier stopped at a tall oak tree. He rested his palm against the bark and stared at the wrinkled lines detailing the tree. Like each line represented a memory of his own past.

Sophia watched him closely and she noticed his eyes were glossed over with sadness.

Reaching out to him, she wanted to find a way to take on some of his burden. Although she didn't know what the cause was, she wanted to take his pain. Her fingers lightly touched his shoulder, as she said. "Is everything alright?"

Glancing at her fingers, he only stared for a couple of heartbeats. His eyes shot up to meet hers and he abruptly wrapped his hands around her waist and pushed her against the tree.

"How uncomfortable do I make you?" he breathed.

"Not very," was all she said.

The hand that was once around her waist now slid around her neck. Xavier brushed his thumb along her skin tentatively. The memory of where his hands had been ignited that new fire in the pit of Sophia's stomach, and she found herself staring at his lips.

"Are you going to..."

"Bite you?"

Sophia was going to say 'kiss me.' But now that he had mentioned it, an anticipation began rising up her legs. He could easily overpower her and drink from her if he wanted to. Xavier was stronger than her, but she knew he wouldn't. Even when he was trying to push her away she trusted him. She knew his humour, all of his different masks were just that. A thin veil to hide his deepest hurt.

"It would be a shame to leave a mark on this pretty little thing." he traced a thin trail down her neck.

The conversation with Jack entered her mind, and the question escaped from like it was a natural conversation between close friends."Did you murder those women?"

A flicker of pain washed over his mask. Possibly because he heard doubt in her tone. "I've told you already."

"But why did they have bite marks on their necks? Your face was covered in blood."

He stared at her, breathing her in.

"I do not feed on living people. Like I said, I do not live off blood. I need it every once in a while to keep my strength." He hooked up a smile. "Those women were already dead when I found them."

"Wouldn't it be easier to kill someone as opposed to finding ones who are already dead?"

"That requires strategy, and choosing a victim every time. I do not want to hurt anyone, I was raised this way. If I were to become a murder, I would forever be on the run. It is exhausting having people chase me," he cocked his head to the side. "It is a whole other story when women chase me." Sliding his hand away from her neck, and hooking his thumb under her chin, he brought her eyes to look at him. "You are the most fun to be chased by."

"I never chased you."

"No?" he teased.

Her chest heaved as she watched his gorgeous face, only inches away from hers, breathe her in.

With flushed cheeks, she was about to deny it but she knew it wasn't a lie. Her face said it all. Sophia was drawn to him the very moment they met. Xavier intrigued her, and in his own bizarre way, she was certain he held an affection towards her from the moment they met. For he didn't care about the rules of keeping her past a secret. He must have been informed upon entry to the orphanage that he was to keep it hidden from Sophia. It would be a foolish mistake if they let him speak freely to her without warning.

But he still put the pieces in place. All with a silly nickname, he told her exactly what she was the moment she stepped into his bedroom. The night she heard him play.

At this moment Sophia had no idea what to do with her hands. She wanted to reach out and grip his shirt and pull him into another passionate kiss, but she felt like that was the last thing Xavier needed. A distraction from the pain infecting his heart.

Sophia was becoming increasingly aware of every slight movement of his fingers around her waist. "I-I..." she stammered, mentally kicking herself for coming across as childish. "I want to know more about you."

"You do not need to know," he muttered, brushing his lips across the scars on her cheek.

"Tell me anyway." she sighed, refusing to give into his touch.

He scoffed. "You're very persistent." his smile lowered. "What would you like to know?"

"Are your parents as sarcastic as you?"

When his face hardened, and there wasn't even a ghost of a smile on his lips, it was made clear that his family was the source of his pain.

What had happened to them?

"I don't want to talk about them."

"Have you ever loved?" Sophia moved onto a subject she wasn't so sure she wanted to hear the answer to.

Xavier dropped his hands from her waist and took a step back, putting a wide gap between them. She could feel herself breathe again.

"Why do you ask?"

"Curiosity."

His eyebrows furrowed together and he was looking everywhere but at Sophia.

A rush of jealousy filled Sophia as it was clear someone in his past broke his heart. She couldn't help but imagine Xavier intimate with a woman much more beautiful than herself, with his hands tangled up in hers. She imagined she would have no signs of scars on her face and radiated confidence. She pictured her with golden hair which reflects the sun and her eyes to be as blue as the clearest oceans. She pictured him happy and smiling. With someone he felt confident enough to share all of his secrets with.

"What happened to her?"

"I never answered your question," Xavier huffed. "Do you enjoy making assumptions about other people?"

"I want you to have confidence in me," the tears warmed her eyes. "I want to take whatever burdens you face and throw them into the lake."

"Sophia!" he yelled in frustration. "What would be the point in that? If I give a large piece of myself to you, only to watch you throw your own life away by marrying a man you're not in love with? How does that make any sense?"

She bit the corner of her cheek and dropped her gaze. It sent a pinch to her heart when she saw the look of anger on Xavier's face.

He was right. What right did she have to take away any burdens, when she herself couldn't even deal with her own. But she cared about him so deeply that she wanted to be there for him. "I'm sorry, I was only-"

A rush of panic fueled her lungs. Everything in her life had truly fallen apart. She pushed herself off the tree, hoisted up her skirt and dashed deeper into the unknown forest. Running so fast that she couldn't even see where she was going.

Nothing had gone right for her ever since she stepped foot into Lord Paine's office. No, nothing went right since she first arrived at the orphanage. Her life was full of nothing but loneliness and disappointment. Even the one person she called a true friend was anything but that. All those years he wanted something more, wanted her as his wife. Now she had met a man, who captivated her heart and mind and there was no possibility of them having a life together.

If only she had rejected Jack's original proposal. If only she put it off, and she could have let him down easily. Then it would have been less complicated. There would be less time wasted, less feelings hurt. But it was too late. Whenever she tried to fix her life she only seemed to make matters worse.

Suddenly, her foot caught under a raised branch. Causing her to fly forward through the trees, and eventually landing on a leaf covered ground. Her arms were stretched out in front of her, and she couldn't bring herself to raise her head. Sophia was severely out of breath, only then did she realise just how far she must have run to be this winded.

The scar on her forehead was throbbing and she feared she may have opened up the wound.

The ground suddenly began shaking at her feet, like the entire earth was quaking beneath her fingers. Sophia wasn't sure if she was hallucinating or if this was actually happening.

The vibration was shortly met with a stomping sound, and it was getting louder and louder. It was like someone had picked up every tree in this forest and shook out their leaves.

Then, everything stopped. Everything went silent. The stomping, the quaking earth. Silent.

"This is very interesting," a voice hissed from close by. It was as if a snake had managed to find the ability to speak. Each 'S' was dragged out in such a sinister way that it sent a chill down Sophia's spine.

"It's not very often food comes to my door, usually I am the one looking for it." he chuckled.

Somehow, Sophia managed to conjure the strength to lift her head. When she got an eyeful of who - or what - was standing in front of her, she was sure she had fallen into a dream. A very realistic, bizzare dream.

Fur covered, bear-like feet stopped in Sophia's view as the creature shifted his weight to examine its prey.

Sophia bawled her hands into weak fists and she tried to force herself to get up. It was like her body was rejecting her, not allowing the numb feeling to thaw. Mud stained her face and tangled in her hair as her lifeless eyes looked around. She was confident that the creature thought she was dead.

The creature dropped to his knees and she had to repress a scream when she saw his face. It was not of a man but of a serpent. He flicked out his tongue every couple of seconds as it danced quickly in front of her. Its eyes were an unnatural shade of green, with black slits for pupils.

If he were only a few inches taller, he would be taller than the trees in this forest.

This was the last way she expected to die. In the hands - or claws - of a monster. Sophia should have fought harder with her body to get up and flee. Even if she managed to get to her feet, in one step he could easily catch her.

She maintained eye contact as the monster opened its mouth wide, revealing the rubber tongue drenching its mouth with saliva. Fangs larger than the population of rats in London, sank down ready to engulf her in one big bite. She closed her eyes waiting for her demise, until a loud screech bled in her ears.

Suddenly the monster cowered back, as if it was suddenly hit with a blinding pain. When Sophia's eyes found the monster again, a large black hole had burned into his chest. As though the sun had been brought down to be directly aimed at the creature's chest.

The monster was wounded, but he still stood.

A firm hand gripped around Sophia's frozen arm as she was dragged up to her feet.

It was Jack, he held her up with his free arm and only when she huddled close to his chest did she see that his other hand was glowing. Much like the golden light that surrounded his entire body that night in the infermany.

Had Jack caused such damage to the monster with only his hand?

Sophia didn't know what to do. All she could do was watch as the creature regained his footing, drops of blood now spilling from its mouth. "If it isn't the little warrior of God." the creatures' eyes changed to a black liquid and were targeting Jack.

The creature's gaze shifted behind the pair, and a hiss of approval danced around his tongue. "Now he's my kind of person, a fellow demon."

Xavier emerged behind Jack, with a casual stride in his step. As though this was nothing more than a cheap show at the circus.

Xavier shifted his weight and let out an annoyed sigh. Like he was just disturbed from a peaceful sleep. "I wouldn't label myself a demon. I am far too sophisticated for that."

The demon looked confused. "You're siding with *him*?"

He shrugged modestly. "I wouldn't say siding, I'd call it protecting my prey."

When Xavier spoke about Sophia being his prey she felt Jack's hand tense around her waist. The world was spinning at her feet and she could feel herself spinning with it.

The demon hissed. "You are in my home, she stumbled down here so I have every right to catch whatever human steps here."

Sophia clung onto Jack's shirt like a frightened kitten. She was so confused as to what was going on.

"That would be a shame, but I'm afraid you're out of luck." Xavier mused. "For she is not fully human. You could even call her a fellow demon if you were brave."

Demon?

"Leave this woman," Jack demanded.

The demon hissed. "Demon or not. You are trespassing in my home, what's mine is mine."

"Leave her," Jack persisted. "And I will spare you. You know I can cast any demon to Hell if I wish."

Xavier suddenly went stiff at Jack's words.

"What makes you think I am not already going there?" the monster crooned.

Jack glanced at Xavier with a menacing look on his face. Xavier mirrored his gaze with a raised eyebrow.

"Did I ever tell you what happens when one demon bites another demon?" Xavier mused.

Was this a dream? The way Jack and Xavier regarded one another in this moment was like two old school friends. Maybe it was all of the adrenalin from this unusual moment.

"No, I don't believe you have." Jack replied.

"Well, the blood acts as a sort of poison if too much is exchanged from one to the other" Xavier looked over to the monster. "I could show you the trick, unless...he is willing to step away."

The creature chuckled. "You really think you weak little boys could stop me?"

"Are you rejecting my offer of walking away?"

When the demon gave no reply, Xavier knew his answer. He bowed over, as if ready to start a duel. "As you wish."

Before Sophia even knew what was going on, Jack gripped her wrist and ran with her behind a tall oak tree. Shortly after releasing his hold, Jack ran back to Xaveir's side.

Sophia just stood and hid behind the tree, in a state of show and awe at the two men that despise one another, now working together to take down a creature from a fairytale. It was a small ray of hope that perhaps they could one day get along. Yet, that would be far into the future.

"Mr Green, would you care to lend me a hand?"

"It would be my pleasure."

After a beat Jack, the glow dancing across Jack's hand had now illuminated brighter than the sun. His hand disappeared in a ball of light, and before the creature had time to react, Jack shot a ray of light from his hand. It seemed to take a toll on him, this ability that Sophia had never seen before. For each shot of light made the demon stumble back, whilst also bringing Jack to his knees.

With the monster now blinded by the intense light, this gave Xavier his opportunity to leap into the air, higher than any man could jump, and land on the wiggling neck of the serpent. The demon didn't look as if it was putting up much of a fight. It tried its best to shake it's spindly neck, to force Xavier off but his grip was too strong.

Jack released one last ball of light to the creature's chest, causing it to collapse down to the ground with the help of Xavier.

Xavier quickly knelt to the ground and Sophia witnessed his fangs slide out of his mouth. He rolled up the sleeve to his coat and bit into his own arm, with his blood staining his teeth he then bit into the demon. It shrieked an ungodly sound which made Sophia press her hands to her ears.

When satisfied he was dead, both boys got to their feet with their chests heaving up and down trying to catch their breaths.

"Well," Xavier began. "This was unexpected." His eyes shot up to meet Sophia who was shaking in fear. "It looks as if you owe us men your life. A couple hundred pounds should do it."

She was too frightened to think of anything to say.

Xavier wiped his mouth over his sleeve, and spat out any excess blood staining his mouth. "Nothing worse than the taste of demon blood."

Jack said nothing, as he hunched over with his palms pressed into his lower thighs, trying to regain his breath.

At the same time, the two men both stepped forward to find Sophia and ensure she was all right. Her eyes averted to the demon and noticed that there was some movement coming from him. Her voice was still weak and she couldn't bring herself to even move.

Suddenly the demon was on his feet and running straight towards her. Xavier and Jack didn't react quick enough, the demon threw them aside like they were balls of paper.

Xavier's back slammed right against a tree and left him nearly unconscious.

When Jack fell he simply rolled and wasn't as badly injured.

This was it.

Sophia was ready to accept her fate. She closed her eyes and waited for her death to come.

When suddenly a bright, blinding blue light flashed across the entire forest coming from an unknown location. Seconds, even minutes ticked by she wondered if the death was painful at all. Since she was still standing without anything as much as grazing her skin.

When she slowly opened her eyes and expected to see the gates of Heaven, instead she was still in the forest, alive and well.

When the blue light disappeared, so did the demon as if he was never there in the first place.

It was only when she looked to where the creature was once standing, stood an unfamiliar man holding a crystal-like shape toward the sky. There was something about him that made Sophia want to run to him, and wrap her arms around him.

His hair was a dark shade of brown with slits of grey above his ears. His face was that of a handsome gentleman one could find blending in at a politician's meeting. The man was slender in build, with long pale fingers.

When he lowered the crystal he used to banish the demon, Sophia stared at his elegant movements as none of what just happened seemed unusual to him. The stranger released a breath and looked around the chaotic sight, and that's when Sophia met this man's eyes. He held the same green eyes as her own, and a face she was certain she had seen once before, only now he was older.

The crystal in his hand was letting off a luminous glow, as powering down.

The stranger shoved the crystal into his breast pocket, like it was nothing more than a quill.

The man glanced over at Sophia, and he lingered there for an uncomfortable amount of time. There was no doubt there was a recognition between the two. The way he looked at her just now was no coincidence.

Then he ripped his gaze away to the two boys lying on the ground. He walked to Jack first and pulled him to his feet by the scruff of his shirt. "Don't you know not to mess with a demon that powerful?" he shoved him hard so Jack stumbled back a few steps.

The stranger then headed to Xavier and did the same to him. Blood was still staining his mouth and his eyes were rolling back. "You of all creatures should have known better. You should have known he wouldn't go down that easily."

This man knew a lot about creatures. Sophia assumed it was other creatures that knew of one another, but if this man was who Sophia thought he was, he had to be human.

Xavier half smiled, stumbling on his feet like he was intoxicated. "I wanted to show off my brute strength to have that lovely lady swooning."

Sophia watched the stranger carefully. She tried her hardest to remember but her mind was blocking her from doing so.

"What was that?" Jack asked, as he limped over to meet this stranger.

He pulled the crystal back out from his pocket? "This?" he looked down on it. "Believe it or not this is much stronger than any mere power you hold in your own angelic hand. It is a device which I created made of pure magic, energy and crystal."

"Magic?" Xavier scoffed. "Magic is nothing but fairydust."

The stranger looked over at him with a small glare, a glare that Sophia had shot to Xavier many times. "And vampires are from horror stories," he shrugged. "To anyone who has no knowledge of their existence, that is."

"You're an inventor." Jack said as a matter of fact, and cut their conversation short.

He nodded in agreement. "Yes, it has taken me ten years to get it perfect. I could even rival God with this power." he tossed it in the air and caught it in his hand, like it was a mere stone. "No offence." he offered Jack, but he didn't seem fazed by it.

"Let's see how powerful this thing is then." Xavier reached for the crystal but the stranger pulled it away swiftly.

"Sorry," he smiled. "Created to only be used by me. I can't risk certain people getting a hold of this and selling it on. That's what my other inventions are for."

Sophia was slightly taken aback that she was leaning her weight against a tree, struggling to breathe as the three men were happily chatting away about a tiny crystal. "If I could interrupt." Sophia finally found her voice.

All three men turned around, yet the stranger kept his gaze to the ground. It was as though he couldn't bring himself to look at her again, but so naturally met Xavier and Jack's gaze.

Xavier pressed his finger to his lips, "Hush, men are speaking."

Sophia crinkled up her nose and pushed herself away from the tree.

She stormed over to the stranger and reached out her hand in an offer of a handshake. "I wish to show my appreciation for you saving my life."

The stranger simply stared at her hand. Eventually he reached over and accepted, still not looking at her.

"What is your name?" she demanded.

It took him a moment. "Christopher."

When he spoke his name a flash entered her mind. It was Sophia as a child, in an unfamiliar room, she was lying on her stomach with a colouring pencil in her hand. She was poorly drawing a white pony with a bushy tail. She remembered feeling full of excitement to show someone, but then the memory abruptly was snatched out of her mind, like it never existed in the first place.

The silence filled the forest, as Jack and Xavier realised what Sophia was thinking.

"We got into a carriage accent yesterday, not far from here." Jack said, suspicion lacing his voice. "Do you know where it has landed us?"

"Well, currently you are standing in my front garden." Christopher said. "So, you are in Derbyshire. If you crashed near here I can only imagine it is another one of these demons that caught the scent of a human travelling alongside you, and tried to have his dinner."

"How have you known demons are here," Xavier asked, folding his arms over his chest.

Christopher oddly smirked at the question, like he was in on some sort of joke. "I can't give away all of my secrets to strangers, now can I?"

Jack visibly didn't like this answer, but he decided to let it go for now. As all three of them knew exactly who this man was.

"Thank you," Sophia could feel the years of tears clawing their way up her throat. This man was her father, she was sure of it. In looks alone she couldn't be more certain. "For saving us."

"Don't give him all of the glory," Xavier stepped in. "I bit my arm to kill that creature, now I am no longer a sight for perfection..." he looked down at his pale arm now with a wound.

"That little trick works on lesser demons. That one would have only been wounded for a short period of time before regaining his strength. Far too powerful to be defeated by something so insignificant."

"I don't tend to take advice from people who aren't demons," said Xavier.

"Fine by me, next time you're up against something like that, don't expect me to rescue you." Christopher said, with a playfulness in his tone.

"How did you know we were in some form of trouble?" asked Jack, clearly trying to dig for information. To justify his scepticism.

"I was just taking a stroll, and the crystal changes from white to blue whenever it senses a demon." he held it out in front of Xavier and the crystal was still a light shade of blue.

Sophia too was sceptical of his answer. Although Christopher had mentioned this was his 'front garden' why would he carry around a crystal that so easily banishes demons? Unless, there truly was more than one demon lurking around this forest.

"It's a shame it doesn't wipe out *all* demons present." Jack said, snidely.

"Sadly no," Christopher scoffed. "It is designed to defeat one type of demon at a time." he dropped his hand on Xavier's shoulder. "You're lucky, my friend."

"Where are you staying?" Christopher swiftly changed the subject.

The three of them stole glances between one another. Trying to work out the best answer to give.

But it was Sophia who spoke up, "Actually," she nervously tucked a strand of her brunette curls behind her ear. "We were actually on our way to meet a scientist. Would you happen to be Christopher...Cole?"

Please say yes, Sophia pleaded internally. *Please tell me that all of my years of searching for meaning are coming to fruition.*

"Yes," Christopher answered, and he finally looked up at Sophia. That recognition was back, and his eyes trailed over the scars on her cheek. Then Christpher swallowed hard, and Sophia was sure a sudden glimpse of guilt washed over his face. "And you're Sophia?"

He didn't say her last name, as if he didn't want to go into detail of their similarities.

"I am."

The air was still filled with an awkward silence, and now the tension was so thick that it could be cut through with a knife. "Well...I was expecting you. Please, follow me and I will be happy to have you three as my guests."

As the three composed themselves and trailed behind Christoper to his house, Jack said what they were thinking. "Isn't all of this very...*convenient.*"

"I must warn you," Christopher called over his shoulder as he was quite a distance ahead of everyone. "I am having a ball tomorrow night at my manor for business purposes. You are more than welcome to join. After everything you have been through it looks like you could have a night to relax and have a good time."

"Very convenient," Xavier muttered to the group.

Chapter Twenty

Christopher didn't live in a regular house, it was a mansion. Well, a mansion was an understatement, it was more of a castle. He tried to downplay it when they arrived but all three of them stood in awe with their mouths gaping open. Sophia certainly didn't feel welcome with her tattered dress, and bloodsoaked forehead.

It was secluded in the back of the forest, not a sign of life anywhere. Christopher mentioned he was having a ball tomorrow night, how would anyone be able to find this place?

The brick walls were painted a pure white, with a vast drive. There was even a miniature fountain upon the walkway. There were a few potted plants that just blended into the extravagance.

Inside was far more luxurious. Everything about this place had the same elegance of the orphanage, only it was a lot brighter and bigger.

Christopher showed each of them to their separate rooms. Sophia was last to be shown her room, and a wave of unexpected nostalgia hit her chest. Digging through her memory she couldn't remember standing in this room, she had never left the orphanage for more than a few hours before. But there was something about this powder blue wallpaper with a herron pattern that felt familiar to her.

Not much stuck out to her. The double bed at the centre of the room was just that, a bed. The furniture, wardrobe, desk, and vanity did not give her the same feeling. But something about this wallpaper, the shape of this wide room made her feel emotional.

She had to know. Sophia couldn't hold it in anymore, otherwise she might burst. "Christopher-"

When she turned around she realised he wasn't there. She was left alone without another word.

Why did he seem to avoid her? Did he truly not know she was his daughter? After so many years, he still couldn't stand to be around her.

Back in the forest it seemed to pain him to look at her.

But why?

Words could not describe how refreshed Sophia felt after having a long hot bath and a good night's rest.

The three of them had breakfast brought to their rooms by one of Christopher's servants.

Sophia kept to herself most of the day, trying to come up with exactly how she would approach Christopher. She considered outright telling him who she was. Yet, she thought that might be foolish, and a bit overwhelming. So, she decided to try and have a civil conversation with him, and find out more about him. His interests and his life. Then she would hopefully find the perfect moment to tell him he was her father.

Tonight would be the perfect opportunity. Balls were ideal for socializing. Guests had already arrived from each corner of the UK.

Sophia was still getting ready in her room, with the help of one of Christopher's servants. She was quiet, like Stella. But unlike Stella, this maid seemed to be focused on getting the job done as quickly as possible. Sophia certainly didn't feel a desire to open up a conversation with her.

Christopher had an array of dresses, but there was no woman who seemed to take residence in this place. Perhaps he just kept them for emergencies, like tonight. He did seem like the type to have parties every other day, so maybe these dresses were spares for guests who might get a bit too tipsy.

The ballgown he gave to Sophia was beautiful. It was a silk orchid colour, tucked in at her waist allowing her curves to be shown off. Whilst the skirt of the gown exploded with a gorgeous layered mesh, she felt like a princess. It was more of a revealing dress that she was used to, it showed off a small amount of cleavage, accompanied by elegant cut off shoulders.

When she stole a glance at her reflection she took in more of the details. Her breasts swelled from the square rim. Her brunette curls cascaded down her left shoulder, and small strands of hair tickled her rosy cheeks.

Sophia couldn't help but blush, as she felt a rare confidence about her appearance. Even with the scars, she felt beautiful.

It was wrong that she was looking forward to seeing Xavier's reaction to her attire. For neither him or Jack have seen her so made up. She never had a reason to before. Cassandra never once hosted any sort of party, therefore there would be no reason to look nice.

A breeze rolled in from the open window, causing a shudder to trickle down her back.

Once the servant left, Sophia took another look at her reflection. She traced the scars on her face with the tips of her fingers. There was not enough makeup to cover up such harsh slashes, not if she wanted to look like a clown at least.

There was a gentle tap on the door.

It was Jack.

Upon entering he was taken aback by her radiance and couldn't control the gasp which escaped past his lips. "I've never seen you so made up," he smiled. He was in a dark green suit accompanied with a new sleek black cane.

Christopher really had everything covered.

Jack's hair was neatly combed to one side, making his bright coloured eyes pop. It gave them more of a sparkle than usual, which Sophia never thought possible.

Once he realised they were alone, Sophia's cheeks flushed and she looked to the ground out of embarrassment. "I've never had such a beautiful dress."

He stepped into the room and reached into his pocket. "I have something for you," he pulled out the locket which he'd bought for her many years ago and brushed his thumb across it. "I picked it up before we left home. Would you wear it?"

Without hesitation, she nodded; she felt it was the least she could do. She turned to the mirror and watched him slide into the reflection. Jack draped the chain around her slim neck and clasped it into place. It naturally lay flat on her chest. She watched his every movement in the mirror, and realised that the happiness she once felt when she saw him was replaced with guilt.

When he finished clasping the necklace he ran his fingers through her brunette curls. As if by instinct, she rested the back of her head against his chest.

It hit her like a ton of bricks in this moment, when she realised just how much she missed the relationship she once had with him. How they would laugh at the silliest of things, their days reading under the willow tree and the strong bond of trust they once shared.

Jack's fingers slipped down to her arms, leaving a trail of goosebumps in his wake.

"You're so beautiful." he muttered with a pained expression on his face.

Dropping his gaze, she couldn't bring herself to look at him. "I do not deserve your kind words."

"We will have to find another church to get married," he ignored her. "For it doesn't look like we will make it back in time for your birthday." he watched her sad expression drop lower as each second ticked by. "I want you to open your heart to me," his fingers danced lightly across her skin. "Instead of you insisting that you do not love me. If you were more accepting ... you could grow to love me."

This caught her attention, causing her to snap up her gaze and meet his eyes again in the mirror. "You should be grateful I am not in love with you, for I cannot turn you to stone."

"To have the love of my life as my wife is all I could ever ask for." his eyes were focused intently on hers, like he was looking right through her. "To have her love me in return is everything I could ever want, regardless of the dangers." He pressed his lips against the back of her head. "You're worth all of that to me."

Jack had left without Sophia, she claimed to not be fully ready although there wasn't anything she could add to her attire without it appearing as too much.

In all honesty, she just needed time to compose her thoughts. Each time she spent time alone with Jack, it was as if he poured a bucket full of guilt over her shoulders, completely drentching her. It wasn't intentional, of course, but it made her dread seeing him, which in turn caused more guilt to shadow her.

Sophia finally mustered the courage to leave her room, and as if fate was teasing her, Xavier was down the hall, also exiting his room. He seemed to be struggling to button up the sleeve of his shirt under his black dress coat.

It was wrong for the amount of joy and warmth that filled her body when she saw him, how she wanted to run to him and wrap her arms around his smooth neck.

It would be rude for her to turn her back and walk away from him, and she'd be lying to herself if she wasn't interested in what he thought of how she looked.

Clutching her hands in front of her skirt, she took slow steps to him, not taking her eyes off his profile. Her heels clapped against the wooden floor and she was surprised that he hadn't noticed her coming.

As she approached, she dipped her head to find his eyes, "Xavier?" she said, innocently.

Surprised, Xavier snapped up his head with his dark eyes wide. When he took in Sophia's dolled up appearance his lips slightly parted and she could have sworn she saw his breath hitch.

Sophia couldn't fight her pleased smile. She dropped her head to look down at her extravagant gown, "It's lovely, isn't it? It was so kind of Christopher to lend me such a dress for tonight." she looked up to meet his eyes, his expression hadn't moved, like he was in a state of shock. "Arriving in ripped and dirty clothes wouldn't exactly be appropriate for a ball."

It was then she noticed that Xavier had been given new clothes also, a fresh formal attire that consisted of his signature colours of black and white. With a daring grey waistcoat buttoned up at his torso.

To her surprise, he didn't say anything. Instead, he dropped his head and walked away.

Sophia stood wondering what she had said wrong. Was her dress too revealing? Had she somehow offended him in such a short time?

The room was filled with idle chatter and an orchestra playing beautifully, making the atmosphere much calmer.

Sophia stood alone looking in on the party from the corner. She wasn't sure what to do with herself, since Xavier was nowhere to be seen and Jack had been dragged off by a beautiful young woman. She seemed to captivate Jack's attention and he didn't glance back at Sophia to check her wellbeing.

Not that she minded, she could see him knocking his head back and laughing. Sophia was glad to see him happy.

Every guest clearly came from money, just their clothes were a sign of high class.

"You might have your man stolen away tonight," Christopher was suddenly beside Sophia, with a glass of brandy on the rocks in his hand. His eyes were on the beautiful young woman sinking her claws into Jack. Her face was sculpted out of the finest of marble. Her snug gown hugged at her legs, which left very little to the imagination.

"You see that woman?" Christopher pointed to the woman with Jack. "She is a Siren, she can lure a man by just the sound of her voice."

She looked over at Christopher with a panicked expression.

He simply chuckled. "Do not worry, the worst she will do is take him to her chambers. I know her too well, she is just looking for fun."

Sophia frowned. "Jack would never do anything so foolish." The thought of her best friend being intimate with a woman he just met, sent a pain through her heart. She knew she had no right in questioning what he did with his life but she knew his character. She felt like too much was changing and it was overwhelming.

"You don't seem to be having fun." Christopher said it was more of a statement than a question.

Sophia dropped her shoulders, and dared to look up to him. The words were always lost when she met Christopher's gaze. So much she wanted to say - to ask - but she couldn't. She was too afraid of what his reaction might be. She had been rejected from everyone in her life, but she wasn't so sure she could handle it from her father.

"May I ask you a question?" Christopher asked, looking down at his glass and pretending to be interested in swirling around the brown liquid.

"Of course!" Sophia said, a bit too passionately.

"Your name is Sophia Cole, yes?"

She swallowed down her anticipation, "Yes."

Christopher still didn't raise his head. His eyebrows furrowed together, internally debating what he was going to say next. Whatever it was, Sophia wanted to shake him to spill out whatever he wanted to say. "Can't be much of a coincidence, can it?"

When his matching green eyes met her own, there was a softness in his eyes. A sincere look of longing but also sadness.

"You look just like your mother."

Sophia's heart swelled to an uncomfortable size, it was too big for her ribs to contain. Her mind went blank as she stared at him. The tears were outlining her eyes now, but she was smiling at the same time.

All of the years she felt lost, seemed like a waste. For her father was but a carriage ride away.

The questions she had compiled vanished from her head, she was too focused on not collapsing. But her body seemed to act on its own accord. She slammed herself into his chest, with such force that Christopher actually stumbled back a few steps.

Before returning her embrace he placed his glass down on the table, and wrapped one arm around her back and his other hand cradling the back of her head.

The rest of the party seemed to vanish, as Sophia held on tight to her father. It was everything she ever dreamed of and more. He seemed to need this just as much as she did. How could Cassandra keep family members apart for so many years? Just because he was human.

The pain seemed unjustified for her reasonings.

They stepped out of their embrace, and Christopher brought both of his hands to her cheeks and took in the sight of his daughter with a smile of disbelief. "I have missed you, my darling Sophia." Christopher heard a crash coming from the opposite side of the room, and two aristiracts had launched into a drunken screaming match of nonsense.

When Christopher dropped his hands, he released a tired sigh. "I must see this, but we will catch up later."

Sophia gave a tight smile as she fought with every fibre of her being not to cry.

It was fast approaching her birthday. Less than a week away now. That had to be the first thing she asked her father, why he would agree to her marrying with such an unfair time limit. If there was a way she could get out of this, it made her angry that all of the hurt and broken relationships would have resulted in nothing.

Jack had excused himself from the ballroom, and the Siren was also nowhere in sight. Sophia wasn't stupid, she knew exactly what he was doing. If she was being completely honest, she was happy that he had managed to find himself a girl who wanted to share in that side of a relationship, for Sophia could never imagine giving herself to Jack like that.

Sophia stood awkwardly in the corner of the room, practically blending into the walls. She had nothing in common with any of Christopher's guests, why would she? They were all ridiculously rich, and she had no money to her name. Even her savings would be worthless to these people.

How could she stand still after what had just happened?

She needed to take a walk. Even if it was around the building, she didn't care. Sophia needed to take in everything that had happened, not only tonight but these past few months.

Sophia decided to leave, but she wasn't ready to return to her room. Instead she gave herself a tour of Christopher's home. It was bizarre to think that this could have also been her home growing up. If she was permitted to stay with her father, all of these halls and rooms would be free for her.

She was surprised at the amount of artwork that filled the walls and rooms; there were never less than two pieces in a room. The paintings were gorgeous, and each unique from the last. Some landscapes and others portraits.

But one painting in particular caught the eye of Sophia out of all the rest. It was less perfected, more amateurish. A set of three stood out in the upstairs lounging area. One was of a small white jack russell holding a large stick, another of a beautiful lake that had a rainbow sky, and the third was - what appeared to be - a portrait of Christopher. It was certainly a beginners painting, as it didn't resemble anything she would imagine someone paying for.

As she looked closer, she noticed thin white initials painted in each corner of the three paintings.

T.C

The same initials as her mother.

Could these really be the paintings of her mother? These couldn't be paintings that he had picked up at a market, as all other pieces of art were extravagant and perfect down to the last stroke.

Sophia should have felt more joy, but she felt sick and lightheaded.

It only seemed to solidify all the years in the orphanage, thinking she was abandoned and alone, was a waste. Was she ripped away from her father without even a care of what she wanted? Because she was a creature and had to be locked away?

Sophia made it back to her bedroom without passing out, in the corner of her eye she noticed Xavier's door was wide open. It was then she realised that he never did come down to the ballroom.

Against her better judgement, she stepped away from her door and visited Xavier's room. She wasn't sure why his door was wide open, as everything appeared to be perfectly placed, nothing seemed to be touched.

Sophia's eyes found a silhouette leaning his weight against the balcony. The light from the moon outlined his body with an illuminating glow. Her heart was beating in her ears knowing that it was Xavier. It suddenly became uncomfortable to breathe, and it wasn't because her dress was so tight, though she knew that that didn't help.

It was as though she was drawn to him, like a moth to a flame. She was walking towards him, and with each step a new set of nerves would kick in. Her hands were sweaty, her breath shook and warmth filled her eyes as she approached him.

Stepping through the arch, she could see him clearly. He had his back to her, the light breeze ruffled his hair to the left, revealing his soft pale neck. She almost wanted to laugh that he was dressed in all black, was he allergic to colour?

"Xavier?" she called, in a timid voice.

He didn't turn around, almost as if he wasn't surprised she was there. Instead, he dropped his head between his shoulders. He had been acting odd ever since he saw her in her dress, had it offended him somehow?

Sophia stepped beside him, and he immediately turned his head away from her, as if he couldn't even look at her. What had she done to cause this reaction?

It took a lot of will for her not to cry. Jack was upset with her, and she wasn't confident that she could fix what they once had, and now Xavier?

"When we return to London, I will be leaving."

The glass wall around her heart had been dropped, completely shattering the piece of hope she had. "What?"

Finally he said, "It's starting to become overwhelming." Xavier turned his head so she could see the profile of his face. His lips were anchored down and his eyebrows were slightly arched. She had never expected to witness such a sad expression from Xavier, a man who prided himself in being unfazed by such serious events, now looking like he was attending a funeral.

"What is?" Sophia inched forward, eager for an answer.

Xavier shook his head, and tilted his head towards the stars. It was then that she noticed he was breathing heavily. Was he aching as much as she was?

"Simply being around you," Xavier replied. "I cannot watch you marry him. Start a life with him. I cannot do it, and please do not ask me to."

Sophia opened her mouth, but she couldn't find the words. Instead she said the first thing that came to her mind, "I'm sorry."

Xavier only laughed, "There you go again, apologising for other people's feelings. Doesn't it get tiring?"

"What else can I say?" her fists clenched at her sides, the tears were beginning to form. "No matter what I say it won't make you feel any better. Even that wasn't enough to get you to simply look at me!"

Xavier then looked at her, his face solemn.

Sophia suddenly felt naked, like all of her clothes had turned to ash, revealing her vulnerability. To hide her watery eyes, she buried her face into his shoulder and gripped her fingers onto the material of his jacket. "I don't understand why you tease me," she quivered, breathing in his scent as she buried her face deeper into his arm. "You push me and push me until you feel like I am going to break. How can you be so cruel as to kiss me and now you tell me you wish to leave? Was that just to confuse my heart and you could then have fun at my expense?" she wanted nothing more than to pull his face to hers and kiss him like the world would end. She wanted that electrifying feeling against her fingers, and it looked as though he might give it to her.

Xavier turned his whole body so he was now fully facing her.

Before she could meet his eyes, his hand cupped lightly around her scarred cheek and he brushed his thumb across her skin.

She looked up with wide green eyes instantly lost in the pools of black.

"You truly think that it is you who is about to break?" His voice was low, coated with a deep rasp. "I find myself falling for you, Sophia. Look at you," a sad smile pricked his lips as his eyes danced across her face, causing her to blush. "How beautiful you are. I cannot tell you how much I ached when you approached me earlier, looking like you do. I wanted nothing more than to take you into my arms and kiss you without consequence."

"I find myself falling for you," he continued, pressing his forehead hard against hers, closing his eyes. This was difficult for him to admit, clearly. "You tease me just as much as I do you. I love your reactions to my playful words, and to know that you would never say anything to harm anyone. It is always amusing to see as you attempt to conjure a response to me. You fill me with a joy that I thought had vanished years ago."

He was so close, just like at the lake and he continued to itch forward. His warm breath tangled with hers and Sophia suddenly felt conscious that she was breathing too loud.

"Xavier-"

"Please," he sighed, his breath shaking as his hand circled around her waist. He raised his head, and Sophia suddenly felt disappointed that he didn't kiss her. "Please don't say anything that could break my heart."

Sophia reached up and lay her hand flat over his heart. They always seemed to be in perfect rhythm with one another.

Were his words the truth? Or was this one big game? She was slightly reluctant in allowing her heart to give in entirely for she feared he would break it. Yet, she could no longer deny the yearning desire to be held by him, to kiss him...to have a life with him.

"And when I hear Jack..." he continued, with a poison in his tone. "Claiming you as his wife, like you are some insignificant prize...it makes me want to rip his eyes out."

"I am sure he feels the same way about you."

"No, he doesn't because I-" he bit back, like he had to consider what he was about to say was worth it.

Sophia had to know, he was already so open with her, what was the point in stopping now?

"You...what?" she whispered.

His back straightened as he looked down on her through his thick black lashes. His black eyes were intently locked on hers, like what he was about to say was the most serious thing he would ever admit. "Because I actually love you." he started shaking his head. "The way he treats you is not love. Begging you to be his is not something you do to someone you claim to love. You should accept their decision no matter what. I would do that for you. If I believed you truly loved Jack, I would not be here with you right now. I would have escaped the orphanage the minute I had the chance." Xavier let out an unamused laugh. "And believe me, I had many chances."

Because I actually love you.

I actually love you.

It was the sweetest thing she had heard in her life. Xavier loved her, and by his confession she knew he was serious.

Sophia swallowed the lump rising in her throat. "You stayed because of me?"

He didn't answer because it was obvious, and she wasn't entirely sure why she asked, but she felt like she needed the clarity. Somehow his silence was the clarity she needed.

"Sophia," he said, taking a step back so he could hold both of her hands. "I know you need to be married in three days.. I know that -"

That sent a sharp pain through her heart, how could she forget?

"What I need to know is," not once did his eyes waver from hers. "Could you see yourself falling in love with Jack?"

In her mind she immediately answered, but saying it outloud was oddly painful. Although Jack wasn't here she knew it would hurt him. She shook her head, "No."

"Could you see yourself falling in love with me?"

Her face was suddenly hot, burning even. Was what she had felt towards him love? No, she was certain she'd known if she had fallen in love with him. Xavier just admitted he loved her, and from her understanding, once she fell for him and their eyes locked he would turn to stone.

This terrified her, because she knew she was falling fast for him and what control do people have when they fall in love?

There must be an indication, otherwise how would people know exactly when to say it? But what he said didn't sound ridiculous, and she knew in her heart that she didn't want to be away from him any longer, so her answer was. "Yes."

Xavier didn't hide his relief as he smiled, a genuine smile that sent her heart into a flutter. He brought up one of her hands to his lips, and he grazed a kiss across her knuckles. "Sophia," he muttered against her skin. "Marry me."

Chapter Twenty-One

"Hannah, will you please just go back to your room?" Robert was growing tired since it was close to midnight and he required sleep.

Hannah was in the dining room, with sweat dripping from her body causing a small puddle to trail behind her. She was draped in a ratty blanket and pacing around the room, mumbling something to herself.

"Do you not know what the night is?" She sounded as if she was talking to herself.

"Yes," Robert huffed. "It is a full moon which is exactly why you need to go back to your room."

The moon was close to being in the centre of the sky, and that was when the change would happen.

Shooting daggers with bared fangs, Hannah stood her ground with a frantic look on her face. "To be locked up like a prisoner? Why is it me? Why do I have to suffer? What makes you so special that you can control yourself?"

"Please, Hannah we have talked about this before-"

"Because I was deprived of oxygen when I was born is not a reason!" she screamed.

Storming over, with her footpath leaving a trail of fire, Hannah curled her upper lip and began growling like a dog. Robert could see the animal was ready to break out of her. He wasn't sure if he was prepared for this, he was still sore from their previous encounter with a full moon. Fearing some old scars may reopen.

"Is it because you're a man and it makes you stronger than me? Tell me the real reason," she shoved him back, hard.

It pained him to see his twin in this state. Her eyes were bloodshot and the animal was soon to replace her. He tried everything he could to help her fight it. On the days that she was well, the days she was actually his sister, Robert would help train her anger by exercising and finding methods that could work for her.

So far nothing worked.

The only way she was kept from running a rampage amongst the orphanage was lining her room with silver. She had no furniture left for her to break in her wolf form. She would thrash herself around, and Robert would be in the room with her for as long as he could withstand.

Even in his wolf form she was far stronger than him, and Robert was certain he would die at the hands of his sister. As time went on he realised there was nothing he could do to prevent the beast in her heart.

"Tell me the truth, you coward!" she pushed and pushed until she was cowering on her knees. "You're a coward! Tell me why it is only I who gets in this state."

She was touching on a nerve. His twin and closest friend, the one he spent his entire orphan life protecting, was throwing insults at him. Pushing him away, it sent a pain in his chest. Sometimes he found it hard to control his own temper, and she certainly tested the wolf inside of him tonight.

"You coward!"

"Father tried to strangle you as a child!" he burst out. "He despised having a girl, he thought it showed him as weak. In doing so it caused you to repress power early on. It must have triggered a response to let loose on your power, and you never try to hold yourself back!"

Hannah's eyes welled with tears and she quickly turned to her common friend, anger. "You're lying!"

"You asked for the truth."

Hannah arched over, clutching her hands into her scalp. Her back arched as her dress began to rip in multiple places. Clumps of brown hair emerged out of her skin, and her muscles were swelling, no longer being held back by the flimsy material of her dress. Her fingernails grew twice the size and transformed into things sharper than butcher knives. A single swoop from one claw could tear down an entire wall without even breaking a sweat.

Hannah's cute button nose made a crunching sound, like it had just been broken in multiple different places, as it broke out into a long snout. Her ears were coated with fur, and stood sharp at either side of her head.

Standing before Robert was no longer his beautiful sister; instead it was a beast on hind legs.

A werewolf.

"Hannah, it is me, your brother." he tried to reason with her when he realised she was about to attack him. This technique never worked but he prayed that one day she could control it, and recognise that it was her brother standing before her.

Hannah knocked her beast body back and howled at the full moon, shattering the windows in the dining room with it's high pitched sound. Her eyes were hungry for blood and Robert was the only available victim. Releasing a throaty growl, with saliva hanging down from her bared fangs, Hannah began slowly prowling towards Robert.

He fell back after tripping over one of the chair legs. Robert was rarely frightened of Hannah, as he usually had the safety of the silver lining her bedroom walls to keep him safe. But now that she was here, out in the open with not even a plate of silver in sight, Robert was afraid.

Robert scrambled back onto the floor and headed straight for the door. He considered transforming himself and tackling her that way. But the years of trying to repress her, and fighting back with her every month had tired him out. He was too weak to even want to shift into his wolf form.

Why didn't she just listen to him? Tonight was the first night she was outside of her room when the sky was centred with a full moon.

Hannah could just as easily break down this door and kill everyone inside.

When Robert scrambled for the door he was surprised it opened for him. He didn't waste his breath as he bolted for the door in one quick leap.

On the other side was Albert. He reached in and grabbed Robert by the scruff of his shirt and assisted in dragging him out of the dining room.

When Albert slammed the door shut, he locked it. Not that that would do much good for their situation. Hannah was howling and already throwing her body at the door. Splinters of wood were flying from the door. All it would take was a few more attacks to the door for it to fully break down.

Cassandra, and for some reason Stella, were also present. Robert couldn't deal with any personal drama right now, as he avoided eye contact with Stella at all costs.

"You promised you would keep her under control," Albert shook him by his shirt. "People could get killed!"

"I have controlled her alone for years," Robert snapped back. "I slip up one time and suddenly I am completely wrong? Maybe if I had some help this would have been prevented."

Albert released his grip and glanced over at Stella, who simply bowed like she was taking a silent order from him. She too was avoiding Robert's gaze, after everything that had happened these past few weeks, she couldn't handle seeing his face.

"I hate to ask, Stella but we need a guard on this door...."

Stella only curtsied and shut her eyes. Channeling her power through her mind until her hand illuminated with a red energy. It seductively danced around the palms of her hand, kissing the tips of her fingers. Stretching out her arm, the red energy began to enclose around the door, and the entire wall.

Voices began whispering in her ear this time, telling her to consume her power. Embrace it, and take down this wretched building and all of the people who hurt her.

Before she could give in, she snatched the power back and pushed down the burning sensation that wanted so desperately to escape.

Robert was staring at Stella now, and as she composed herself and the red light had vanished from her hand. He noticed that a long patch of her golden hair now had a strip of red. It certainly wasn't there before, and when Stella looked around he noticed her once deep brown eyes were now the shade of blood red.

"That should be around the entire room," Stella said to the ground, feeling embarrassed. "There should be no way for her to escape. It will vanish by sunrise."

"Good," Albert took Cassandra's hand in his and squeezed it. Like he was ready for this to be the end, and needing some moral support.

Shortly after, Albert released Cassandra's hand and flared his nostrils. An anger boiled in his ears as he pointed an accusatory finger at Robert. "Do not let this happen again."

"Albert," Cassandra began. "You should not be so hard on Robert, he was just-"

"Endangering the lives of everyone in this orphanage," this was the loudest Robert had heard Albert yell, he was usually the calm one out of the couple.

Albert stormed away, leaving a trail of smoke behind.

Cassandra sighed. "I must apologise, he has a lot of stress. We do not blame you for this, but precautions must be discussed for the safety of everyone else who lives here."

Stella and Robert were now left alone.

Robert knew that the 'precaution' meant his sister's death. He gritted his teeth and punched the glowing wall. The second his knuckle made contact with the wall, it sent a burning fire up his entire arm. He retreated back and released an aggravated yell of agony, cupping his hand around his wrist to ease the pain. "Fuck, fuck, fuck!"

"Please stop," Stella said, timidly. "That wall is specifically to keep werewolves contained."

He raised a firm hand as if he had heard enough. "Do not tell me what to do," he snapped.

She bit the inside of her cheek. "I was simply thinking of your well being, *Sir.*"

"Shut up," he snarled.

These past few days Stella had sudden, unusual pains in her stomach. They were back now, and she felt a hot bile rising up her throat. She tried to fight it, but it was too late. Her body hunched over, and Stella threw up on the ground in front of them. If she had just walked a few inches closer she could have soaked Robert's shoes. Yes, she would be humiliated but it would be a form of revenge for his behaviour towards her.

"What is the matter with you?" he looked down at her in disgust.

As he started to walk away, Stella slowly rose and straightened her spine. Her red eyes fixed on the back of his neck as he walked in a smug stride.

How he can treat a woman like nothing more than a piece of dirt at the end of his shoe, just because she worked as a housemaid.

"I'm pregnant."

That made Robert pause. Stopping in his place, abruptly.

Instead of the look of sheer anger on his face like she expected, he looked over with wide eyes. Although Stella couldn't tell what he was thinking, there was no doubt that a rush of fear crept into his mind.

Stella lowered her head and regretted telling him the way that she did. It only made her decision become all the more difficult.

Chapter Twenty-Two

"Oh my," Sophia said in an exasperated breath.

Sophia had almost convinced herself she was dreaming. Months ago she feared she would not find a husband in time for her eighteenth birthday. But she had now received her second proposal, more than she had ever expected in her lifetime.

Her heart had a different reaction to this proposal. She had to clamp her mouth shut before blindly agreeing to it. How could she accept when she was still engaged to Jack. That wouldn't be fair.

Yet, she didn't want to reject Xavier either.

This was all too much.

Sophia fled from the balcony without giving Xavier a response. She didn't dare look back to see his reaction, as she knew it would only make her turn around and leap into his arms.

Barging past guests that were wandering the halls, she could not find her voice to apologise. In every direction there seemed to be a group of drunk men grouped together, either singing or shouting. Christopher really let his guests run wild amongst his home.

There was only one door in front of her that seemed to be an option for her. It was the closest to her, so she swung open the door and ran inside, and slammed the door behind her. With her eyes closed she pressed her back against the door with her chest panting.

How did she get herself into this situation? If it wasn't for that letter she would be back at the orphanage and living the life she grew up to believe was normal.

"I thought you had finally started to enjoy the party," a voice said from within the room.

Sophia shot open her eyes and found Christopher sitting at his desk. With his screwdriver in one hand and an oddly shaped device sitting in the other.

Stacks of papers were scattered around the room, this place was much different than the eloquent rooms in this manor. It was more disorganised, but Sophia guessed that if he was a scientist the last thing he would be concerned about was how tidy his workspace was.

"I have to say that this is a first for someone to barge into my office."

Sophia pushed herself away from the door. "My apologies, I just-" her mind wandered back to Xavier on the balcony. He was pouring his heart out to her and all she could do was run away. She knew that her feelings were developing fast for him. Now that he loved her, she had very little time to prepare herself to lose her sight to stone. How does one even go about preparing for something like that?

"Shouldn't a host be attending his own party?"

Christopher shrugged his shoulders as if he wasn't interested. "I only host these parties so the drunk fools will fund my inventions. There is nothing better than asking drunk people for money. Works every time...almost."

Sophia giggled. "It's amazing how a few drinks can completely change a person."

Christopher scoffed and shook his head, dazedly. "So, where are those two lovely fellows who were accompanying you? Was I right about that one lad? Going off with the siren?"

"The last time I saw Mr Green he was in fact with the siren but I have not seen him since, and Mr Howell is..." she sank her teeth into her bottom lip. "Dealing with some personal issues at the moment." she let out a sad breath as she dropped her shoulders.

"Are you all right?" there was a surprising concern in his voice.

Sophia gave him a tight smile with no actual answer.

Christopher swiveled in his chair and placed the screwdriver down at his desk. He still held the device he was working on, as if too frightened to let it go. "Would you like to talk about it?"

Sophia's breath caught, it was such a fatherly thing to say. It was like he was always a part of her life, and this was a regular sort of conversation they would have.

"May I ask you something?"

Christopher leaned his weight forward, resting his elbows on his thighs. "Of course."

"Why did my mother write that will," Sophia was nervous. "Why did you agree to her request that I marry by my eighteenth birthday?"

Christopher dropped his head, hiding whatever reaction he had. It took him a moment to compose himself, but when he did, he did so with a sigh. "Your mother was very ill. She had me write up the letter for her, and as her dying wish she wanted to ensure you were looked after. She wanted you to find a husband to protect you. And if you were to find a husband in that orphanage you would not be so alone."

"It has caused my life nothing but hardship," Sophia was angry now. Not satisfied with the reasoning behind the letter. "This forced engagement has done nothing but make things worse. Isn't there anything you can do to stop it?"

Christopher shook his head, "It was signed with a seel, and once in the hands of Lord Paine it can't be adjusted."

"But I-"

"Life isn't always fair," Christopher's tone was serious. "We all must do things that we don't want to at one point in our lives."

An awkward silence fell upon the room. It seemed like no matter what, Sophia would have to be married in three days time.

"Besides," Christopher turned back around so his legs were tucked under his desk. "You seem to be quite taken with that young man."

"Mr Green is..."

"Not him," Christopher laughed, as if that would be the most ridiculous idea in the world. "That vampire. He is very smitten with you, reminds me of when I met your mother."

A sweet smile grew on her lips at the mention of her, it seemed to avoke pleasant memories for Christopher.

"I'd love to hear more about her."

Christopher froze suddenly, his smile quickly washed away.

Feeling like the air was growing thicker, Sophia brushed her hand along his desk and her eyes ran across one of his papers. A hand drawn diagram of a circular device with many arrows and notes pointing around it. It was difficult to read his handwriting as it looked as though he wrote it in a rush. However, Sophia could make out the name of this device scrawled out in large letters at the top

Everlasting Life.

"A new invention?"

Christopher picked up the sheet of paper that caught Sophia's attention and examined it, "Yes, actually. It is the purpose of this party. I need to get all of the money I can for the supplies to build the final version." he gave a little shake to the device he was currently working on. "This is a prototype."

"What does it do?"

"I would probably talk your ear off explaining the finer details of how and why it works. Essentially, it brings the spirit of a loved one back. There would be no need for loss if we could simply take hold of that person's spirit and have them here as if they never left."

"But doesn't grief make us into stronger people? The loss makes us appreciate what we have left."

Christopher shook his head. "Although that is true, loss can turn a man over to insanity. There is enough unhappiness in this world as it is."

It hadn't fully clicked in her mind that Sophia was standing and talking with her father. She could see the passion in his work, just by how he described them. It only made her excited to find out more about him, what other interests he had, and maybe soon he could talk of her mother.

"It still needs work. At the moment it can only bring back a person's fresh loss. I haven't figured it out yet, but the stronger the pain in someone's heart the more likely it will work. I want to build it so that shouldn't matter."

"How can that be possible?"

"As ridiculous as it sounds, love is the strongest component to this invention. Of course, I have materials to make these phenomenal inventions work, but it all comes down to the person in its presence. The heart pumps a secret message to the person you think about, and the spirit will respond to that message. If they love you back they will appear."

"That sounds quite sad." The idea of someone not showing up because they did not reciprocate the love they felt was heart wrenching.

A clear gem sat in the centre of the device, when Christpher moved it around Sophia noticed an odd red liquid swirling around inside. It looked like blood was spinning through the gem to have it powered. For a prototype he certainly added a lot of decoration, with engraved roses and thorns outlining the edges.

"How do you make it work?" asked Sophia.

"Like I said, currently it works with a fresh loss. It is one of the things which needs modifying." he grazed his finger across the gem. "When someone comes within a short distance of this device, the gem will glow a pure white and that glow *should* take the form of that person's lost loved one."

Just as Sophia was about to dive into more questions, like what the red liquid was that seemed to be the main component of this device, there was a knock on the door. She didn't look over shoulder to see who it was when they entered.

Her eyes were entranced by the device in Christopher's hand, as the gem inside began glowing.

It was certainly getting brighter as the seconds ticked by, and the little vial of liquid housed within the gem was emptying, soon filling the room with an overwhelming bright light.

Everyone shielded their eyes, as the light was so bright it dared to blind anyone that looked directly at it.

Chrisopher dropped the device to the floor, unable to handle its power.

After a beat Sophia lowered her arm and the blinding white light had now faded, and standing before her was a beautiful white figure hovering over the device. The waves of her raven black hair fell gracefully over her shoulders, her eyes were closed like she was in a peaceful slumber. She was dressed head to toe in white, resembling that of a nightgown.

"Lucy," a voice from behind breathed.

Sophia snapped her head around to find Xavier standing there. His thin lips were slightly parted and his eyes were wide and full of pain. His face was paler than ever before. Fists had now curled at his side and his black eyes were glassy, like he was on the edge of crying. He swallowed the lump blocking his throat, and it was like Sophia could feel the pain he was feeling. There was so much coating his face that none of the masks could cover it.

She glanced back at the girl Xavier had named Lucy, and saw the remarkable similarities between her and Xavier. Both dark haired with pale skin, strong jaw lines along with other strong facial features. Her nose was small and thin, as opposed to Xavier's bigger and bumpier nose.

Lucy's eyes shot open abruptly with a glazed stare in her eyes, like she was on an elusive drug.

Even their eyes were the same, from shape to colour.

With her eyes open she looked even more beautiful. Her long eyelashes brought out her black eyes and her red lips parted as her eyes locked on Xavier's. There was a small hint of recognition in her face, but that soon fell back into a blank stare.

"Lucy!" Xavier stepped in front of Sophia, becoming the main view of Lucy.

"I know not of the name you speak." she spoke like she was in some sort of trance.

Xavier was pained, and ripped his gaze away from Lucy. It then fixated on Christopher's in a rage so fiery that he could burn this entire manor down. "What have you done?"

"Proving that my invention can be a success." Christopher was staring at Lucy with a fascination.

"Your invention?"

"Yes, the soul of a deceased person can be projected through that device," he pointed to the circular device lying flat on the floor. "It still needs perfecting. But I am so close to finishing my life's work."

"It needs destroying!" Xavier yelled. He was focused on keeping his gaze on Christopher, like the mere sight of Lucy pierced a dagger through his heart.

"Think of how many people's hearts will be fixed knowing they can see their loved ones again."

Xavier aggressively shook his head. "You are disturbing their peace. How is that fair?"

"Why should the living go through all of the suffering? The dead can no longer feel, they are nothing more than spirits, I am not actually hurting them."

"So you're doing this out of the kindness of your own heart? You don't gain anything from this?"

Christopher wore a wicked smile, "Well, of course a profit will be made."

That added fuel to Xavier's firing rage. "Put Lucy's soul back where it belongs."

"Curious, how did Lucy die?" Christopher punched a hand into his trouser pocket, and stared at Xavier with a squint in his eyes. "She must have died before her heart stopped beating."

Xavier couldn't bring himself to look at anyone. His mouth clamped shut and his jaw was tense. Sophia could see his pulse pounding in his neck.

"It appears as if she has not accepted that she is dead," continued Christopher. "For she does not know who she is or where she is, which means she cannot cope with the fact that her life was taken before she was ready."

Xavier shut his eyes as if relieving a painful memory.

"I have heard about you, Mr Howell. Accused of murdering women, and put up in that *wretched* orphanage?"

So Christopher must not have been happy with Sophia being taken away to the orphanage, as he spoke of it with a bitterness in his tone. Like he wanted to wash his mouth out before saying the word again.

"How do you know so much about me?"

"I have my sources."

Xavier was about to protest until Christopher bent down and picked up his device, causing the image of Lucy to collapse. "Now get out," he snarled. "I have work to do. You are welcome to stay in my home as long as you see fit."

"You are welcome to meet the end of my foot, you bast-"

"Xavier," Sophia cut him off before he could finish. She pressed her hands on his chest and began escorting him out of the office.

Xavier stepped back in an odd sort of daze, like he couldn't figure out what to do. Internally debating whether he should leave or punch Christopher in the face.

Sophia closed the door behind them and when she turned back around, Xavier was storming down the hall with his fists at his sides and his broad shoulders arched.

She couldn't leave him alone with such a rage built up inside of him. Worried for his safety, she picked up the skirt of her gown and ran after him.

Following through the entire house, constantly calling his name, Xavier ignored her and stormed out the front door and stomped down the front steps leading to the front garden. Small white stones crunched underneath his feet as he was prepared to walk back into the dangerous forest in which he fought that demon.

Sophia somehow managed to catch up to him, she gripped the sleeve of his coat and halted in his direct path. Xavier tried to side step her, but Sophia was there at each attempt to block him.

There was a look of pure anger creasing his face. His fangs were now present and digging into his lower lip. It looked painful, like at any second he could draw his own blood.

Carefully reaching out, Sophia grabbed a fist full of his shirt and clung to him. She was far too afraid to let him go and possibly get himself killed.

Xavier couldn't stand still, constantly shifting his weight, and ready to break out into a run at any moment.

"How can he think that is okay?" he barked. "To bring up *my* sister without permission? Not letting her rest after all these years."

Of course it was his sister. They looked related in facial features alone. Sophia felt a rush of guilt that she was growing far too familiar with.

"How did she die?" she said in a calm tone. Not wanting to anger him more, but she could tell he'd been bottling this up for a while.

His fangs slowly retracted into his mouth as his breath became shallow. The memory was flashing into his mind and Xavier reached out to Sophia's wrist. Lacing his fingers around her wrist, his grip was tight, as though without it he wouldn't have the strength to stand.

Releasing the material of his shirt, she slipped her hand into his hair at the side of his head. "You can trust me," she breathed.

"She was murdered," gritting his teeth, fighting with everything he had not to cry. "Along with my mother and father."

Sophia had assumed that something had happened to his family. The way he would talk of his mother, and desperately hoping that the woman at the bar all those months ago was his sister.

"I found them." the tips of his back hair caused a shadow to form over his eyes. "A week after my seventeenth birthday I came home and they were just...there. Together in the living room. Dead."

"Xavier..." she wanted to weep for him. No one should ever have to go through something like that, never mind witness it.

"I couldn't find my brother, but I can only assume he managed to escape." Xavier raised his head, his eyes glossed over. "But I don't have much hope since I haven't seen him since that day. I can only imagine he was caught and killed in a different location."

"Did you ever find out who did it?"

Rolling his eyes around, he grinded his teeth together. Xavier was struggling to regain his composure. "I'm certain Lord Paine had something to do with it, for their refusal to join the orphanage. I have no proof, obviously."

"Whoever did it knew they were vampires," he said. "For they knew the only way to kill one of us. All of them had a stake through their hearts."

Sophia could picture it, bloody corpses in a living room and a young Xavier walking in as if it was a regular day. Only for it to turn into the worst day of his life.

When he met Sophia's concerned eyes, he pressed his fingers against the scars on her cheek. The ice around his heart thawed when he took in her appearance. "You're so beautiful."

Shaking her head, she didn't want compliments at a time like this. She didn't want it to be another excuse for him to distract himself from his pain. Smoothing her hands over his shoulders, she took a small step forward.

This was the real Xavier. A caring man who was just injured from the traumatic events of his past. It was obvious the slight digs and teasing jokes were a cover up to hide his true self from people.

Moving her hands down to his waist she snuggled her face into his palm. When he cupped his hands over her cheeks she found her eyelids become heavy as they inched closer to one another. Just as their lips were mere inches apart Xavier let out a sigh of laughter.

"What is it?" she looked up at him with big innocent eyes.

"Whenever we are close to sharing a moment I remember that you are promised to another," he pressed his forehead against hers. "I meant what I said on the balcony. My offer still stands."

"What about Jack?"

"You really want to marry a man you could never love?" Xavier said. "I'm not going to lie to you and say he won't be mad at you. He'll probably be furious. But he'll get over it, because he'll want you to be happy."

Sophia chewed on her bottom lip. Her heart had decided a long time ago that Xavier was the one for her. She just never wanted to admit it fully to herself.

"But," Xavier continued, dropping his voice. "If you truly want to marry Jack, if you think you will be happy with him. I'll let you go."

Her fingers gripped on tighter around his waist, as if afraid he would walk away at this very moment.

Tears filled her eyes. How would she break it to Jack, that she was to marry another man over him? It wasn't right to lead him on all this time. Perhaps one day he would thank her, for she could never offer him a fulfilling life if she resented him for taking away her opportunity of love.

Jack had always looked after her, even as a child he was always the one there for her. But now it was time for Sophia to take care of herself. And make decisions that are best for her.

"I will marry you." A single tear trickled down her cheek. "But only when I tell Jack." Her shoulders shook as she felt she was finally releasing a heavy burden weighing down on her heart.

Xavier brushed a tear away with his thumb. "Why are you crying?"

"Knowing I am going to hurt my friend, and leading him up this road. It wasn't worth it. In the end, all he will get is a broken heart and it's all my fault." She chewed on her bottom lip. "You are not concerned about marrying a woman who isn't in love with you yet?"

Both of his comforting hands slipped around her waist. "I'm already deeply in love with you. And if you feel you could love me in the future, what difference does it make when we marry? I'd only end up marrying you anyway."

"But I will turn you to stone, my world will be stone?"

"So you cannot have love for that reason?"

"How can I risk your life?" her face felt puffy from crying.

"Do you want to live your life without me?"

"I don't think I can," the thought of Xavier no longer being in her life pulled hard at her heart strings and that they may soon snap. "What if I turn you to stone?"

"Then I will make one handsome statue." A smile grew on his lips and he pressed his mouth against hers tenderly. He held her close as her arms wrapped around his neck. The small bit of stubble around his chin was tickling her as they kissed. Their hold of one another grew tighter with each passionate moment. Xavier's hands began travelling around her body as his mouth searched for hers.

"We'll figure something out." Xavier promised against her mouth.

When his hands slid around the back of her neck, that fire was back. Sophia knew that Xavier was the only man who could ever fill her up with such a desire, such a longing that it made her ache.

"I didn't think I'd have to take time to convince you to marry me," he mumbled against her lips with a smile. "I thought my devilish good looks would have been enough."

Chapter Twenty-Three

Xavier walked Sophia back to her room, and she felt like a great load had been lifted from her shoulders. When walking beside him she was unsure of what to do or what to say. He must have noticed her nervous nature as he pulled one hand out of his coat pocket and slipped it around hers. "I could see you were itching to hold my hand."

"You make me sound desperate," she blushed.

Xavier chuckled, not denying it.

They stopped at her door and she slid her hands around his waist and looked up at him with her big eyes and a cheeky smile on her lips. "If we are to be married then you need to stop with the insults. A husband is meant to honour his wife."

Xavier lowered his lips to meet hers with a smile. "And a wife is meant to obey her husband." he melted into her for another kiss and she was smiling the entire time.

In the bad deal of cards her life had been held up until now, it felt as though Xavier had finally offered her a fresh hand.

Something she could actually work with, a life that could make her happy. There were still many things they had to work out, there would be consequences to their love but Sophia knew she could deal with it with Xavier at her side.

"Sophia..." a heartbroken voice said from behind them.

Sophia ripped away from Xavier and spun a half circle to find Jack, with a look of utter despair plastered on his face.

His silver tie was loose down his chest with three of his top buttons undone. Jack certainly didn't arrive at Christopher's ball looking like that. That siren must have shown him a wild time, with his once combed over blonde hair now sticking up in multiple directions.

Xavier's chest broadened, as though he was ready to fight with Jack.

"I need to speak with you," Sophia said, her hands sweating from nerves. She had no idea how Jack would take this news. But what she was sure of, she had to do it alone. Xavier couldn't be here. Jack would only see it as her rubbing it in his face.

Sophia turned to Xavier, and offered a reassuring smile. "May you leave us?"

Xavier wasn't sure whether he should. Jack didn't exactly have a clean record of keeping his calm, especially when it involved Sophia. But Xavier could see in Sophia's eyes that she desperately wanted this, so he decided to respect her wishes. "I'll be in my room if you need me."

A thankful smile tickled Sophia's lips as she watched him disappear into his room.

Turning back to face Jack was difficult. What possibly made things worse for her was that his expression was unreadable. If she had to pinpoint it, she would say he looked tired.

Sophia gestured to her bedroom door, "Shall we go inside?"

Jack shook his head, the ends of his blonde hair brushing his forehead. "I'd rather just get this over with."

"You don't even know what I want to say-"

"It's not hard to guess, Sophia." he sounded so defeated. Like he was ready to give up the fight.

Sophia had to tell him straight. There couldn't be any confusion between them. The string of false hope had to be cut right now.

"I can't marry you Jack." Sophia said with her broken glass heart. "I won't marry you."

Instead of losing his temper, like she had come to expect, Jack only nodded with a purse of his lips. "I'm surprised it took this long." he ran a hand through his disheveled hair, then ran his palm over the length of his face before dropping it down to his thigh. "What's your plan then? Live on the streets?"

Blood rushed to her cheeks, and she couldn't meet his gaze when she announced, "I...I'm...Xavier proposed to me," she stole a glance, and Jack's face paled. "And I said yes."

"This is a joke, isn't it?" there was a hint of a laugh in his words. Like Jack was desperately turning this into a joke, he needed her not to be serious.

"No, Jack. I'm marrying Xavier."

As hard as this was, she had to at least look at him when giving him this news. "I am marrying him because I think there is a chance for me to marry a man I could fall in love with."

Jack's eyes searched her face, for any sign that this was a cruel joke. The all too familiar look of anger overtook his face, his neck rising in red. The final straw was when he looked down at the necklace hanging on her chest. Jack had that commissioned for her many years ago, as a token of his love to her. Now what was it? A piece of jewelry that she could rub in his face? Mock him with the idea that he ever thought she could love him in return.

Suddenly, Jack stormed over, reached for the locket and ripped it from her neck.

It sent a pulling pain around the back of her neck and she stumbled back with fresh tears in her eyes, "Jack..." she breathed with disbelief.

"I have done everything for you," he yelled in her face, his nose scrunching in disgust and the locket held in his fist. "Everything, just in hopes you would see that I actually *care* for you."

"I never doubted that." Sophia's voice shook.

"Do you want to know why I came by your room tonight?" Jack took a small step back. "Because I was guilt ridden for going to bed with a woman from Christopher's party. I was so ashamed! But now I wish I never wasted my breath. I should have stayed and continued to fuck her, like you've clearly been doing with that murderer!"

"That's enough," Xavier had stepped in. Sophia didn't even hear him coming. "Go and sulk somewhere else." he wrapped his arm around Sophia's shoulder and opened up her bedroom door.

Escorting her inside, like she was a delicate doll, she felt like her heart had crumbled into a million pieces.

Jack eyed her every movement as she stepped inside of her room, seeing the red mark around her neck from where he had ripped the chain from her.

"I'm sure there are plenty of drunk women willing to let you relieve your stress." Xavier said, with a mocking in his tone.

Jack swung for Xavier and punched him across the cheek. It was such a movement he was growing used to doing that he almost perfected his hook. He let out all of his anger through that punch and it clearly showed, since Xavier was actually hurt.

Xavier held his cheek and breathed in quickly from his teeth. "I have lost count of the amount of times you have swung for me," his voice sounded like his mouth was full of cotton. "You need to control that temper of yours."

Sophia stepped in front of Xavier and it was her turn to take control of the pair of them. "Leave Jack, you aren't helping anyone."

So he did.

Jack left without having to be told twice. Only the sound of his shoes could be heard, clicking against the varnished wooden floor. Gradually fading away into the distance, along with any hope of rebuilding their relationship.

Sophia placed a comforting hand on Xavier's shoulders and guided him into her room. He cradled his face as he slumped down onto the edge of her bed. "I am impressed that he'd managed to hurt me. With a little bit of time he could actually become a threat."

Sophia grabbed his hand and pulled it away from his face to examine the damage, and whether Jack had managed to leave a mark. It was still early so chances were a mark wouldn't appear until morning.

"I feel as if my cheek has its own separate pulse."

"I'll go get some ice," she didn't get the chance to take one step before Xavier hooked his fingers through hers. "I'll be okay," he looked up at her with his heartwarming smile.

Grabbing the material of her mesh skirt, he pulled her so she was standing in between his legs. Sliding her hands around his neck, their eyes found each other.

Xavier was still smiling as his eyes scanned her face, making Sophia feel naked.

"I should really go and get some ice, otherwise your face might swell."

"It will only make me look dangerous." he chuckled.

When she reached out her fingers to touch his sore cheek, Xavier flinched back with a sharp hiss.

"Who is it you are trying to impress?" she asked. "I am to be your wife, which means there will be no other women in your life."

He shrugged his shoulders. "I suppose I could live with that."

Releasing the material of her dress, he reached up to cradle the back of her head and pulled her lips to meet his. Xavier pressed hard against her and a gasp escaped from her with the fire which trailed its way down to her heart.

As if the kiss had taken control of her body, Sophia hooked her leg around his waist and straddled his lap. They moved in rhythm together without their lips breaking apart. Xavier's hands made their way under her dress and laid flat against her thighs. The moment their skin made contact, he released a groan as he pushed his face to hers.

Sophia could feel his arousal pressed against her, and she was happy that she gave him this sort of reaction.

Xavier slipped his hands around to the back of her thighs, and picked her up effortlessly. He positioned her head in between her two cushions and his body acted as a blanket over hers.

Her hands were lacing through his thick black hair and pulling him closer.

One of Xavier's hands cradled her cheek and the other held tightly onto her waist. Their kiss was fuelled by passion, but Xavier was still gentle with her, like she was a rose ready to wilt.

Hours could have passed by with them tangled together, the heat only rising with each kiss.

Sophia's body was craving for more, she needed him. With her eyes closed the entire time, she found his coat and guided it off his firm body. Xavier assisted by throwing it to the floor.

Xavier then undid the buttons of his waistcoat, and in a fast motion dropped that next to his coat.

This still wasn't enough, she wanted to feel his skin against her fingers. He wanted him to ravish her and show her just how much he claimed to love her.

Her fingers found the buttons of his shirt, and she clumsily undid them, again dropping his shirt to the floor, so now he was completely shirtless. Xavier's muscles tensed around her body as her hands trailed up his firm back. Just this simple touch sent a pulsing urge to her core.

Xavier wrapped his muscled arm around her, and he held her like he never wanted to let go.

The happiness that burst from her heart was overwhelming. All she wanted was to stay like this forever, but if Xavier wanted to take this further she knew she wouldn't stop him. The nerves began to rise up her chest. She tried everything to push it back down, but now that they made their presence known they weren't going anywhere. She wanted to give herself to him but right now she wasn't sure that she was ready.

The proper thing to do was to wait until marriage. What if she fell in love with him on their wedding day? She wanted to *see* him when they made love at least one time.

It was Xavier who pulled away first. When she looked up at him with a bare chest she found herself blushing.

She could see the perfect line of his collarbone as he held himself up by his elbows. "Are you all right?" he asked, with his eyes searching her face.

When she settled back down to reality, she'd noticed she had been shaking. She hoped Xavier didn't think she was afraid of him. It was just her nerves taking control of her body.

"I'm sorry," he pressed his lips against her forehead and pushed himself off.

She sat up and watched him as he scrambled to find his shirt. Even underneath his clothes he was everything she imagined a god would be. If she tried to describe it to anyone, people would think it was a description of a handsome prince from a book. Only, this prince had scars.

"I hope you are not upset with me," she said, her voice shaking.

He looked at her with an unreadable expression. "Why would I be upset with you?"

"For not..." she blushed at the idea.

Xavier watched her with the same expression as he pulled his shirt back on, and covered up his beautiful chest. He kissed her swollen lips gently. "I said it once, and I will say it again. I will not make you do anything you do not feel comfortable with." Xavier took her small hand in his, and grazed her knuckles. A sweet small smile tickling his lips. "Besides, it's not fun if only one person enjoys it."

Robert sat with his head in his hands, trying to piece together everything that had happened in the past twenty four hours.

Stella sat opposite him in her chambers, and she nervously rubbed the top of Duncan's head. He acted as a sort of guard dog against Robert. He must have seen him as a threat to Stella, and would not keep his black eyes from him, offering up warning growels if he got too close.

"You are sure it is mine," he broke their silence.

She bit back all feelings of offence and gritted her teeth. "Yes, for you are the only person I have recently..."

Robert rubbed his jaw and let out a groan.

"I-I still have not decided on what I want to do," she mumbled.

Surprise crossed his face as he asked, "What do you mean?"

Stella shrugged, and thought she was being quite clear. "About whether I want to keep it or not."

"You are not getting rid of my child," his eyebrows furrowed together. "If this is about your reputation as a woman and your future-"

"That is not the issue. A relationship with a man was never anything I had intended." It was like her heart was constricted by rope. She patted the top of Duncan's head when he began nuzzling his wet nose against her knee, without keeping his glare off Robert.

"I don't think I can..."

"And why not?"

With trembling hands, Stella lowered her head, unable to meet his eyes. She couldn't look into the eyes of the man that hurt her so many times. The man she had fallen in love with, and tossed her aside as some sort of plaything.

"It is too dangerous," she was purposely giving short answers, hoping that that would be enough to show she didn't want to talk about it.

Robert looked at her as if asking her to elaborate on her words. "Because..."

"Because of what I am." her eyebrows knitted together and she held her belly, thinking that there was a life growing inside of her and she would have to take care of it. She wasn't sure she could do it. For one day she could lose control and could hurt an innocent person.

"Cassandra has always kept your identification a secret, why is that? What are you?"

Rubbing her temples, she considered telling him of her heritage. If they were going to be raising a child together he must know of her past. Her chest was growing tight and it was getting harder and harder for her to breathe. "I've never actually been given an official title." Stella sighed. "But, I am...I'm the daughter of Lucifer. A Princess of Hell, if you will."

Robert's eyes widened and didn't hide the unexpected shock that paled his face. His mouth hung open and his eyebrows almost flew from his forehead.

"I had managed to escape from my father because I did not want to be involved in such evil doings," embarrassment crept up her spine. "If I lose my temper or I use too much of the power I possess, then the darkness will take a hold of me and I will lose myself to the devil."

Robert let out a heavy sigh. "Cassandra knows this?"

All she did was nod. "She does not know the extent. Cassandra knows I have a power, and it can be dangerous if used too often. But she does not know of my true past. I have a feeling she might suspect it."

"Who is your mother?"

"Similar to the story of Jesus only opposite, my father got a woman pregnant with nothing but pure evil in her heart. She died whilst giving birth to me in the Underworld. I escaped when I was thirteen..." she stopped herself. Stella shared too much already.

"Why did your father not try to find you?"

She licked her dry lips. "My father is cruel," she stated the obvious. "He torments me from the Underworld. Mostly, with visions of the pain I will experience later in my life. I haven't had one in a while, but when they do come it's tortuous. He occasionally likes to send me harsh images unrelated to me that no human could see and still hold their sanity. My father expects me to go mad, and he'll easily be able to coerce me into returning to him." She swallowed the lump in her throat and she began shaking. "I do not want to hurt people," she clung onto the edge of her dirty apron and gritted her teeth. "I want nothing more than a family and to be happy, but I am terrified I will unintentionally hurt people."

"Is that why some of your features have changed? Like your eyes and hair?"

Stella touched the new strip of red in her hair, "This is new. I can only assume that every time I overuse my power, a part of me is filled with darkness. It must be a reminder from my father that I belong to him, along with my powers."

"Will the baby be born evil? With the blood of a wolf combined with the blood of a..."

"Devil," she answered.

Robert nodded slowly. "Will it be too strong?"

She shrugged her shoulders. "The way I see it is, no one is born evil but they are taught it from a young age. I was the lucky one who learnt that my father's evil ways weren't right, if I raise this baby to be only good it will grow up knowing how to be good." She stared down at Duncan who was looking up at her with sad black eyes. "At least I hope."

"I am not concerned for what the baby will be," Stella choked out a cry. "But I'm concerned about harming it."

"I won't let you," he reached over and attempted to hold her hand but Duncan broke out into a fit of barks and bared his teeth as a warning.

Robert flinched back and gave a puzzled look to the dog. "I am guessing he does not like me, where did you get him?"

"I rescued him. Please do not tell Mrs Green, I do not want him to go back onto the streets."

"You are full of secrets, I guess it is always the quiet ones with a lot to hide." Robert flashed a genuine smile. "I won't tell her anything."

Chapter Twenty-Four

"My birthday is tomorrow," Sophia and Xavier were strolling around Christopher's garden. It was a vast field with gorgeous tall trees shadowing the grass. The entirety of Christopher's house was something from a dream. Sophia half expected small pixies to giggle and emerge from the bushes to sprinkle their magic around.

Xavier was squatting down at the small pond that was covered with lily pads. He was throwing stones into the water that swans had claimed as their bath. One hissed at him and flapped open its beautiful white wings.

"Well, you ruined your chance at becoming my pet," Xavier mocked. There was a faint bruise on his right cheek from where Jack had punched him two nights ago.

"Xavier," Sophia sighed. "Tomorrow is the last day we can be wed."

"Do you ever wonder if animals could talk?" he ignored her, staring down at the swans. "Perhaps if you encourage them, they might do it. I wonder which animal I would have the most in common with."

"A pig."

Xavier chuckled. "Well, I was going to say a strong gallivant horse."

"Please Xavier," she felt the sun burning the top of her head, she regretted not bringing a hat. It was oddly a warm day for May. The powder pink hat she left on her nightstand would have gone so well with her dress too.

"I am stressed. If you have changed your mind I wish for you to tell me because I will need to go out to the town find a drunk man and convince him to-"

In one turn, Xavier was now standing in front of his bride-to-be. Taking her hands in his, he brought her knuckles to his lips and kissed them. "Calm down, I have not changed my mind. We shall be married before your birthday ends. As much as I am full of rage towards Christopher I'm sure he could have something arranged in a gorgeous place like this."

"When?" she persisted. "I would prefer it sooner rather than later."

"I do not remember you being this eager to marry Jack," he shook his head. "I must hold women to desperation."

She ignored his comment and jabbed her finger into his chest with a point. "I shall find Christopher and request his help with our marriage, whilst you stay here and play with the swans." Rolling her green eyes around in her head, Sophia huffed. "It's the least Christopher can do considering he agreed to that blasted will."

As she walked away, her target was set on her father. In the distance she heard Xavier let out a grunt. "Ow! It bit me!"

This was the man she was going to spend her life with. She couldn't help the childish grin that grew on her face as she headed inside.

Searching the halls, Sophia quickly found her father sitting at his desk in his study. He was still wearing the outfit he'd worn from the party two days ago.

Had he been working on nothing but this device?

Not wanting to intrude, she knocked on the door. This startled Christopher, causing him to drop his screwdriver and snap his head up to face Sophia. When he realised it was only her, he released a long breath and seemed to relax in his chair.

That odd behaviour didn't go unnoticed. He seemed so tense before, barely taking the time to blink when working on the *Everlasting Life.*

Christopher's eyes were lined with red, and bloodshot. But he still held a welcoming smile, even if it was slightly forced.

"Are you all right?" Sophia stepped into the room and examined her father's face. Up close she could see that his green eyes were wild, and his pupil had expanded so far out it almost covered his entire iris.

Christopher put down everything he was holding and held his hand under his nostrils, inhaling a long breath. "Yes, I-I...I've just been very busy."

He was stammering, frantic.

Sophia was uncomfortable seeing her father this way, but she supposed he must be tired if he had no sleep and was working his brain for hours. "I need to make a request."

"What is that?" Christopher couldn't keep his hands still, shoving them in and out of his pockets.

"Well...as you know, I have to be married by tomorrow. As it's my birthday."

She wondered if Christopher remembered her birthday?

"Is there any possible way you could help put together a service for myself and Mr Howell? Or if you know any churches we could visit?"

"Hmm," he grumbled as he poured himself a glass of whisky. "What about that blonde fellow? I was under the impression you two were to marry." He glanced up at her and saw a pained expression. "Have I touched a nerve?" he took a sip from his engraved glass.

"It is complicated," she sighed. "I would rather not dive into it, I just need to be wed to Mr Howell as soon as possible." She cocked her head to the side and fiddled with her gloved fingers. "No later than tomorrow."

He nodded as though that was the most reasonable request he had heard in his life. "Mr Howell didn't strike me as the type to settle down."

Sophia quickly shot up her eyebrows and decided not to respond.

"You're willing to become the wife of an accused murderer? *And* a vampire?"

"I trust his word that he is innocent." she tried to not lose her temper as she stood her ground. "And what he is does not matter to me. For he accepts me exactly how I am."

Christopher smugly shrugged and took another sip. "Whatever you say," he dropped his glass onto his desk and rummaged through his draws. "But I will organise a wedding. With such short notice it will not be a fairytale. You will have a priest, and a couple of guests. I will find a dress for you too, but that is the best I can do."

For that to be 'the best he could do' seemed like everything Sophia could ever want in a wedding.

Never in her life would Sophia have imagined that her father would take on such a big responsibility for her to be married. But months ago she didn't even know that he was alive. Now he is going out of his way to find her a gown, and save her life from the streets (even if he was an equal part of causing this scenario).

Sophia opened up her arms and wrapped her arms around his back, holding him in a tight embrace.

There was a hesitation that couldn't be denied. But Christopher still held his daughter just as tightly when he eventually returned the hug. His fingers were shaking against her back, and Sophia wondered what cocktail he had that made him so erratic today.

"Thank you," she mumbled into his shoulder.

Christopher's breath hitched, as he moved his hand to cradle the back of her head. Holding his daughter as though afraid of letting go.

Stella wiped the sweat from her brow with the back of her hand. Now that her working day was done undid the bow of her apron as she approached her bedroom door. Her feet were pulsing and she longed to lie back on her mattress and rest.

Before she could step inside of her room she was greeted by Duncan wagging his scrawny tail. His tongue was sticking out as he panted with excitement.

Feeling a rush of love towards this dog, she closed the door behind her and opened up her arms as she knelt to the floor. Giving Duncan a few minutes worth of back rubs and ear scratches.

"I know what you want," she pulled out half a loaf of bread from the basket at her bedside. Stella dropped it to the floor and

Duncan scooped it up in his mouth and ran to his bed and indulged himself.

There was a sudden unexpected knock at her door, and Stella shot up in fear of Cassandra finding Dunca. The dog didn't seem to notice, as he was happy eating.

"Who is it?"

The door creaked open and Robert greeted her with half a smile. She watched him suspiciously. She hadn't seen him since their conversation about the baby. Ever since then she has gone out of her way to avoid him. She hadn't even changed any of the beds on that floor to avoid bumping into him.

"I hope I didn't disturb you." he invited himself in slowly with his hands tucked behind his back.

It was clear that he was uncomfortable and flustered. His golden eyes could settle in one location. Eventually he looked at Stella, who was just as uncomfortable and flustered as Robert. If not more so.

When he didn't say anything, and just stood in her small room all he was doing was taking up a lot of space. "Sir, I really need-"

"I thought I would give you this." Robert cut her off, and thrust out his hands from behind his back.

Clutched in his large hands was a present. He even went out of his way to wrap it in crinkled paper and a tight attempt at a bow.

This was the last thing Stella expected from Robert. It was impossible for her to bite back a smile when she took the present and look at the awful attempt at a bow.

"What is it?"

"Open it."

Stella unraveled the silk bow, and ripped open the paper. Inside was a small piece of material that looked no bigger than a handkerchief. When she tucked the remnants of the paper under her elbow, she lifted out the material. It unraveled to be a small white dress.

Fit for a small baby.

Stella felt like she might cry, she tried her best to fight it back. Looking at this item it had hit her that this was something for a small person, someone that would be hers to nurture and care for.

She covered her mouth with her hand and turned her back to Robert.

"I still haven't made a decision."

When his hand dropped over her shoulder, Robert turned her around to face him. This was the first time she had noticed the lines across his face. All of the day to day stress he was under caring for his sister. He was twenty three but looked like a mature thirty year old.

"I will help you. I will ensure you won't harm our child."

She shook her head. "No, Sir. You deal with enough."

"No formalities, speak to me as you would a friend."

A friend? After all they had shared, after everything she had given to him?

"I have spent my life in anger and resentment towards my sister, and I feared I would run out of time to have a family and be happy. You have given me the opportunity and I promise to not leave your side."

She thought back to the way he had treated her, and how his behavior had suddenly changed. She didn't trust it.

What if something like this was a wakeup call that Robert needed? For that same man to be standing in front of her, gifting her baby clothes and pleading to aid her. Maybe there was hope they could create something wonderful.

Then, just like any sunny day there is always one cloud to block the rays of light. A sudden flash appeared in her mind. No longer was she standing in her bedroom with Robert, now she was on the floor of the entrance hall to the orphanage. Heavy rain hissed down the cobbled steps and she was sure she was screaming.

There was a towel wrapped around her shoulders, and Cassandra was cradling her in her arms, but not in a comforting way. In a way to keep her restrained.

Stella's gaze was fixated on one of the carriages that was hardly ever used, now parked in front of the orphanage, with a driver at the reins. It was reserved for events that Cassandra and Albert may need to attend. Which was rare.

Then Stella saw what she was shrieking about. Inside of the carriage was Robert and a baby held in his arms. There was a panicked and pained look on his face as he yelled something to the driver, and Stella could only watch as they rode away out of her life, for good.

Stella stumbled back into her reality, snapping out of her vision almost gave her whiplash.

Robert watched her with concern.

Everything Robert was doing right now was an act. To get on her good side so he could steal away their baby.

Stella bawled her hand into a fist and repeatedly punched him in his chest. "You want to take my child away from me!" she cried. "You think you can possess me to get your own way!"

Confusion coated his face. "What? Stella I-"

"Get out!" she cried.

This rage that was building in her chest made her punches harder to his chest. Unfortunately for Stella, Robert had plenty of practise restraining someone. His hands tightly gripped her arms as she flailed about desperate to break free.

"I am not going to take it away!" he yelled.

"You will," she snarled. Duncan was at her side barking at Robert with his sharp teeth bared. Robert just ignored him and focused his gaze to Stella's eyes.

"I saw you!" she screamed, her hand clutching around her stomach.

"What?"

Stella's bottom lip was quivering. "I had a vision of you taking our child away!"

Robert thought back to their conversation, and how Stella's father would send her visions to corrupt her mind. He cupped his hands over Stella's cheeks, pulling her to look at him. "Stella, I would never do anything like that. It's just your father trying to get inside of your head."

When she met his golden eyes, she found herself calming as she took in the details. There were a few brown spots in his eyes. Each time she looked into them, she noticed something new. Not only had he managed to calm her down, but she felt like she believed him.

Before she knew it, Robert's hand was lightly pressed against Stella's stomach. Her eyes followed his hand, and she nervously placed her palm over his knuckles.

When she looked back up at Robert, it was the first time she had ever seen him smiling. There was always such a serious and troubled look on his face. Like every moment he struggled to find peace in his heart. But something she had inside of her made him happy.

They stood like that for a while, neither of them said anything as they soaked up this moment of uninterrupted happiness.

Stella found herself drawn to him like a magnet. She reached up and planted a kiss on his lips.

When she realised what she was doing she snapped herself back, locking her gaze to the ground. "I-I'm sorry," she mumbled. "I don't know why-"

She was swiftly cut off when Robert hooked his finger under her chin, pulling her to look at him. His golden eyes scanned her face, and soon his mouth locked with hers. Wrapping his arms tightly around her body and holding her close as they kissed.

Duncan started barking again, interrupting them.

Robert pulled away and looked down at Duncan, laughing. "You might have to share her from now on."

Chapter Twenty-Five

It had finally started to settle that this time tomorrow Sophia would be a married woman.

It was safe to assume that Sophia would not be getting any sleep tonight, for all of her nerves would be electrocuting her awake.

It did give her a chance to reflect on the past three months, and the hardship that has been endured. Not only herself, but Jack and even Xavier too. When Jack had calmed down, she knew she had to make amends with him. She had no idea how, or if he even would forgive her, but she knew she had to try.

Christopher got straight to work after Sophia had requested a wedding ceremony. Although his odd behaviour earlier today did sprinkle unease in her stomach, she just had to hope that it was a one off thing. That he had been working himself too hard to work on his invention. He had mentioned it was his life's work, not something anyone would want to work haphazardly on.

Sophia couldn't stop thinking about Xavier. Oddly, it wasn't just about their wedding, the main thought that occupied her mind was the idea of intimacy. She feared as time got closer to her wedding day the sooner she would fall in love with him.

She wanted to experience everything with Xavier. The more her mind raced the more she had convinced herself that she wanted to be able to look him in the eyes when they made love for the first time.

Just the thought of him sent her heart into a race.

It was hard to believe the man she first met in a prison cell was going to be her husband. That this man, possibly the most handsome man she had ever met, loved her.

Sophia was nervous, but she had decided that tonight she was going to give herself to Xavier.

Later that night, Sophia found Xavier in the drawing room alone. He was standing in front of the fireplace, with the light from the fire causing a golden glow to outline his silhouette.

Xavier seemed to be lost in thought, with his hands clasped beside his back and his eyes watching the yellow and red flames dance in the logs.

When she stepped closer into the room, the lavender silk of her gown brushing against her legs, she stopped behind him. He must not have heard her enter as he hadn't even stolen a glance to see who had entered the room.

With a sweaty palm, Sophia tapped Xavier on the back. Releasing his hands, and jolting him out of his own mind, he turned around to face Sophia. A welcoming smile grew on his lips, and her heart fluttered in her chest. She was so grateful that a man like Xavier would look at her like she was a precious gem. One that he felt so lucky to be in possession of.

"Isn't it bad luck for the bride to see the groom the night before the wedding?" Xavier teased.

"We aren't exactly going for tradition, are we?"

Xavier peered over his shoulder and took a note of the time. It was five minutes past midnight, when he turned back to Sophia he said. "Happy birthday."

Xavier slipped his hands around her waist and kissed her mouth.

This kiss only made her more nervous for what she was about to request. But, in her heart she knew this was what she wanted. All of Xavier, and for him to have all of her.

"May you come with me to my room?" Sophia asked when she pulled away.

Xavier slipped his fingers through hers and held her hand. "Lead the way."

Inside her room held so much more significance now that Xavier was present. He had no idea what thoughts were swirling around in her mind. She never even considered the possibility that he could reject her.

Sophia stared at him, doing her best to take in every detail of him. Not that it was difficult, Xavier was the type of gentleman that if you saw him in passing along the street you would remember him forever.

His black hair wasn't cempt but naturally ruffled over his forehead. She loved how thick his eyebrows were. His dark eyes that she could spend eternity falling into.

"Is everything alright?" he broke her chain of thought. "Was there something you wanted to discuss here?"

"No, nothing like that." She sank her teeth into her bottom lip and took his hands in hers. Her face was bright red, she felt as though she might spontaneously combust.

Sophia had never considered this before, of course she knew what sex was. If she did this with Xavier before having his hand in marriage then he could easily ruin her. If he slept with her and never saw her again, her life would be so much worse.

Yet, she trusted Xavier. She wanted to do this with him because she *wanted* to give everything and experience everything before she would lose her ability to look into his eyes. She wanted to make love to him with no fear of accidentally catching his eye and turning him to stone.

That would certainly be an awkward predicament.

"Did I tell you how beautiful you look tonight?" He stepped to her and slid his hands around her waist. His fingers spread out across her hips and every slight movement from Xavier's hand caused Sophia's heart to catapult out of her chest.

Xavier dipped his head to meet Sophia's gaze, it's strange how anxious this made her now. Knowing that one day an innocent look in the eyes could result in her dearly beloved becoming a statue.

"Are you sure all is well?" Xavier said, and shortly followed up with a kiss to her forehead. "What did you want to discuss here? You seem a little off."

Sophia released a shaky breath and finally raised her head to meet Xavier's black eyes. Oh how she loved to get lost in them, she could stare and get sucked into the deep black pools of ink that were his eyes. She had to savour little moments like these, soon she would have to rely on her memory.

She reached up her palm and cupped the side of his face, her eyes following her thumb as she brushed his smooth cheek. The bruise had faded from this morning, but it was still present on his cheek.

A faint smile appeared on her lips as she entranced herself with the smooth texture of his pale skin. She snapped her eyes again to his, "Kiss me?"

Xavier didn't even hesitate. With her hand over his heart, Xavier dipped his head and brushed his lips across hers. It was his turn to cup her cheek, he always favoured her scarred cheek. Whether he knew it or not, he was telling her that he thought she was beautiful, even with her scars slashed across one side of her face.

It was so easy for Sophia to get lost in Xavier's kiss, he made it so simple for the rest of the world to just melt away at her feet. In this moment she needed him closer, she craved to be touched in places she never even knew she could be touched.

Sophia leaned in for more, her breasts were now pressed firmly against Xavier's broad chest. When he snaked his arm around her back, holding her close, Sophia could feel a spark igniting her body.

It was when a small moan escaped from Sophia's lips that Xavier pulled away and rested his forehead against hers. They were both panting hard, their breath intertwining.

"Sophia..." he said her name with caution wrapped in his tone. It was as though he knew where this was headed before she could even say anything.

"I know that we are to be married tomorrow, and this *should* wait until then but..." Sophia couldn't bring herself to speak louder than a whisper.

"But...I'm afraid."

Xavier pulled his head back and looked down to Sophia, his thick eyebrows slightly raised like he was concerned. "Afraid of what?" He too was whispering, as if they were afraid if they spoke too loud it could burst this intimate bubble forming around them.

"I'm afraid that I'll fall in love with you tomorrow," her cheeks were now as red as her favourite rose. "I know I am falling for you, and I am so afraid of not having the chance to *see* you when we make love for the first time."

Xavier lowered a hand from her waist and slid his fingers through hers, to assure her he was there.

Sophia smiled up at him, all of her nerves now in her throat. "I...I want you to make love to me...tonight."

Xavier didn't hide the surprise in his eyes, his dark eyebrows twitched and his lips parted ever so slightly. He dipped his head and the moments of silence weren't reassuring to Sophia. A sudden panic pricked in her chest, what if he was going to call off their wedding? What if he realised just how fast this train was moving and he wanted to leap off while he still had the chance.

Sophia couldn't stand it anymore, she couldn't linger in this silence. "Have you changed your mind?"

Xavier snapped his head up, his gaze immediately locking with hers. He brought up his warm hand to the side of her face and grazed his thumb across her skin. "No, Sophia." His eyes were serious, and he was speaking to her in a tone that she had to believe in him. "I just don't want you to regret it. I don't want you to wake up in the morning wishing this wasn't how we..."

"I won't regret it," she took a small step forward. "I know that I want this...with you."

"Are you sure?"

She answered with a small nod and a smile crept up on her lips. Her eyes soon fell to his chest, it was effortlessly rising and falling, and the rhythm settled any fear Sophia had lingering in her chest.

Slowly, Sophia raised her hands and gripped the material of Xavier's dress coat, he didn't move as she did so, and began slowly slipping it from his shoulders until it dropped to the floor. Sophia didn't take her eyes from his chest, his breathing now rapid.

This wasn't something an unwed woman should do, she shouldn't be alone with a man in her room full stop but she didn't care. It's not like anything in her life could be considered normal, and people would look down on her regardless of her actions, simply because she lived in the orphanage.

The only thing Sophia cared about in this moment was Xavier, and taking in every single detail of his body so she could have the full experience. She had to memorise every curve, every blemish, every single detail of his body.

Xavier didn't even flinch when Sophia moved her hands to the buttons on his shirt, she froze for a second considering whether she was ready to see him shirtless but deep in her heart she knew. She knew she needed him.

Delicately, Sophia began unbuttoning Xavier's crisp white shirt. The lower she got the more of his pale white skin was revealed. It was like unwrapping a gift, and anticipating with excitement what could be inside. She could feel her bottom lip trembling as her lower stomach began to ache, and an impatient desire coursed through her veins.

When she undid the last button she pressed her hand to his firm torso and slid her fingers under the material of his shirt. She kept her eyes locked to his chest, still watching the rise and fall of his shoulders.

He felt so smooth under his clothes, like what she imagined sleeping on a cloud would be like. As she slipped her hands higher she felt an unusual raised texture to his right peck. Acting on her own accord, Sophia went to push back the material of Xavier's shirt - just as she did with his coat - until Xavier's hand gripped her wrist lightly. Halting her.

Sophia snapped up her head to meet his gaze, afraid that she may have unintentionally done something wrong.

"We don't have to...if you're not-"

She smiled, reassuringly. A wave of relief went through her. She had zero experience being intimate with a man, she had read about sex in books and she wasn't completely naive to the act but she had no idea what to do in this moment. "I want to," she replied. Then resumed sliding off his shirt from his shoulders until he was standing in nothing but his black trousers and shoes.

A gasp slipped from her lips when Sophia saw a long healed scar over his chest, that was what her fingers made contact with. It looked old, like the scars on Sophia's face, a raised white surface that reached to his shoulder. It appeared as though someone had slashed him with a blade, Sophia didn't even want to begin to imagine how painful that must have been.

She frowned when her eyes trailed down to his torso and noticed that there were more scars, only fainter, across his rib cage and lower stomach.

Xavier still held her wrist, he was making circular motions with his thumb along his skin.

"How did you get these?"

Xavier shrugged like it was nothing, which bothered Sophia. The idea of anyone hurting him sent an uncomfortable pain through her heart. He released her wrist when she moved her hand to the scars along his torso, she individually traced each line in a somewhat state of disbelief.

"That was for beating a gentleman at poker who wasn't very happy that I cheated."

Sophia didn't say anything, instead she slid her fingers up to a long scar across his ribcage.

"That one was from a bartender who chased me down after not paying my tab." Xavier chuckled at the memory.

Sophia found it odd that he was a vampire and yet even he could be caught off guard from an angry human flailing around with a knife.

Her hands moved up to the large scar across his chest, it started just above his nipple and it looked to be the most painful of them all. The others were mere scratches in comparison. Based on how raised the scar was, it must have been a deep cut.

"This one," he exhaled a sigh. "Was from the remarkable Lord Paine himself. After my first day in his prison I made an...unflattering remark in regards to his wife. It resulted in him taking a wooden stake to my chest." Xavier shuddered from this memory. "Any deeper and he would have pierced my heart, and I wouldn't be standing here with you."

Such a violent act from a man who sat at his desk for most of the day, looking bored with the world.

Although her life has been nothing but chaos since Xavier showed up in her life, she couldn't imagine herself without him now. Her life would have been empty and miserable, and she most likely would have still been Jack's bride.

"Now you know how to kill a vampire. As simple as taking a stake through the heart."

The scar didn't seem like an attempt to kill Xavier, as it was a long line of a scar. It could be seen as more of a threat, to show Lord Paine had it in him to kill. Maybe that's why Xavier suspects Lord Paine of killing his family.

Sophia pressed her lips against the scar on his chest, and trailed small kisses along it, just as Xavier did with the scars on her cheek. It was an odd feeling knowing that the two men she held closest to her heart also held scars, only theirs were easily hidden. It made Sophia wonder if she hadn't acquired the scars on her face would she too have kept hers a secret. Perhaps Sophia had wasted too much time giving her scars such weight, Xavier and Jack walked with theirs every day with little to no acknowledgement. Maybe it was time for her to let it go.

Xavier put both his hands onto her shoulders, dipping his head with a sweet smile on his lips. "I'm not in pain, if that's what you're worried about."

"I just don't like the idea of anyone hurting you."

Xavier smiled, and kissed her deeply. Completely stealing her breath away. "And I to you," he muttered against her mouth.

He held her in a tight embrace as they kissed, anyone outside of this room was insignificant. Sophia soon melted into him, all of her fears and insecurities washing away with the taste of his whisky coated lips.

As their kiss intensified, Sophia wrapped her arms around the back of his neck and pressed her body against his. When Xavier's hands circled her waist, and his hands pressed against her back, an involuntary moan escaped from her lips causing Xavier's grip to tighten around her.

Sophia was feeling things she had never experienced before, a deep lust for more. Her hips were drawn to Xavier, and she was tingling from head to toe. The world spinning at her feet.

Xavier broke their kiss only to trail a fiery heat down her neck as his lips grazed her skin. Sophia gripped his thick black hair in fistfuls as he kissed his way back up to her lips.

For a moment Sophia pulled away to drink in the hungry features of his face, she had no idea she could cause such a reaction from a man but he looked as though he yearned for her. Possibly more than she did for him at this moment, which she thought was not possible.

"May you undress me?" She asked, struggling to catch her breath.

Xavier simply nodded, and slowly turned her by her waist so her back was facing him. Sophia gathered her hair and positioned it over her shoulder so it would be easier for Xavier to see.

Before he even began pulling at the strings holding her dress together, his warm breath hit against her neck, causing her to bite her bottom lip. Xavier only made it worse by trailing kisses along the back of her neck.

The more her dress started to loosen at the back, Xavier began trailing kisses at every new patch of skin that was revealed.

Sophia's heart thrashed against her ribs after every kiss and she wasn't sure how long she could last just standing and waiting for him to undress her.

Xavier made a trail back up the back of her neck, all the way to her ear. She could feel the goosebumps rising on her arms as his hot breath hit against her skin. "I don't think I ever told you," he whispered so quietly in her ear, that if she didn't listen carefully she would miss what he had to say. "I loathed the idea of living in that orphanage. But..." she could feel him smile. "It's possibly the greatest and only blessing this world has given me in years."

Sophia looked over her shoulder to get a good look at him. Her eyes wide with anticipation, her heart was practically hammering in her ears. She knew exactly why he never wanted to call the orphanage a home. It resulted in the loss of his entire family, the people he cherished most, and to hear him say this brought warm tears to her eyes. "Why?" She asked, not once taking her gaze away from his.

"Because it brought me to you."

Finally, Xavier finished tugging at the strings and the gown was now hanging on by the sleeves. With the dress no longer pressed against her chest, Sophia felt like she could breathe.

That was soon met with the nerves and realisation that Xavier would soon see her. No clothes, no barrier between him and her exposed body.

Then the fear crept in, what if he didn't like what he saw. He wasn't the only one with scars on his body, but he wore them as though they didn't exist but hers were itching and burning into her skin every day. She couldn't go one day without being reminded of them. At least Xavier knew where his scars came from, Sophia didn't have the comfort of knowing how she acquired hers.

The dress was now completely loose but Sophia still held it up, psyching herself up to reveal her naked body. Xavier was patient, wanting to ensure she was ready. That she wouldn't suddenly change her mind, but she knew that would never happen.

Xavier slipped his hands to her bare arms and guided the dress down, and it soon fell into a puddle circling her body.

Sophia was suddenly frozen in place, with her naked back to Xavier. She didn't know what to do or how Xavier would react.

She had never stood naked in front of anyone before, other than Stella - even then she only saw her naked a handful of times when she needed assistance with certain corsets and undergarments.

Xavier swallowed and his fingers pressed into the arch of her back, and then his left hand traced a line along her shoulder blades, and she knew exactly what shape he was tracing.

It was another scar.

Sophia dropped her head, almost ashamed of herself.

"I did not know you had more scars." He said in a low, hushed tone.

Before she could open her mouth to say something, to apologise, it was cut short when she felt his featherlike lips brush across her scar. He kissed her just as she did him, and the sudden rush of pleasure was back and stronger than ever.

He turned her by her waist to face him. Sophia's movements were stiff as she turned to face him, her breasts on full display. When she faced him his eyes trailed down her chest and along the remaining scars across her ribs and two slashes down her left thigh. Whatever it was that caused the scars, they were only to the left side of her body, the right was blemish free. Not even a faint mark to be found.

"You're so beautiful, Sophia." Xavier said, in a tone that made the corners of her eyes fill with tears. It was so sincere that it was difficult to hear because it was the exact opposite of what she would tell herself.

Xavier saw the uncertainty in her face, and his response was to get down onto his knees and kiss the scar across her ribs. Once he was done there he dared to move to the two slashes across her inner thigh. When his mouth made contact she felt a warm aroused spark, and she couldn't help but knock her head back and feel each individual movement of his lips.

Xavier got back to his feet and slid his hand through hers, "I mean it, Sophia." He looked deep into her eyes that were full of lust. "You are the most beautiful woman I have ever laid eyes upon. I would feel the same even if you hadn't a single scar on your extravagant body."

Heat pricked her cheeks, and she surprised herself by pulling him to the bed. They didn't sit for a while. Sophia unfastened the button holding up Xavier's trousers, and after a deep breath dropped them to the floor.

She felt rude for staring but she couldn't look away. The length of him was almost intimidating and she couldn't help but turn into a volcano.

"Are you nervous?" Xavier asked, thinking she was looking to the floor but her sights were captivated by *something else.*

Sophia nodded, even though she was caught up by the sight of him it had started to sink in that this was real, and she was going to have sex with Xavier.

"I...I have never....I have never done this before," she was fumbling over her words. Obviously she had never done this before, Xavier knew that but she felt like she had to admit she was completely new to all of this. She didn't know what to do, or where to put her hands.

"I know."

"You have?"

Xavier nodded but she couldn't see because she couldn't raise her head from the ground. "But never with anyone I cared for."

Although Sophia hated picturing Xavier with other more attractive girls, she appreciated his honesty. He could have easily lied to her to spare her feelings but she was a little relieved that he knew what he was doing, so she could have some guidance.

Xavier's finger hooked under her chin and tilted her head to face him, her eyes were wide with anticipation. "It's the truth, Sophia," he kept saying her name, he had done so many times before but tonight it made her body tremble. "I've never cared or felt this way for anyone other than you. You are the only woman I have ever loved."

His free hand held her waist, the tips of his fingers were like feathers as they grazed her skin. It was like he was leaving a trail of fiery passion after each simple touch.

Xavier sat on the edge of the bed, and slowly guided Sophia's thighs to wrap around his waist. She could feel his cock pushing against her and she instinctively wanted to thrust her hips against him but she managed to compose herself. Straddling him, she looked down at him through her long eyelashes, drinking in the intoxicating features of his face. His sharp jaw, the crook of his nose and his upturned eyes that housed pools of black ink.

The feeling of their skin grazing against one another was like swimming in a bath of ecstasy. Their mouths once again collided, Xavier's hand slid around her back and pulled her closer to his chest. Sophia couldn't hold herself back this time, her body was reacting by thrusting her hips against him, stifling Xavier to moan against her mouth. His deep husky moans only provided more pleasure for Sophia's ears, like she was listening to the perfect symphony.

Sophia slid her hands into his raven black hair and grabbed fist fulls as she opened her mouth and invited his tongue inside. She was panting and moaning so much that she feared she might collapse. Her swollen breasts brushed against his chest, only adding more pleasure to an already steamy exchange.

This was just kissing, Sophia was already feeling an aching desire to have more of him. Her legs spread apart more as she needed to feel him, all of him.

Soon after, he picked her up and gently laid her down in between the large, powder blue pillows. He blanketed her body with his, and watched her intently for only a moment.

The ends of his black hair tickled her nose. "Beautiful."

The more he said it the more she wanted to believe him.

Sophia smiled and felt her cheeks flush as she wrapped her arms around his neck and pulled him down to her until their lips locked again. Xavier trailed kisses down her neck, over her breasts, until he got dangerously low...between her legs low.

Sophia couldn't keep her gaze from him, she watched as he spread open her legs. Sinking her teeth into her bottom lip, she waited and anticipated what his next move would be. When a wicked smile formed on his mouth the lower part of her body ached.

Surely he's not going to...

Before Sophia could finish her internal sentence Xavier did exactly what she thought he was not going to. The second his tongue made contact between her legs a burst of light filled Sophia's vision. She released a strong gasp and gripped the sheets beneath her. Xavier flicked his tongue in a rhythm that made her body crave more. She arched her neck, unable to control herself, biting back the screams that were rising in her throat.

When Xavier pulled back, Sophia's body was craving and demanding more. So much so that it was physically painful. Instead of giving Sophia what she wanted, Xavier kissed her stomach and her firm breasts, ensuring to flick his tongue across her erect nipple before meeting her face. He positioned both of his elbows and each side of her head, his entire body blanketing hers.

"Are you sure you're ready?" He asked, brushing any stray hairs away from her face.

Sophia bit her bottom lip and gave a quick nod as her response.

Xavier adjusted himself and suddenly she felt him slowly push inside of her, and it was shortly followed by a quick sharp, intense pain in her lower body. Her body jerked up in response and Xavier cupped the back of her head as she buried her face into his shoulder.

Xavier continued to move with her, pushing in and out. It was painful at first but then it slowly dissolved into an overwhelming amount of pleasure. Sophia wasn't sure if she could clamp her mouth shut to keep quiet. At this rate everyone back in London would be able to hear her. Or this household would think there was an earthquake.

Sophia tried to make the most of looking at Xavier as they filled each other with pleasure, the hungry look on his face made her body quiver. The deep look of concentration and his gritted teeth as he pumped in and out of her was certainly something she could never forget.

Xavier buried his face into her neck, his deep growls playing like a symphony so close to Sophia's ear. Then, the world around her stilled and she felt as though she had drifted onto cloud nine when Xavier's grip tightened around her.

Then her world fell into a pleasurable state of bliss.

How could Sophia possibly sleep after the night she and Xavier shared. He didn't seem to have any trouble, as he lay on his side and seemed to be gone to the world. In such a peaceful slumber, Sophia watched him as his chest rose and fell.

Sophia clutched the blanket close to her chest, and she couldn't fight the glee that rose in her throat.

Xavier was so handsome, she silently prayed that one day a law would pass that he would not be permitted to wear a shirt when in her presence. A body like his should not be covered by the unworthy material that was his clothes.

"I can feel you watching me," Xavier spoke, but seemingly still in a slumber.

Xavier then opened one eye, and when he caught her bashful expression a grin stretched across his face.

Although they had shared an intimate night together, and Xavier's hands had been all over her body, Sophia was suddenly aware that under the thin blanket she was completely naked.

Propping himself up, Xavier leaned his weight on his elbow. His raven black hair was wild and sticking out in multiple different directions, all thanks to Sophia requiring something to grip onto.

Bringing the blanket up to her nose, Sophia hit her coy smile behind the material. Xavier raised a playful eyebrow when he noticed this and shuffled closer to her. He positioned one of his hands over her waist and the other beside her head. "Are you hiding from me?"

Sophia tucked the blanket under her chin, "Perhaps."

Xavier moved his hand that was beside her head, and began stroking Sophia's hair back from her forehead. "Is your body off limits to me now?"

"I'm afraid so," she whispered, a playfulness lacing her tone.

An eyebrow quirked on Xavier, he lowered himself down until their lips were but inches apart. "I'm sure I can rectify that."

In one swift motion, Xavier slid himself under the covers and Sophia rolled onto her back and excitedly anticipated how he was going to 'rectify' this situation.

Already, his hands were all over her waist. Soon that was followed by his soft feathery lips trailing heat along her navel.

A giggle bubbled in her throat when his hands started traveling up her body.

Xavier kissed all the way up her torso and along her right breast. He lingered there for a while, trailing his mouth and flicking her erect nipple with his tongue.

Sophia ached at his touch, and he knew damn well that she did. She was almost certain she could feel him smiling.

Adjusting himself, Xavier's head emerged from under the covers and he was now face to face with Sophia. His entire body was leaning over hers, squashing her slightly. Both of his elbows were positioned at either side of her head, with one hand brushing back invisible hairs from her cheeks. "That did not seem to be very off limits."

Before she could respond, Xavier kissed her deeply. His fingers dug into her hips, and Sophia bucked her hips in response. Moaning into his mouth as the fire ignited in her chest.

"We need to rest," she said breathlessly against his mouth.

Xavier's reply was with trailing kisses from her jaw and into the arch of her neck, only adding fuel to her fire. "We're to be wed in a couple of hours," she whispered, her hands gripping onto his hair. "I do not want to pass out when taking our vows."

"I'll save us some time and say them here," he said, making his way back up to her mouth and pressing his lips against hers.

"I, Xavier Howell."

Kiss.

"Do take thee..."

Kiss.

Sophia was struggling to hold back her laughter as she playfully swatted his arm.

"Sophia Cole..."

Kiss.

"To be my lawfully wedded wife."

Kiss.

"In sickness and in health, whether fat or skinny-"

"Xavier!" She shrieked and rolled him onto his back, both her legs were straddling his waist as she looked down on him, her body on full display in front of him.

"You are so wicked," Sophia trailed her finger along his chest, tracing the line of his prominent scar.

"I have a question," Sophia said.

"Hmm?"

Knowing what she was about to ask, it wasn't exactly well timed but she had to know.

Scanning his face with her eyes, he looked very tired. His eyes were drifting to sleep but it was obvious he was enjoying the view too much to go to sleep.

"Couldn't you drink my blood? Since I have human blood?"

Xavier watched her, clearly unsure of what to say. He let out a nervous breath and brought one hand up to slide around her neck. "I don't think you quite realize how painful it would be to have your skin pierced with fangs. Plus, I wouldn't want to leave a mark on your pretty neck."

Rolling her eyes, she said. "I have plenty of scars, a couple teeth marks would be nothing more than a blemish."

His face fell into a frown, so she changed the subject. "I have another question."

"Is the only thing that defines you as a vampire is that you have fangs and drink human blood?" She asked, cocking her head to the side. "Or do you have more secret talents?"

Xavier lifted himself up, so his back was resting on the headboard. "It's more complicated than that."

"How so?"

Running his palm over his face he let out an amused laugh. "Well, the main 'advantage' I suppose is that I am immortal...or I will be."

An eyebrow raised from Sophia, asking him to elaborate.

"Immortality for vampires isn't simply living forever. We can die, just not easily once we *become* immortal." Xavier explained. "At some point in my life, it could be today or it could be in fifty years, my heart will stop beating and I will remain frozen in the age that my heart stopped." Xavier smirked. "I am just hoping I am lucky and it happens early. I don't want to be eighty forever."

This sparked a small bit of anxiety in Sophia. If he stopped aging, and remained young forever, on his arm as the years went on Sophia would look like his grandmother and not his wife.

Swallowing her fears, Sophia asked, "Is it painful?"

Xavier merely shrugged. "I don't know."

"Did your parents go through it?"

He shook his head, "They died before it happened to them. You can't kill a vampire as easily with a single stake through the heart once they've changed."

Sophia didn't fully understand it. She didn't fully understand herself, but they had the rest of their lives to figure it out.

Taking in the rugged details of his face, her eyes focused on his crooked nose. She tapped his bridge, like she was testing it worked. "What happened to this?"

"So many questions," he sighed and pushed himself up, slipping his hands around her bare back. "I think we've done enough talking." Xavier buried his face into the crook of her neck, and trailed kisses up to her jaw. As much as she wanted to give into him, Sophia wanted to get to know as much about him before he became her husband.

Pushing him back was like a punishment, "Tell me."

"You are confident that this is a result of something? My scars were an obvious indication and if that wasn't the same case for my nose, and you weren't so lucky with your guess, I would be highly offended."

Swatting his forearm, she pushed, "Well?"

"*Well,*" he mimicked her. "The story isn't as interesting as you might think, perhaps I should leave at least one thing a mystery."

"We are to be married, and that means no secrets."

A smile curved his mouth, "Fine. As children my father wanted us to try feeding off animal blood to prevent the risk of being caught feasting on corpses." he explained. "On one of these trips, he trusted my sister and I to hunt a deer, our garden was infested with them. They were like rats."

Sophia softly giggled at that, and continued to intently listen. She enjoyed hearing Xavier talk about his past, she could feel the warmth radiating from him.

"It was Lucy's turn to capture the animal. Everything was set up for her perfectly, it should have been the easiest hunt that we had ever done. But for whatever reason I still cannot comprehend," he was smiling at the memory, whilst also trying to wrap his head around it. "She jumped out to pounce on it but she froze like *she* was the prey. Instead of the deer fleeing, like most would, it charged at her. Causing my sister to bolt and run right into me when my back was turned, screaming like she was escaping a house fire. When she charged into me, I fell face first onto a log, resulting in my once perfectly chiseled nose becoming a broken mess. It was disgusting, blood everywhere."

"I can imagine," Sophia was surprised at the simplicity of a story, there was no brawl or demonic attribute to his story. It was something that could have happened to anyone.

"I never let her forget it," he said, his smile growing, causing the corners of his eyes to crease. "When she would tell me to do my chores I would remind her of what she did. That wore thin very quickly, her responses soon became: *a broken nose doesn't affect your hands.*" His smile soon faded, like he was abruptly reminded that he would never see his sister again. Not the real Lucy.

"I am sure you were just as much of a nightmare as a child as you are now."

Suddenly, Xavier flipped Sophia so she was on her back and his body acted as a blanket. One hand circled her waist and the other propped himself up beside her. "Most definitely," he said as he brushed his lips across hers.

"Tell me you love me," she muttered against his mouth.

She felt his smile widen as they kissed, followed by a laugh through his nose. "I love you."

"Again?" she giggled.

"You are such a pest," he said. "I will get my revenge."

Before he melted into her, Sophia said. "And how will you do that?"

"By making it very difficult for you to walk down the aisle tomorrow."

Chapter Twenty-Six

The wedding came together without a hitch. Now all Sophia had to do was meet Xavier down the aisle and get married. Christopher must have had a secret love for wedding planning. He managed to transform the ballroom into something out of a fantasy with such a tight deadline. The maids were discussing how they spent hours clipping white roses from the garden and decorating the ballroom with them. Sophia was yet to see it, but the way the girls described it, she could only imagine something from a fairytale.

Sophia liked to imagine that Christopher did this for her only. Since Christopher had missed all of the important moments in Sophia's life, at least he could be a part of her wedding.

As one of the younger maids focused on her hair, she couldn't help but think of Stella. She was the only person she wished could get in a horse and carriage and attend her wedding. But it would be something to look forward to when she returned to the orphanage. She would talk her ear off about how marvelous this day was.

Yet, Sophia had a sinking feeling in the pit of her stomach. Something she couldn't quite put her finger on. As though she would never see Stella again, and get a chance to tell her wild story of how she fell in love with a vampire.

All Sophia could do for now was enjoy being the centre of attention. It's not something she ever wanted to get used to, but she made an exception for her wedding day.

She decided to have her hair down, with a couple of pieces from the sides joined together at the back of her head, and braided down her back. The rest of her hair curled naturally down her back. She couldn't wait to feel Xavier's hands run through it.

Biting down on her lip, Sophia blushed as she thought of the night they had shared. It had been only hours since she had seen him last and she already missed him. His hands had touched every single part of her body, made her feel things she never thought possible. How her heart pooled with warmth at just the thought, she knew it wouldn't be long until she fell in love with him.

The young maid finished up her hair.

The elderly lady that was sitting in the corner, fiddling with a long piece of lace and a sparkly object, got up out of her chair and met Sophia at her vanity. Appearing in the mirror, she looked frail. Old enough to be her grandmother. With her slender fingers, with veins bumping her skin, she slid the sparkled object over her head. Like she was being crowned as a Queen.

A delicate, simple headband sat atop her head with the veil attached to it. It felt odd to wear a veil without her dress, but looking at her reflection she knew that whatever dress Chrsitopher could supply wouldn't matter. She would feel like a princess today, all because of a headband and a veil.

"The dress has arrived," Christopher burst in the door. Luckily Sophia wasn't naked as that could have been a very awkward start to her wedding day.

Christopher looked proud as he held in his hands a pure white gown. It was almost blinding how white it was. As she got to her feet and hurried over, leaving trails of excitement in her wake, she was mesmerized by the intricate details of the skirt. With a weightless layered lace of the skirt it looked spacious to walk in, that cut out her fears of tripping up down the aisle. It would pinch in at the waist and the sleeves would reach her knuckles with a matching lace pattern as to the skirt. It wasn't the dress of her dreams, it was so much more than that. It was beautiful. Almost too beautiful, Sophia wasn't sure if she was worthy of wearing it.

She trailed her fingers across the soft material and Christopher put it in her hands.

"This is beautiful," she couldn't put into words how grateful she was. "How did you get a hold of such a stunning dress in such short notice?"

"It was your mother's," he admitted.

When the shock appeared on Sophia's face, Christopher said. "It would be nice to see her daughter wear it for her wedding."

Sophia would not cry. She had done enough of that, but the ache which came along with it was still present. It always would be.

"I'm your daughter too." she whispered, as though she had to keep reminding herself.

Christopher smiled, sadly. He reached out his hand and cupped her scarred cheek, brushing his thumb along one of her scars. Soon she would ask how she acquired them. He must know, for the sadness in his eyes as he took them in reminded her of a guilty conscience.

"My beautiful Sophia." he whispered. "My darling daughter."

When Christopher realised there were maids present, he dropped his hand and cleared his throat. As though he was embarrassed for them to witness him in such a vulnerable state. "Mr Howell is ready in the ballroom. So, when you're dressed the maids will take you there."

"Wait!" she called before he turned to leave. When Christopher looked over his shoulder to look at her, he looked fearful of what she was about to say.

"Would you...would you give me away?"

Christopher's eyes, the eyes he gave to Sophia, widened. Why would this be such a shock? A father giving away his daughter happens daily at weddings.

"I'm sorry that this all seems sudden," she brought her hands together and chipped away at her nails. "This is all so strange but...I am sure I am not the only girl who wants her father to walk her down the aisle."

Due to the amount of time that had passed without an answer, Sophia was certain he was going to decline. Perhaps she was rushing into trying to develop a relationship with her father.

That was until Christopher said, "I would be honoured."

The ballroom was fully transformed into an elegant setting for a traditional wedding. The theme Christopher went with was white and silver. Sophia wondered if this was how her parents' wedding looked when they married.

The entire room radiated sophistication, and a timeless elegance. There were no details that felt like too much - too in your face. The most that was done was the addition of the white roses on every chair. The colours were clearly carefully selected, as there was no piece out of place. To top everything off, the room was lit with tall candles, twinkling in every corner to really set this romantic mood.

Christopher managed to scrounge together a few guests. No doubt from one of his many parties. Sophia was glad that there weren't too many strangers present, as it would feel like she was stealing the identity of someone else's bride. She almost convinced herself that this wasn't for her, but for a princess.

A maximum of twelve male guests stood in suites and elegant dresses. They all had white deck chairs with a silk ribbon wrapped around each one.

With her arm tightly grasped against the sleeve of Christopher's coat, her eyes were shielded with a white linen veil. Her eyes scanned the room only caring for one man, soon she found him.

Xavier.

Of course he would steal the entire show. Just standing in a black and white suit, his hands clasped together in front of him, he could steal anyone's breath away.

Sophia was so used to seeing him with disheveled and untamed hair, but today he's actually styled it. It made him look so formal, so classy. Like he belonged with the rest of these rich aristocats.

He was so handsome, and when his onyx eyes took in the sight of Sophia she saw his lips art. Xavier sucked in a long breath, as his chest rose and fell.

Was he nervous?

Xavier had to be careful. If he kept looking at her like that, like she is the most beautiful woman to have ever existed, Sophia would fall in love with him any second.

Xavier managed to find her eyes through the veil, and not once did he look away.

The room vanished so it was just the two of them. Sophia had to compose herself, otherwise she might release her father and sprint to meet her future husband.

As soon as they reached him, Xavier took Sophia's hand in his and squeezed her fingers, almost as if he was reassuring her he was there. She was eager to raise her veil to get a good look at him.

Before turning to the priest, Sophia turned back to Christopher. She wrapped her arms around him for a tight embrace, and his grip felt loose around her waist. Perhaps he was too frightened to ruin her dress by holding on too tightly.

For so long Sophia felt alone in this life. With no one who could understand her. But now, she was embracing her father. The only family she had left, and he seemed to accept her for all of her scars. He would help her discover her past.

And now, her future seems brighter. She would be marrying a man that filled her heart with a golden glow. A man she would one day fall in love with, and possibly have a family of their own.

When Christopher released Sophia, he joined the rest of the guests at the seating area. He sat on the front row with his fingers laid flat against his upper thighs.

The priest began the ceremony with Xavier grazing his thumb across the back of her knuckle.

Sophia tried her best to concentrate on what the priest was saying, but she couldn't but be aware of Xavier's soft touch.

After today she would no longer be a Cole, the name which held mystery in the past few years. Today she would become Sophia Howell. The name which gave her a new beginning, a new life with Xavier by her side.

The ceremony was shorter than she'd expected, she always thought weddings went on for hours but it rushed by. When Xavier slowly raised the veil and placed it behind her head, her vision was still obscured by the tears in her eyes.

Xavier and Sophia exchanged vows and sealed the promise with a kiss, but no ring. There wasn't enough time to have rings made in such short notice, but there would be plenty of time after today to have that sorted.

The kiss was enough to prove Xavier's loyalty to her. He kissed her like there was no one else present, with his mouth searching hers, unlocking the secrets to her heart. Xavier was so gentle as he cupped her cheeks, like he was scared she would break.

That was it, they were married. Sophia let out a sigh of relief that her future was safe. She looked through the unenthusiastic applauding crowd and hoped to find Jack's face, but he was nowhere in sight.

Xavier had his hand around her dainty waist and kissed the side of her face. "You look beautiful, Mrs Howell."

It felt strange to hear someone say her new name, she almost didn't realise he was talking to her. It sent a burst of joy through her heart. She pecked him on the lips and all the maids quickly began clearing away. Of course these men and women would only come to a wedding if it involved a party afterwards.

Christopher was on the other side of the room, with his back against the wall. He was looking at Sophia, and there was sadness in his eyes.

Excusing herself from Xavier's arm, she met with her father.

"Thank you for organising this," said Sophia, dipping her head.

She still had so many unanswered questions. Where could she even begin to ask about her life. She would love to hear all about her mother and how they met. It would take her a lifetime to ask all of the questions she wanted answered.

"Please, enjoy your wedding. I know you have many questions, and I will answer them, but enjoy being the bride today."

The formality in which he spoke was disheartening. What did she expect? Already he had shown her more love and kindness than she had expected.

All of these years, being apart from one another must have been hard on him. Maybe even harder than it was for Sophia.

At least for Sophia, she didn't have memories of him. So there was nothing for her to miss, nothing for her to reflect on. But for Christopher, his child that he cradled in his arms. A baby he made with the love of his life, taken away from him simply because of who he was.

When Xavier met them, Christopher patted him on the shoulder. "Congratulations, what better excuse to get drunk."

Xavier didn't do much to hide his distaste. Sophia knew that tomorrow was going to be full of fights and raised voices, with her husband demanding to destroy the device that brought his sister's spirit back.

Xavier was about to open his mouth to say something but Sophia squeezed his hand tightly. "Leave it alone for today," she whispered as a warning.

With a lick of his bottom lip, he considered it for a moment. Then his shoulders slumped slightly as he admitted defeat. "Fine, but it will be a battlefield tomorrow."

Sophia only smiled faintly. She was happy to be married, and to a man she was falling in love with. She was just hurt that Jack did not attend. Surely word must have gotten around that she was marrying today. Not that she could blame him entirely. They were already on thin ice these past few months, but the other night surely caused a crack.

Maybe this really was the end of their friendship.

Xavier stepped into her view, taking her hands in his. "Are you alright? That's not the face a bride should be making on her wedding day."

Bringing her shoulder up to her ear, she said. "Jack isn't here."

Xavier touched her cheek. It was clear he didn't know what comforting words to offer her at this time. As much as he disliked Jack, he knew how much Sophia cared for him.

Enjoy your wedding.

Christopher was right. This was supposed to be a day of celebration. For today she would leave the broken pieces of her heart at the door and attempt to put them back together tomorrow. Today was about having fun and enjoying her first day as someone's wife.

Sophia raised herself up on her toes and kissed Xavier, "Let's enjoy today," she said as she lowered herself down.

Xavier mirrored her sentiment and kissed her forehead.

Throughout the day more guests piled in and everyone was having a merry time getting drunk. Most had forgotten that two people were celebrating a marriage and just focused on the free drinks.

Sophia didn't mind. She was happily dancing with Xavier within the crowd of people. It reminded her of how they danced that night at the lake. When they first kissed. She never would have known the next time they were to dance like this would be at their wedding.

She had already lost the veil that one of the maids crafted for her. Sophia remembered putting it down at the refreshment table, and turned her back for one second only to find it gone when she had returned.

As much as she tried to enjoy her wedding day, she couldn't help but think of Jack. These past three months have been a mess. Sophia knew that if she could go back in time and change everything, she would in a heartbeat. She would have rejected Jack's proposal and tried to salvage their friendship from there.

But she can't go back. She can waste her energy each day wishing she could turn back the clocks, warn her younger self of all the mistakes she would make. But it would be a waste of time. All she could do now is try to make things right.

The worst thing out of all this, the hurt that Jack had endured from Sophia resulted in nothing for him. He didn't get the girl he was in love with all of his life. Jack went through so much, just to be tossed aside.

"I know you're thinking about him," Xavier broke her chain of thought, resting his chin on the top of her head.

"I am concerned for him," Sophia sighed, pressing her cheek flat against his chest. The rhythm of his heart soothing her soul.

"There's no doubt he heard of our wedding taking place today," said Xavier. "But he may just be in his room."

"I know but-"

"If you're that worried for him, go and talk to him. You can come back when you're satisfied you've done everything you can." he pulled her at arm's length and kissed her.

"You do not mind?"

He shrugged his shoulders. "I am sure I can find ways to occupy my time, I may be intoxicated the next time you see me though."

She brushed her lips against his, when they broke apart Xavier said, "I'm sorry, I am sure this isn't the wedding you dreamed of." He took her hand in his, grazed his thumb across her finger where a ring should be. "I promise I'll make it up to you."

How did he turn into the sweetest gentleman? Unless he was always like that, and he had finally let the mask fall only for her. "You don't need to do any such thing."

Pressing her lips to his cheek, she waved goodbye and went to search for Jack.

Chapter Twenty-Seven

Jack's bedroom was her first destination, but was disheartened to find it empty.

Half an hour had passed and Sophia was running out of options where he could be.

The drawing room.

The garden.

All empty.

Sophia was ready to give up and make her way back to Xavier. Jack could have left for all she knew and she would be spending her wedding day wandering the halls. Another day couldn't hurt. The more time he had to himself the better, she supposed.

Just when Sophia was about to turn around and leave, she realised she was in a part of the manor that she had never been before. She was standing in a hallway which was lined with doors that matched the rest of the building. Only...there was something in her chest telling her she had been here before. Not recently, but at some point in her life she had walked this hall.

The wallpaper was different from every other corridor. The walls were a grey chevron, and it hit her like a ton of bricks.

Her dreams.

This was the wallpaper that the door from her dream sat on. She was sure of it. There wasn't a detail that made her think otherwise.

Suddenly, she found herself running, checking every door in the process. They were all brown, but the one from her dream was a distinct eggshell white, with four cracks in the door.

It was getting darker the further she was walking into this hall. The candles were appearing less and less on the walls but when she reached the very end of the hall she found it.

Standing alone, a white eggshell door with exactly four cracks down the wood. Sophia wasn't sure whether she had fallen asleep and she was back in a very vivid dream.

When she reached out to the handle, it felt real in her hands. It felt like a cold doorknob against her fingers. For a while she just stood there, with the doorknob in hand. Would this answer the questions that her mind had blocked out for years?

Sophia suddenly felt sick, like whatever was in there would be something she couldn't unsee.

Turning the knob she opened the door, and was greeted by a set of stairs going down. Just like her most recent dream. This was the furthest her mind would let her remember about this door.

It would be very inappropriate to go snooping around her father's house, especially after everything he had done for her wedding. But, there was a voice screaming at her to go down. That there was something she needed to see, and that this would be her last chance.

She took a deep breath and descended the stairs, her fingers shaking the entire time.

There were a lot of stairs, and she had to pick up the ends of her dress to prevent it from getting dirty.

When Sophia reached the bottom, the room was filled with darkness. The only light source was from a crack in the wall leading to the outside. With that light, she was able to find a lantern and some matches.

She was too scared to stay in the dark for much longer, so she lit a match and the lantern.

It didn't take long for the room to fill with light from this single lantern.

Sophia raised the lamp to guide her way around the room, and then she saw what her heart already knew was here. A woman chained by the wrists to the concrete wall. She was more of a skeleton than a person, with skin stretched across her bones. Her hair hadn't been maintained in years, with knots that could never be untangled. And within her hair were clumps of dirt that coloured her once golden hair. This woman's head was hung between her shoulders, just like Xavier when she first met him. Blood stained her dirt covered feet and her hands were sliced with nail marks, like she had been trying to inflict pain upon herself.

Dressed in nothing but a grey dress, that was ripped all over the skirt, it was covered in stains. From blood to urine, Sophia wondered how she had managed to live like this? And *why* was she down here.

As Sophia approached and the light shined more details along her arms and legs, Sophia could see large dots scattered across her skin. Like someone had been injecting her every day with a small needle. There were some scars that were old, but others looked brand new.

Sophia stepped closer to her, cautiously.

The woman couldn't see Sophia, for her eyes were completely covered with a piece of thick grey cloth.

"E-excuse me." Sophia trembled.

The woman snapped her head up and clenched her fists. "Help me," there was a strain in her voice. This woman couldn't speak any louder than a whisper.

When she snapped out of her shock, Sophia ran to the woman and began fiddling with the chains at her wrists. She needed a key to unlock her. Why would Christopher have a woman chained up in his basement? Did he know she was here? He seemed like such a put together gentleman. He couldn't have been the one to do this to her. Her father couldn't be this kind of man, it was impossible.

"I need a key," Sophia stammered.

"I never see where he puts it," the woman began crying. "Please, help me. I have been here for over eighteen years. Living off bread and water, I need to get out." Her pale lips were cracked in multiple places, and dried blood stained her mouth. She was as dry as the desert, desperate for even a single drop of water. "A-a boy was here earlier. He heard me crying...he tried to help and then he...he...."

"You are neglecting your guests, Sophia." Sophia turned and found Christopher standing at the bottom of the stairs with his hands punched into his trouser pocket, leaning his body weight against the frame of the stairs. A black shadow crossed his face, and he suddenly seemed unrecognisable.

The woman's head shot up, like a dog that was alerted to an intruder. "Sophia?" she breathed, and the woman suddenly began thrashing her body forward, trying to break free from the chains. Her teeth were bared, grunting as she used any strength she had left to break free.

Sophia could not show that she was frightened of him, she could not show any sign of weakness. With her hands balled at her sides, she released her bottom lip from her two front teeth. "Why is she in this state?" she asked, trying to repress her shaking voice.

Christopher ignored her and walked further into the room and to the woman in chains.

Sophia's eyes followed him as he squatted down, avoiding getting dirt on his clean suite. With a smile on his face he grabbed the woman's boney cheeks and pulled her to face him. She sat frozen as his hot breath hit her face. "If only you could see her wearing your dress."

The woman let out a whimper and tried to shake her head free. His grip only grew tighter and his smile creased into a rage.

"You're...you're my..." Sophia had lost all words.

This wasn't the Christopher who walked her down the aisle, the man she longed for in a father. This was the frightening erratic Christopher she caught a glimpse of all of those nights ago.

If only she hadn't brushed off his behaviour, if only she had seen the warning signs that he was a lunatic.

Forcefully, Christopher pulled the woman's dirty face closer until the ends of their noses touched, "Our Sophia is all grown up and married. To a murderous vampire, aren't you proud, Theresa?" He dropped her face without any care of it hurting her. "He will probably have her killed on their wedding night."

Theresa made a noise in the back of her throat and shot out a ball of spit, landing directly in Christopher's face. Her chest was heaving from a struggling breath.

Sophia wanted to move, to go seek help but she was frozen in fear. She tried to tell herself to pick up her legs and head for the door. Get Xavier and have him free her mother. But another part of her couldn't leave this woman, for Christopher could do something to her.

Christopher glared down Theresa and slowly raised himself to his feet, casting a shadow over her limp body. He looked down on her with disgust, like she was nothing more than a bug at the end of his shoe. Raising his hand in the air, he swiftly struck her across the cheek. The slap was hard enough to make her cry out in pain.

Sophia could not just sit back and watch this unfold. She couldn't just stand here, she had to move her feet and get help.

In a flash of adrenaline that finally kicked in, she whipped herself around and bolted for the stairs. Sophia scrambled up the concrete steps, her lungs filling with fire as she panicked to break free. She could see the closed door, it was only a few steps away.

When she finally made it to the top she gripped her hand around the doorknob and twisted. It was locked. The more panic filled her lungs the faster she tried to turn the knob. A desperate cry escaped her throat as she tried barging the door with her shoulder.

It was useless.

Christopher had locked them in.

She sucked in a long breath and was about to scream for Xavier, when a rope was draped around her mouth and the only noises she could make were muffled.

The sides of her mouth were burning from the rope scratching against the corners of her mouth. She did everything she could to kick out her legs and break free from Christopher's hold, but she was powerless. Christopher had a strength that was too powerful for her to overcome.

He dragged her back down the stairs, the back of her heel hitting the concrete steps and shooting a pain through her legs.

Not even with her free hands could she swing for Christopher or break free from the burning rope.

When he dragged her back down to the bottom of the stairs, Christopher threw her down to the ground next to Theresa, causing her head to hit against the wall.

Sophia reached up behind her head, checking there was no blood. When she brought her hand to her face to inspect, there wasn't even a drop.

Christopher grabbed both of his daughter's wrists, like she was nothing more than a ragdoll, and chained her in the same position as Theresa.

Christopher pulled the rope away from Sophia's mouth and threw it to the ground. "Like mother, like daughter, I suppose." Christopher grumbled as he dropped the keys into his coat pocket.

Sophia shot her head to Theresa and opened her mouth but couldn't bring herself to speak. She attempted to thrash her body and somehow break herself free from the chains but it was hopeless, she was trapped.

"I could stay down here and go through my dastardly plans, but I'm sure you'll pick it up as the years go on."

Christopher punched his hands in his pockets, playing with the keys as he walked up the cobbled steps. Before he left he looked over his shoulder as if ready to say something, but decided better of himself and continued up the stairs.

When the door closed, she heard the click of a lock. He'd trapped them here, chained to the wall in a basement.

Sophia fought with all her strength to slip her hands through the shackles, her hands were turning red in the process and she was sure she was about to lose circulation.

It was hopeless, she was stuck in an empty basement for possibly the rest of her life.

"I'm sorry," sobbed Theresa.

Sophia stared at the wall in front of her, her eyes followed the spiders climbing into their webs and opened her mouth with tears spilling from the corner of her eyes. "Was he lying?" she chewed her bottom lip and gritted her teeth. "Are you my-"

"Yes."

"How do you know I am your daughter, you are blindfolded?"

She shook her head, her arms falling limp. Her wrists were bound tight, with red marks burned into her skin. How long had she been down here?

"I have a hole in my heart. I knew it from the moment you spoke." Her sobs were becoming louder but she sounded too weak to cry. "My baby who was taken from me, is now here after eighteen years."

"Taken away...?" her head was hurting. "I assumed you were dead. I was given a letter from The Council...addressed from you."

"No," she whimpered, like an injured dog. "None of this was supposed to happen."

"I need answers. You have to tell me what's happening. Why am I here? Why is my father keeping us captive?"

"I'll start from the beginning," she held a deep breath and began her story. "I am a gorgon, a creature that seduces men and turns them to stone when we are sick of them. It was only ever supposed to be for fun. I have surely had my fair share of torturing men for entertainment." She stifled a laugh. "Then I met Christopher in a local pub. He was trying to be taken seriously as an inventor, and no one did. They called him crazy and the things he discussed were far from human capabilities. I found him interesting - and handsome - so I was the first person to listen to his crazy ideas. After that, he courted me and we fell in love. We eloped and I found out I was pregnant with you.

"As time passed, I felt a heavy burden about my past and what I am. I told him the truth, that I am a gorgon. At first he was skeptical and I proved it to him by turning one of his lab rats to stone. He seemed...excited and asked permission to use my blood for experiments. I agreed, not seeing the harm and I trusted him. What I didn't realise was, he was injecting himself with my blood and some other concoctions. It was a ridiculous idea that he could somehow give himself supernatural abilities. Instead it drove him mad, and he is addicted to it."

That's why he was so erratic that night. Sophia thought. *He must have been high off of gorgon blood.*

"As I got closer to the delivery date I became concerned when I saw notes lying around for an invention which involved experimentation on our baby - you." Theresa's head dropped as she relived the memory. "So I left. Before I even got to the forest that crowds this manor, he caught me and tackled me to the ground. He dragged me back to the house and tied me up here with a blindfold covering my eyes so I couldn't turn him to stone. He delivered you...whilst I was in agony and chained to the wall...he took you away and I never got the chance to hold you...to see you, not once."

Sophia felt as if she should be crying. She wanted to, but with one question answered it caused more questions to spin in her head. "So, was it Christopher who wrote the letter? About me getting married?"

Theresa nodded. "There was never any money, and if you weren't to marry, nothing would have happened. He wrote the letter when you were taken to that orphanage. He knew it could mean one of two things. That you would seek him out knowing he is alive, then he would use you like a cow and drain you of all your blood for his inventions and his addiction. Just like he did to me."

Which is what happened, and Sophia felt foolish for giving him what he wanted.

"Or he assumed you would one day breed with another creature after a forced union. He planned to steal that child and extract its blood for his inventions. Nothing he has made has worked. Nothing that is worth money, at least."

"What has he made?" Sophia was numb all over. She wasn't even sure if she was speaking. "I know of *Everlasting Life.*"

Theresa scoffed, clearly she has heard of it before. "He's made all sorts of devices that work. One that can mimic my abilities, turning people to stone. And other trinkets that no one wants to buy."

"How did you know about the letter?"

"Christopher is a cruel man, he wrote the letter in a way of mocking me. He read it outloud before he sent it to Lord Paine."

Lord Paine had some involvement in this. It was obvious, but what would he get out of everything? He seemed bored with

Sophia's very existence. Why would he go out of his way to deliver the letter as instructed by Christopher?

Sophia hit the back of her head against the wall and felt her chest rise and fall. Her friendship was broken for nothing. All of this could have been avoided yet Christopher had to go along with his sick game.

She couldn't figure out what she should be doing, laughing in disbelief or crying. Her emotions were so muddled she ended up doing both.

"What is funny?" Theresa asked, almost frustrated.

Sophia shook her head with an uncomfortable feeling of anxiety in her chest. "That letter was the start of everything crumbling. How could a stupid piece of paper break someone?" her head was throbbing and she was feeling claustrophobic. She pulled her wrists back from the wall in another attempt to break free. It once again proved to be useless, she was only causing herself more injury. "We need to get out."

"If there was any way, don't you think I would have done it by now."

Chapter Twenty-Eight

An hour had passed since Sophia had left Xavier in the ballroom. He thought she would have been back by now. Maybe it wasn't the best idea to let her go to Jack alone, especially after his violent outbursts. Xavier decided to go and look for her, at least for his own peace of mind. He searched the entire manor for Sophia, but concern swelled after every door he opened and found her not there.

There was no sign of her, or Jack for that matter. Sophia wouldn't have left, she never had a habit of wandering off and she certainly wouldn't do it on her wedding day.

Xavier arrived outside of Christopher's office and the bile of hatred rose in his throat. The memory of his sister, summoned like she was nothing more than an object for show, still contorted his heart with rage and grief.

Curling his hands into fists, Xavier stormed into Christoper's study without the courtesy of knocking.

When the door swung open, almost flying off his hinges, Xavier wasn't prepared for what he witnessed.

Christopher was standing in the corner, hunched over like a creature from the sewers. With his left arm stretched out as straight as a plank of wood, the other was holding a needle against the vein on his wrist. The needle disappeared into his skin, and the red vial used for his inventions was being injected into his body.

When Xavier saw this, he froze in place for a moment, he was unsure of what he was witnessing exactly. And taking in the manic and wild appearance that Christopher had turned into, only made the fear for Sophia's safety heighten.

Christopher's eyes were bulging out of his head when he met Xavier's gaze. It didn't stop him from injecting the entire red fluid into his body.

Finally Xavier snapped out of his state of shock, and barked. "What the hell are you doing?"

Christopher retracted the needle from his arm, the smell of iron filled Xavier's nostrils. The air filled with an overwhelming stench of blood and Xavier could feel his heart pounding with desire. This wasn't a healthy reaction for him, Christopher only had a small drop escape from him. How long had it been since he fed? He was so caught up with Sophia that nothing else mattered to him.

Luckily he wasn't at a point that would make him go on a rampage, his father taught him well to repress any animalistic urges to satisfy his cravings.

But there was another stench in the air that made Xavier's stomach churn. When Xavier's eyes found a small bottle of red liquid opened on his desk, he knew that's what Christopher had just put into his body.

Christopher followed his eyes, and tried to retrieve his bottle but he was too slow and Xavier reached it first.

Picking it up, he brought it up to his nose and took a small whiff. It was such a strong potent force that it made him take a few steps back and curl up his nose. This wasn't human blood, it was the blood of a demon and Christopher had injected it into himself.

When Christopher tried to frantically roll down his sleeve, he wasn't fast enough to hide the countless dots and scars across his arm. How long had he been doing this to himself?

How was he alive? A human shouldn't be able to withstand this kind of blood in their system. But Christopher clearly hasn't gone unaffected. His teeth were grinding together, and his brown hair was sticking up in multiple directions as his hand scratched over the place where he just injected himself.

"Why don't any of you knock?"

"Where's Sophia?"

"Lost your wife?" The playfulness in his tone was unsettling.

"She's missing, it's not like her." Xavier chose his words carefully. It was useless trying to play games with him. His first priority had to be finding Sophia and ensuring she was safe.

Christopher extended his arms, the tips of his fingers violently shaking, the pupils in his eyes having expanded to almost cover his entire iris. "As you can see I'm all alone. Why don't you ask Mr Green?"

Xavier didn't let the obvious jab get to him. He inadvertently looked around his desk again, searching for something that could provide him with clues to Sophia's location. All that was present was a bunch of scribbles and drawings of future inventions, each outlining the materials required.

Then Xavier's eyes caught on a framed photograph, tucked away in the midst of the chaos.

Christopher stiffened when he followed Xavier's eyes.

"Could you leave now?" There was a pleading in his tone.

Xavier ignored him and picked up the old photo frame. Inside of the frame was a girl in black and white, no older than five. She had a bright, toothless, smile. Her hair was wild, and clearly hadn't been brushed in days. She was clutching a brown bear in her small hands. Her face was smooth, not a scar in sight.

Suddenly, the frame was snatched away from Xavier's grip and being thrown into a draw. Christoper pressed the palms of his hands into the desk, hunching up his shoulders.

"I'm not going to stand here and pretend that you are a good man," Xavier said. "Just because you are my father-in-law. If you can stand here and tell me that you have no idea where Sophia is, then it will prove how little she meant to you."

Christopher's eyes couldn't focus on one place. He scanned the room in such a panic, internally debating with his own conscience about how to answer.

Xavier couldn't waste his time and stand and just wait for Christopher to make up his mind. "You aren't deserving of her." his palms were sweating as he curled his fingers into his palm.

Xavier then left Christopher in his state and searched every corner of the manor, twice. He decided the next best place to search would be the forest in front of the manor. Although, he doubted he'd find her there but he couldn't completely rule it out. Something could have spooked her whilst talking with Jack, causing her to run out.

He followed a familiar trail leading to the crash site, everything just as chaotic as the last time he saw it.

Once again, there was no sign of Sophia. His heart defiled like a balloon with several punctures to it.

Xavier turned to walk away, but stopped when he heard a grumbled "Wait." echo around the forest.

When he turned to follow the sound of the voice, Xavier walked past a few trees and then saw Jack emerge from the darkness. His suite was completely torn, like he had just wrestled with a bear and lost. Drops of blood trickled out of his nose, and his usually tidy hair was ruffled with spots of mud tangled into his locks. He limped to Xavier, one hand cradling his ribs.

"What happened to you?" Xavier couldn't hide his amusement.

Jack practically fell on Xavier's shoulder, his feet dragging against the floor.

"Is Sophia with you?" asked Xavier.

Jack shook his head, shaking crumbs of dirt onto Xavier's shoulder. "No, but I fear for her." Jack managed to stand, but he still kept a firm grip on Xavier's shoulder for support. "I fear Christopher is going to do something to her."

"What do you mean?"

Jack was panting, struggling to catch his breath. "Christopher has a woman chained in his basement. She's been held captive for years."

"We must hurry back," Xavier said. As he turned to sprint back to the manor, Jack clutched the sleeve of his coat, halting him. "What are you doing? You said so yourself, you're concerned for Sophia's safety."

"I can't just waltz in through the front door," Jack snapped. "Christopher caught me with the woman he tied up. He struck me in the back of the head as I tried to set her free. He dragged my body back to this crash site, thinking people would assume I died in an accident. He didn't take into account how much pain I can endure."

Xavier turned to face him. "Then what do you propose we do?"

"We'll look around for another way in. Preferably, so we are undetected."

Xavier grumbled, feeling impatient. "What does it matter if he sees us? What could he - a human - do?"

Jack shook his head, mirroring Xavier's impatience. "I don't want to risk him hurting Sophia."

"For once, I agree with you Mr Green."

Jack smiled at that. "Let us hurry. We can't waste any more time."

They rushed back to the manor, Xavier was slightly in front as Jack struggled to keep up. They scoured the building. There were countless windows and the door leading to the garden, but nothing that could give quick access underground.

"I knew there was something off about Christopher," Jack grumbled. "I am certain he caused our crash. I have not seen a single other demon in this forest. He must have somehow let that one loose."

"When was the last time you saw her?" Jack asked, swiftly changing the subject.

Xavier froze, there wasn't exactly a good time to bring this up with him. "At our...wedding."

Jack froze too. His lips parted, visibly stunned. "She married you?" he breathed out. He knew that they were to be wed but he didn't expect her to actually go through with it.

Placing a hand over his heart, he pressed his back into the brick wall, tilting his head toward the sky. All the time he spent planning their wedding, imagining their life together, all he had done was keep her from finding real love with someone else. For she married him within days, yet Sophia seemed uninterested in planning with Jack.

Xavier stood awkwardly, rubbing the back of his head. "If it's any consolation, she left looking for you. She was worried about you."

Jack lowered his head to face him.

Xavier was surprised by his reaction, he was sure he would flail his arms about and attempt to get in another punch. Instead his expression was blank, with the only hit of emotion given away by his eyes. An array of emotions could be seen swirling around the pools of blue.

"Do you love her?" Jack finally asked.

Xavier dropped his hand to his thigh and replied. "Yes."

"Does she love you?" These questions clearly pained Jack, but he had to know.

"Not yet," said Xavier. "But she said it won't be long until she does."

Jack let out a deep breath without saying another word about the subject. He already endured the pain from his wings, and a hit to the head today, he couldn't take any more.

Jack picked himself up from the wall with a wince, and limped to Xavier's side. He looked at Xavier for a long moment and cupped his hand over his shoulder, giving it a light shake.

Sliding his hand down, Jack turned with his head hanging. "There might be a way back here."

"Jack," Xavier said, softly. "She does love you. I know this isn't the best time but...please don't leave her life."

With his head hung low, Jack found a suspicious patch of oddly placed leaves and branches. He quickly knelt down and began pushing everything aside.

"Here!" Jack proclaimed.

A square door leading underground sat in plain sight. It was a pretty pathetic attempt to keep it hidden. Not that a regular person walking by would need a reason to find this door suspicious.

"A door," Jack shook the black handles. "It's locked."

"Out of the way," Xavier took Jack's place. His hands gripped around the cold black handle and, as easy as picking up a pen, he flung the doors open, breaking the chain and lock in one swoop. An echo traveled down the stairs leading into darkness.

Chapter Twenty-Nine

Sophia had all but given up. The more she pulled on her shackles the more her wrists pulsed in agony.

She and her mother sat in silence, with very little left to say. Sophia knew this was her chance to ask questions but with how bleek the situation was, what was the point?

Her mind wandered to Jack, was he safe? Did he just leave without saying goodbye? How could she blame him if he did? After everything she has put him through these past three months, she wouldn't blame him if he completely cut her out of his life.

All of the times he stood by her side. Offered her a marriage with little to no thought, all because he loved her and wanted her safe. Yes, he had his own intentions but Sophia knew deep down that he did everything, put himself through so much pain, because he cared for her. Oh, how she wished she showed him more respect toward his feelings.

Before she didn't understand Jack's feelings towards her. How he could feel the need to be that one and only person by someone's side forever. At times she thought he was exaggerating. But now that she found Xavier, and she was falling deeper and deeper into the pool of love, she was slowly starting to understand. Sophia knew that she'd hate it if Xavier flaunted another woman in front of her. If proclaimed he never loved her, even if it was to be honest, that it would crush her soul.

And that's exactly what she did to Jack.

Her mind drifted to Xavier, her husband. In such a short amount of time he opened up her world and helped the truth shine. He too, saved her and gave her the opportunity to love, even if it came with a consequence. Not only had he helped her feel a sense of freedom, but she felt like he truly understood her.

"I have made such a mess of things," Sophia sighed, thinking out loud. "I never expected *this* would be how I would be spending my wedding day."

Theresa was silent for a while. Sophia would steal glances to check she was still breathing. She was. Theresa just seemed to be consumed by her turmoil. When she spoke, it was more like she was in a trance. Looking back at her own life and trying to figure out how she ended up in this position. "I truly loved him."

Sophia looked over to her.

"Even now," continued Theresa. "I hate myself for still loving him."

Suddenly, she was interrupted by a loud bang coming from the corner of the room, and rays of light revealed a wooden staircase that was originally hidden by the darkness.

Sophia shot up her head as two long black shadows extended across the stairs.

Jack and Xavier.

She opened her mouth to extend her joy but all she could manage was a whimper.

"Sophia," Xavier breathed and ran to her. The second he was in front of her, without a moment of hesitation, he gripped onto the black chains holding her up, and pulled them out of the wall. As if snapping a stick, Xavier broke the shackles from her wrists, setting her free.

Dizziness overwhelmed her mind, and she practically fell into his arms.

Xavier held her up as he embraced her. One hand looped around her back and the other in her hair. He planted kisses on the side of her head, and squeezed her so tightly as though he was seconds away from losing her.

Sophia stepped back and looked up to Xavier, who was wearing a face of relief.

A loud thud and the sound of rattling chains caused Sophia to turn around swiftly. It was her mother collapsing after Jack released her from her eighteen year shackles. Jack summoned the light to his finger and cut through the shackles.

Theresa coughed and took a sharp inhale of breath, which soon turned into an intense sobbing.

Leaving Xavier's arms, Sophia dropped to her knees in front of her mother. She reached behind her head and undid the knot to her blindfold. Slowly, she dropped it to the ground beside her. After eighteen years of darkness it took Theresa a couple of minutes to adjust to the light.

When her blurry eyes finally sharpened, she looked upon her daughter. She took in every single detail of her face and cupped her hand around her cheek. It was hard to tell exactly how many features she inherited from her mother because of how frail and thin she was. But there were small things she recognised from Sophia's own reflection, like the shape of her lips and the bridge of her nose.

Theresa brought both hands to her daughter's cheeks and cried as she held her for the first time.

Sophia could feel that she was shaking. Her fingers were so thin, Sophia could feel her bones graze on her cheek. "My beautiful girl," Theresa sobbed, tears staining her cheeks.

The corners of her eyes cracked as she smiled. She needed to get out of here, if Theresa was held like this for any longer she would die.

Theresa threw her arms around Sophia, holding her as tight as she could. She cried into her daughter's shoulder, and she could tell that this was something she had been desperate to do for eighteen years.

After a couple of minutes of the room falling still, Jack placed a hand on Sophia's shoulder. "We must leave."

Sophia nodded. Breaking apart from her mother was difficult, as Theresa clung to the material of her dress, afraid of letting her go again.

When Theresa finally released her grip, she took Sophia's hands as she helped her to her feet. Theresa fell the second her legs extended, and Jack caught her and held her up in his arms. She looked up at him, with a grateful smile. "Are you my daughter's husband?"

Jack wasn't very good at hiding the pain in his eyes. "N-no." he glanced at Xavier, and grumbled. "He is."

Theresa didn't hide her surprise as she looked at Xavier. "So Christopher was right. You're married to a vampire?"

"Please, save the introductions for later," Jack hoisted Theresa up into his arms and cradled her like she was a child.

"Yes, please do." A voice chimed from the stairs that Sophia was dragged down. Christopher casually walked into the room, and Theresa nestled her face into Jack's shoulder. Resembling a child frightened of a stranger.

Xavier instinctively pulled Sophia close to his chest. His breathing was heavy as his grip tightened around the sleeves of her torn wedding dress.

With his hands punched into his pockets, Christopher mused when he saw Theresa free of her chains. "What do you plan to do? Take her to that prison?" his playful tone set a layer of unease across the room. "She'll be just as much a prisoner there as she was here." He reached his hand to grab Theresa's wrist, until Jack stepped back.

"You cannot be that deluded," Jack scoffed. "That *this* is an option to be considered."

"I need her here." The playfulness was gone, vanished in a blink of an eye. As though it never existed in the first place.

"For your sick inventions." Xavier snarled, his upper lip curling.

"My inventions will only improve humanity."

"You never cared for humanity," it was Theresa who spoke up. "At first you did but...you changed."

Christopher's face soured, his nostrils flaring and his hands shaking as he released them from his pockets. A frightening fury filled his face.

There was a mixture of emotions competing with one another. Amongst the anger a deep sadness was emerging in his watery eyes. His breath was hitching, and he took another step to Theresa, as if silently pleading with her. "You can't leave me, Tess."

Theresa flinched. She looked ready to break, a name he hadn't called her in years.

Sophia tried to step in, to help her mother but Xavier's grip tightened around her.

"Everything you have done is for your own gain. For money and your foolish dream of immortality."

Christopher turned his back to her, his hands came up to his ears and pressed firmly against his skull. Like he was trying to block out her words.

"This - I..." Christopher dropped his hands from his head, and stared at the wall. The green of his eyes trailing along every single crack that made up this wall. The prison that he created to keep his wife.

"After eighteen years," Christopher whispered, dropping to his knees. His hands falling limp at either of his sides. "Only three of my inventions proved to work. As prototypes, not one device had fully come to pass." he looked over his shoulder, tears spilling from his eyes. "Three."

"The torture of this woman ends," Jack towered over him. "If you cherish these inventions more than your wife, then you are not a scientist. You're a monster."

Christopher just sat there, his chin resting on his shoulder and his eyes frantically looking around - unable to find anything to focus on as his thoughts swirled around in his head.

He looked pathetic. The ends of his disheveled brown hair now shadowed his face, hiding what emotion he was currently feeling.

The tense silence was suddenly echoing with laughter. Christopher's shoulders shook as he lifted his head and locked his gaze to no one in particular. Christopher's face fell as he shot back up to his feet and began pacing in the small space. He gripped his hands into his hair and began yelling inaudible sentences.

"Why did you do all of this?" Sophia yelled out. Breaking Christopher's rantings. "The arranged marriage? Were you truly going to use it to kidnap me? Or take any future child I had?"

"This bitch wasn't going to last for much longer," Christopher snarled. "I needed new blood to experiment with. Since that *orphanage* houses so many creatures, if you were to breed a child that could provide so many possibilities for future inventions."

Sophia felt as though she might throw up. "You would steal my child? Your grandchild?"

"You wouldn't be able to," Jack said. "You're not to step foot inside of the orphanage."

"What do you mean?" asked Sophia.

"My mother told me about your father," Jack sighed. "Of course I didn't realise just how much of a lunatic he is, but he is the one who gave you those scars, Sophia."

She choked on her breath.

"Oh, shut up." Christopher snarled. "If it wasn't for your mother taking her away none of this would have happened. I wouldn't have to spend years *waiting* for her to arrive at my doorstep. I wouldn't have to make the effort to ensure she travelled through my forest." He abruptly stopped and stared at Theresa.

After everything he had done, after the amount of hurt he had caused to his own family, Christopher's face still softened at the sight of Theresa.

Sophia pulled away from Xavier's grip and cautiously stepped in front of her father. "If you set her free, we will all leave and not a word has to be spoken about what has occurred within these walls."

Even though she was standing in front of him, Christopher couldn't look at his own daughter. "I would have expected to breed a half intelligent child. You don't expect me to believe that this...*whore* will keep quiet about being chained in a basement for eighteen years and drained of her blood." When Christopher insulted her, there was a hesitation in each word. Like he was trying to convince himself that that's what she was. Trying his best to justify his actions, but deep down in his human heart he knew it wasn't true. "Not that any sane person would believe you."

"Lord Paine would." Jack barked.

Christopher knocked his head back and cackled. "Like he doesn't already know?"

"Excuse me?" Sophia breathed.

Christopher waved his hand to end the conversation.

Xavier's hand gripped around Sophia's upper arm and pulled her back. He looked to Jack, "We need to leave, now."

Jack agreed with a small nod and ran up the stairs that they came from, and Xavier dragged Sophia along with him. At first she was reluctant, she couldn't leave her father for she feared what he would do next.

But what could she do? Christopher wasn't to be reasoned with at this point, he was far too past redemption.

Xavier and Sophia followed Jack as he led them away from the house.

They were finding their way back to that abandoned hotel, in hopes for a few hours of rest. Xavier was looking over his shoulder every so often to check they weren't being followed. They were seemingly alone.

Once inside, Jack lay Theresa down on the settee and she immediately fell into a deep sleep. This must have been the first bit of comfort she'd had in years. Sleeping on a concrete floor must have been excruciatingly painful.

Sophia sat on the very edge of the settee, ensuring that she wouldn't disturb her mother. She brushed her sweat covered hair out the way of her forehead and watched her chest rise and fall as she breathed.

Looking at this woman lying in front of her, resembling a corpse, Sophia couldn't comprehend that this was her mother. And of all people to make her like this was her father. How could anyone do such a thing? And how could Sophia be related to him?

She couldn't hold it in anymore. After years of longing for a family, the vivid pictures she created in her head of her mother and father, completely shattered. Everything in her life up until now had been a lie. She didn't even know who she was. It was all well and good people explaining and spelling things out for her in regards to her demonic heritage, but that didn't mean she understood a thing.

As Sophia hunched over and sobbed into her hands, the cold tears trickled down from her palms to her wrists. She had cried a lot recently, but this was the most tears she had shed.

Feather-like fingers wrapped around her wrists and pulled her hands away from her face. Xavier was squatting in front of her, his knees trapping Sophia's legs.

"I don't understand *anything*," she choked on her cry after adding an emphasis to the word 'anything.'

Xavier didn't smile, instead he dropped one hand over her knee and kept one hand around her wrist. "No one is expecting you to understand," he spoke softly. "Not right now, anyway."

Sophia almost jolted out of her skin when a hand touched her back. Whipping around, it was only Jack. She wanted to ask what had happened to him, for he looked like he had been dragged behind a horse and carriage.

"I'm going to visit the town and see if we can get a ride back to London."

Before Sophia could open her mouth Jack was gone.

"He will never forgive me," she muttered as she turned back to Xavier.

"He just needs time."

"I'm sorry...I'm sorry that I caused this. I'm sorry that I dragged you and Jack here, I'm sorry you had to marry me for *nothing*, I'm sorry that I've been nothing but a hassle and a burden."

Xavier slipped his hands around her cheeks and pulled her to face him. His brow was furrowed and his mouth a razor thin line. "None of what you said is true. Christopher caused this, not you. Wanting to find out more about your past isn't something you should apologise for. And in regards to marrying you," he dipped his head to ensure her eyes didn't waver. "If I didn't want to marry you, if I detested the idea, I wouldn't have done it." His thumb grazed her cheek. "Sometimes it can be that simple."

The way in which he spoke with such confidence, did settle Sophia's heart.

Xavier released her cheeks and opened up his arms, "Come here," he whispered.

It took less than a second for her to fall into his chest, her arms hooking around his back and pressing her face into his shoulder.

"I'll make this up to you," he said, his lips against her hair. "I'll give you the wedding day you deserve."

"I don't care about that," she muttered.

"I do."

Chapter Twenty-Thirty

Jack returned an hour later. He'd managed to find someone that agreed to take them back to London first thing in the morning. He requested a hefty payment, Jack gave him half now and he would receive the rest upon returning to the orphanage.

That night, everyone was exhausted from the events which took place. Theresa hadn't woken up since they first arrived at the hotel. Sophia would check on her every half an hour to ensure she was alright.

Jack lay in the corner of the room with his back against the wall.

Xavier lay next to Sophia, he started off the night with his arms wrapped around her but he managed to maneuver himself so he was flat on his stomach and the side of his head resting against the back of his hands.

Everyone managed to fall asleep, everyone apart from Sophia. Her memories of her father's actions wouldn't stop replaying over and over in her head. It made her heart gallop in her chest, ensuring she would get no sleep that night.

Now that she knew what lies beyond that door she constantly dreamed of, she wondered if it would ever appear again. Or would she be haunted by her father's erratic face, envisioning him torturing her mother all for his sick inventions.

She quickly came to the conclusion that she must have seen that door in her childhood, before she was taken away by Cassandra. She must have stumbled across it, and her childhood interest may have caused her to want to go inside. Christopher must have caught her and stressed that she was never to open the door.

Even in her forgotten memories his words still infiltrated the back of her mind.

Sophia's eyes snapped open when she heard the sound of footsteps crunching on leaves outside. Before she had time to react, a cold chill slipped down her spine as the breeze rolled in from the broken windows. A shadowy figure appeared in the hallway, scanning the premises.

Floorboards creaked with his every movement, and when he appeared into the living room, and when the light from the moon outlined his face, Sophia knew exactly who it was.

Christopher.

Her father.

When Sophia watched as Christopher found Theresa sleeping on the settee, Sophia turned to Xavier and began violently shaking him awake.

Xavier grumbled awake, and when he realised the panic that fueled the air he shot up in a flash, his eyes meeting Sophia's. He seemingly asked her what was wrong but it didn't take him long to find Christopher hovering over Theresa. He didn't seem to notice that anyone else was awake.

In a flash, Xavier sprang to his feet. He seemed to disappear from one side of the room to the other, as he was now behind Christopher with one arm wrapped around his neck and the other pinning down his arms.

All of the commotion woke Jack and Theresa.

Jack got to his feet and ran to Sophia's side as she got up.

All she could do was watch as Xavier effortlessly restrained her father, and Christopher fought with everything he had to break free but Xavier was too strong. If he wanted to, he could break his neck as easily as snapping a twig.

Theresa was delirious when she woke, she tried to lift herself up but when she put weight on her elbows, it was too much for her and she collapsed back down, hitting her frail head hard against the arm of the settee.

"We need to turn him over to Lord Paine-"

"NO!" Christopher yelled so loud that it echoed across the building. It could have caused the entire building to collapse on top of them.

Christopher struggled for a while, and Xavier's hold became tighter and tighter around his neck. So much in fact his face was turning blue and he was gasping for air.

"Xavier," Sophia said, calmly. "You're suffocating him."

It took him a second to release his grip on Christopher. But when he did, he opened his arms and Christopher fell to the dusty floor with a loud thud. He held himself up with one arm as his free hand slipped around his neck, ensuring his airway hadn't been ripped out.

Sophia walked around the settee and stood in front of her father, as he heaved and gagged for air. He wasn't the man she thought he was. He was broken.

Then something her mother said replayed in her mind.

I truly loved him. Even now, I hate myself for still loving him.

Sophia knew there were more memories she had to discover within herself. There must have been times in her childhood with him that were happy - normal. She was certain of it. Seeing what he had become disappointed Sophia, deeply. Like a man who promised would change, only to fall back into the same toxic behaviour that made them a monster.

Jack stepped to Sophia, placing a hand over her shoulder to halt her. As if he was warning her that it was too dangerous to be in Christopher's presence. But with Jack and Xavier at her side, she wasn't afraid.

She offered him a weak smile before stepping out of his hand.

What this situation must have looked like to an outsider looking in. A malnourished woman collapsed on the settee, a bride with her gown torn and ripped in multiple places, a groom with a murderous look in his eye for his father-in-law, and said father-in-law gasping for air on his knees.

Sophia slid down to her knees, now at eye level with her father.

All she did was stare at his hands that completely covered his face. He wasn't crying or sobbing, he was clearly wallowing in self loathing.

"You know that this cannot continue," Sophia had so much she wanted to say. But she didn't know how to. For a while, she sat in front of him and hoped the words would come as she looked upon the man who caused so much hurt.

To everyone's surprise, Christopher raised his head out of his hands. Defeat painted his face, his green eyes glassy with regret. "How can everything I have done be for nothing?"

Her chest contorted as she gripped her hands in her lap. Sophia's heart wanted desperately to somehow wave a magic wand and turn back the clocks. Or transport them into an alternate reality where none of this happened. Where Sophia grew up with both of her parents, and the most extreme confrontation they would have was what's for dinner that night.

But Sophia had to stop trying to put herself into worlds of fantasy. This was her reality, this was her life. She had to face it head on, instead of running away.

"I cannot pretend that things will be alright once we leave here," Sophia muttered. "I don't even know what will happen tomorrow."

Christopher met his daughter's eyes, and his bottom lip trembled. The corners of his mouth were anchored down, and it looked impossible to remove the weight. His entire body went numb, his limbs were limp and his mouth hung open loosely.

"I want to hate you," her voice trembled as her eyes pooled with tears before streaking down her cheeks. "After everything you have done, after everything you have caused -" she quickly looked away. "- how could you do such a thing to your wife? To *plan* such horrific things on your child?"

Christopher's gaze never wavered.

Sophia wasn't expecting an answer, how could anyone answer that? But he did.

"I didn't mean for any of this to happen."

It was like he had curled his hand into a tight fist and punched her across the face. Now she was mad, now the anger she felt guilty for feeling rose up above everything else. "This wasn't an accident! You tortured this woman for eighteen *years*. And not once did you think to stop?"

Then a warm hand covered hers, and Sophia shot up her eyes to her father.

He still wore the same expression, like he was in mourning. For what, she couldn't decide. Mourning for the life he could have had if he hadn't taken his inventions too far, for the child that was taken away from him, mourning the years of love for his family that he tossed aside. There was so much for him to grieve over, and it was all caused by his hands.

Sophia was foolish to think that he was sincere, but every time she denied it the look on his face told her it was the truth.

Sophia was a fool.

When Christopher dared to reach out his other hand and touch her scarred cheek, both Jack and Xavier tensed. They were ready at any moment to take him down if he made one wrong move.

Christopher ignored them, almost as if they weren't even there.

There was no doubt in the way Christopher looked at the scars on Sophia's cheek, that Christopher had been the one to cause it. She didn't know how, or why he would be responsible for such violent scars not only on her face but her entire body.

But right now, his face was plagued with guilt and no amount of prayers could purify him with redemption.

"You grew up to be so beautiful," he said. "I'm sorry."

Sophia's mouth opened, lips parted and words failed on her tongue. She wasn't entirely sure what he was apologizing for. It could have been for everything, or only for her scars. But the word 'sorry' was laced with desperation. A plea for forgiveness that she didn't feel was the right person to offer it to him.

When their eyes locked in that moment there was a mutual feeling pooling its way out of Sophia and Christophr's hearts. An invisible string was knotting around their hearts and attaching them together. A string so thin, yet so strong, but even a thousand knives could not cut.

The love of a father to a daughter. In a single beat of their hearts, the unconditional love filled their souls.. Within that beat, as fast as a blink, Christopher froze in place. His skin, once as soft as a pillow now a cold coarse stone that weighed down Sophia's hand and cheek.

Panic fuelled her when she stared at her father, now encased in a statue, frozen in place with the look of guilt forever carved into his face. One second he was there as a real person, and the next he was gone. Locked away into a stone prison for eternity. The years of pain he caused for everyone around him, would forever be trapped here, in this abandoned hotel where no one would ever visit.

When the realisation set across the room as to what had happened, Sophia screamed at the top of her lungs, scrambling back away from the statue she had created. Like it was a monster ready to pounce on her.

Jack was behind her, he dropped to his knees and covered her eyes with the palm of his hand. He held her tightly as she rocked back and forth, the tears spilling in between his fingers.

Sophia wailed as she screamed in agony.

Ensuring not to move his palm away from Sophia's eyes, he used his other hand to drape her into his chest, allowing her to weep.

Within one moment she lost the father she had searched for her entire life.

What would her mother think once she awoke and found her husband as a statue?

She would never be able to look Jack and Xavier in the eyes again.

And her entire world had become stone.

END OF BOOK ONE

Printed in Great Britain
by Amazon